THE LAST RONIN

A TEENAGE MUTANT NINJA TURTLES NOVEL

THE LAST RONIN

A TEENAGE MUTANT NINJA TURTLES NOVEL

ERIK BURNHAM

WITH ILLUSTRATIONS BY THE
ESCORZA BROTHERS

ABRAMS, NEW YORK

Editor: Claire Stetzer
Designer: Brann Garvey
Design Manager: Deena Micah Fleming
Managing Editor: Grace Ball
Production Manager: Julie Primavera

Library of Congress Control Number: 2025950739

ISBN: 978-1-4197-8792-8
eISBN: 979-8-89684-042-8

Printed and bound in the United States
10 9 8 7 6 5 4 3 2 1

Abrams books are available at special discounts when purchased in quantity
for premiums and promotions as well as fundraising or educational use.
Special editions can also be created to specification. For details, contact
sales@abramsbooks.com or the address below.

Abrams® is a registered trademark of Harry N. Abrams, Inc.

ABRAMS is represented in the UK and Europe by Abrams & Chronicle Books,
22-24 Ely Place, London EC1N 6TE and Média-Participations, 57 rue Gaston
Tessier, 75166 Paris, France.
abramsandchronicle.co.uk and media-participations.com
info@abramsandchronicle.co.uk

ABRAMS The Art of Books
195 Broadway, New York, NY 10007
abramsbooks.com

T#1360085

1

RONIN DIPS A HAND into the East River. What had once been water sluices through his three fingers. The river's always been polluted. Now it's a reeking brown slurry.

Three-eyed fish, goes the old joke. All sorts of toxic and irradiated hybrid creatures lurk in the depths of the river that separates Manhattan from the boroughs of Brooklyn and Queens. That was true even before toxic runoff turned the water to brown muck. Before he fled the city.

Before the wall went up around Manhattan.

Through the hazy dusk-light of a foul sky rises the wall, implacable and silent across the river, a hulking gray partition they say you can see from space. Behind it, skyscrapers pierce the gloom.

A lonely shorebird squawks and Ronin swivels his head to take in the desolate reaches of Brooklyn Bridge Park. He imagines an impossibly tall stork picking its way through the ragged pilings at the edge of the river. But there is nothing.

"Only mutant here is you, bro."

The voice comes from right beside him. But when Ronin glances down into the river's oily surface, he sees only his silhouette. A murky reflection of one who is no longer young, whose face is lined with wrinkles set deep into tough reptilian skin. Laughter drifts across the empty park. He can't help but look around, even though he knows it's the ghosts. It's always the ghosts.

One of the ghosts calls him by his name. His real name. It sounds like the name of a stranger.

Years ago, in another life, Ronin had a family. A father and three brothers. Together they had fought to keep the city from becoming the place it is now. The five of them, training and laughing and roaming tunnels and rooftops together. Kicking ass. Living off pizza. It had been a good life.

But now, the turtle's family—and everyone else he's ever loved— is dead, and his name rings false because of it. He thinks of himself as nothing more than a ronin, a masterless warrior.

Though, unlike a true ronin, he has not returned to this once-magnificent city alone.

His brothers' voices have proven more stubborn than death. And just like in life, they love to give him shit. Always chiming in loudest when he's in the mood for peace.

"Sure is cold."

"Forget the temperature. The toxicity level's gotta be off the charts."

"You know who swims in sludge like that? Total freakin' maniacs, that's who."

Ronin dips a toe into the muck. He tries to imagine what it will feel like to submerge his six-foot frame. Well. He's been through worse.

"Not like I can just walk there." Ronin points to the remnants of the Brooklyn Bridge. Its stone towers short and uneven, the road spilling into the water. Cables like braided vines plunge into the stinking depths. Whatever chemical runoff that has turned the river fetid is also corrupting the bridge. Eating it from within as the river pulls it down.

"So unless one of you stashed a boat over here when we were kids," Ronin says, "I don't have a choice. You can always stay behind if it bothers you so much."

"Hey—where you go, we go. You know that."

Ronin pulls an old pair of goggles up over his black mask. "See you guys on the other side."

He steps off the edge of the cracked and weed-choked pavement. The river takes him in with uncanny slowness. A strange miasma burns his nostrils. His feet find jagged rocks, and then after a few steps there's nothing but fathoms of sludge beneath him. Tilting his body forward into a crawl and clamping his mouth shut, Ronin uses his thick arms like oars to propel himself along. The river pulls at his hooded leather coat. The stench gags him.

Minutes tick by. Manhattan's wall seems to loom no larger. A human being would be screwed, he reflects. Flimsy skin melted away by this chemical soup, soft innards seared by toxicity. Ronin's green reptilian skin, on the other hand, is tough and fibrous—and has only grown thicker over the years. He's harder to kill than the wild young turtle who fled the city so long ago. Armored for the path that lies before him now. The path of vengeance.

Eventually the island reaches out to welcome her long-lost son. His fingers brush against a rock and he tilts his body back so his feet can find purchase. Sludge clings heavily to his body as he emerges. Behind him, the river screams the name of the man he has come home to kill.

Oroku Hiroto.

2

THE NARROW SHORELINE IN the shadow of the wall is a landscape of jagged debris. Sections are littered with crossed iron rivets like traps on the beaches of Normandy during World War II. Ronin moves swiftly past them through an eerie, green-tinted darkness and thinks of the books in his father's old library. So much history, gone. One of his two-toed tabi boots catches on a strand of barbed wire that rises from the muck. He bends to pry a metal snarl from the battered leather, noticing that he's lost one of his knee pads in the river.

He takes a moment to check the rest of his gear. Boots, thick black pants, loose-fitting black shirt, and hooded leather coat—grimy but intact. Bulletproof vest, gauntlets, elbow pads—all there. Not bad for a swim through a million gallons of toxic waste. One knee pad is an acceptable loss.

He can feel his brothers smirking at all the gear he wears like he's an infantry soldier on jungle patrol. When they were teenagers, all they needed were their belts, pads for their joints, and masks. But they were smaller then. Moving unobtrusively was a simple matter. Now—

"Now you're a two-hundred-pound mutant turtle, but I'm sure the hoodie will help you blend in."

"Shut up. Lemme think for a second."

"Oh, he needs to think. By all means."

Ronin pats an inside pocket. His prized possession, his father's journal, is dry and safe inside its watertight pouch. He moves his hand to his belt. Throwing stars, smoke bombs, small explosive charges. Line and grapple.

Everything's ready. Ronin turns his attention to the wall.

A low whistle drones in the back of his mind. "Gotta be twenty stories high. At least."

His brother is right: The wall rises to challenge the buildings here at the south end of Manhattan, where the Financial District gives way to Battery Park. Green phosphorescence pours down the cement as if the wall were alive with plankton. He peers up at the glowing undersides of distant clouds and puts it together: light pollution. It's been so long since he's been in the city, he's forgotten how its radiance leaks out in every direction. He tries to pick out the top of the wall in the haze, but it makes his head hurt.

"By any chance, did you happen to pack the world's longest grappling hook?"

There has to be a weakness. Somewhere. He turns left and keeps to the wet dirt at the base of the wall. Ronin figures he's working his way around the southern tip of Manhattan, somewhere around Battery Park. Or at least where the park used to be.

"Stop!"

Ronin winces at the command. When his brothers get too loud, he can feel their voices in his teeth like an electric shock.

"Check it out. Looks like it used to be a gate."

Algae-colored phosphorescence glints off a rusted iron grille. Ronin runs a finger along metal bars. Poured cement clings to the metal in great frozen waves. There's no way to slip through. Even if he'd brought a welding torch, cutting the bars would get him nowhere.

"Somebody meant business when they blocked it off."

Ronin looks up. Thirty or forty feet above the cement-encrusted gate, the wall flares outward in strange crenellations. Pillboxes and sally ports rising into the darkness. At one time, there had apparently been a watchtower here. A vertical strongpoint at the wall's southernmost curl. Plenty of spots to catch his grapple, plenty of handholds to ascend. Much better than sheer concrete. Yes, here is his point of entry. As far as he can tell, it's unmanned. Ronin wonders what they were guarding against. He thinks of the rippling in the shallows as he ventured through the muck. How many other monsters are out here?

Doesn't matter. Ronin unhooks the grapple from his belt. He's the only monster who will be getting in tonight.

"So where's all the laser tripwires?"

"What, like in *Spycatcher*?"

"*Spycatcher 2*'s the one with the lasers."

"When they go to Moscow."

Ronin pauses. He hasn't thought about the *Spycatcher* series in a long time. He loved watching those movies with his brothers, all of them digging in to a couple of large pies from Antonio's, reciting lines to each other, cranking the volume on the synths-and-electric-guitars soundtrack. For once, his brothers bring up a good point. Outside the wall, there's no redundant security. No guards on patrol, no boats in the river, no dogs. He scans the sheer cement to either side of the gate. A couple of old security cameras jut out, barely visible in the deep shadows of the watchtower's overhangs.

"Probably more worried about folks getting out than in."

Ronin reaches into his belt and comes up with a pair of metal throwing stars—shuriken—and flicks his wrist to let them fly. Quickly, silently, with precision born of a lifetime of practice, they find their marks. Glass camera lenses shatter.

"You didn't have to go and waste throwing stars like that! Those cameras are a million years old, who knows if they even work."

"Don't care." Ronin hefts the grapple. "Felt good."

After a few quick spins to build momentum, he sends the hook flying into the night. It bites a piece of metal atop the gate, an old steel bar that emerges from the poured cement. With a single tug, he tests the line. Satisfied it will bear his weight, Ronin climbs hand over hand, bracing his feet flat against the wall.

He ascends through a pocket of city noise. The furious rush of Manhattan envelops him in earsplitting dissonance, and then all is quiet once again. At the top of the gate he clings to a ledge jutting from an old balcony. He unhooks the grapple and stows it in his belt. Now he must free climb. The face of the watchtower is marred by weatherbeaten runnels. Ronin wedges his thick fingers in a groove and works his way up a seam in the concrete. Each ledge or gun slit or balcony is a new and merciful landmark on his journey.

His brothers go quiet as he ascends. Even their presence, so often like an itch in the back of his mind, is diminished. They know better than to startle him now. Ronin narrows his focus to the handholds within reach. He moves underneath the eaves of crumbling ornamentation, clinging to a gargoyle's eroded leer. He breathes in and out and waits for a swirling wind coming up from the harbor to break against the wall. The rush carries an echo of the hated name: *Oroku Hiroto.*

Ronin lets out a low growl that threatens to build into a roar, but he forces himself to remain methodical in his attention. There will be time for urgency when he reaches the city. For now: patience. The muscles in his upper back and shoulders begin to cramp. He is strong, yes—but also heavy. Another howling gust carries with it the stench of the river, and he nearly chokes.

He comes up underneath an overhang that protrudes about a foot from the wall. Doused in shadow, Ronin reaches back with his left hand and works his three fingers over the edge of the stone lip. He takes a breath and repeats the name. *Oroku Hiroto.* He must not fall. Not now. Not when he's so close. He transfers his right hand to the overhang. For a breathless moment he swings out over the dark river. Then he pushes his arm across the ledge and swings his body to one side. The toe of his boot finds purchase. He rolls atop the overhang and stares up into a light-smeared sky. He waits for his heart to slow. Then, pressing himself against the wall, he stands.

"Nimble as a billy goat," one of his brothers says.

"We didn't want to psyche you out before you started, but honestly we gave you a fifty-fifty shot of making it this far."

"I was more sixty-forty."

Ronin doesn't reply. He doesn't want to break the spell. The city glow spills over the top of the wall no more than ten feet above his head. Coils of razor wire unspool. The name on the wind—*Oroku Hiroto*—slithers into his ears. He spins his grapple and lets the line fly. The hook digs in somewhere on the other side of the wall. His arms are numb as he hoists himself up to the top. Like a flipped switch, Manhattan comes to life as he crests the wall, and all at once he is drowning in light.

Ronin is unmoored. New York wears the jittery skin of some other city, and the dislocation nearly brings him to his knees. Below, there is no Battery Park. Low-slung hovels festooned with lights crowd what used to be green space. He traces the makeshift dwellings in haphazard avenues as they ramble toward the base of the wall. Then they cascade upward at a steep curve, ramshackle stacks of huts affixed to the wall by a fever dream of scaffolds and lifts.

He watches a motorbike descend the pillars of shanties, its headlight juddering down narrow staircases and around hairpin switchbacks until it hits the streets and joins a thick knot of traffic crawling toward the edge of the settlement. Ronin lifts his head to take in the towers of steel and glass that rise beyond what used to be Battery Park. In years past, the Financial District would go mostly quiet at night after the Wall Street hotshots commuted home. But now everything's lit up like Times Square. It's not just the billions of gigawatts of lights. That, he'd expected. It's the digital screens of every size dotting the buildings as far as his eyes can see, the reflections of their radiant advertisements prismatic in canyons of glass.

Voices ride the wave and slam into Ronin's ears all at once. The cries of lovers and fighters and food vendors, and, amid the cacophony, his brothers' astonishment.

Halfway between the hovels and the top of the wall, the headlights of antigrav vehicles carve lanes of traffic into thin air. Ronin has seen the airborne cars and trucks before, of course, but not even in Tokyo are so many jammed together in seemingly random array, riding each other's bumpers yet never colliding. The antigrav traffic emits a magnetic whine that ribbons up to the top of the wall. The combined glow of vehicles and screens makes it feel like daytime.

Ronin breathes deep, longing for a whiff of the home he left behind. He finds it underneath the scorched metallic odor of the antigrav engines. A hundred different cuts of meat seasoned a thousand different ways. Cigarette smoke. Urine. The sickly sweet undercurrent of streetside garbage.

"Do I detect a hint of sewer?"

"Ahhh, there it is."

Satisfied, he lets his gaze drift beyond the Financial District. His lips peel back to expose his teeth as he regards the mega-skyscraper that rises above the old giants to dominate the skyline. This looming monstrosity is the home of the Foot Clan in New York, a vertical compound of cramped barracks, training studios, mess halls, armories, and luxury apartments for Oroku Hiroto and his coterie of sycophants. He imagines priceless art spattered in blood, countless Foot soldiers lying broken on the expensive floors, Oroku Hiroto on his knees pleading for his life. Ronin's hands ball into fists. Slung across the back of his shell, his brothers' weapons seem to quiver with the manic urge to be unleashed.

Time to finish this.

3

FROM ATOP THE WALL, the stacks of shanties look frozen mid-tumble, like some giant had tossed a thousand misshapen dwellings down into Battery Park. They appear to be poised on the knife's edge of some great collapse. But now Ronin makes his way down a narrow corridor of surprising integrity. Rebar pokes into the hallway at odd angles. The superstructure has been reinforced with steel, the beams and rods supporting each hut welded to the framework of its neighbor. Strands of holiday lights illuminate the low ceiling. Voices in English, Spanish, Chinese, Russian, and a dozen more languages he can't place drift into the hallway. Between an outer husk of wooden slats of all different shapes and sizes—scavenged, Ronin figures—the brightness of the Financial District leaks in.

Ronin darts across a landing from which staircases spiral in five directions. He curls around a switchback and presses himself against plywood to make way for a young woman carrying an infant in a shoulder sling. An errant nail pokes his shell. He pulls his hood down low and averts his eyes as she squeezes past. In her wake, Ronin sniffs a hint of baby powder.

"Okay. You're finally here, you want to hurry up and finish the job, I get that," a ghost starts.

"But! Hear me out, bro. You don't even know how to get into the tower. You don't know if these people around here are loyal to the Foot Clan."

"You might want to do some recon, is what he's getting at."

He estimates he's halfway down the wall. The wooden-scrap husk opens up abruptly, giving way to a wider lane. Too late, he clocks that he's at a crossing. The rattle of an old motor hits his ears right before the bike comes barreling toward him. He ducks into a doorway. The bike sounds like the old souped-up crotch rockets some of the kids from back in the day would race up the West Side Highway. City lights go hazy in a cloud of gasoline exhaust, then sharpen as a breeze clears out the crossing. The bike's engine gets lost in the cacophony of ground-level city sounds.

Laughter comes from behind him. It isn't his brothers. This is raspy, unwell chortling. It degenerates into a wheezing cough. Ronin turns, hand on the hilt of his brother's sai, as a woman's voice pipes up from the shadows.

"First time in the stacks, big fella?"

Ronin takes in the little room. Four small round tables are lit by the flickering glow of fake electric candles. Only one table is occupied. A wizened old man in suspenders and a loose-fitting long-sleeve shirt brings a white napkin to his mouth as another bout of wet coughing doubles him over. His companion, a middle-aged woman, hoists a bottle of amber liquid in Ronin's direction.

Ronin shakes his head. For all he knows, the Foot Clan has eyes and ears all over this place. He keeps his hood pulled low and turns his head slightly so these people can't get a clear look at his reptilian features.

One of his brothers interjects. "Ask about the tower!"

Ronin ignores the voice. The woman shrugs and upends the bottle for a long swig before slamming it back down on the table. The man takes the napkin from his mouth, glances at a dark blot in its crumpled center, grimaces, and balls up the cloth in his fist.

"Goddamn kids come barreling down Main Street." He sniffs. "No regard for anybody else." He looks at Ronin from behind wet, rheumy eyes. "We ain't all like that, friend. Some of us got manners. Like me and Ezzie here." He takes the bottle and tilts a splash into his dirty long-stemmed glass.

Ronin knows he should keep moving. But this old-timer and his drinking buddy take him back. A vision of something lost—of summer nights and neighbors gathering on the stoops of the Lower East Side—gives him pause. "You call this stairway *Main Street*?"

The man traces a finger through the air, marking a descent. "Runs all the way down into Battery Village, then meets up with the south end of Broadway."

Ronin tells himself it isn't just nostalgia that's made him linger. This is good information. The most efficient route north. Until he has his bearings in this new Manhattan, he'll need to listen to the streets.

"Where'd you come from, anyway?" the woman called Ezzie asks. There's a glint in her eye that Ronin doesn't like. She's peering at him hard, angling for a better look. "Fall outta the sky?"

"Coma," he says. "Seventeen years. Just woke up."

One of his brothers snorts. "Good one."

"My cousin was in a coma," the old man says.

"Here we go," Ezzie says.

"He's in dreamland six weeks before the doc says to me, he says, *Jasper, you're next of kin, he ain't got no one else, so we're telling you, we're pulling the plug.* They needed the bed. And I ain't got the kind of scratch for one of those portable Stockman units, so that was that." The man pours himself another.

"*Stockman.*" The name curdles in Ronin's mouth. So the mad scientist is still kicking. His mind, unbidden, serves up flashes of Baxter Stockman's murderous technology. Firelight glinting off waves of flying mousers, that merciless, unfeeling army of robotic death machines. Ronin shakes off the memory. "He makes *medical equipment* now?"

The woman leans back and folds her arms across her chest. Her wooden chair creaks. The delicate skin at the corners of her eyes creases as she regards him with suspicion. "I think you best be moving along now, friend."

"Coma, my ass," the man says as he flicks a fingernail against his glass and listens to the ping till it dies away.

The gravelly roar of another bike swells from higher up the stack. Ronin takes a step inside the lonely watering hole. He figures these people are too skittish to talk about Stockman—or Hiroto—directly. He tries another angle. "Tell me about the wall."

The man eyes the weapons bristling from Ronin's back.

"I got someplace I gotta be," Ezzie says.

She moves to get up. Ronin's bulk crowds the doorway. He folds his arms. Ezzie thinks for a moment, sits back down, and reaches for the bottle. Outside, Ronin senses a group of pedestrians as they scamper down the steps at his back. A trio, judging by their footfalls. Two of them in heavy boots. Jasper waits for their voices to fade before he speaks.

"The wall ain't just there to look pretty," the old man says in a low voice. "It's a whole goddamn power plant"—he snaps his fingers—"what do you call it . . ."

"Hydroelectric," Ezzie says.

"Yeah. It takes that shit outta the river and gives us clean water to drink and energy to run the city."

"You drink *that* water?" Ronin recalls his journey through the toxic sludge.

"Help yourself," Jasper says, pointing to a carafe of clear liquid on a neighboring table. Ronin doesn't move.

"Stockman is no saint," Ezzie says softly, "but his tech can work miracles. And the Foot Clan makes sure it's well maintained."

"What's in it for them?" Ronin asks.

Ezzie and Jasper share a glance. "You really did just fall outta the sky," Ezzie says. Then she moves a hand through the air around her head. "*Everything*," she whispers.

Ronin fights the urge to join these two at their table. It's been so long since he's spoken to anyone but ghosts. "And Hiroto. He spends all his time up in that tower?"

Ezzie swigs from the bottle. Then she folds her arms across her chest and studies a knot in the wooden table. "You best be movin' along now, friend."

"Watch yourself out there," Jasper says. "Bein' that you just woke up."

With that, Ronin turns and leaves them to their drinks.

4

RONIN LEAVES THE BUSTLING shantytown of Battery Village behind and picks up the southernmost curving tip of Broadway. On the street, he does his best to blend in with the crowd despite his hulking, cloaked frame.

"At least it's still the city that never sleeps," his brother says.

"Silver lining."

The entrance to the Bowling Green subway stop shimmers with holographic train times. Ronin walks right through the bright green messages. He reminds himself that he's officially arrived—his feet are once again treading the cracked pavement of Manhattan after nearly two decades gone. If he wasn't so preoccupied, he might worry about the black hole inside him where the love of his home used to be. Besides the city's ten million pairs of eyes, there are cameras mounted everywhere. Atop streetlights, perched on awnings above corporate lobbies, peeking out from bicycle racks. And it doesn't take a Stockman-level genius to know who's on the other end. Ronin imagines driving his brother's sai through a camera lens, the weapon's sharp point somehow popping out of Hiroto's screen in his penthouse monitoring room, jabbing him in the face, skewering his eye . . .

A piercing whistle splits the night. A big man takes off running. Commotion ripples. Pedestrians bounce off his burly elbows as he moves. From on high, advertisements seem to pour from the frames of their façade-mounted screens. Radiant phantoms of soda cans and kitty litter and cartoon characters and gleaming motorcycles drip down to the teeming streets, painting washed-out film reels over the crowd. The man on the run bursts through a friendly elephant with a roll of toilet paper sauntering down Broadway.

"Uh, you okay, bro?" one of the ghosts asks him.

"I think he's gone into shut-off mode," another responds.

Ronin understands distantly that he has halted in the middle of the sidewalk. New Yorkers grumble as they go around him. He does not care. This bright new skin the city is wearing has wormed its way into his brain. He struggles to superimpose this flickering madness over the home he once knew.

A lanky teenager with tattoos spiraling up his neck waves a hand in front of Ronin's face.

"Yo, this guy's tweaking!"

A second kid peers up at Ronin's slack-jawed countenance. "Aww, damn, he's ugly as hell!"

"And he *reeks.*"

Cracking up, the two kids vanish down an alley.

Ronin shakes off the reverie, suddenly conscious of the odor of river sludge that wreathes his filthy cloak. He keeps moving, but glances over his shoulder to catch the end of the big man's run. The man stumbles and spins on his heel and careens out onto Broadway. A taxi swerves, its driver cursing out the open window.

"At least the cabs are still yellow."

The big man clutches his throat. Ronin catches the glint of a metal flail around his neck.

"Kusari-fundo," he mutters. Weighted chain—a ninja weapon. The big man goes down. A moment later, two black-clad figures emerge from the crowd. Ronin's cold blood runs even colder.

"Foot Clan."

Highly trained ninja soldiers who serve Oroku Hiroto. Warriors Ronin dedicated his life to fighting, alongside his brothers and father,

Splinter, back in the time before the wall. Back when he still had a family to fight alongside.

Ronin stalks toward the melee. One Foot soldier yanks the kusari and wrenches the big man backward on his knees. His grimace of pain and shock is garishly lit by a passing ad for a berry cereal. The second ninja brandishes a tonfa, a short wooden club with a handle like a police nightstick. Light flashes in the red bug-like eyes of the two ninjas' masks.

"Not your fight," one of his brothers cautions him.

"I think the idea is to stay out of trouble till you get to the tower."

The Foot soldier raises the tonfa. The club is silhouetted in the glow of a headlight. Cars give the scene a wide berth. Pedestrians avert their eyes. The weapon comes down on the big man's head. Ronin hears the crack of bone. No one intervenes. Ronin forces himself to stand down. He knows his brothers are right. It would be monumentally stupid to blow his cover before he even gets north of the Brooklyn Bridge. He turns away, melting once again into the crowd on the sidewalk. His own failure to act sickens him.

In the old days, those Foot soldiers would have been the ones getting their bones cracked.

Heading north toward his old stomping ground of the Lower East Side, Ronin keeps to the shadows pooled at the edge of the sidewalk, where light from the screens angles away from the sides of the buildings. He steps carefully through encampments of homeless New Yorkers. Some of the men and women stir as he passes swiftly over their sleeping rolls. Others don't. It seems to Ronin that there are more people than ever living rough on the streets.

With Battery Village far behind him now, Broadway is a canyon defined by rows of run-down office towers. Foot Clan patrols become more frequent, ninjas walking the streets in pairs or trios. Ronin wonders if they are aware of the bad energy they give off, if they enjoy the way the public shrinks away from them, wary and disturbed. He feels their presence as a knot in his gut. Every sighting of his family's oldest foe is another desecration of the memory of his father and brothers, who fought to keep the Foot Clan where they belonged: underground. And now they roam with impunity. Ronin imagines, in vivid detail, cutting every ninja he sees to pieces, the bodies piling high enough that Oroku Hiroto receives word of the rampage in Lower Manhattan.

"Hey, sorry to interrupt the murder daydream, but didn't that used to be City Hall?"

Ronin can feel his brothers nudging him, like a light breeze blowing inside his head. He follows it. Off to the right, behind a wrought iron fence, stands an alabaster monolith at least thirty feet high. Antigrav cars whir around it, carving a traffic circle into empty air. The monument itself spins with aching slowness. Projected on the flat plane of the side facing Ronin is an image of Oroku Saki, the Shredder, archnemesis of Ronin's father, Splinter. Ronin moves closer to the gate and grips the iron bars in his fists, staring up at Shredder's silver helmet and faceplate, the rows of cruel blades that line his armor. The monolith turns to reveal Oroku Karai, Shredder's daughter. Her jet-black hair flows out from her red skullcap. She wields dual katana blades. Ronin bares his teeth. He knows what's coming next. The monolith spins. His heart pounds. The third pillar of the Oroku family comes into focus. Ronin can barely make him out through the crimson stain spreading across his mind. He lets go of the bars and turns away from the fence to stalk across the street.

"Uh, bro—maybe do some breathing exercises real quick, before you do something we're all going to—"

"Oh boy."

"—regret."

Antigrav traffic casts elongated shadows that slice bright holo-ads into dark negatives. Ronin moves through the shifting panels of light and dark, weaving between street-bound cars and trucks. Music and talk radio come and go. He steps up onto the sidewalk and barrels directly into a lone Foot soldier surveying the corner of Broadway and Murray Street. Ronin abandons subtlety and stealth. The Foot soldier does not cry out. He is well trained. A tonfa is in his hand a split second after Ronin knocks him to his knees with a single hard shove. He does not bother showing this soldier respect by applying any art to his attack. This is a street brawl. Ronin leans back. The tonfa whooshes through empty air where Ronin's head had been. Without thinking, he launches a backhand strike and the edge of his fist catches the soldier's skull in a glancing blow. The ninja, staggering, leans into his momentum and tries to exaggerate his fall. Ronin is not fooled by the feint. He delivers a palm heel strike to the place where the ninja ends up and sends the wiry fighter reeling. Pedestrians give them a wide berth. Ronin can read anxiety in the way they hurry along. This is not their business. Surely more Foot soldiers will be swarming in a matter of seconds. Best not to be around when they get here. Ronin takes the ninja by his wrist and wrenches it into a vicious half-turn. This time the fighter's training evaporates and he cries out. The tonfa clatters to the pavement. Ronin takes one step forward and flings the ninja into the mouth of an alley. A single red LED light burns above the back door of a takeout joint.

The ninja hits the greasy cobblestones and comes to rest among piles of black garbage bags. One bag, not quite closed, leaks a thick brown sauce.

"I was skeptical," one of his brothers says, "but you know what, I don't hate this."

The ninja goes for a blade tucked into his belt. Ronin delivers a swift kick to his forearm and the long knife sails into the darkness of the alley. The street noises are muffled in here, the ninja's ragged breaths loud in the quiet. Ronin goes down on one knee. He seizes the Foot Clan fighter by the throat. With his other hand, he yanks the soldier's black mask off. Perhaps Ronin is simply old, but the ninja strikes him as a shockingly young man. He is white with a high forehead and a shock of wavy brown hair. Sweat beads on his upper lip. Ronin sweeps back his own hood and leans into the cone of red light. Ronin grins as the Foot soldier's eyes go wide.

"*Mutant*," he rasps.

"Yeah," Ronin says.

"This one's a genius," one of his brothers says.

"I'm gonna let go of your throat so you can answer my questions," Ronin says, leaning in. He hopes he still stinks like the river. "You try to call for your buddies, access some hidden comm, and I'll break your jaw. You go for a weapon or try to make a run for it, and I'll break the rest of you. Clear?"

The kid nods. "M-my name's Jacob," he says. Ronin can smell the fear on his breath, acrid and biting. "I take care of my mother and sister, I only do this because—"

"I don't care why you do it."

The kid nods again.

"Your boss. Oroku Hiroto."

The kid swallows. "Please," he says. "He'll kill my whole family just for talking to you."

"Then we better make this quick. Hiroto's tower—he live there full-time?"

The kid's mouth opens. He shakes his head. "I don't know what you mean."

"I mean, will I find him there tonight?"

"Tonight? I don't know."

Ronin shoves a cloaked forearm against Jacob's neck. A gurgling sound escapes. Ronin moves closer, pressing harder. Terror dilates the kid's pupils.

"I just mean . . ." He tries to speak. Ronin eases up. The kid coughs. "I just mean I don't know exactly about the tower. But he never leaves Foot City. I know that."

Ronin fights the urge to draw his brother's sai and drive it into this soldier's neck. A red mist blossoms across his vision. He trembles with rage. "You call New York *Foot City* now?"

Ronin picks up the scent of urine. The ninja's pissed himself. "No! Not all of New York. It's just the nickname we have for the blocks around the tower. It's walled off. It's a different world inside."

"You live there?"

The kid chokes out a laugh. "I look filthy rich to you? I just guard it when I'm not on patrol. Please, like I said, I'm no Hiroto worshipper, this was the only work I could get, and my mother's—"

Ronin lowers his arm in disgust. "Shut up." The kid rubs his neck, wincing. Ronin shifts his weight back on his heels, giving the kid a moment.

"Tell me about Foot City. What kind of security are we talking about?"

"Um, plates in the wall that are pressure sensitive so you can't climb or you'll trip the alarms. And then tons of us, of course. Foot Clan I mean. Other booby traps I don't know about. I don't have the right clearance." He pauses. "And mousers."

Ronin reflexively shudders at the mention of the robotic monsters. He shakes off a cascade of painful memories. "So Stockman's there, too?"

The kid looks confused. "Baxter Stockman? In the tower? No. I don't think he ever leaves Roosevelt Island."

An island in the middle of the toxic sludge river makes a good place for a lair. Ronin files this away for later.

"Ask about the sewers," one of his brothers says.

"Chill, okay?" Ronin's irritation flares. "I'm getting to that."

"Um," Jacob's eyes dart from side to side. "Who are you talking to?"

Ronin ignores him. "Tell me: Are there manhole covers in Foot City?"

"Manhole covers?"

"Sewer lids, dipshit."

"Yeah, yeah, I know . . ." Jacob's brow furrows as he thinks. "Yes!" he says after a pause. "There's definitely a bunch of manhole covers."

Blue light splashes down the alley, turning the red LED purple. In his peripheral vision, Ronin catches sight of a radiant tropical beverage floating past the mouth of the alley. He waits for the dim red glow to return. Then he shifts his voice to a low growl.

"What else?"

"That's all I know, I swear!"

"You gonna let your asshole buddies know I'm coming?"

Jacob hesitates. Ronin can practically hear his frightened mind churn.

He gives the kid a quick rabbit punch to his gut. "No," Jacob says after his breath comes back. He shakes his head. "No way."

Ronin glares at him. Then he gets to his feet. Jacob's eyes are white shining orbs peering up fearfully from the gloom. He shows the kid the black Foot Clan mask still crumpled in his fist. Then he tosses it into the darkness at the other end of the alley.

"Find a new job."

And he's gone.

5

JONES SHOVES THE DOOR to Hilty's Pub with her shoulder and steps inside. Rank humidity slaps her in the face, along with the mingled odors of sweat, leather, and stale beer. She peels off her riding gloves and flexes her fingers. The throttle on her motorcycle has been giving her shit lately, and her hand is sore from pulling it tight to open up the engine. The juke in the corner's blasting dub and the bassline rattles in her chest.

Some wastrel staggers out of a corner booth and gives her a fist bump without stopping. "Sup, Jones." And the man is gone, whirling off across Hilty's sticky floor to glom onto some other tight-knit cabal of Lower East Siders.

Jones looks over her shoulder. Hilty's single square window is begrimed with filth. Totally opaque. It's force of habit to check on her heavily modded bike, even though nobody—not even the most hard-up LES resident—would dare snatch one parked in front of Hilty's. That would only bring those inside *outside*, and those inside were people you did not want to mess with.

Besides, the bridges and tunnels have been sealed off for years. Anyone dumb enough to jack her bike for a joyride would be stuck on twenty-two square miles of island. Easy enough to find, then break. You could be sure about that, and Jones has a health respect for certainty. It's a rare commodity in the city these days.

She sidles past a crew of mechanics in their spot by the bar.

"Hey, we don't serve kids here!"

Jones peers beyond the mechanics. The bartender, an old-timer everybody calls Wink, is spiraling a wet dishrag along the bar's age-pocked wood. He's mean-mugging her, the wrinkled flesh of his face a map of contempt. He plops the dishrag on the bar and points to the door. Jones folds her arms across her chest and glares back. Then Wink's face breaks into a grin. One of the mechanics looks from Wink to Jones and shakes his head. Same old joke. Never gets old. Wink picks up a broom and rams its handle up into the middle of an ancient, dusty ceiling fan. The fan musters a low, desultory spin.

Jones makes her way to a sunken booth in the back corner. A poster on the wall advertises some ancient punk show. There are no holo-ads in Hilty's, no screens of any kind. Drinking here is like stepping back in time. The dreadful bathrooms are even covered in graffiti—Hilty's doesn't spring for Stockman Klean-tech to combat vandalism.

At the edge of the table, she puts her hands on her hips. "You guys wanna make some room?"

Four heads turn to her. A granite slab of a man speaks first. "Maybe you can go get a high chair," he suggests.

"Maybe you can drink river sludge, Crunch."

He lifts his pint and makes a show of examining his half-drunk beer. "I think maybe I already am? Wink really needs to change the taps."

He shrugs and drains the glass. Shirtless but for a black leather vest, the veins in his muscles are like fat worms trapped just beneath his skin.

"You know when the last time these taps were changed?" The equally imposing man next to Crunch pipes up. "You could get a taxi to take you across the bridge to Brooklyn."

Jones gives the second man a nod. "Nice vest, Scrape. New pickup?"

Crunch and Scrape are practically brothers, and Jones, as an only child, is a keen student of their dynamic. They orbit the same fashion universe but don't quite overlap, like variations on a theme. Crunch is bald, Scrape rocks a mohawk and ratty goatee. Crunch likes classic leather vests, Scrape goes for canvas with studded epaulets. Sometimes it seems to Jones like they want desperately to do the identical thing—same clothes, same hairstyles—but social anxiety is getting in the way. She has often longed for a non-awkward way to tell them she supports whatever weird aesthetic choices they want to make.

"Nah," Crunch says. "He just washed it."

Scrape refills Crunch's beer from a pitcher that looks like a coffee mug in his massive hand. "So what's the good word, Jones?"

"I don't know. No words are good, lately."

Across the table from Crunch and Scrape, a young Chinese guy named Breaker in a beanie and sporting an immaculate mustache slides over, patting the booth's duct-taped leather. "Plenty of room over here on the fun side of the booth."

Jones takes him up on it. She can feel the metal springs through the worn cushion. "Thanks, B."

She'd met Breaker a year or so back when a couple of Triads were giving her a hard time over in Seward Park. Jones could've handled things herself, but she appreciated that someone stuck their neck out. Breaker would do anything for anybody. Loyalty—that's another thing she has a healthy respect for. And she'd found it in these freaks.

The fourth guy in the booth doesn't look up from the small gadget he's tinkering with. It looks like a radio, but who knows. Lug rarely speaks, and his eyes are hidden behind visor-like sunglasses that clip to his temples. Jones has never actually seen his eyes. Except for his unruly hair, gaunt face, and slender hands, she's never seen any part of him. He favors long-sleeve jumpsuits and steel-toed boots.

"Hey, Lug," she says, "keep it down over there."

Everyone waits for his lips to twitch into the hint of a smile.

"There it is," Scrape says. The men all drink.

"Thanks for the glass, guys." Jones indicates the empty table in front of her. "Bunch of gentlemen, seriously."

Crunch pushes a full pitcher toward her. "Get chuggin'. You got some catching up to do."

Breaker yanks the pitcher away by the handle. Beer sloshes onto the floor. Jones imagines an acidic hiss as it hits the tiles. "You're underage, Jones."

She grabs Breaker's glass and drains half a beer before he can snatch it back. The warm, foamy ale tastes like motor oil. She fights the urge to gag. Better off pouring the beers at Hilty's into your bike instead of down your throat. Jones swipes the back of her hand across her mouth. "Like the cops give a shit about some Rock Bottom dive."

"Ha!" Crunch's big palm slaps the table. "*Cops*. That's a good one, Jones."

"I thought I saw one of our boys in blue last week," Scrape says. "Turns out it was just a mailman."

"It's not the cops I'm worried about," Breaker says. "If your mom smells booze on your breath again, she'll break me in half."

"My mom says the cops actually used to patrol Rock Bottom," Jones says, "before the wall."

"Sure did," Breaker says with authority. "There were detectives, too. When somebody got killed back then, they actually tried to find out who did it."

"To be fair," Jones says, "somebody gets killed today, everybody already knows who did it."

"Yeah," Breaker says, "but back in the day, they actually used to get arrested."

Crunch elbows Scrape. "This guy's talking like he was there."

"I'm older than you," Breaker points out.

"You're *twenty-four*," Scrape says. "That makes you older than me 'n Crunch by one year, old-timer."

Breaker slides the pitcher back over to Jones. "Your mom asks, it was Lug who gave you the beer."

Next to him, Lug leans in closer to the exposed wiry innards of the device. A portable soldering iron emits a ribbon of white smoke.

Jones glares at Breaker, then holds the pitcher with two hands and upends it to pour beer down her gullet. She forces down her gag reflex at the oily taste. She's seventeen, tall and muscular, and tonight she wears dark purple riding leathers with a matching bucket hat and goggles. The outfit makes her look older and helps her blend in. Just another biker cruising through the fluid subcultures of the Lower East Side.

She slams the pitcher down on the table. "I do love blaming Lug for things."

Crunch nods. "It's the best."

Suddenly, Lug looks up from his work. The soldering gun poised in his hand. The jukebox dub rattles the framed posters on the wall. "Hey," he says.

Jones is astonished. They always rag on Lug day and night and he never says a word.

"Shit, man," Scrape says gently. "We're sorry, we didn't mean—"

"*Shhhh!*"

Jones is taken aback by the fierceness of Lug's voice. "Lug, what the hell, man?"

Lug cocks his head like a dog straining to listen. His visor shimmers in the dim light. "Can't you guys hear that?"

The crew goes quiet. Jones tries to sort through the noise around her. There's the thick, syrupy bass of the music, the chatter of Hilty's patrons, peals of laughter, an occasional shout, glasses hitting tables—all of it bouncing off the bar's low ceiling. She frowns at

Crunch across the table, whose bushy eyebrows furrow into a V. He shrugs.

"You got us, Lug. What are we hearing?"

"I think someone is messing with our bikes."

Scrape looks around the table. "Is he, like, doing a bit?"

"Hold on," Breaker holds up a finger. "You know what, I think I hear it, too. The way Lug rebuilt those engines, they don't sound like your average set of wheels."

Jones can't hear anything except Hilty's din, but she slides out of the booth. "We might as well go see what's up. Beats sitting here listening to you guys talk about the olden days when the cops still showed their faces in Rock Bottom."

"Ah," Crunch says, rising to his full height, ducking his head like a penitent beneath the ceiling. "It was a gentler time all around, lads."

The crowd parts without looking, warned by Rock Bottom instinct that Crunch and Scrape are coming through. Breaker and Lug follow, with Jones at the rear.

Outside, a row of air-bikes crouch like dormant beetles. An ancient Harley sits on its kickstand, a tiny Maltese in goggles inhabiting its sidecar. Twin Jet Spiders gleam. There are skinny little Needles and clunky old Yamasakis. Jones's gaze sweeps across Breaker's polished black Street Bob, right next to Lug's lime-green Corsair, Crunch's blaze-orange Triumph, and Scrape's vintage purple Scout . . .

"You have got to be kidding me," she says.

The space where she'd parked her cherry-red Softail Slim is empty. Light shines in a dime-sized drop of oil on the pavement, the only remnant of her bike, her one true love. Jones begins to pace in a circle. "What the *hell*." Her bike isn't the flashiest. It would have been tough to steal. She eyes the other motorcycles with sudden contempt. There are a dozen junk boxes that would've been easier pickings. Why'd the thief have to single hers out? Her face is burning.

She wants to rip off her hat and scream at the sky. But she controls herself and screams at passersby instead.

"Did any of you see who jacked my bike just now?" A middle-aged couple averts their eyes as they pass. "Hey! I'm talkin' to you!" They hurry down the street and melt into the crowd. Jones flags down a teenage girl. "You see who took my bike?" She waves a hand at the empty space where the bike used to be. "You know which way he went?"

"Jones," Crunch says.

She ignores him. "Hey!" she stalks over to a man in a canary-yellow suit carrying a battered briefcase. "You see who took my bike?" The man shakes his head and quickens his pace.

"Jones!" Crunch takes her by the arm. "Easy. We'll find the bastard."

She shrugs him off and looks at the faces of her friends. Anger knots her stomach. She rips off her hat and runs a hand through her sweat-slicked hair. Then she turns to Crunch. "Who would be so *stupid*?"

6

RONIN LEANS FORWARD AND opens up the throttle. The tires bite the pavement and the bike surges ahead. He chose the red Softail at random, snapped the ignition, and started it with the tip of his brother's sai in place of a screwdriver. The theft had taken forty seconds. Nobody shot him a second look. He needed speed, and he found it in this bike. The throttle's a little sticky, but other than that, he can't complain. Now the eyes of the streets won't see a mutant turtle, just some jackass in a black outfit cruising east on Houston.

Ronin weaves between a bakery van and a taxi. He catches a whiff of freshly baked bread. The cab driver curses out the window. A gold chain hangs from his rearview. Ronin smirks. His brothers must be loving this.

"Yeah, till you get pancaked by a semitruck."

"And we go forever unavenged."

Ronin swerves around a beat-up old sedan. "You guys have been really dramatic since we got to the city."

The ride is a peculiar mixture of nostalgia and wonder. Antigrav traffic cycles above the streets in a dreamlike parallel to the free-for-all of earthbound vehicles on Houston. Light from holo-ads filters down through the whirring rows of air-cars, casting splotches of reds and yellows on familiar buildings that are no longer as he remembers them.

Ronin hangs a left to pick up the Bowery, heading north. His mind overlays old signs and awnings over the sterile new buildings

he speeds past. The pub where Casey Jones liked to have a nightcap after a long shift busting heads. The coffee shop with April O'Neil's favorite blend. A hundred different manhole covers and sewer grates, all of them leading to the labyrinth he and his brothers called home, with the lair as its underground nerve center, where their wise old father, Splinter, would be waiting for them . . .

The old signs and awnings flicker away, leaving behind new facades in their wake. Gone, too, are the friends he'll never see again. The father he'd buried in foreign soil.

The whine of the bike's engine coalesces into the hated name. *Oroku Hiroto.*

He grits his teeth.

"Easy, bro."

He twists the bike's throttle, handlebar gripped tight in his fist. The engine revs. The saddle vibrates. The exhaust pipe gives off a fierce heat that travels up his leg. He comes up fast on a furniture delivery truck with a grinning sofa emblazoned across the back of its trailer. At the last second Ronin careens around the truck and hangs a left onto Eighth Street. The bike fishtails, tires shrieking on the blacktop as he eases the throttle. He's heading west now, and the landscape of Lower Manhattan shifts before his eyes. It's as if the city has shed yet another skin.

Ahead, blotting out the smog-blurred moon, Hiroto's megastructure rises atop four skyscraper-sized stanchions to challenge even the World Trade Center. A glass canopy spreads out from the main tower like an apron, covering several blocks of Manhattan in an artificial sky.

Foot City.

Jacob's words echo in his head. Only people with money can afford to live there. The rest live under the thumb of the Foot Clan patrols, eking out a living at street level, the place they call Rock Bottom. He figures anybody in between rich and poor lives in those sterile new buildings he sees everywhere, holo-ads shining in their windows. All of these people, in ways big and small, trudging through their lives in service to the man who watches them from his magnificent tower. Eighth Street passes in a riot of noise and fluorescence. Ronin's vision narrows to a tunnel that pulses with his racing heart.

"Bro . . ."

He imagines yanking back on the handlebars and with brute strength willing the bike up the side of the tower, leaving Rock Bottom behind as he rockets into the rarefied air that Hiroto poisons with his breath. Crashing in through a penthouse window, jumping the bike onto the man's lavishly appointed table, splattering his art collection with the ruins of his feast, aiming the front wheel straight at Hiroto's wide, terrified eyes—

"Bro, look out!"

Ronin cranks the bike sideways and skids to a stop in front of a sheer, nondescript barrier rising from the middle of the road. Crumpled fast-food bags and glass bottles are strewn along the wall's cement base. Six-inch spikes poke up like railroad ties hammered up from under the street.

"Shit."

He should have noticed the sudden change in atmosphere. Sixth Avenue is a desolate no-man's-land. High above, the tower seems to hover atop its stanchions. Foot City's glass canopy stretches for several blocks in every direction, tinting the sky a dark shade of red.

"You can't actually drive through walls," one of his brothers says. "Not sure if you knew that."

One boot on the ground to balance his bike, Ronin peers deep into the blood-colored night. He bites back a growl of rage. No one surrounds this city—*Ronin's* city—with a massive wall, then carves up the West Village into a fortress to keep out the have-nots.

A sudden movement catches Ronin's attention. His hand goes to his brother's sai. A section of the wall opens up. From this perfect square emerges a mechanical arm, triple jointed, tipped with a narrowing point. The point of the arm seeks out yellow-and-green scrawl: graffiti letters, bulbous and vibrant. Ronin squints to make them out. *DIE FOOT DIE.* A motor grinds quietly. The tip of the arm traces the letters, erasing the paint, leaving bare cement in its wake as if the message was never there.

"Stockman," Ronin mutters, thinking back to Jacob's intel. The mad scientist in league with the scion of ninja royalty. Pressure-sensitive plates. Secret traps. Scaling the wall is out of the question. There's bound to be more formidable tech inside the walls of Foot City, too. Mousers and worse creations.

But there's no such thing as perfect security. He turns the bike around.

Gotta be a sewer around here somewhere.

7

FROM ASTRIDE HIS BIKE, Ronin gazes through a chain-link fence into a sunken loading dock—a drab cement space carved out of the bedrock a dozen feet below street level. One side of the dock is the base of a massive stanchion. Ronin surveys the construction. Steel reinforced with the same matte-finish polymer that provides the framework for all the soulless new construction that grows like a mundane fungus through Manhattan. The sight of it tweaks his simmering anger up a notch. He suspects it's another Stockman innovation. His eyes catch movement. A team of workers in orange jumpsuits and caps pile out of a Bizley Fuel truck with Jersey plates. Besides the chopper access for the one-percenters, Hiroto must have a secret land route in and out of the city. Three of the Bizley workers connect a hose to a large metal tank shaped like an oversize lozenge.

A low mechanical heaving—some unseen winch—slots into place. A gust of stale, sour air rises from the dock, displaced by whatever machine's come to life to deal with the influx of fuel.

And there, just beyond the truck, Ronin sees it: a round metal grate, slapped on the side of the dock that meets the stanchion. He can feel his brothers' collective energy tick up, like a sudden gasp inside his mind.

"That right there? That's a sweet, sweet sewer entrance," one points out.

"The best kind, too. The ultrarare vertically situated manhole cover," another ghost adds.

"Just walk right in like it's a door. Remember to wipe your feet," suggests the third.

Ronin's eyes catch movement at the margins of the loading dock. It's a forlorn place but not forgotten. Machinery clanks. A row of yellow bulbs blinks on, off, on, off. Another foul gust catches Ronin in its updraft.

"You shoulda stole a glider instead of a motorcycle," a ghost tells him, "then you coulda sailed down there like Snake Plissken!"

Besides the orange-clad Bizley team, Ronin picks out a trio of Foot Clan guards. They pad softly on patrol, wraiths in the darkness.

"Think you can take 'em all out before they report the mutant turtle loose in the city?" He can hear the caution in his brother's voice.

Ronin looks from the guards to the workers to the truck to the sewer entrance. "Don't have to take 'em all out. There's this thing called a *diversion*."

"I know what a diversion is."

Ronin's lips peel back into a smile.

With his dead brother's sharpened sai, he quietly severs chain links until he can peel back a segment of the fence large enough for a three-hundred-pound mutant turtle to ride a motorcycle through. The workers' voices swell as they laugh at some private joke. Just some contractors out on a job. Ronin tries not to lump them in with the Foot Clan, with Hiroto, but he wonders how far the rot spreads. You can't always draw a hard line between the innocent and the guilty. City's always been like that. Even before the wall. With one hand, he frees a grenade from his belt. With the other he releases the motorcycle's hand brake and rockets forward. The bike roars off the edge of the street and arcs beautifully above the loading zone. At the peak of his jump, he wedges the grenade behind the bike's speedometer. *Three*. He angles the bike toward the fuel truck's massive tank and pushes off the seat. *Two*. He leaps away from the doomed bike.

One.

The bike crashes wheels-first into the fuel tank. Ronin hits the pavement and rolls away from the truck.

The explosion comes a split second later: percussive blast followed by shock wave. Ronin's feet are in the air and he's slammed hard to the pavement. Molten metal flung from the sides of the truck hits the stanchion at his back. Ronin feels the heat singe his mask. He shuts his eyes and turns away. Sparks eat holes in his cloak. A dull pain radiates from his shell. He notes distantly that he took a piece of shrapnel. Down on one knee, he surveys the dock. Black smoke roils from the husk of the truck, its sides peeled open like a metal flower in bloom.

Someone cries out. Foot soldier or fuel truck grunt, Ronin can't tell. He doesn't poke around the wreckage to find out. He coughs up tarry phlegm and spits on the stanchion. Then he scampers to the manhole. With a lifetime of practice, he enters the sewer and replaces the cover behind him. Outside, muted voices call out for their colleagues. He imagines shell-shocked men staggering through the black smoke, and he wonders how many of them made it. He tells himself he didn't know the explosion would be so powerful. It's a feeble lie.

"Well, that was real graceful," one of the ghosts says.

"Worked, didn't it? We're inside." Ronin shakes off thoughts of families waiting back in Hoboken for fathers and husbands to come home. If there's a scale in the afterlife to balance his accounts, he'll be standing before it soon enough.

"Check out the wall," another voice says. "About a million cables down here."

"And junction boxes," the third points out. "That means computers. Maybe you can download a map of the tower."

"No time. *Up* is the only direction I need." Ronin shoves heavy fiber optics aside and ducks into a tunnel. His boots disturb a layer of muck. Rats scurry. Warmth gathers in Ronin's belly. Home at last.

An access ladder glimmers in the sickly half-light. He grabs a cold rung.

"You should be more methodical," a ghost admonishes. "You can't rely on luck a hundred percent of the time. It won't last forever."

"Doesn't need to last forever." Ronin squeezes his bulky frame through a shaft that narrows as he climbs. The shrapnel embedded in his shell scrapes the wall. It feels like a splinter he can't extract, an itch he can't scratch. "Only needs to last a little bit longer."

8

RONIN LIFTS THE MANHOLE cover and peers out into a new world, his masked eyes darting back and forth. Shades of salmon-colored light filter down from the vast glass apron that blossoms out from Hiroto's tower. It's like he's at the bottom of a coral reef, gazing up at the faraway surface.

"It's so peaceful . . ." The wonderment in his brother's tone—almost an appreciation—stokes his ire.

"Mmm," he grunts. At the same time he admits to himself that Foot City does resemble a classic utopian vision—the future city he'd always imagined, fed by sci-fi and classic comics. The streets look newly paved. The sidewalks are uncracked and free of litter. The facades of the buildings are polished to a high sheen.

"No cars," Ronin points out. No wonder it's peaceful. Citizens roam freely as if browsing an open-air market. He catches impressions of latex skirts, glimmering cardigans, shoes that mimic bare feet. Weird shit that must be the height of upper-class fashion. Laughter drifts down into the manhole. Carefree, lilting voices. The clink of glasses from a sidewalk wine bar.

"Look up, genius."

Ronin does—and beholds an orderly rotation of antigrav traffic. The vehicles hum along, boosted by their dully glowing maglevs. He expects to smell the telltale burnt-metal odor of the engines. Instead he picks up a neutral scent. Vaguely floral but not cloying like heavy perfume.

"Filtered air," one of his brothers says. "These people got it all."

"You couldn't pay me to live in this department store showroom," Ronin says. He sets the manhole cover aside and begins to clamber out of the sewer.

BIP BIP BIP BIP BIP BIP . . .

Ronin curses at the sudden persistent alarm that blares down the street.

"Maybe if you'd spent a little more time with those junction boxes," a ghost says, "you'd have a better idea of the security waiting for you up top."

Ronin is already exposed. He can feel the well-heeled eyeballs on him. Nothing to do but finish climbing out. He kicks the manhole cover back into place. The alarm doesn't stop. A woman in an asymmetrical dress gasps at the sight of him. A man in a visor takes her arm and hustles her away. A mother shoos her two children onto the sidewalk.

Ronin buzzes with tension. He is an interloper here, a smelly freak who crashed a dinner party. He doesn't give a shit about the way rich people perceive him, but he's attracting too much attention. The metal in his shell throbs. He drops into a fighting stance, swivels his head. Everywhere, people flee like he's a monster. Panic twists their sculpted faces.

"I hate this place," he mutters. It dawns on him what else Foot City is missing, besides the bumper-to-bumper traffic: no holo-ads peeling themselves off sun-bright screens to stalk pedestrians with promises of new low prices on frozen mozzarella sticks and car stereos. Sensory overload's for the riffraff outside the loving arms of Hiroto's canopy. Residents of Foot City are spared the hard sell.

A young boy peers up at him, open-mouthed, speechless. His mother rushes into the street to yank the kid away. She slides a hand to shield the kid's eyes as if Ronin is a true abomination, a nightmare vision for a child to fear.

Three uniformed Foot soldiers materialize in the wake of the dispersing throng. They stand opposite Ronin, the empty blacktop between them, braver citizens lining the sidewalks on either side like spectators at a parade. The Foot soldiers' black body armor and the sidearms on their hips set them apart from the ninjas outside the walls. The jagged three-toed spikes of the Foot Clan emblem adorn their uniforms.

"Halt!" one of the soldiers calls out in a hollow, digitized voice.

Ronin shows his palms. "I'm not moving."

The crowd murmurs. Ronin figures it's the first time these soft citizens have ever seen a confrontation. It's like a lurid scene from Rock Bottom got beamed into Foot City.

The soldiers approach. Ronin clocks their inhuman gait. Methodical yet stilted.

"Put your hands behind your head and get on your knees." That voice again. Like it's coming from a speaker tossed down a well.

Ronin's certain these soldiers are robots. He shakes his head. Stockman's fingerprints are all over this place. These soldiers aren't the first androids Ronin's encountered. But their sophistication makes him less sure of his chances in a fight. Their sleek, dark armor betrays no obvious weak points.

"Apprehension protocol," one of the androids commands. The other two spread out to either side in a flanking maneuver. The trio approaches slowly. Ronin figures their decision matrices are humming, waiting to see if he'll fight or flee so they can adjust tactics. He shifts his weight from one foot to the other, feeling a lightness of being course through him. The spirits of his three brothers make their wishes known, that they want him to attack these enemies, to feel the glory and rage of a fight through his pulsing adrenaline.

Ronin wears their weapons on his back—one sharpened sai, one katana, a simple wooden bō staff, a pair of nunchaku—and his brothers urge him to take the much-loved, battle-scarred weapons into his hands.

"Not here," he mutters.

Not when there are kids lining the street, curious little faces peeking out from between their parents' legs. A stray blade goes flying, a shuriken gets deflected, and the scale that weighs his deeds plummets hard toward irredeemable. So he pulls three silver pellets from his belt and smashes them down on the blacktop. The pellets crack open, releasing chemicals into the filtered air. Jets of thick, opaque smoke rise and swirl. In seconds, Ronin is obscured completely. Bystanders fade to silhouettes in the sudden haze. Ronin moves swiftly and silently through ranks of frightened citizens fanning their faces, carving fleeting trails of fresh air through the tenacious cloud. He darts into an alley between residential towers. The narrow space defies what he knows about alleys. No piles of trash bags, no overflowing dumpster, no sour smells or sleeping rolls of houseless people. Nothing but sanitized polymer to either side as his boots hit uncluttered pavement.

The alley spits him out onto an empty tennis court. A single floodlight spills a white glow that casts an elongated shadow from the net. Across the court, Ronin spies a row of darkened balconies capped with striped awnings. Spectator boxes. Without hesitation, he crosses the court to an old-time wrought iron lamppost. A silly anachronism, but lucky: Its decorative flourishes give him handholds for an easy climb. Ten feet above the court, Ronin leaps from a perch atop the light to the balcony. He climbs over the side, ducks down behind the partition, and raises his head to peer across the court.

"Those androids gotta be stocked with all kinds of tracking tech," Ronin says to his brothers.

"I bet we see them in three—"

"Two—"

"One," Ronin says under his breath. A moment later, the trio emerges from the mouth of the alley.

"Nailed it, bro."

The androids fan out to either side of the court as if they're getting ready for a match. The third android pauses by the net.

A red beam emanates from the android's helmet. It sweeps back and forth along the ground. Ronin has the uncomfortable sensation that it's picking up his scent like a hunting dog.

"That won't be too hard. You reek."

The beam freezes. Then the android lifts its head and the thin red line rises up the lamppost, jumps to the balcony partition, and pierces the darkness above Ronin's head. He glances over his shoulder. The red dot hits a mirror above a wet bar and goes prismatic. Spokes of laser light refract.

Then it blinks off. Darkness returns to the spectator box. Ronin lifts his head to peek out at the court.

The android is standing by the lamppost, staring up at Ronin's balcony. Then it draws a blade. A long, familiar blade.

"Robot security with a *katana*?" His brother sounds indignant. Ronin is offended by the sight. A walking piece of Stockman tech wielding an ancient weapon that true ninjas dedicate their lives to studying. He makes a fist. Everything about Foot City is a parody, an imitation. Hiroto cleared the decks—took out Ronin's entire family—to make way for a soulless vision. The insult drives him from his hiding place.

"You guys are about to get your wish," he tells his brothers. Adrenaline courses along his half-shell and imbues their weapons with life. The shrapnel's dull ache melts away. He vaults over the balcony's edge and lands in front of the android. Without giving Ronin a moment to square off, the robot attacks.

Its strikes are fast and vicious, its form perfect. Ronin feels the wind of the blade as it whistles close to his face and neck. Yet he doesn't feel threatened. The attack is metronomic and predictable. The android swings the katana with the rote mimicry of kenjutsu—Japanese swordsmanship—but there is no heart behind the technique. It's like fighting a chess simulator. It knows all the moves, but it's vulnerable to brute force.

If you're sick of the game, you simply break it.

Ronin slips, evades, then counterattacks. He lands a flurry of rapid punches. His jabs shatter the android's faceplate. A human hand would be ripped to shreds, but his tough reptilian skin protects his knuckles. He rolls his shoulder back to dodge the katana's downstroke. The android gives him an opening. Ronin's fists connect—one-two—with the robot's head. Fragments of faceplate scatter across the court like sleek black puzzle pieces.

The blade drops. The robot crumples. Ronin watches the lights on its helmet flicker and go dark. He fixes his hood and scans the court for the other two androids. They stand at their respective baselines, perfectly still, staring at him.

He extends his arms. "You waiting for an invitation?"

They do not move.

"What the hell?" he says to his brothers.

"Filming you," one suggests. "Sending the video back to the nerve center."

"Hmm," Ronin says. With a sudden flick of his wrist, he launches a shuriken at one of the androids. It leans to the side and the pointed silver star whips harmlessly past its head and embeds itself in a lamppost with a soft *thunk*.

The android straightens and makes no attempt to counterattack.

"Have it your way," Ronin says. Their behavior unsettles him. He wishes they would draw their weapons, fire some Stockman death ray at him, charge him with their own katanas drawn. But they keep up the statue act. He gives them a wave. Then he moves toward a set of double doors under the spectator boxes, shifting his focus to the tower and all that lies ahead. He takes four steps before the whirring of a servomotor halts him. Metal scrapes against the court's hard surface. Ronin sighs. He turns to watch the downed android regain its footing. Its legs buckle then right themselves. It moves like a puppy learning to walk.

"H-halt," it tells him. Ronin is puzzled by the quaver in its voice. An emotional stutter, an almost human hesitation. Maybe he'd punched it hard enough to damage its processor.

The android lurches into a fighting stance. Its frame trembles, then goes perfectly still. The whirring sound ceases. Ronin waits. The robot does not advance. Likely waiting for Ronin to strike first. The secondary androids make no move to intervene. He considers the weapons slung across his back. Sai, katana, bō, nunchaku. All that remains of his brothers. He reaches back and grips the handle of the katana. Matching this robotic ninja blade for blade seems poetic. But then his stomach curdles, and he releases the handle. This soldier is an abomination. It has never trained. Never studied the ancient techniques Ronin's father passed down to his four sons. This thing before him now has only ever been *programmed*.

It isn't worthy of facing his brothers' weapons.

He draws his tonfa instead. Twin batons of iron-reinforced wood. If blunt force fails, the tonfa are equipped with an electromagnetic pulse generator built into each shaft. An EMP ends this fight before it begins, but it isn't subtle. One blast could bring all of Foot City's security down on him.

Ronin twirls the batons. He shifts his weight to his back foot. The android scans the movement and leaps forward. Its speed is impressive considering its broken face. The mechanical arm spins its blade like a child's toy. Ronin takes in the fluidity of the advance, the inhuman grace. An untrained fighter would be cut to ribbons. But Ronin reads movements like words on a page—years of repetition and honed instinct telling a story he's heard a million times before.

Ronin splits his energies. One tonfa blocks the katana's down-stroke while its twin strikes the robot's head. Ronin's control is absolute, yet even he is a little stunned by how much power he puts behind the single blow. The robot's connective tissue frays at the neck. Its head cocks to one side and it regards Ronin with a certain sad bewilderment. Then the cords of plastic, metal, and wiring give way with a sizzle. The android's head slides off its ruined neck and hits the ground. Each bounce leaves shards of faceplate on the green court.

He glances up at the other two androids. They stare back with implacable calm, long shadows stretching to the bistro tables that line the far wall. Their inaction makes him angry.

"Hey!" he calls out, waving his tonfa like he's landing a plane. "I just killed your pal, you gonna do anything about it?"

"Nah," a ghost says. "They know they can't beat you. They've already done the calculations, or whatever."

Ronin stows his tonfa in his belt. "So what are they gonna do, then?"

One of the androids speaks. "Suspect located in Recreation Zone 661. Requesting air support."

"There you go."

"Reinforcements. Classic."

Ronin glances up. The pinkish glow descending from the glass apron is the color of a late summer sunset. He wonders what form *air support* will take. He tunes out his brothers' chatter and gives the android's severed head one last look. It seems to glare at Ronin from the wreckage of its helmet. Something glints: a soft hint of life. Ronin takes a step toward it.

"What the hell?"

He goes down on one knee to examine the jagged pucker of the ruined faceplate. He reaches out and snaps off a shard. Behind it lies the pale, blotchy skin of a human being. A single unblinking eye stares back at him. The pupil is ringed in metal. Ronin has witnessed countless deaths. He is certain there is still intelligence behind that eye. It widens with fear of the unknown, and then the void takes hold. The eye goes glassy and dark.

"Is there a *person* inside that armor?" one of his brothers asks.

"Looks like some kind of cyborg. More synthetic than human."

The third voice quivers with disgust: "A synthetic ninja? A *synja*? What kind of sick freak does that to someone?"

"The reason we're here," Ronin says. "That's who."

He stands. The other two androids are gone. Air support's gotta be zeroing in. Time to move. He kicks open the nice white doors beneath the spectator boxes. A deadbolt pops through the frame. He pads through an empty café, its tables set for tomorrow's breakfast service, then stops for a moment. He permits himself a deep, steadying breath. Another. The very first lesson his father taught him and his brothers comes back to him now, Splinter's calming voice ringing in his head.

Strike hard.

Fade away into the night.

Never lose focus.

9

"HALT!"

The strained electronic command of another synja echoes across rooftops of Foot City. A warning shot grazes Ronin's hood. The androids—cyborgs, whatever—are better shots than they are martial artists. He darts behind a row of boxy HVAC units. High ground ought to give him the advantage. That's why he scrambled up the first fire escape he saw. But an army of synjas is swarming, pouring across the rooftops all around him.

He takes a moment to consider his predicament. A localized alert blares from speakers on every block of the streets below. Ronin grits his teeth. Good that the civilians are off the streets. Bad that the whole city-within-a-city knows he's here. A second shot caroms off the HVAC's steel casing at his back. He senses movement on the rooftops across the street. Clocks black helmets everywhere.

"Good news is, you're not being hunted."

"Bad news is, you're being *herded*."

Ronin agrees with his brothers. The synjas are moving him like a pawn to set him up for the ending Hiroto's chosen for him.

He imagines a barrage of rockets. Homing missiles fired from some Stockman drone swooping down from the canopy. The Oroku Hiroto he remembers won't have a problem taking out a city block to kill the last surviving mutant turtle. Collateral damage means nothing to a man like that.

A third high-caliber round takes a chunk out of the corner of the HVAC box. Ronin shields his eyes as bits of torn metal pepper the air.

"Might want to do your deep thinking on the run," a ghost prods.

He scans the rooftops. Foot City's enclosure has skewed his sense of direction. He can't map his line of sight onto the larger city. All he knows is Hiroto's megastructure, the lynchpin of Manhattan's inner fiefdom, rises just a few blocks ahead. This close, the tower is a provocation.

"Architectural nightmare is what it is," one of his brothers says.

Another snorts. "Nerd."

The structure tapers up from a foundation that spans several blocks. Tiers of glass like terraced earthworks pour down the sides, frozen in liquid metal frameworks. It looks to Ronin like every light is burning in thousands of residences. The middle section narrows to a standard skyscraper's width, shining with an off-white, sterile application of the polymer that repeats throughout the city. Ronin's eyes sweep upward. The top third of the tower juts out in gradations like the prow of an ocean liner. He imagines Hiroto at the top, gazing across his territory like Alexander the Great, *no more worlds to conquer.* And capping the roof, so high he can barely make it out, is upsloping ornamentation stolen from a Japanese temple, from which the canopy blossoms to define the enclave.

Footsteps patter across the rooftop. Ronin breaks off his observation.

"Seriously," his brother warns, "time to go."

He springs from his hiding place. Shots ring out. Rounds slap into a rooftop doorframe. White splinters pock the night. Ronin cuts left, puts a water tower between himself and the synja. He could turn and face down the android, but by the time he destroys it, a dozen more will swarm him. He leaps across an alley, lands hard, rolls on the rooftop to absorb the shock. Dull pain shudders inward from his shell. He's just shoved that goddamn shrapnel in a little farther.

Across the silver-tiled roof, past a gazebo twined with flowering plants, Ronin climbs a trellis and vaults over a low wall and winds up feetfirst in a shallow pool. Speckled koi fish scatter at his intrusion. A worried face glances out a massive window.

"Sorry," Ronin says with a wave, but they vanish behind a heavy damask curtain. Beyond the pool, twin stone cherubs spit jets of water into an antique fountain.

"Tennis courts and rooftop koi ponds," a ghost says.

Another one chuckles. "Long way from the sewers, huh."

Ronin keeps moving. On the other side of the gazebo, he comes to the building's edge. Instead of another alley, he finds himself standing just underneath the support beams for an elevated train track that runs above a layer of antigrav traffic. Huge letters in a whimsical calligraphic style tell him he's looking at the Manhattan Dragon. Shadows of the tracks slant down the canyons of Foot City. A snubnosed train whooshes past and the wind in its wake nearly knocks Ronin from the edge of the building. Passengers pressed to windows blur past. He watches the glow of the maglevs recede.

His brothers argue about whether or not he should turn and face down waves of synjas. He ignores them. They sometimes forget that he is *one* and not *four*. Mobs are harder to face alone than with your brothers by your side.

A shot grazes his shell. Ronin leaps across empty space, his heart racing as he's weightless and vulnerable for a long moment in the air. He clutches a support beam, wrapping his arms around cold steel. The beams hum with maglev vibrations, an eerie current that suffuses the Manhattan Dragon's tracks like a distant memory of an electric shock. He climbs around the opposite side of the beam to put steel between his body and the synjas. He's at least a dozen stories high, still partially exposed. Those guns find their mark up here and it's a long way down. So he climbs. Higher ground is his only plan.

A moment later, he's pulling his aching bulk through a maintenance access panel. He crouches on a narrow metal catwalk that runs parallel to thick copper-hued tracks.

"Manhattan Dragon," a ghost says with disdain.

"What's wrong with the subway?" his brother asks.

"Trust me," the third says, "these people don't go underground."

Ronin clears the tracks in a single leap. Now he's on the empty platform. A sign flashing with LEDs tells him the next train's in seven minutes. A curvilinear vending machine offers rows of sweets he's never heard of.

"Ten bucks for a lousy candy bar?"

Ronin waits a moment, ignoring his brother. Synjas come seething across the tracks after him, black-clad androids scuttling like crabs. He rushes to the edge of the platform. The polymer wall comes up to his shoulders, tiles decorated with ornate dragons. He peers over the side.

"Air support incoming," one of his brothers points out.

A sleek black antigrav car breaks free of the traffic flow beneath the elevated tracks. As the car ascends, the red symbol on its roof enlarges. Foot Clan insignia, same as the jagged toes on the androids' armor. He waits until the car is a dozen feet below his vantage point at the dragon wall.

"You can take 'em, bro. All of 'em."

Ronin considers this as a train approaches. The tracks hum with energy. His brothers' anticipation surges through him. The only way to release the pressure is to start the fight.

"Halt!"

He throws a look over his shoulder. A handful of synjas have crossed the tracks. They scamper up onto the platform with uncanny grace. Some draw katanas, others aim their silver double-barreled pistols.

The train whisks into the station. The maglev hum builds to a mosquito whine.

"To be a true warrior," Ronin reminds his brothers as he gets low to the ground, "you must know when to crouch . . ."

Potential energy in his calves and thighs becomes kinetic.

"And when to leap . . ."

He launches himself above the synjas as they close in. A blade carves empty air in the place he had been a split second earlier. Pistols fire. He comes down atop the moving train. There is a jolt of dull pain through his knees and hips. Then he is balanced and upright. The train slows to let its passengers off. The synjas heads' swivel as he rides past.

The antigrav Foot Clan car rises above the wall and matches speed with the train. Ronin grins at the tinted windows.

"But most importantly . . ."

Three steps and he's off the train's smooth back, soaring through the air, arms outstretched—a diver at the top of his arc.

"When to fly."

10

A RAVEN ALIGHTS ON a bank of curved flatscreen monitors to peck at birdseed in a small bowl. Its brothers and sisters whirl above its head as it takes a seed in its beak and rises from the monitor to join the riot of black wings circling the domed ceiling atop the vast penthouse suite of Oroku Hiroto's grand residence. Five stories. Open-concept plan. The raven passes over the dozens of monitors that display the output of Hiroto's supercomputer. Surveillance videos, security reports, dashboards for the departments that keep Foot City running, conference calls between siloed underlings. The raven joins a trio of its brethren as they swoop low over a white marble table, dive into Hiroto's dojo, tighten formation to bank up a short staircase to Hiroto's bedroom, then soar through a humid arboretum where their wings rustle the leaves of orange trees. Mist descends from unseen sprinklers. The birds spiral above their keen-eyed master, whose long dark hair glistens with simulated dew. He plucks a dangling orange from its branch. The birds emit low gurgling croaks as they pass over Hiroto's head and vanish around a corner.

Hiroto offers the ripe fruit to the burly man at his side, a black-armored soldier who carries his helmet under his arm. "Orange, Captain Ikusa?"

"No, thank you, sir." The captain strolls over to a glass wall beyond the trees. Hiroto joins him a moment later, dropping orange peels on the damp floor. A low-slung Stockman Klean-tech bot scuttles behind him to hoover up the refuse. Hiroto eyes the mechanical roach-like cleaner with bland interest. His team swept it for bugs, same as all his in-house Stockman machinery. Yet he can't help but picture the scientist at the center of a nest of surveillance, keeping an eye on Hiroto's inner sanctum. The men he fights. The women he beds. The interminable one-sided conversations with his mother.

The irritating security breaches he's forced to deal with.

Hiroto dismisses the notion of Stockman's spying. He gazes out the window, south across the city, and chews an orange wedge. He grimaces at the taste. Flat. No tartness, no real flavor. He tosses the fruit over his shoulder. It splats against the teak floor. There's a low whirr as the Klean-tech bot scoops it up. The skyline of the old Financial District etches itself against the night beyond Foot City. Hiroto's own reflection ghosts the glass. He meets his sharp-eyed gaze and tucks a strand of jet-black hair behind his ears.

"My mother always said Manhattan was no place to grow citrus," Hiroto says.

"Well, sir." Ikusa gestures toward the small indoor orchard at their backs. "I think you proved her wrong."

Hiroto picks a white spongy pith from his tongue and flicks it away. The orange's bad taste lingers. "Yes, I did."

Hiroto stares out across the city. *His* city. He shifts his weight from one foot to the other. There's a slight strain in his calf from sparring. He'll need an ice bath later. He chooses a distant skyscraper, traces its edges in his mind, and tries to connect some emotion to it. That faraway building is *his*, he tells himself, just as Foot City is *his*. He alone decides whether it stands or falls. With a single command, he could have it detonated, the rubble cleared away. An empty lot in its place. Records of its history permanently deleted. What did the warriors of old do? *Salt the earth.* Make sure nothing ever grows in its place. The city as it stands now is his, yes; but so is its future, its past. The wildest dreams of his family, exceeded. By any measure he is a man of achievement, of purpose, of fulfillment of all earthly promise. He leans forward so that his forehead is pressed against the glass.

Next to him, the chief of his security clears his throat.

Hiroto straightens up. "Captain—did you *like* my mother, back when we were children?"

Ikusa frowns. "Sir, I . . ." He pauses and starts again. "I respected Oroku Karai. We all did." He pauses. "She was a formidable warrior."

Hiroto nods. Platitudes. But what did he expect this man to say? How strange, to watch an old friend begin to hold his tongue, to shape his replies with care. He ought to be used to it by now, this icy remove between himself as the leader of the Foot Clan and everyone else in his orbit. He reaches into his pocket and retrieves a handful of birdseed. He holds out a clenched fist and then opens his hand. A moment later, a raven is perched on his wrist, pecking at the snack. Even his ravens he must bribe with food, or else—

"Are you all right, sir?"

Hiroto lifts his arm and the bird takes flight. He ignores the question. "So what is it about this rogue derelict from Rock Bottom that sent you seventy-seven floors out of your way this evening?"

The captain hesitates. "As you know, ordinarily, we'd have snuffed out the intruder immediately."

"Yes, yes." Hiroto waves a hand. "Insubordination from the lower classes can have a galvanizing effect if left unpunished. A single spark is all it takes. And then"—he makes a fluttering motion with his fingers—"rebellion."

He imbues the word with disgust for the captain's sake. But inside, his stomach knots with excitement. He often dreams of barricades in the streets, masses storming Foot City, pitched battles on every corner. And in his dreams he descends from his tower like an avenging angel, unleashing his fury, painting the streets with blood.

"Yes, sir," Ikusa agrees.

Hiroto waits for him to say something genuine. But the underling act is all-encompassing. A shell of obsequiousness grown hard around his old friend.

"I was in the dojo when the alert pinged," Hiroto says. Gingerly, he shifts his weight to his sore leg, letting his calf bear the strain. Some nameless sparring partner had almost tripped him with a swipe of his bō. Hiroto had recovered quickly and pulped the soldier's face with a palm heel strike. "I figured that was the last I'd hear of it."

"Right, sir. As I said, ordinarily, you'd only find out about it after we'd already dealt with the problem, in tomorrow's security briefing. It wouldn't be the kind of thing I'd personally come and trouble you about."

Hiroto takes a deep breath and tries to banish his impatience. "I understand that, Captain." He lets coldness shape his tone. He takes another breath and a memory surfaces: a weekend at the Foot Clan's retreat in the mountains upstate, just Hiroto and his mother, Ikusa and his parents, and a few other high-ranking families. Hiroto and Ikusa bashing each other with pool noodles, cannonballing off the diving board, splashing the adults on their lounge chairs . . .

Hiroto brings himself back to the present. "Yet here you are." He tries to smile. From the look on Ikusa's face, it is a grotesque parody. He relaxes his facial muscles. Somewhere, a raven squawks.

"Yes, well . . ." Ikusa trails off. Hiroto frowns. His old friend is a battle-hardened warrior. What could be making him nervous?

Ikusa produces a tablet computer from a slim case.

Hiroto leads his old friend out of the orchard and into a small antechamber. Swords in ornate scabbards decorate the walls. Tachi and katana blades. Curved tantō daggers. All of them crafted by master bladesmiths. Ikusa eyes the weapons. Hiroto reads anxiety in his craggy face. They sit together on a wooden bench, Ikusa starting a video on the screen. Hiroto recognizes one of the recreation zones, somewhere in the middle district.

At the far end of a tennis court, one of his synjas is squaring off against a burly opponent in a black hooded cloak.

The camera zooms. The lens goes fuzzy for a moment, then sharpens to a crisp image of the intruder evading the synja's katana with astonishing grace and fluidity. A human would have been spurting arterial blood in seconds. Mechanical, perhaps—yet the intruder does not move like Stockman tech. When its counterattack comes, it is swift and vicious. A flurry of blows to the head. The synja's faceplate cracks.

The footage switches angles. The lens closes in on the intruder.

Hiroto's pulse hammers in his skull. His vision swims.

He is looking into the eyes of a ghost.

The ghost glares directly into the camera. *"What are you waiting for?"* The voice is deeply worn with age and torment. Hiroto finds that he is clutching the bench, squeezing the fine wooden slat as if he intends to snap it in half.

This cannot be. The mutant turtles of the Hamato Clan, and their rat father, are long dead. He alone defeated the enemies that his mother and grandfather failed to destroy. He alone has come to rule the city these abominations schemed to conquer.

"Is this real?" The words escape his lips before he can tamp them down. Could it be a ruse of some kind? A clever costume? Digital manipulation?

Ikusa pauses the video. Hiroto senses the man does not know what to say. "I assure you, sir, it's most definitely—"

"Play it again," Hiroto says. "Just the last thirty seconds."

Ikusa swipes a finger across the screen. The creature once again raises its arms in provocation. *"What are you waiting for?"*

Hiroto shivers. The skin of the creature's face, scarred and weathered, moves naturally with each breath. His teeth are yellowed with age and hard living. Spittle flies from his moist tongue as he speaks. And the way he fights . . . this creature has the grace of one who has studied martial arts for a lifetime.

This is not a fake. It is one of his greatest enemies, resurrected.

Instantly, the most plausible arc of this creature's existence unspools in his mind. Years spent in hiding, keeping despair at bay with a single-minded focus on revenge. Yes, he can see the fury in the mutant's eyes as he knocks the head off the synja with a single tonfa strike. Avenging his father and brothers stokes the fire in his belly. Gives him life. Hiroto has no doubt the turtle has come back to Manhattan to kill him. He imagines this task has consumed the turtle, festering as it hid in some forsaken hole, biding its time, alone with its memories . . .

"Sir?"

Hiroto envies this beast's life of simple, narrow-minded brutality. This mutant turtle does not need to pretend to care about administration, or the petty complaints of the privileged, or enforcing a precarious order among the underclasses.

"Sir?"

Hiroto recalls that each of the brother turtles had been defined by a mask of a certain color: red, purple, orange, blue. And he remembers their names: Raphael, Donatello, Michelangelo, Leonardo—along with their mutant rat of a father, Splinter. His grandfather's archnemesis. But this turtle's mask is black, like his cloak. So which one is he?

"*Sir?*"

Hiroto turns to Ikusa. "I'm right here, Captain."

Ikusa stows the tablet, gets up from the bench, and waits for Hiroto with his hands behind his back. Hiroto scans the weapons on the wall. His heart pounds. Adrenaline surges through him. He feels alive, his routine existence suddenly infused with a vivid new energy. Heat pulsates behind his eyes, through his temples. Hiroto rises to his feet. He feels like he could keep ascending through the penthouse's domed roof, through Foot City's canopy, soar above the city like one of his ravens, up through the clouds, into the stratosphere.

"What are your orders, sir?"

"I killed him once, Ikusa. I can do it again."

Hiroto mentally selects an ancient katana from the wall, feels the grip in his hands as he turns to face the surviving turtle on a rain-slicked sidewalk in a dream. His body awareness spikes. He can sense, acutely, the beds of his nails, the valves of his heart, the whorls of his fingerprints.

"He's on the run in the middle district," Ikusa says. He eyes his master curiously. "But we've established a perimeter and called in air support. He's essentially surrounded. The only question that remains is, how do you want to handle this?"

The command to *stand down* is on the tip of Hiroto's tongue. Let the bastard through. All he has to do is tell his security chief—his childhood friend—to call off the synjas, the squads of Foot soldiers, the Stockman tech he is no doubt itching to activate.

In old times, when the clans waged open war and honor was paramount, the decision would be a simple one. Hiroto would step out of his tower and face the intruder himself, driven by hatred of an ancestral enemy and respect for a warrior who has every right to be seeking revenge. The two of them would battle for the honor of their clans—Oroku and Hamato—and the outcome would decide the fate of the city itself.

"Lethal force is duly authorized." The words come out flat and dispassionate. "Do not take him alive." In his mind, he returns the ancient katana to its place on the wall.

He simply cannot risking losing the world his mother and grandfather always dreamed of. The world Hiroto willed into existence on their behalf. He has seen the turtle fight. One split second lapse in attention, one well-placed strike at an artery, and the power of his clan, the respect and fear of millions of citizens, all goes away.

"Execute him on sight."

Ikusa seems to relax. These are the expected directives. "Yes, sir."

Hiroto turns away so his childhood friend cannot see the pained twist to his face. A raven lands on the hilt of a blade and pecks at an embedded amethyst. Hiroto can sense Ikusa lingering.

"That will be all, Captain."

Hiroto waits until Ikusa's footsteps fade. Then he extends a hand. There is no birdseed in his palm. Just an offer of fellowship. The bird flies away.

Hiroto lets the outstretched hand play along the scabbard of a katana inlaid with swooping ornamentation and mother-of-pearl shrines. There is always a chance the turtle will best his entire army of warriors, his synjas, and Stockman's mechanical fighters. A chance he will ascend to the penthouse, bloodied and battered, yet alive.

It's best if this intruder, this ghost from his past, dies somewhere far below, Hiroto tells himself as he takes the katana off the wall.

But there's always a chance he'll make it through.

11

RONIN LANDS HARD ON the hovering vehicle's roof, denting the black aluminum alloy. The antigrav engine vibrates up his legs, and a fierce headwind nearly knocks him off his feet. He throws himself down flat and reaches for the driver's side door handle. The lights of Foot City fly past. The car speeds up. The wind peels back his lips.

The car veers from side to side. Ronin's body slides along the roof. His grip falters. A billboard hews into view then disappears. The driver steers into a spin. G-forces roil Ronin's guts.

Summoning brute force, Ronin pries the door off its hinges and tosses it to the streets below. The synja at the wheel sticks its head out and rotates its neck to glance up at Ronin.

"Halt," it tells him.

Ronin grasps the side of the cyborg's helmet and wrenches it halfway out of the spinning car.

"Halt!"

A swift kick sends it flailing away. No time to watch it smash on the distant pavement. The car, still spinning, tilts on its axis. The roof goes vertical. Ronin climbs and flips over the frame where the driver's side door had been. He drops into the cramped interior. His head pounds. The car is a pendulum, swinging from nothing. Antigrav traffic glides around it, horns blaring. Ronin folds himself into the seat. A vast field of digital readouts curls around him. A control yoke in place of a steering wheel is jammed between his knees. A light on the dash begins to blink.

"Is that light important? It seems important!" one of his brothers shouts.

He flicks a switch nearest the flashing light. The car turns upside down and rockets forward. His foot hits a pedal. He yanks the yoke, trying to right it. The antigrav engine whines. A fresh alarm sounds. The car launches upward, loopy and wild like a bottle rocket's trajectory. The underside of an antigrav truck passes within inches of his windshield. Blue static from the truck's lifts scorches the glass. Ronin tries to press the yoke back to its resting position. It doesn't move.

"The controls are jammed!"

"Do something, man!"

"I'm trying!" Ronin yells. He works a leg free, lifts his knee to his face, and slams the yoke down with the heel of his boot. The car rights itself. G-forces smack into the side of his face, pressing his cheek into his teeth.

"Look out!"

Ronin has time for a single absurd thought: There's exactly one billboard in Foot City and he's going to hit it. Friendly cartoon Foot soldiers wave at him in vintage LED array. Then the car crashes into an animated face. Sparks fly. A spiderweb of cracks sizzle across the windshield. He throws a reflexive hand over his face as the car grinds through a landscape of tiny lights. Then he's out the other side. The car noses down toward the streets below. The engine groans. He feels like he's being shoved from behind as the car begins its death spiral. An antigrav delivery truck clips the side mirror and glass whirls away.

The ghosts scream in his head. The car pitches down toward a green awning: Angela's Famous Deep Dish.

"Chicago pizza?! This place sucks."

Ronin wrenches the yoke back. The instrument panel flashes in protest. The engine winds down like a toy with a dead battery. A strange weightless silence takes hold. The yoke breaks off in Ronin's hand and he tosses it out the open door. The roof of a five-story building comes up fast to meet him. There is nothing more he can do.

The world goes bright white then returns in sickening jump cuts.

The car is back in the air. The impact should have shattered his spine. He knows this, dimly, in the back of his mind, like you might know an old friend in a dream.

Cut.

He lifts off, tilts back, the canopy looms, then the car slams down again, shedding metal pieces that scatter across the silver rooftop.

Cut.

The car slides into a shrieking skid and crumples against the side of a neighboring building. Ronin blinks away a surge of full-body pain. Then he sucks in a ragged breath and climbs out the wrecked frame of the driver's side door. The car, a smoking husk, settles into itself with a metallic hiss.

"Smooth moves," a ghost says. "You couldn't even fly ten feet in a straight line."

"Shut up," Ronin says. Or tries to say. He falls to one knee. The rooftop goes fuzzy. There's a picnic table, he thinks. With an umbrella that he clipped on the way in. He blinks the world back to coherence. Then he drags himself to the edge of the roof.

"Better keep moving."

Ronin coughs into his fist. "Easy for you to say."

But his brother is right. The smoking wreck of an antigrav car is a flag planted in the middle of Foot City. He straightens his left arm. His shoulder pops. The troubling thought surfaces once again: He should be dead. Or at least paralyzed. Yet somehow, here he is. Walking around. He tells himself not to dwell. Any landing you walk away from is a good one. And he managed to get nearer to his objective. The base of Hiroto's tower is a few blocks away. Vengeance is so close he can taste it.

He spits blood off the roof and moves on.

12

RONIN HUDDLES IN THE shadows of an industrial-grade water purifier. The machine's low vibrations soothe his sore back. From the darkness of the warehouse roof, he gazes up at a dizzying feat of engineering. The megastructure rises from four pylons, smooth windowless cylinders of high-gloss polymer. Each one is at least ten stories above the street. The focal point of this vast hollow beneath the tower is an open cargo bay the size of a football field. Antigrav security and delivery vehicles flow in and out, rising up into the tower's belly in one lane and descending in another.

"About a mile too high for your grappling hook."

"Mm." Ronin watches. And waits. He notes the precise timing of the vehicles. If he lets his vision go slack, a miasma appears. A smeared lens in the air. Antigrav engine emissions, like heat shimmer on blacktop.

One of his brothers sighs. "Think you just ran outta miracles, bro."

"Same as it ever was," Ronin says. He pushes the words out through a swollen throat. "I stopped believing in miracles a long time ago."

Ronin pushes himself off the purifier. Instantly he misses the back massage. The edge of the warehouse is a low barrier, no higher than his knees. Security prowlers like the one he just hijacked patrol the airspace around the warehouse. He wonders idly what the Foot Clan keeps locked up in there.

"Diamonds."

"Swiss chocolate."

"Spare parts for mousers."

Ronin tracks the incoming loop of another antigrav prowler. Black, tinted windows, red insignia on the roof.

"Hey, wait."

"You gonna discuss this with us first?"

He ignores his brothers, backs up for a running start, and takes off.

"Not again!"

He thinks about what a stupid plan this is as he reaches for the prowler gliding past him.

Come on . . .

Ronin's fingers snag the edge of the running board. Before the headwind knocks him off, he adjusts his grip and presses himself flat against the underside of the car. The toes of his boots slot neatly beneath steel exhaust panels. The smell of hot metal fills his reptilian nostrils. He clings on as the antigrav car loops around the far end of the warehouse, then joins the traffic stream headed up into the tower's massive bay. His arms ache. The shrapnel in his half-shell sends fiery jolts into his back.

The car ascends past the rim of the access bay. The atmosphere shifts like a color gradient. Another skin for the city: cold, blue, efficient. Ronin waits for the floor to slide into view. Then he lets go of the car, hits the slate-colored tiles, and rolls behind a stack of mammoth crates. He peers out across a cavernous docking bay. White beams from wall-mounted spotlights streak across the steel and polymer hangar. He catalogs vehicles parked in clusters: boxy troop transports, sleek interceptors, tanks, hovercrafts, even what looks like a Harrier jump jet. Articulated, piston-driven limbs work in mimetic rhythms to clean windshields and assemble engines. Silver androids—worker drones without fighting gear—unload antigrav trucks. Ronin spies cases of wine, barrels of produce, trays of freshly baked bread he swears he can smell from his hiding place.

He follows a little cleaning bot's journey around the perimeter past soldiers moving heavy weaponry. They work in teams, transferring rocket launchers, grenades, and long guns to tram cars that glide toward an archway at the opposite end of the hangar.

"That's gotta lead to the upper levels."

"Too bad it's inconveniently located on the other side of the platform."

"Just gotta get through the Foot soldiers with military-grade equipment, is all."

"Well then," Ronin says, "I better get a ride."

"See, I knew you were gonna say that."

"It's like every two seconds there's a new vehicle."

"Since when are you a *vehicles* guy?"

Ronin waits for one of the silent electric trams to cruise past his hiding spot. He catches the silver blur of a tram through a gap in the crates—and hesitates. Doubt throbs in his aching head. Once he steps into view, the alert will spread through the tower. Every soldier at Hiroto's disposal will come down on him. Mousers. Synjas. Tech beyond his imagination.

"Screw it."

Maybe they won't expect a direct attack. Ronin springs from his hiding place and rushes the tram. He launches himself at the driver in a linebacker tackle. His shoulder impacts the side of the driver's head. There's a satisfying crunch—the guy's human beneath the mask—and the driver slumps in the seat. Ronin shoves him off the tram and swings into place behind the controls. In a cup holder, coffee steams. A photograph of a young woman holding a baby girl is taped to the panel. He finds the gas pedal with his foot.

"Hey!" A Foot soldier rushes to the aid of the fallen driver. "Stop!"

Ronin jams a boot down on the pedal. The tram zips forward. His peripheral vision catalogs enemy reactions. Foot soldiers in formation bringing weapons to bear. Others frozen in place. Long guns taking aim. Android workers unloading trucks, unbothered. Spotlights sweeping across the floor. Ronin squints against the sudden glare.

"Get down!" a ghost screams inside his head. Ronin ducks below the panel as bullets pock the tram's steel siding. A shuriken embeds itself in the seat cushion inches from his thigh. The eruption of noise bounces around the hangar, a wall of sound and fury. He pulls two flash-bang grenades from his belt. Small, cylindrical, the size of double-A batteries. He tosses one to the left and one to the right in high arcing lobs. A moment later, twin percussive blasts pop. Ronin shields his eyes from the blinding light that flares from the detonations. The tram is knocked around like a boat in a hurricane. He shuts his eyes and holds onto a handle. Phosphenes burst orange and pink along the backs of his eyelids. The treads leave the tiles and the fishtailing vehicle swings perpendicular to its path toward the archway. Ronin dives out of the tram and rolls forward into a cloud of soot-colored smoke, the aftermath of the grenades.

A pair of Foot soldiers appears, like silhouetted wraiths. Ronin strikes out with his fists at the soft parts of their armor: kidneys, neck, upper arms. As if on autopilot, he finds a tonfa already clutched in his fist coming down on a helmeted head. He delivers an elbow to a throat and the Foot soldier staggers back into the smoke. Whirling, the tonfa an extension of his arm, he hears the crack of bone in the sightless gloom and smiles. He handles his attackers one by one and moves on. No time to make sure they stay down. He has to keep moving. The injured cry out, wallowing in confusion, littering his wake.

Ronin darts for the archway. The air clears. Bounding up a stairwell, hemmed in by tight corners and narrow passages, ragged breathing echoes back to him. Sterile corridors come and go. His only concern is up, always up. The tower's lowest levels are a desolate maze, a warren of maintenance rooms and catwalks and low-hanging nests of pipes. The atmosphere brings to mind a submarine's guts. Bare bulbs in yellow mesh cages flicker as he moves past. He breaks into a run. A familiar utility closet comes and goes, its door ajar, red and blue lights blinking in the darkness. He stops, panting.

"Am I going in circles?"

"We got bigger problems, bro."

"You hear that sound?"

Ronin cocks his head. A high-pitched mechanical whine rings in his ears. "Yeah. Air conditioners. Boilers. Whatever."

"The sound isn't uniform," a ghost says, like he's an idiot. "It's getting louder. Something's coming this way, fast."

The oncoming threat slides around a corner in a blur of fluid motion. Ronin drops into a low fighting stance and flexes his fingers, itching to choose the proper weapon. In seconds, he takes in this new opponent's gleaming white armor, bladed forearms, inline skates instead of feet. Full mechanoid. No upgraded Foot soldier or cyborg fighter here. Bright red eyes the size of golf balls.

As it approaches, Ronin takes in the robot's combat speed. Its skates leave shimmering black trails like mica on the polished floor. Far beyond human. Beyond synja. Letting it get too close is a mistake. But he can use its mobility against it.

Its voice is a metallic croak. "Lethal force authorized."

"I can dig that," Ronin says. He draws a trio of blades from his belt, long and skinny, like throwing knives with no handles. He steps to one side and waits for the robot to commit to a shift in momentum. There will be a tipping point when the machine is going too fast to stop or dodge—

Now.

He flings the blades. One strikes the head and two bury themselves in the torso. The wounds trail a shower of sparks. The metal shell is thin on an attacker built solely for speed. The robot spasms. A bladed forearm swipes at empty air.

Ronin sprints ahead, closing the gap on his own terms. It's always better to control the flow of battle. Master Splinter said that once.

"It's actually from *Spycatcher 3*," his brother corrects him.

Either way. Good advice.

He extends an arm sideways and clotheslines the malfunctioning robot. Something pops in his wrist and he shakes it off. The robot goes horizontal, slamming its head against the floor and careening into the wall. Then Ronin is upon it. He gouges an eye with the butt of a tonfa. The automaton's arms flail. Motors whirr and grind against themselves. He hammers the tonfa down into the robot's skull, windmilling and bashing it with his other hand like he's driving a stake into the ground. Motors die. An acrid smell rises. Silence falls over the corridor, sudden and jarring. The mechanoid is inert. Dead. He kicks it twice to make sure.

"Very elegant," a ghost says.

He rotates his wrist and winces at the sharp pain. "I got it done."

Ronin goes down on one knee and pulls the wreckage of the mechanoid's head up toward him. He peers into the one good eye. No light blinks back at him. But maybe its internal comms are still functional.

"Sending toys to do your fighting for you, Hiroto?" Ronin growls into the lens. "I'll see you soon, you—"

13

"—GUTLESS COWARD."

The mutant turtle's face pixelates into static. The feed goes dead. Hiroto sits at the center of a panopticon of monitors and blows across the rim of a mug. Steam from his jasmine tea fogs a screen that displays Captain Ikusa's pained expression. Surrounding Ikusa, five additional monitors display various members of his security team. A pair of IT overlords, the head synja programmer, and Baxter Stockman, the mad scientist himself, deigning to join them from his Roosevelt Island headquarters. While the scientist is not strictly part of the team, Hiroto has summoned him for a different, albeit related, reason.

Elsewhere, alerts are screaming. Feeds from across the tower show the carnage littering the mutant turtle's wake. Wounded Foot soldiers, mechanoid fighters turned to scrap.

Hiroto winces and silences the alarms, sips his tea and sets the mug down on a coaster. A raven squawks, its tone petulant. Hiroto looks at each face in the monitors in turn, then levels a lingering glare at Ikusa. He tries to quell the turmoil raging inside him. He has not been this excited since he executed his plot to destroy the Hamato Clan so many years ago. Passion that has long since deserted his heart is bringing color and shape to his world. But he can betray none of this sentiment in front of the ones who serve him. As head of the Oroku Clan—and, by extension, the city itself—he must never let the ruthless mask slip. And so, on this night, his old friend Ikusa will bear the brunt of the rage he summons without much effort.

He grits his teeth. "Captain Ikusa, why am I looking at a terrorist infiltrator inside the lower levels of my tower?"

A raven punctuates his inquiry with a throaty *grawk*.

Ikusa's reply is soft and deferential. He bows his head. "I make no excuse for the intruder's continued advance. I have failed you." Ikusa rises from his chair. His broad armored chest fills the screen. Hiroto watches the captain strap on a pair of long daggers. "I will confront him myself."

Hiroto grips the mug so hard its handle snaps off. They are all of them performative, playing roles for each other's benefits. This is why the mutant is still alive, he thinks. The core of the Foot Clan has eroded. Years of unchecked power and mechanization has dulled its edge. He tosses the priceless ceramic shard aside. The bot hurries over to scoop it up.

"Stand down, Captain."

Ikusa returns to his seat.

Hiroto glances across the displays. He reads fear in every face except Stockman's. Hiroto has not set eyes on the scientist in many years. He studies the hybrid visage, a fusion of man and machine that resembles a living experiment. The face that peers back through the monitor is knotted with runnels of scarred flesh. Wormlike protrusions that pulse as if imbued with a heartbeat. Gleaming metal inserts are grafted across his forehead and down the sides of his face, a medieval half helm of densely filigreed circuits. And yet the most inhuman aspect of Baxter Stockman is his eyes. They are nothing but red embers in hollow sockets, the afterglow of a life spent hunched over lab equipment. Hiroto shudders internally. A miasma of isolation and obsession bleeds from the monitor.

Hiroto turns his attention back to Ikusa and imagines ending this meeting with five simple words: *Let him come to me*. His leg bounces under the desk. It is never enough to spar with his elite Foot soldiers, to parry the blows of the highly trained, the fastest, the strongest, and in turn break their ribs and shatter their noses. This is all just foreplay with diminishing returns. But to fight such a warrior as one of Splinter's mutant turtles, one-on-one!

Hiroto allows himself a moment to entertain this fantasy. Then he brings a fist down on the table to banish it. "More!" The monitors bounce. Agitated birds break formation. One of the IT technicians jumps in his chair. The other's head darts back like a snake's. Hiroto grins at his direct reports. "More soldiers, more synjas, more everything. Unleash it all. See that he goes no farther."

In his mind, the turtle battles through all of them: every last warrior of the Foot Clan, each smaller battle inflicting fatigue and injury by degree, until he reaches the penthouse half dead and vulnerable, his tough reptilian skin crosshatched with raw wounds, for Hiroto to finish off before the approving eyes of his ancestors.

Hiroto glances up at a raven, still as a statue, perched on a monitor, regarding him with disapproval. The bird knows his mind.

"*I'm not going to take the chance,*" he hisses at it.

"What was that, sir?" Ikusa says.

Hiroto lowers his eyes to the monitors. "What was what, Captain?"

Ikusa shifts in his seat. "Nothing. It's just—what if this intruder is only the spearhead of a much larger infiltration plan? If I am to bring all our resources to bear on this one single—"

"Do it!" Hiroto screams. Then he takes a breath and tucks a wild strand of hair behind his ear. He moderates his voice. Projects calm. Slows his heart rate. "Now, Captain."

Ikusa bows quickly and signs off. A black screen with the red Foot Clan insignia replaces him.

Hiroto swivels and finds himself looking at the bushy, owlish eyebrows of the synja programmer. He struggles to recall the man's name. He wonders if they've ever spoken before. Why is the programmer even at this meeting? Did Hiroto summon him? He can't remember. The man's presence irritates him.

"You're fired," he says. The programmer blinks. His face contorts. The pair from IT stiffen in their seats. Stockman remains silent and unmoved. His map of scars ripples in some unseen heat shimmer.

"Sir, I—"

"Do you live in the tower?"

"Y-yes, on fifty-six, with my wife and our three daughters. We're very happy here, and the girls—"

"Be out by tomorrow morning."

Stockman's avatar emits a low, strangled hiss. Hiroto gazes deep into the programmer's watery eyes. He tries to summon a feeling, an emotion, attached to what he has just done to this man. But he finds himself completely unmoved. The summary judgment, the power to change the course of an entire family's upward mobility, does not even accelerate the beating of his heart. Perhaps he should have the man killed?

He waits. Sits with this new thought while the man squirms in his chair. Considers a public execution.

No. The man means nothing to him. Having him killed would provide no uptick or downturn in his mood. It would be like watching the Klean-tech bot scoop up a dead carpenter ant.

He sighs. "Never mind. I rescind your termination."

The man's eyes go wide. His lip trembles. "Thank you, sir, you really are everything they say about you, strong and fair and—"

Hiroto ends the meeting for the programmer and the IT lackeys. On a central monitor he watches real-time footage of the mutant turtle cutting his way through a mob of Foot soldiers. Men and women who took a vow to give their lives for the Oroku family do so now, before his eyes, as the turtle parries, counters, feints, strikes, draws blood, administers death strokes. The mutant enters an elevator and emerges a moment later on the fifty-ninth floor. Behind him, the elevator car's silver walls are painted in blood. Black-clad ninjas are sprawled on the floor. The turtle moves down the hall, into the jurisdiction of another set of cameras, another surveillance net.

Ikusa's words echo in his head. *The spearhead of a larger infiltration plan.* He dismisses the idea. This turtle is the last of his kind, half mad with bloodlust, a creature of pure vengeance. He is not working with some shabby group of revolutionaries to change the system. He is simply here to kill the man who destroyed his family.

Hiroto understands. It's what *he* would do.

Stockman clears his throat. The sound is like a wheezing engine. With a twinge of reluctance, Hiroto turns his attention to the scientist. "Here I am." Stockman's voice is eerily bifurcated, two voices in dissonant harmony. The strains of man and machine in a perilous coexistence. "Attending a meeting of astonishing insignificance. Why? Enlighten me, Hiroto." Lips flicker into a quick smile, there and gone. "Please."

Hiroto blinks. When they first met, Baxter Stockman had been a strange, obsessive man whose dark skin was already fading to gray after a lifetime of hunkering away in a lab. But Hiroto had recognized genius in the man's unorthodox methods. Through Stockman's innovations, Hiroto had been able to transform New York City. Mass-produced androids and cyborgs that allowed the Foot Clan to control the populace, food synthesization plants located in Inwood that provided enough vegetable matter and animal protein to feed millions of residents, electricity generated and freely provided by tech built into the wall that surrounds the island—all of it had sprung from Stockman's brain.

He knows that others draw parallels between Stockman, the scientist on his island, and Hiroto, the ruler in his tower. He has seen the underground newspapers turned out by the Rock Bottom presses. But Hiroto is nothing like Baxter Stockman. He sits at the apex of a storied clan, a family cloaked in historical significance. His every action echoes back through the decades and forward into a future where the Oroku family only grows more powerful. By comparison, Stockman is a lone freak, a man who replaces his aging, decrepit body parts with circuitry and metal. He does not host lavish feasts for the city's upper echelons and entertain beautiful women who flock to his penthouse. Hiroto doubts he even eats real food anymore.

"You were there when we wiped out the Hamato Clan." Hiroto gets down to business. "The rat and his turtles."

One of Stockman's eyes flares with brightness while the other eye goes dark. Then they recalibrate. His upper lip twitches. "Yes. It is given to me in my dreams. I can show you."

"Show me . . . your dreams?"

"They have degraded. But yes."

"No, that's all right, Baxter." Hiroto makes a fist beneath the table. The scientist's voice is worming its way into his skull, forming a cold knot in his forehead. "How could this turtle have survived?"

Stockman sighs. The keening sound roils Hiroto's stomach. "This conversation is a small and distant thing to me." Stockman's head turns to the side, revealing a metal port where his ear ought to be. Hiroto recoils. Raw flesh throbs at the rim of the port. What kind of man does this to himself? The scientist gazes at something off-screen that has stolen his attention. Hiroto senses he is about to hang up the call.

"Wait!" Hiroto digs his fingernails into his palm. "I've patched you through to our security feed. You've had time to watch the intruder, the way he fights."

Stockman's head snaps back with uncanny quickness. "He has a sixty-three percent chance of killing you."

"Take care in how you address me!" Hiroto snarls. Then he composes himself. He lowers his voice. "You serve at the pleasure of my clan," he says. "And you preside over your little Roosevelt Island because I allow it." He sits back in his chair. "Store that fact in your dreams, or whatever it is that you do with important information these days."

Stockman stares blankly into the monitor. Hiroto unclenches his fists and wipes his palms on his thighs. He glances at a security camera feed and watches the mutant turtle yank an unconscious Foot soldier up off the floor and press his eye into a biometric scanner. A door opens. The turtle drops the body and enters. Inside the room, two androids brandish naginata, their long curved blades glinting in the washed-out light of the security camera.

"Android 11-E." Hiroto says without taking his eyes off the security feed. "The prototype."

"Yes," Stockman says.

On the screen, the androids fight as one, programmed with every technique and battle strategy in the Foot Clan's arsenal, the Orokus' unique style playing out before him like a martial arts clinic. They feed off each other, one spinning and the other striking. One blocking and the other feinting then delivering a blow that should have decapitated the turtle. But the mutant is tireless. He moves like liquid, some kind of poured solder, hardening into steel at the moment of impact. Hiroto can feel the intruder's hatred through twenty-six floors. It comes up through the polished teak and marble of his penthouse. He can see it writ large on the screen as if the turtle's fighting stances spell out hieroglyphs, each bend of the knee and lock of an elbow another indictment of Hiroto's murderous savagery.

A *sixty-three percent chance of killing you.*

"Is it ready to be deployed?"

He watches the turtle drive his katana through the neck of an android, where its connective tissue is most vulnerable. The android falls. Hiroto blinks.

"The 11-E prototype has a forty-seven—"

"*Stop!*"

Stockman goes quiet. A coil of flesh like a prominent vein swells in his forehead, bulging against an embedded piece of metal.

"I don't need your analytics," Hiroto says. "Numbers don't mean anything in a fight. There are too many variables."

"The 11-E prototype is awake and online," Stockman says.

The screen goes dark as the scientist abruptly signs off. Hiroto mashes buttons to bypass his security hierarchy and issues commands directly to the computer.

"Deploy the mousers. Activate prototype 11-E."

A raven flies low, disturbing the air about his head. On the screen, the mutant turtle slides a sai under the second android's chin and the light in its eyes goes out.

14

ALL THE FLOORS IN this tower run together. Ronin is trapped in an endless film loop of sparse dojos, plush hallways, kitchens, maintenance closets, server farms, mailrooms, elevator shafts, stairwells. All of them littered with the wreckage of androids and the broken bodies of Foot soldiers. His muscles ache. Every few steps, his vision swims. His reptilian skin is cut in a thousand places. His left hand is swollen, fingers sprained, and his grip barely closes. But he is still moving upward. The ambient sounds of the tower—air conditioning, hum of the lights, shuffle of residents getting out of his way—coalesce into a whispered name: *Oroku Hiroto.*

"Your destiny's at hand," Ronin says to no one. His voice is raspy and soft. Maybe a camera picked it up. Maybe Hiroto heard him.

"That's a cool thing to say," a ghost compliments him.

"Very Shakespearean," another agrees.

"Name one Shakespeare play," the first retorts.

"I know it when I hear it."

Ronin shakes his head, focusing up when a Foot soldier springs from an alcove, almost catching him in the side of the face with an iron-clawed glove. Ronin ducks away from the second swipe and drives his brother's staff into the ninja's gut. Then he twirls the bō and brings it down hard on the back of the ninja's skull. He moves on. Behind him another body crumples to the floor.

Ronin turns a corner into a large room with a familiar musty vastness. There are rows of books on shelves, glossy transparent covers, computer terminals. Some kind of library. His weary mind scans the decor. Bright cheery signs extol the joys of reading. *Your ticket to other worlds.* Sounds nice. He keeps moving. Beyond the shelves is a giant hollow, as if someone took a chunk out of the middle of the tower to create a glass-lined atrium. Outside, the lights of Foot City press in with a twinkling leer. This close to the glass apron that flows from the top of the tower, the lights are bent into red-shifted smears. Vertigo sets in. He rubs his eyes, looks up, counts the overhanging floors. Even reaching for his grappling hook tires him out. He's not sure if he can make the throw to the next level. But he has to try.

There's a familiar clank that comes from everywhere and nowhere. An eerie tingle crawls up his spine.

It's a sound he hasn't heard in years. Not since he lost his family. The sound of an approaching mouser. Of many approaching mousers. Dread rises. When he moves, it's through molasses. The rhythmic *clank-clank-clank* gets louder. The floor vibrates. He feels the swarm before he sees it and flashes to metallic jaws mindlessly chomping. He has seen them inflict carnage in his past life: the two-legged automatons tearing limbs from bodies, leaving tendons dangling like wet ropes. Each one a mechanized shark attack.

Ronin draws his tonfa and drops into a fighting stance. His knees pop.

Scores of chihuahua-sized robots burst through the shelves, jaws clanking, metal teeth shining. Books fly from their perches like stunned birds. For a split second he is rooted to the floor. Something's wrong. The robots are coming at him from *above*. An attack formation that should not be possible.

"These mousers can *fly*, you gotta move!"

Radiant light flashes. A blast of concentrated heat singes his elbow. He dives for the floor, rolls out of the way as little pockets of energy burst around him. His left shoulder explodes with pain as it's grazed by the energy pulse. His mind races, lands on upgraded weapons systems, laser beams. Stockman has been busy. The atrium's behind him, with its free fall into open space. Bad move to let the mousers herd him over the edge. All he can do is head for the stacks, into the swarm, staying low, knees screaming. Beams carom off the metal shelves, punch smoking holes in books. Steel jaws catch the hem of his cloak and shred the fabric. He scrambles behind a row of dusty encyclopedias. With his back to the leather-bound tomes, he draws his tonfa. On both batons he thumbs a pair of hidden switches. A mouser tears into volumes A through J. He can smell oil in its jaws. He flips the switches. A silent wave of energy ripples out from the pulse generators inside the tonfa. He feels an itch behind his teeth. A moment later, the clang of metal cascades throughout the library. Mousers hit the floor like a hundred dropped bowling balls.

Ronin lets out a breath. One of the dead mousers rolls to a stop at his feet. He scans the dual spikes jutting up from its bottom lip, the four squat piggish limbs, the antenna for a tail. His eyes go to the ceiling. How many more stories are there in this infernal tower? Blood leaks from torn skin where the laser grazed his shoulder. He pushes himself to his feet with a groan and works his way down the stacks. At the end of the row is a large reading nook crammed with beanbag chairs and stuffed animals. He tries to imagine the children of the tower, offspring of Foot City's one-percenters. In a corner of the ceiling, a security camera looks on impassively. Ronin stares into the lens and flips it off. Next to the poster is a long bank of floor-to-ceiling windows. He tries to figure out how high he's climbed, how many more floors left to go. He finds himself staring at a beanbag chair. A quick rest won't hurt. He could just sit for a minute or two—

Heavy steps sound from behind him. Ronin takes a breath, lets it out. A hulking shadow is reflected in the glass.

Not good.

He turns to behold a no-necked cyclopean monster emerging from between the stacks. Bipedal, with a gorilla-sized body made from that pseudo plastic polymer and a single red eyeball for a head. Some kind of lens with a dark pupil at its center dilates, taking the measure of Ronin. He scans it in turn for vulnerabilities and finds none. Its joints are armored, its weak spots protected. His brothers are quiet.

Ronin stows the tonfa and draws the katana. The blade is crusted with blood. How many dead soldiers did he leave in his wake? How many are still ahead? He does not feel like himself. He does not feel like anyone at all.

The robot charges. Its legs move like pistons, driving its big body straight toward Ronin. He sidesteps, using the giant's momentum against it. Becoming part of the flow of its attack, driving his sword into an armored clump of wire where arm meets torso. The sword glances off hard polymer. Ronin spins as the machine moves past. The machine is faster. Ronin leans back as a forearm as big as his head misses him by an inch. With two hands on the hilt he drives the sword toward the same armpit. This time he strikes from underneath, thrusting upward. This time the sword cuts deep.

Sparks fly. The robot staggers, mimicking dizziness.

"You tweaked its balance," a ghost says. "It's going down!"

The behemoth reels like a punch-drunk boxer. Its whirling arms sweep board games and action figures and stuffed animals off a shelf, metal claws tearing a divot out of the drywall and shredding a poster of a squirrel sleeping on a stack of books. The black pupil in the red orb dilates madly.

Ronin steps back and lowers the blade. The sight of the hulking mouser destroying itself gives him a rush of adrenaline.

He looks into the security camera. "This the best you got?"

In the space of a single second, the gorilla android regains motor control and springs forward with astonishing quickness. Ronin's instincts take hold. He ducks, whirls, dodges—but he's not fast enough. The robot's heavy arm is wrapped around his neck. The metal torso spins, wrenching Ronin off his feet. He twirls through the air fast enough to feel g-forces pressing against his body. His legs swing like deadweight. His fist hits polymer and pain rockets up his forearm. The robot barrels toward the windows with Ronin held fast in the crook of its elbow. He can't breathe. The robot has his windpipe clamped.

He reaches for the sai. But the robot accelerates like a speeding car. He knows what's about to happen. He just can't believe it. Not when he had gotten so close.

Glass shatters. The library vanishes. Ronin screams into the void as they fall through the cool, clean night air inside Foot City's protective bubble. Disbelief and regret clog his mind. Blood rushes in his temples.

The curved edge of the canopy looms closer and closer, distorting light in all directions. Ronin catches a glimpse of the top of Hiroto's tower. He had been so close to the penthouse. So close to avenging his family.

The robot extends an arm and with a hydraulic blow puts a fist extension through the thick tempered glass of the canopy. The impact barely slows their momentum as it delivers them to the mercy of gravity. Ronin flails wildly. The robot's grip tightens as they plummet into the West Village. Wind shrieks in his ears as the street rises up to meet them. The buildings seem to sway, to bend in toward them, urging them down faster and faster. Lights flare behind his eyes. His breath is trapped in his throat.

Operating on instinct, his hand finds the grip of the sai. He pulls it from his belt and blindly stabs the robot's armpit once, twice, three times, twisting the blade on the way out, ripping into the guts of its circuitry. The behemoth spasms. Its hold loosens. Ronin kicks free. At least he won't die in the clutches of one of Stockman's abominations.

His brothers scream inside his head. He tells them he is sorry. He tried. The wind is a thermal updraft.

"I'll see you soon," he says.

Then he crashes into the concrete, into darkness.

15

JONES FOLLOWS CRUNCH AND Scrape as her two pro wrestler-sized friends shoulder their way through pedestrians. She marvels at their technique. Using the gentlest of nudges, they clear a path for Jones, Lug, and Breaker. They barely make contact with anyone as they move with quiet, mannered purpose.

Jones points to the back of Scrape's retro vest. Some previous owner embroidered a massive raccoon between the shoulder blades.

"Cute," Breaker says. "Nothing says Scrape's aesthetic like a trash panda."

"Hey, Lug." She turns to their mostly silent comrade who brings up the rear. "Nice work installing that tracking chip on the bike. The foresight was just, chef's kiss."

Lug nods, the slightest hint of a smile on his face.

"But it would have been cool to know about it before tonight," Jones says. She doesn't want to come down hard on the guy. She's grateful for the tracker—her Softail Slim would be in the wind without it—but it's still a little weird. Not like Lug creeps her out. He's a solid dude. One with lots of secrets, is all.

"Sorry, Jones."

She reads a genuine apology—even a whiff of sorrow—in his tone. As always, his eyes are shielded by the visor.

"All good," she says, punching him in the arm. He flashes the screen of his handheld. Blank map grid. No pin.

"Signal still lost?"

"Disappeared a while back," Breaker answers for him. "But your skell definitely took the bike to the edge of Foot City."

Jones chews her lip. "Of course he did." She hates it here—the edges of the exclusion zone in the middle of the walled city. Ground zero for the Foot Clan, playground for the elite. The whole place makes her itchy. "Bunch of assholes."

"Who?" Scrape doesn't turn around.

"Everyone except you, buddy."

Across the street, the perimeter of Foot City rises. A holo-ad zips across the wall, a neon sports drink hydrating a thirsty mob like a crop duster airplane. Jones has heard her mother talk about how there are no ads inside Foot City. Rich people are treated to peaceful nights while constant marketing slop is aimed at the lesser citizens.

"Jacked right outside Hilty's," Jones mutters. Her mood's as dark as her lipstick. "Unreal."

"We'll find it," Breaker assures her. "It's around here—"

A cry goes up from the streets. The kind of abrupt emotional release where you know you're about to be caught up in the thick of some wild New York shit. Jones swivels and notices the people around her are looking straight up, so she follows their gaze.

"—somewhere."

It's impossible to miss: a hole in the side of Foot City's shimmering apron. A puncture wound in the glass where it arcs down to meet the top of the wall. Looks like something shot off the rear of the tower, punched through the canopy. She strains her eyes against the night sky. Then she sees it: a shiny white object separating from a smaller, darker blot. It's like a space shuttle uncoupling from its rocket. The shiny thing's clearly metal, some piece of malfunctioning tech that blasted itself straight out of Oroku Hiroto's precious tower.

Jones turns to Breaker and Lug. "Robot swan dive."

And then the crowd breaks in every direction. Crunch scoops her up. His unruly chest hair scratches her face. "Put me down, Crunch!" she hollers.

But he's running and there's nothing she can do. She pops her head out from under his arm as the white object comes down a block away. The ground trembles first with the impact, then a split second later with the explosion. A fireball surges upward. Dispersing onlookers scream as they flee. Smoke and concrete dust fill the air, making Jones's eyes sting.

A moment later, the darker object hits the ground in the place she'd been standing, gawking up like a moron. This one doesn't explode.

"Oh god." The sickening *thwap* echoes in her head. Organic. Not a robot, or one of those cyborg synjas. A person. Someone alive mere seconds earlier, now dead. Crunch sets her down on the sidewalk, drags a handkerchief across her face, then wipes his own eyes. Jones moves to see around his bulk.

Crunch sidesteps to block her view. "You don't want to look."

"Move!"

Breaker lays a shaky hand on her shoulder, his complexion a little green. Lug gazes down the block, impassive behind his visor, watching people begin to congregate at the crash sites.

Jones shakes off Breaker's hand. She flanks around Crunch and bounces off Scrape. He looks at his brother, ashen-faced, and shakes his head. "Let's get outta here."

Jones stares him straight in the eyes. "I'm not leaving without my bike."

"Place is about to be crawling with Foot Clan," Crunch points out.

Jones takes off toward the wreck. The crowd is already reassembling, speculating, talking shit. She sidles into the ring of onlookers, contorts herself to push to the front of the circle. A fine white silt swims in the air and she coughs and spits phlegm at the concrete. She squeezes past a woman with an electric guitar strapped to her back and stops.

The jumper has landed face down and cratered the pavement. He's a big guy, dressed all in black, limbs splayed at strange angles. An arsenal of ninja weapons bristles from his back. Cracks in the concrete radiate from his prone and broken form. Jones can't stop her mind from spinning. What had been running through the guy's head as he busted through the canopy a million miles above the streets?

Regret hits her hard. She should have listened to Crunch. She didn't need to see this, to have this dreadful image lodged in her mind.

Then the jumper moves. Just a small twitch at first. But enough to startle the crowd. Jones looks on, astonished. The impossibility of what she is seeing drags her abruptly into some other realm, where supernatural shit is actually real. The jumper lifts an arm, jams an elbow against the cracked pavement, hoists himself off the ground. The crowd steps back. Nobody wants to be too close to this bewildering resurrection. His massive hands make fists. He groans in pain, then mutters something she can't hear.

Her eyes scan the top of the tower. The little hole in the side of the Foot City canopy has gotta be sixty stories high. This guy should be pulped. The streets should be spattered with his guts. And yet, the hooded figure drags one leg up, bends his knee, and plants his foot. Blood leaks from his misshapen face, but she's seen worse beatings in underground cage fights. The guy's deformed in ways she can't put her finger on. As big as Crunch and Scrape, but underneath his torn cloak, his torso bulges. She wonders if his bones are protruding. Slowly, he gets to his feet, nearly collapses drunkenly to one side, then rights himself. The crowd parts in reverential silence to let him stagger away.

Breaker appears next to her. "Why do I get the feeling you want to follow that guy?"

She watches as the jumper kneels, slides a manhole cover aside, and vanishes into the sewers.

She looks at Breaker. "I think he's the one who jacked my bike." She finds herself startled by her own words. The theory is still half-baked. But she talks it through. "Only a total stranger to Rock Bottom would steal a bike from outside Hilty's. So we tracked his ass to the edge of Foot City. Then this guy comes flying out of Hiroto's tower, craters the blacktop, and gets up and walks away."

"Could be a coincidence."

"Yeah." Jones eyes the blood at the rim of the dark hole in the street that leads to the sewer. "Could be."

A filtered metallic voice crackles. "*All citizens disperse immediately!*"

Jones scans the crowd. A smooth metal skull and red visor appears. The synja muscles its way to the now-empty crater.

Jones lowers her voice. "Here comes the dipshit patrol."

"We gotta split," Breaker says. Instead, Jones moves to stand in front of the open manhole. It's all she can think of to do. She knows she's too small to hide it completely. As soon as the synja turns her way, he'll know where the jumper went. Breaker shakes his head and cozies up next to her. Crunch and Scrape clock what she's doing and slide in behind her, their massive figures obscuring the sewer entrance. Lug saunters over a moment later. Jones folds her arms across her chest. Just a casual hangout. Nothing to see here. The sports drink ad zooms across the wall behind them, trailing brilliant droplets of neon sweat.

A liquor bottle arcs from a ragged gathering on the opposite side-walk, aiming for the synja. Jones watches it come down. It's a good throw. Right on target. But the cyborg redirects its trajectory with the tip of his katana without breaking stride. He doesn't bother to hassle the troublemaker, instead investigating the crater. He sheaths his weapon and places a hand over the broken sidewalk. A bright lattice issues from his metal palm and forms a conical beam. The synja shines the beam over the edges of the crater, the blood, the displaced chunks of pavement. Then he straightens up and activates his comms.

"All units—the terrorist is still alive. Repeat: The terrorist that infiltrated Master Hiroto's tower is still alive."

"Hey!" Jones waves an arm, flags down the synja. Then she points east down the avenue. "The dude you're looking for went that way!"

Breaker's posture stiffens. Tension oozes from his pores.

The synja advances toward them. "You were told to disperse, citizens."

Jones holds up her hands, palms out. "I don't want to be a problem. Just trying to help. The guy was moving pretty fast. Never saw anything like it."

The synja is eerily motionless. Something behind his visor makes a low clicking sound, like a distant cricket.

"You're lying," the synja says after a moment.

Jones opens her mouth to protest, to insist that she saw the dude take off running. Then she remembers who she's talking to. Not some lowly Foot soldier. These newer model synjas are equipped with biometric polygraphs. Real-time data on whether or not organic citizens are being truthful.

The synja's hand rests on its holstered sidearm. "I am detaining you under—"

The manhole cover comes down on the cyborg's forehead like a coin being dropped into the slot of a retro arcade game. The synja's early warning system sends a forearm up to block the heavy steel disc, but the force of the blow smashes his wrist against his visor. Jones hits the deck. Breaker dives the other way. Scrape barrels in as the synja draws his pistol. Crunch retracts the manhole cover and lifts the disc above his head. Scrape yanks the synja's arm and the shot goes wide. The cyborg goes for the hilt of his katana but his damaged hand flops uselessly. Crunch brings the manhole cover down again. The synja darts backward. The steel disc scrapes along the side of the cyborg's armor, churning up sparks.

Scrape is lunging low, wrenching the cyborg's gun hand away from Jones and his brother. Locked in a stalemate with Scrape, the synja delivers a roundhouse kick at Crunch. The armored instep glances off his shoulder, spinning him around.

Jones ducks as the manhole cover shoots from Crunch's grasp. The disc caroms off the wall behind her. At the same time, the synja overpowers Scrape, flinging him away. The cyborg levels the pistol at Jones.

Then the synja stiffens. Goes up on his toes like a ballerina. A web of static electricity crackles from his neck to form a cowl of bluish white energy. The synja collapses to reveal Lug standing behind him, holding a small taser-like device. Lug gives Jones a nod, then pockets the device and walks away. Scrape stands and brushes concrete dust from his vest and nudges the synja's scarred armor with his toe.

"Thing's fried," he says.

Jones lets out a breath. "Thanks, Lug!" she calls after him. Then she turns to Crunch, who's staring down at the fallen synja. "Nice move with the preemptive strike."

Crunch rotates his arm, massages his shoulder, winces. "He almost had me there, Jones. These things are strong as hell."

"Next time you lie to a synja . . ." Breaker starts. "Actually, just don't. Don't lie to a synja. I don't want to be the one who has to tell your mom you're in some Foot Clan holding cell. She already hates me."

"She doesn't *hate* you, she's just overprotective."

"Two things can be true."

"We gotta make ourselves scarce," Crunch says. "Foot's gonna be swarming."

"You guys scatter." Jones heads for the sewer entrance. "I'm going after the diver."

"Let it go, Jones," Scrape says. "We'll scrounge you up a new bike."

She climbs into the hole, wrapping her hand around a blood-smeared rung. "It's not just the bike. I got a feeling about this guy. He could be someone we want to know. Or not. But either way, I gotta find out."

She lowers herself down the ladder.

Above her head, Crunch says, "Just be careful, all right?" and replaces the manhole cover with a sharp *clank*.

She climbs down into a dark abyss and finds wet blood on every rung.

Jones hopes the guy doesn't bleed out before she gets to him.

16

HIROTO CLIMBS THE STEPS to the elevated platform in his penthouse that holds the stasis chamber. He pauses and takes in the handcrafted silver pedestal that supports the long glass cylinder. Behind the glass, nutrient-rich fluid the color of a tropical sea surrounds the occupant in stasis. She floats in some liminal state between life and death, her dark hair untouched by gray despite her now-advanced age. Preserved like a mosquito in amber, as beautiful and strong as the day she was pulled from the river. Hiroto watches the tendrils of her hair waving languidly like strands of seaweed. He places a hand on the glass just above her eternally youthful face.

"Hello, Mother." He turns and retrieves a monitor from the bank of medical equipment feeding her and recycling her waste and providing stimuli for nervous system function. The monitor is attached to a long articulated arm, and he pulls it into her line of sight. He flips a switch and the electrodes around her eye sockets stimulate the muscles there. Her eyes snap open.

As always, he half expects Oroku Karai to sit up, shatter the chamber, rip off her electrodes, and command him to fight a bigger, stronger boy who will beat him without mercy until Hiroto learns to improve his fundamentals. He shakes his head. No, she will never again speak a word to him, much less give him orders. He has no idea if she can even hear or see him. But he likes to think she can.

Karai had been the Foot Clan's fiercest warrior. She would be enraged at the idea of being kept alive in such a fashion. The woman he knew would have preferred death to this half -life. But he is the one making the decisions now. And he has decided that she will bear witness.

"I have something to show you."

He keys in commands on a small tablet. The monitor above his mother blinks on, displaying shelves, books, cheerful decor: one of the tower's residential libraries in a paused clip from a security camera.

"We had an infiltrator," Hiroto explains. He looks into his mother's wide eyes, the pupils swimming in fluid. For some reason, he's pulled into a memory of a trip to the mountain retreat upstate, Oroku Karai and Ikusa's parents sitting on the back patio, surrounded by silent masked bodyguards, all of them watching Hiroto and Ikusa spar with blunted ninjatō blades. Hiroto remembers the heat of that summer afternoon, the sweat soaking his sleeveless tunic. Ikusa came at him with a complex series of feints, and Hiroto was absorbed in the flow of the movement. Then a small object pelted him in the side of the head. And another. He dared not break his focus. But as he parried and turned, he saw her out of the corner of his eye: Oroku Karai tossing grapes from a glass bowl at him. He knew it wasn't a test of his concentration. His mother was simply disgusted with him. Ikusa had hit puberty first and was bigger and stronger. Hiroto had not yet learned how to compensate with speed and tactics. But in that moment, Ikusa had understood what was happening without Hiroto saying a word. Suddenly, the boy's grip on his ninjatō faltered and Hiroto sent it flying into a topiary swan. When he turned to bow at the onlookers, his mother had already left to go inside. Karai had naturally understood that Ikusa had forfeited. While his mother never again spoke of that afternoon, Hiroto knew it would have been better if Ikusa had simply overpowered him fairly.

Hiroto clears his throat, comes back to the present. His mother's eyes stare up at him, unblinking. "One of the mutant turtles we'd assumed to be as dead as his brothers and the rat." He lets the news sink in. Karai floats impassively. Ravens soar above the platform to join their brothers and sisters in circumnavigation of the penthouse dome. Hiroto lets the footage play for half a minute. He watches along with his mother. On the screen, the cloaked, hulking figure faces down a swarm of mousers, dodges energy beams, triggers some kind of EMP in his tonfa, sends the robots crashing down, dead. The turtle moves along the stacks and stops at the carpeted oval of the children's section, lined with beanbag chairs and low shelves. He turns to the camera, stares into the lens, and flips it off.

"Crass," Hiroto says. "He thinks he can infiltrate our home, move up the tower with impunity."

When Android 11-E moves into frame, there's a satisfying moment when the turtle does a quick double take at the sight of its new foe.

"I had the foresight to commission a new weapon," Hiroto says. "Watch."

He has seen this battle play out a dozen times, but imagining it through his mother's eyes gives him a new appreciation of his own strategic genius. The true measure of power isn't fighting battles with some antiquated sense of honor. It's in designing a framework for the enemy's annihilation without risking everything you've built. On the screen, the android and the turtle crash through the library window, out into the night.

He peers down at his mother. *This is why I am standing here, and you are lying in that stasis tube.*

"Coward," she says.

Hiroto blinks, frozen in place. His mother stares back. There is no life behind her eyes, only the unbeing of stasis. He waits, heart pounding. But there is nothing. He shakes his head. Of course she cannot speak. Besides, his mother is wrong: He is no coward. The impulsive version of himself would gladly have faced the turtle, gladly have died gloriously in battle, but then what would happen to their family empire? A true leader must consider all the angles. Honor is one thing. Practicality another.

"Bastard," his mother says, her voice coming from everywhere and nowhere. The ravens repeat it back. The word bounces off the underside of the dome, spinning like a ball in a roulette wheel. *Bastard. Bastard—*

"Master!"

Startled, Hiroto jabs the tablet. The screen goes dark. He looks up to find that Captain Ikusa has joined him on the platform. Ikusa wears his fierce, horned armor. Quickly, Hiroto maneuvers the screen back to its place. He doesn't know when Ikusa arrived. How much he's seen.

"Master Hiroto." Ikusa glances at the stasis chamber, where Karai's eyelids are stretched open, her pupils staring out through the blue-green liquid. "I'm sorry to interrupt. This couldn't wait."

Hiroto keys in a command and his mother's eyes close. He sets the tablet on a side table and smiles at his old friend. "Captain Ikusa. You know, I was just thinking about our trips upstate, when we were kids. The mountain retreat is still in the family, but nobody's ever there. It's a shame to let it sit empty year-round."

Coward. A raven flies low through the platform. *Bastard.*

Hiroto ignores the bird. Ikusa shifts his weight from one foot to another. "Well, I can't imagine you have much time for a vacation these days, sir."

Hiroto's heart sinks a little, then he feels an immediate rush of shame at his own disappointment. He can't expect Ikusa to suggest a trip to the retreat. The only way they will ever travel to the mountains together is if Hiroto commands it. Then Ikusa will dutifully obey. These roles have emerged from the chrysalis of their friendship. There is nothing to be done about it.

For a brief hateful moment, he blames Karai. He imagines taking one of Ikusa's short swords and stabbing a thousand holes in the stasis chamber, watching the precious life-giving fluid spill across the floor while his mother's vitals collapse, the machines shrieking their warnings . . .

"Why so empty-handed, Captain?" He smiles. "Did none of the turtles' weapons survive the impact? Not even a bent sai blade for a trophy?"

"No, Master." Ikusa bows low. "I fear you won't believe me when I tell you the news. I can scarcely believe it myself."

Hiroto's smile falters.

"The terrorist survived the fall."

Hiroto stares at his old friend. Then something opens inside his chest and he bursts out laughing. It feels wonderful. It feels like a release. Ikusa takes a step back. Hiroto tries to compose himself and issue an order, display rage and disappointment at the head of his security forces. But laughter wells up from deep inside and his body trembles. He doubles over. Tears spring to his eyes. The ravens, keyed to his moods, swirl in agitation.

"Sir . . ." is all Ikusa can manage.

Hiroto holds up a hand. He'll be all right in a minute. The news is not remotely funny. He knows this, of course. And yet he laughs and laughs.

17

RONIN SLINKS THROUGH THE dimly lit sewer tunnel. Familiar sounds close in around him: wet footfalls in the muck, echoes of dripping pipes, scurrying rats in the shadows. Every few steps, his legs buckle and he staggers into the wall, leans against it to steady himself, keeps going.

All the while, the battle with the gorilla android replays itself in his weary mind. He imagines himself evading its grasp, driving a blade through some unknown weak point in its armor. The fantasy overtakes him and he smiles through the pain. A lucky shot! That's all it would have taken. If he had feinted left instead of right before—

"Don't beat yourself up, bro."

"Sidewalk already did that for you."

Fine. But he also could have waited in his crater for the Foot Clan to arrive. Gone down fighting. Let the synjas finish him off, taken a few more with him.

No.

He'd known from the start this would be a suicide mission. But dying in the street at the base of the tower he'd almost climbed— that's not how he wants to go out. He's alive now, and he plans to stay that way. He'll retreat to the old lair, heal up, and return for Hiroto's head.

At least, that's the plan. But the lair's more than two miles away. And in the thirty-two minutes since he pulled himself out of the crater, he's barely made it a hundred yards through the sewers.

One step at a time. He repeats this like a mantra. Puts one foot in front of the other. Each breath burns his lungs. He feels like he's just run a marathon. Or one of those ultramarathons for psychotic people, a hundred miles in the Nevada desert. His legs are impossibly heavy. It's like his feet are strapped to cinder blocks.

One step at a time.

He tastes iron in the back of his throat. He sucks in a breath and blood goes down his windpipe. He coughs so much, it feels like his chest is threatening to cave in. Then blood jets from his mouth and paints a section of moldy brick dark red. His head spins. He holds onto the slimy wall to keep from collapsing.

One step at a time.

He doesn't move. It ought to be a simple matter, but his legs don't obey. He can't even feel them anymore.

Movement catches his eye. In the shadows beyond the reach of the tunnel's maintenance lights, three dim ghosts watch him, their eyes glowing softly.

"I'm sorry I failed you," he tells them.

"It's a setback, not a failure," one of his brothers calls out from the dark.

"You're still alive!"

"Which means you're not done yet."

Yes. His brothers are right. He just has to make it to the lair. Then he can—

A new coughing fit stokes the fire in his chest. The pain spreads down to his thighs, up into his face. It would feel so good to sit down, just for a moment. Then he finds he's already lowered himself to his knees.

He waits for the coughing to stop.

He tells himself to get up.

Nothing happens. Blood dribbles down his chin.

"Get up." His voice is a faraway transmission. "Get up."

He makes a fist and hammers his thigh. It doesn't feel like anything at all. He has gone as far as his legs will take him. He will not make it home.

"End of the road," he tells his brothers.

"But what about Hiroto? What about—"

"Quiet," Ronin says. "No more talking. Please."

He gathers his strength, then strips to the waist with slow movements. Now that he has made the decision to go out on his own terms, he feels a bit of strength return. Enough to get him through these last few minutes.

He sets aside his shirt and jacket, belt, goggles, pieces of protective armor he wears over his forearms. All of them ravaged. His father's journal is next. Holding the worn leather-bound book in his hands, he thinks of Master Splinter. More than anything else, he'd wanted to make him proud. But in the end, it had been too little, too late.

He lays the journal on the ground before him. Then he places alongside it the weapons of his family.

A simple wooden bō staff.

A single pair of nunchaku.

An atypical sai, sharpened at the tip to make it more deadly . . .

And a katana, the end of its blade broken during the fall from Hiroto's tower.

Four distinct weapons to fit the unique personalities of four brothers who had been so different, and so alike.

Ronin unzips a side pocket in his pants and produces a small bag. From the bag, he removes four strips of cloth: one red, one blue, one orange, one purple. The masks he and his brothers had grown up wearing. He carefully places the masks over the weapons. Metal and wood peek up through the eye slits.

Ronin misses his brothers so much. He glances into the shadows. The three figures are more distinct, their outlines sharper, their features beginning to coalesce out of the darkness.

He is closer to them now than ever before, inhabiting the border-land between life and death.

He picks up the broken katana and thumbs the edge of the blade. Still sharp. It'll do. Enough strength in the steel to pierce his tough reptilian skin.

"Dude!" a ghost calls out. "You don't gotta do this."

"Yeah, think it through!"

Ronin lets his eyes go slack. The ghostly figures melt back into the shadows. "I'll see you guys real soon."

He turns the shattered sword inward, rests the tip against his belly. "I'm sorry, Father. I failed. Please forgive me."

18

JONES SLOSHES THROUGH THE mire, tracking the jumper. It isn't hard. The guy's a mess. Stumbling, moaning, crying out in pain, coughing. The fact that he's apparently hurt bad strikes Jones as the weirdest part of all this.

Jumper craters the pavement and dies, that's the natural order of things.

Jumper craters the pavement and pops up unscathed, that's some truly supernatural shit.

But this maniac steals her bike, infiltrates Foot City, takes a flying leap off Hiroto's tower, survives—but is still kinda messed up?

Jones doesn't know what to make of it all.

A rat crosses her path. Big fat sucker. She knows there are millions of them down here, an underground society that perpetuates itself no matter what kind of drama's playing out on the streets above.

The coughing gets louder. Jones turns a corner. Just ahead is a massive silhouette in the dim red glow of a service light. She moves on tiptoes, quietly angling for a better view. Then she sees it—just a flash, there and gone: red glint on steel. The guy's holding a blade. What looks like a big knife, pointed straight at his stomach.

Jones can't believe it. She feels herself come unglued, the strangeness messing with her mind. This guy survives a quarter-mile swan dive onto blacktop, then heads into the sewer to commit seppuku? She holds still, not daring to breathe. This guy could be a total psycho. If she approaches him now, he might change his mind about gutting himself and turn his bloodlust her way. Maybe eat her brains and save her ring finger for a trophy.

But fear can't override her compulsion to help. And, if she's being honest with herself, to satisfy her curiosity.

"Hey, big guy!" she calls out, stomping toward him, making a racket on purpose.

The silhouette straightens. Its head turns. It tries to call out—"Who's there?"—but the words are swallowed up by a fit of wet coughing. Jones stops. She doesn't know what to do. The hacking worsens. The blade falls from his hand. Relief washes over her. She prides herself on being tough, but she doesn't want to watch someone drive a blade into their guts.

He collapses onto his side, racked with a gurgling moan. Jones rushes to his side. His weakened voice pleads. She leans in close and tries to make out what might be his last words. "My brothers"—she thinks he says—"my brothers are here."

She rolls the big guy over on his back, where she finally gets a good look at his face: round where it ought to be angular, oddly featureless yet still expressive.

"Holy shit."

Blood stains his wide mouth. She lays a hand gently against the side of his face, just beneath the strip of black fabric he wears like a mask. The flesh is tough, almost fibrous. And cold.

Jones's reality turns inside out. "You're a mutant turtle!"

The turtle blinks, tries to speak, then lies still.

19

RONIN FINDS HIMSELF ENVELOPED in darkness. Not a cold void but a warm cocoon. His pain is gone. He exhales without coughing up blood. The simple act of breathing is practically ecstatic. He turns over, reveling in the softness of his surroundings. It feels like Saturday morning, sleeping late in a soft bed—a peace he hasn't felt in many years. He can't remember how he got here. For the moment, he doesn't care.

Then a voice pierces the calmness: "If you guys don't wake him up soon, I'm eatin' the last bagel."

The voice doesn't come from inside his head. Ronin opens his eyes and pulls the blanket from his face. His old room in the sewer lair greets him. Posters of flash-in-the-pan punk bands, teetering stacks of comic books on a salvaged bookshelf, empty pizza boxes, half-finished model kits. Scrounged lamps and fluorescent bulbs give the whole place a yellow tint. It's exactly as he remembers it.

At the foot of the bed, emerging from a bright glow as if backlit by the sun, his brothers appear, bright-eyed and full of life. All three are teenagers again, like no time has passed. The weight of the empty years without them lifts. He can barely remember his life before this moment.

One of his brothers kicks the side of the bed so hard he almost falls out. "Hey, Sleeping Beauty—wake up. We got things to do."

They dress themselves in battle gear: colored masks, leather belts, wrappings for their joints. Ronin watches, entranced.

He sits up and winces as sharp pain jabs him behind the eyes. "Oh man. Who smashed a cement truck into my skull?"

"More like a fleet of cement trucks."

"Yeah. We've seen prettier things pulled outta the East River in spring."

He rubs the back of his head. Then he swallows and pain flares. His throat is raw. Is he getting sick? He remembers a coughing fit, doubling over, alone in the sewer tunnel. He shakes his head. "I had a weird dream."

"Good weird, or bad weird?"

Steel flashes red in his mind. A sinking despair takes hold. "Bad."

One of his brothers lays a hand on his shoulder. "Well, you're home now. You're safe."

Ronin wants to believe it. But already the room is too bright, his brothers beginning to diminish into the glow. "Home," he says. "The sewer lair." Maybe if he speaks it aloud, the edges of the messy room will come back into focus.

"What, you were expectin' the Ritz or somethin', twinkle toes? And who said you could use my favorite blanket?"

Ronin's brother tosses a pillow at him. It bounces off his head. As it falls away, the sewer lair explodes into light that swallows his brothers, the posters, the comic books, the lava lamp.

"No," Ronin says. He reaches out as if to grab hold of the lair itself, but it slips through his fingers. "Wait!"

Pain swells deep within his chest. His throat tightens, his head aches, his muscles cramp. A terrible thirst takes hold. He feels like he's aged a hundred years in a second.

And then another voice from the past calls out from beyond the light.

"Thank God, you're up."

The voice yanks him fully back to consciousness. And yet there's a moment of total disconnection. It feels like he's awakened from one dream into another.

Once again, he's in his bed in the sewer lair. But the whirlwind of teenage detritus is gone. The light is dim, a blue-gray wash that's easy on the eyes. Scavenged medical equipment huddles against the wall by the bed: IVs clamped to old coat racks, a fridge-like machine that beeps at regular intervals, a boxy old-school screen that displays EKG signals in mustard-yellow spikes.

Slowly, he becomes aware that he is the subject of the equipment's monitoring. There's an IV in his arm, electrodes stuck to his chest, bandages crisscrossing his entire body. His wounds have been dressed. So the visit with his brothers hadn't been a trip to the afterlife, just a stolen moment before waking up. In reality, he has been saved by the woman standing at his bedside holding a tray on which a bowl of chicken soup steams. She comes into focus and he is once again ripped from his moorings.

"*April?*" It can't be. April's dead, along with everyone else he ever cared about. "Is it really you?"

"Yes," she says. "It's me."

At the sound of her voice, Ronin breaks into a grin that hurts his battered face. His oldest friend in the world, back from the dead, with a smile as warm as the soup. Her reddish-brown hair is streaked with gray, and crow's feet gather at the corners of her eyes. Otherwise she's unchanged. She's even wearing her yellow leather coat and dark jeans. He decides not to dwell on how this moment came about. At the same time, he shoves down the memory of what he was about to do to himself back in the tunnel.

April sits on the edge of the bed, leans in, and lifts a spoon to feed him. Light moves across her forehead. Ronin catches sight of a mass of scar tissue knotted on the left side of her face.

"I'm so relieved you're finally awake," she says. "You really had me worried, Michelangelo . . ."

NEW YORK CITY: TWENTY YEARS AGO

APRIL PACES HER APARTMENT above the 2nd Time Around antique shop. She passes through the dining room and fusses with a chair, the salad tongs, an errant cloth napkin. A monstrous roast turkey anchors the feast, trimmings flanking the white ceramic serving dish. All of it says traditional Thanksgiving.

April O'Neil and Casey Jones have been planning this dinner for weeks. She adjusts a fork, takes a sip of red wine to calm her nerves. She looks across the dining room at Casey, where he's fixing a too-long polyester necktie in the mirror by the door. He shakes his head, undoes the tie at the neck, begins again. He's nervous, too, she knows, though he'd never admit it. They're probably putting too much pressure on themselves. Casey even trimmed his scraggly hair and scrounged up a collared shirt and clean black jeans. April's in a cozy brown cardigan over an orange turtleneck. It's got 1970s basement vibes. The nostalgia is comforting.

April tops off her wine. "What the hell is taking them so long? You told them six thirty sharp, right? Everything's getting cold!"

Casey loops the tie through a loose knot at his throat. "Maybe we should've told them we were having pizza."

"You *did* tell them it was special, right? That it's not just a regular old holiday meal . . ."

Casey pulls the tie. The knot tightens. It hangs too long, well past his waistline. He shrugs at himself in the mirror. "Relax, April. You know gettin' from the lair to here is always a pain in the ass." He joins April by the feast, lays a hand on her shoulder to siphon off her anxiety. "Just give 'em a little time. They'll be here."

April sighs. "But all this food . . ."

". . . is *fine*, babe." Casey laughs. "I'm more worried about screwing up the toast later."

"Are you nervous to tell them?"

"Sorta. But it's a good kind of nervous. They're family, you know?" Casey takes April's hand and lifts it, allowing the engagement ring to sparkle in the flickering light of the old apartment's not-quite-up-to-code fixtures. "I still can't believe you said yes."

"Well, I used to think I'd end up marrying you out of pity, then I couldn't wait for you to ask me. Took you long enough."

"Sorry 'bout that. It's just"—Casey gives April's fingers a light squeeze before letting go—"the streets never really showed me how to care about anything but myself for most of my life. Which sounds stupid, 'cause I wouldn't even *have* a life if it wasn't for you and the guys."

Casey clears his throat and turns away. April wishes her boyfriend—no, *fiancé*, she reminds herself—would feel more comfortable sharing his emotions more. But she figures they've got a lifetime together. Eventually he'll cry in front of her, and she'll show him how much love she has to give, and he'll understand that it's okay, that it only makes him stronger.

"Speakin' of the guys," Casey says, deftly segueing, "I think you're right. They're takin' their sweet time, and I'm starvin'."

"I'll call Donnie and find out what's—"

The front door explodes inward. Framed in the doorway is Raphael's squat, muscular frame. His fist leaves a bloody splotch on the wood.

"Make a hole!" Raph yells as he bursts into the apartment. "Incoming!" Blood clings to his feet and smears the floor. He blows past April and Casey and stumbles to the table. "We got ambushed!"

"Raph, you're hurt!" April says. The turtle ignores her.

"Ambushed?" Casey grabs his Louisville Slugger, chokes up on the grip, and eyes the open doorway. "By who?"

"We got away," Raph says, "but . . ." He glances over his shoulder. Then he swipes a big green arm across the table. The Thanksgiving spread clatters to the floor. Cranberry sauce and gravy spatters the area rug. The massive turkey lands with a wet *thud*.

April steps in mashed potatoes as she reaches for her friend. "You have to let me look at you."

Raphael bats her hand away. "Forget me. It's Master Splinter."

April doesn't have a chance to ask what happened. Two of Raphael's brother turtles, Michelangelo and Donatello, appear in the doorway. Master Splinter, their sensei—their *father*, really—is propped between them, arms across their broad shoulders, furry brown head lolling. The mutant rat's gray-brown fur is matted with blood. A pained moan escapes him.

"Raph! Where?" Michelangelo yells. His tone is jarring: Mikey, the party animal, is deadly serious. April's anxiety ratchets up. She meets Casey's eyes and finds the gravity of the situation reflected in them.

"Over here!" Raph calls back. "Get him on the table."

"April," Donatello says, "grab the med kit."

Michelangelo and Donatello lift the elderly rat onto the table with gentleness that breaks April's heart. They set him carefully on his back. Splinter's maroon robe is in tatters. The old mutant's blood soaks the lacy white tablecloth. To think that just a moment ago the table had held a magazine-worthy Thanksgiving feast, and now—

April snaps out of it. From a junk drawer she retrieves her makeshift medical kit—an old lunchbox filled mostly with bandages and aspirin—pulls out two pairs of scissors, and tosses one to Donatello. Then she begins snipping off Splinter's robe with her own pair. The mutant rat's head thrashes back and forth. Michelangelo holds it steady. April is dismayed to find the robe's fabric sodden with blood. Under all that fur, Splinter is severely damaged. She has to find the source. "Donnie," she says. Her voice is calm and measured. "Help me cut away his clothes so we can assess the damage."

Donatello stares at the scissors in his hand as if confounded by them. "I don't know where to start, April, I—"

She gives him a sharp look. Shock is setting in. No time for that now. She slaps the bare skin of his shoulder. "Hey! Donnie! Focus!" He blinks at her. "We need to find which wound's the most dangerous."

Donatello takes a deep breath and lets it out. "Yeah . . . okay . . . sorry." He shakes his head. "I'm good."

He begins to snip at the collar of Splinter's robe.

Casey stalks back and forth from the table to the wall, hands gripping the bat. "Who the hell ambushed you?"

Raphael snorts. "Who do you think?" He rubs his jaw and spits out a tooth fragment. "Foot bastards."

"Big strike team," Michelangelo adds. "I don't know how they knew exactly where to find us, but they jumped us as soon as we came outta the sewers."

Splinter begins to cough. Blood mists along Michelangelo's arm as he tries to hold his father still. April pulls the scissors away, not wanting to accidentally injure the old mutant. Donatello follows her lead.

Splinter pushes out a single word through the coughing fit: "Leonardo."

Only now does April realize the eldest turtle isn't here with the others.

Michelangelo takes Splinter's hand in his own. "Rear guard, Sensei. Leo was making sure the rest of us got clear."

"Screw this," Casey says, pointing the tip of the baseball bat at Raphael. "C'mon, Raph. Let's go make sure Leo got out."

Raph's fists are clenched. "Damn straight. It's body count time."

"Stand down, Raph."

April's head swivels toward this new voice. Relief washes over her as Leonardo steps into the apartment. The fourth turtle stows his katanas on his back and heads for the table.

"We're good for now," Leonardo says. "I shook the last of the Foot back in the subway. Looked like they might be running toward the East Side. The docks, maybe."

Casey lowers the bat. "What happened with the truce, Leo? Thought we got past all that shit with them."

"Honestly, I'm surprised it lasted as long as it did." Leo shrugs. "How's Father?"

"He's lost a lot of blood," April says. "Donnie and I are doing the best we can, but without a real doctor, I don't know if we can save him."

Splinter's body goes still. He lets out a long sigh and begins to mutter softly. April and the turtles lean in.

"This war . . ." he whispers. "Just a matter of time. Oroku against Hamato . . . always. Karai . . . trying to end it once and for all."

"Shh," Michelangelo says. "We got you, Sensei."

Leo looks at Casey. "Could you bring the van around? Now that he's stabilized a bit, we can bring him to Dr. Lee."

"On it," Casey nods. "You want shotgun, Raph?"

No reply. April glances around the apartment. The red-masked turtle is gone, and April knows exactly where he went. After an attack like this, he's going to want blood. She meets Leonardo's eyes. He shakes his head. "Goddammit."

Raphael pops up from the sewer tunnel and sniffs the air. Briny river stench. Diesel fuel. Dead fish. He's as far east as the Lower East Side gets, a jutting bulge into the river a few blocks south of the Williamsburg Bridge. Just ahead, the motionless arms of dormant cranes angle above the loading dock. He creeps up from the tunnel and hits the streets, melting into the shadows. Another smell hits him: blood. He bares his teeth, draws both of his sai. He moves through darkness, the weapons extensions of his forearms.

Past the docks' office, a single-wide trailer with ratty blinds and darkened windows, the scent grows stronger. He pauses at the edge of the trailer and looks out upon a flat expanse, a graveyard of old shipping containers and crates. There are ninjas gathered in the darkness: dozens of Foot soldiers, many splayed out on the ground or curled up, attended by comrades as they cry out in pain. Raph smiles at their agony. Relishes it. Wishes to inflict more.

But there are many soldiers who stand up straight, unhurt—for now. Raphael calms his heart, forces himself to remain hidden. They will pay, but first he must observe. No use rushing into a lopsided fight if she isn't here. He grips the sai tighter. His weapons have a mind of their own, a pleasant hum, a longing to rend flesh and rupture internal organs.

He thinks of Splinter, moaning on a bloody table in April's apartment. His eyes roam the black-clad ninjas, selecting the ones who will die first. Truce breakers, all of them. He doesn't know why his father trusted the Foot Clan to keep their word in the first place. Oroku Karai is ruthlessly ambitious. Letting her power grow unchecked has been a mistake.

The ninjas still able to stand come to attention. A hush falls over the gathering. Raphael follows the shift in energy to a crate at the far end of the docks, where a woman climbs atop it. The long trailing ends of her crimson headband flutter in the crisp November wind. She's flanked by four high-ranking Foot soldiers brandishing tall yari spears.

"I gave you one simple command."

Her voice is clear and strong. Some of the Foot soldiers flinch as if she struck them. Raphael imagines flinging a sai at her face. He idly judges the arc, the trajectory, knowing it would be foolish. But, oh, the satisfaction of watching the tripointed blade bury itself between her eyes . . .

"Kill the mutants!" She sweeps her gaze along those forming loose ranks at the back of the crowd. The ones Raphael will cut through first. "That's it! A single task. Bring your far superior numbers to snuff out *five* sewer dwellers." She paces back and forth on her platform. "And yet here we are. Five sewer dwellers in the wind but *alive*, and the Foot Clan cowering on the docks, nursing wounds, wallowing in failure so thick"—she tilts her head and gives the air a theatrical sniff—"I can smell it. And it's a *bad* smell. A smell that *offends* me." She prowls to the edge of the container, leans down, points at a Foot soldier. "Does it offend you?"

"Y-yes, Master."

She cups her ear. "*What did you say?*"

"Yes, Master!" The response is louder this time.

"Yes! I would imagine it does! Because you *reek of it*."

She straightens up, extends her arms. "The truce between the Foot and the Hamato Clans has been broken. We must finish what we started. We must wash off the stench of failure!"

Karai glares at her fighters while murmurs spread throughout the crowd. Behind her, silent implacable cranes rise into the black, starless sky.

Raphael knows he won't get a better chance. He springs from his hiding place. A hunter. An animal. A ninja turtle unleashed.

"Blood has been spilled!" Karai shouts from atop the container, her voice resounding across the ranks of her warriors. "And there is no turning back now. We finish this tonight!"

"Yeah," Raphael shouts. So much for stealth. "We do."

A Foot soldier turns, startled. His eyes go wide as Raphael opens his throat with a swipe of his sai. First blood on the weapon is like chugging coffee—his adrenaline cranks up. A sprawled, wounded ninja reaches for Raphael's legs but Raphael kicks him in the face and the man goes limp. A third soldier leaps off a crate and Raph skewers him through the chest with both sai and flings him to the ground. Raph grins. He can see the deaths of these ninjas a split second before he inflicts them. In his mind's eye a neck is stabbed, an artery severed, a belly eviscerated, and then he makes it so as if guided by some all-powerful god. Raphael whirls. Men and women cry out and beg for their lives on their knees. Some remain silent. He doesn't care either way. They all die at his hand.

"And so!" Karai shouts, pointing at the disturbance in her ranks. "Our failure finds us. Destroy the beast!"

Raphael laughs. He wants Karai to throw wave after wave of fighters at him. An emptiness fills him. Some ninjas attack without pause and march stoically into the next life, drowning in blood. Others hesitate, and he reads the fear in their movements. He revels in their terror at the moment of their deaths. These, the cowards who broke the truce and ambushed his family.

He delivers an elbow and feels a nose shatter. Then he thrusts forward and carves out an eye. The soldier's hands go to his face and Raphael severs eight fingers with one stroke of his sai. He leaves the soldier writhing on the ground and moves on to stab a belly, twist, and remove meat with his blade. There are no faces, no distinct fighters, only targets and then wounds.

The Foot soldiers begin to organize around him. Their ranks bristle with katanas. Raphael gives himself over to his training, Splinter's teachings guiding his movements. He finds himself in the air, upside down, blood-soaked sai finding strange angles to puncture Foot soldiers.

A blow to his shell knocks him to one knee. Dull pain courses through his back. Something whistles past his ear. A stinging rush opens up on his shoulder.

Arrows. He can sense two lodged in his shell. A katana comes at him in a vicious downward slice. Raphael's sai finds the hand that grips it and a scream hits the air. He tosses a ninja away like a discarded toy. Up ahead, Karai looks down upon the carnage.

"Quit hiding behind these scrubs!" Raphael screams. "Let's finish this once and for all." He snaps a neck without taking his eyes off Karai. Becoming a machine of brutal precision has been easy. A split-second thought of Splinter bleeding out on April's dining room table and he's inflicting spin kicks, finishing ninjas with sai swept apart to half sever heads from bodies.

"Yes . . ." Karai is in the air, impossibly high, silhouetted against a crimson moon. Her hands clutch a pair of long swords. ". . . we will."

An arrow slides along the top of his skull, a glancing shot that still cuts too deep. Blood runs in his eyes. He wipes it with the back of his hand. Karai hits the earth softly, bends her knees, then closes the gap between them. Raphael knows his shell is bristling with arrows. He thinks one might be lodged in his left thigh but doesn't care to look. Karai fills his field of vision, a lithe fighter, dark hair flowing from beneath her bandana. Raphael's mind goes as red as the moon.

As red as his mask.

Raphael bellows as he severs the jugular of a soldier in front of him. Jets of warm blood spatter his face. All at once Karai is coming over the top with a katana and driving a knee into his solar plexus and slashing at his calves. Raphael staggers back, deflecting steel with his sai. The kinetic energy of her attack vibrates up his arm. He feels the eyes of the Foot soldiers on him. If he delivers a killing blow to Karai, they will slaughter him with arrows and shuriken and spears. He won't be getting out of this alive.

This dawns on him like a distant star, its light barely reaching Earth. He will never see his brothers, or Splinter, or April and Casey again. There is sadness somewhere on the horizon, and longing, and regret. But no time to wallow. Right here in front of him is the object of his rage, katanas whirling. And he must kill her to make his own death count for something.

If he is going to be gone from his brothers' lives forever, then he will make sure Oroku Karai is, too.

That will be a fair trade for the future of the city.

Karai feints and Raph parries nothing but air and then they are too close for the katana blade to find its target so Karai smashes the kashira—the end of the grip—into Raph's face. He spits blood. She stomps on his foot. He backhands her across the face and her head whips to one side. He follows with a roundhouse kick that cracks a rib and sends her flailing. She skids on the dirty ground but stays on her feet.

Her angular face is ruddy with exertion. Blood leaks from her nose. At her back, a dozen ninjas wait with arrows notched.

"My soldiers failed to take your head," she says. "But I will not."

Raphael knows he should keep his mouth shut. That's what Splinter and his brothers would caution. Let Karai spit all the venom she wants. Let her emotions guide her. Remain stoic. Wait for her weaknesses to reveal themselves.

But he isn't his brothers. He's Raphael. And he's rude.

"Go to hell, Karai."

She comes at him, darting to one side, her attack like a dance. Her fighting style is slippery, quick, surprising. He traps a katana between the triplicate blades of a sai but she pulls it free with a metallic *shink* before he can pry it from her grasp.

It's like she has three limbs. He feels like a guy at a blackjack table trying to count cards. He's monitoring so many things at once he's losing track of the real game. They mirror each other strike for strike. For an eerie moment Raph thinks she can see his moves before he makes them. The fire in her eyes, her sheer force of will, makes him wonder: Deep down, what is she fighting for?

Blood stings his eyes and Raphael unleashes a flurry of quick blows. He is vaguely aware that the momentum of the fight is taking them toward the river. Karai digs in, dodges low, and the vicious swipe of a sai whistles over her head. Raph's back is half turned as he recovers. He swivels, bringing a sai down on the flat of her blade, guiding it away from his neck. Her voice echoes in his mind. *My soldiers failed to take your head. I will not.*

Karai's vow triggers an instinct, a chain of cause and effect that takes a microsecond to inform his next move. If she wants his head, then her second katana will be at odds with what he reads in her narrowed eyes, and his own deflection must—

"Hrrraaaagh!" Raph screams as Karai buries her katana deep in his side. The blade cuts a fiery path through muscle and sinew. His breath goes ragged. Karai smiles. They both know his lung is punctured. She withdraws the blade and a geyser of blood fans out on the ground as he spins and lands a deep gash to her lower back. She screams.

"Kidney for a lung," he rasps. Already short of breath. Gotta move faster.

The wetness of the blood on his side gives Raph a new plan: Change the field of battle. If he can get Karai in the river, the edge will be his.

He fights through the pain and pushes her backward with a volley of rote punches and kicks. Herding, not fighting. She dances just beyond them, easily out of reach. He senses the gathered ninjas move as one, loosely ringing their leader and her mortal enemy. At any moment Karai could command them to rush in and finish the job for her. But Raphael knows her honor and hubris will not permit it. His breath comes in wheezing gasps. His vision swims. He manages to slice a chunk of flesh out of Karai's upper arm. She cries out and returns with a downward slice that barely misses his eye. His cheek erupts in searing pain.

Karai's second blade comes across his neck. Raphael leans away and feels the wind of the steel's passage.

"You missed!"

Karai shifts her weight as a fulcrum for another strike. Her back foot rests on the edge of an old dock, long out of use, all rotten wood and gull shit.

Raph lunges. He gets low and plows his shoulder into her gut. He feels the breath go out of her in a rush. An arrow rips into the back of his knee. Soldiers scared he's about to drown their master. The pain is a distant alarm. He dismisses it. A moment later, the cold, dark water of the East River closes in around them. Karai's screams are muffled and dreamlike. The whole world has gone quiet, and yet their thrashing limbs emit a dull roar.

Through jets of bubbles, Raph catches sight of her twin katanas, lost in the shock of hitting the water. They drift into the depths and vanish.

He lets one sai go and grips her tunic with his free hand. Weaponless, she bites down on his wrist. The pain is nothing to him. Let her chew his fingers off. He'll carve out her eyes and some East River monster-fish will eat them whole. As Karai flails, he slides his hand up to her throat. He holds her gaze and wills her to know what he's thinking: that she is done. That she is going to die here, in the dark, at his hands.

Her eyes go wide with understanding. The cold and the pain and the knowledge of his own death melt away. It has all been worth it for this: Karai had not taken a breath before their plunge. Even if she had, Raph is a mutant. He can hold his breath much longer than a mere human. All he has to do is wait and nature will take its course.

Watching her drown, he thinks of Splinter. He tries to project thoughts of his father, the wise old rat, into her mind, so it's the last thing she sees before she dies. His remaining sai is in his other hand. He could end this now. But he chooses to let her die slowly. Raphael is conscious of the dishonor in denying his enemy mercy at the end. He stretches his lips into a smile and decides he doesn't give a shit. Her face goes slack. She quits struggling.

Then something changes. He catches a glimmer in her eye. A flicker of—what? Hope? He squeezes tighter. Too late, he thinks he should have stabbed her and been done with it.

Her arm is already reaching over his shoulder. She pulls free a small push dagger that had been lodged in his shell. Everything is slow motion down here. There is only Raphael and Karai. They are their own world.

Raphael knows what is happening. He knows what will happen. And yet he is in a strange limbo state, where no matter what he does or how he twists in the water, he cannot avoid his fate. It has happened, it is happening, it was always going to happen. He lets go of her throat to put a thick forearm in the way of the blade. But the cold steel is already biting his throat. Without even willing it, his other hand buries the sai into the flesh of her upper back. At least he can die knowing that he took Oroku Karai with him. It was always going to end like this anyway. She gives the push dagger one last shove before her body goes limp in the water.

A burning, tugging sensation in his neck tells him his carotid artery has likely been severed. There is very little pain, but already his hands and feet are distant things. His strength vanishes. The sai floats away. He watches the depths take his beloved weapon. Perhaps he could swim to the surface, float around till a barge picks him up at dawn. But this is a thought belonging to another turtle in another time. It does not connect to something he could actually do. And so he gives himself over to the river. Karai's blood mingles with his own in the dark and filthy water. There are moments of his life he wishes to revisit. Memories with his brothers, scampering across Manhattan. They flash past with impossible speed, too fast to savor. And as darkness overtakes his vision, the memories flit away into confusion.

The last thing he sees is Karai's ninjas diving into the river to claim her.

20

HOME.

Drab cement walls. Bad light. Cracked floors. Scavenged furniture. Crooked chairs. Knife-scarred table. Chipped pots and pans on sagging shelves. Fridge that sounds like a backfiring engine. Sulfurous water from the tap.

Nice to see that nothing's changed.

Ronin paces the kitchen, slipping into a past he'd both worshipped and tried to forget. It's been a few days since his fall, since he almost reunited with his brothers, and now that he's well enough to get out of bed, every inch of this place holds a memory. He stops near the bathroom door and leans over to inspect some faded ink lines on the wall. For five years, Splinter had charted the heights of his young, growing turtles. Donatello had been so proud of pulling ahead at year three, and then everyone caught up by year four. Ronin eyes the cabinet door beneath the sink, hanging at an angle from its hinges. Raph had kicked it, frustrated over some trivial thing. Probably Splinter making him a peanut butter sandwich instead of a grilled cheese. In the early days, Raph's anger was pure petulance. Splinter taught him control, discipline.

Ronin sighs. All that training didn't keep Raph from getting himself killed. He runs a hand along the edge of the sink. No dust clings to his finger. April keeps this place spotless. His thoughts turn dark. Who is he to judge his brother when he's only here because of his own suicide mission?

Looking for distraction, he rifles through a drawer. Electrical tape, mismatched cutlery, AA batteries, a box of waterproof matches.

Ronin takes a seat at the rickety wooden table where he'd shared thousands of pizza dinners with his brothers. He pulls a match from the box, strikes it, and watches the flame burn down to his thick, scarred fingertips. The match fizzles out. A thin wisp of smoke vanishes into the air and takes his name with it.

Ronin is a moniker for someone who's lost everyone they've ever loved. For him, for Michelangelo, that's no longer true. He sits up straight in his old, creaky chair. Michelangelo. The name creeps under his skin like a benevolent virus. A nostalgic link connects him to the turtle he used to be, long ago. Always up for a joke, a party, a way to deflate the seriousness of life in the city.

"This whole April-still-being-alive thing is nuts, huh?" The voice belongs to Donatello.

Michelangelo glances around the table. His three brothers are here with him, looking crisp and sharp. He wonders if his straying so close to the border between life and death has given them more power to materialize in this world. It's a nice thought. Steaming teacups sit before them.

"Hard to believe anyone survived what April did," Leonardo agrees.

Raph chuckles and leans back in his chair, folding his hands behind his head. "Talk about miracles—right, Mikey?"

"Yeah." Michelangelo strikes another match. "Last thing I remember from back when I saw her last is the explosion. I was out of it pretty bad when I finally came to. Couldn't remember anything for days. And by the time I did . . ."

Inspired by his brothers' inexplicable tea, he gets up to make his own. He sets an old kettle on the stove and putters around until he finds some looseleaf oolong in a cloudy mason jar.

"Explosion, huh? I guess I kinda missed that one," Raph says.

"No 'kinda' about it," Donnie says. "Remind me, Leo, *why* did he miss it?"

"I dunno, Donnie—couldn't have been because he flipped out, ran off, and did something stupidly hotheaded again, would it?"

"Hey!" Raph pounds the table with a fist. "How many times has my stupid hot head saved all your asses, huh?"

"Not enough," Michelangelo says.

Raph swivels in his chair. "Oh, you got somethin' to say, Mikey? At least I didn't try to off myself at the first whiff of failure."

"Don't give me that!" Michelangelo yells to the phantom Raphael. "I fought beside you in every battle—even the idiotic ones you started—and you still think you have the right to judge me?"

Michelangelo turns away from the scrutiny of his brothers' unblinking eyes. "You all knew what my mission was in the tower. It was a one-way ticket from the start. For our father. For our family. For our honor . . ." Michelangelo trails off. When he turns back to the table, his brothers and their teacups are gone. Ghosts are better at vanishing than any ninja.

A shrill whistle steals his attention. He takes the kettle from the stove and scrounges up a pot and spoon. As he works, he talks to his brothers. He knows they're still listening. They're always listening.

"Look, I should be dead. That fall should've killed me, but it didn't. No idea how, or why, but I'm still here. I lost a battle, but the war goes on."

Satisfied the tea is properly steeped, Mike pours himself a cup. "We've all had so much stolen from us." He blows steam across the surface of the mug. "I swear to you all, I will finish what we started. What Master Splinter raised us to do." Mike raises his cup toward the empty table. "The last Oroku must die."

21

"MICHELANGELO!"

April makes her way into the kitchen. Her threadbare robe is belted with a fine piece of silk. Mike remembers it from Splinter's collection. His father possessed so many wonderful things. Old-world artifacts, Hamato Clan heirlooms. He's glad to see one put to use. Splinter would have approved.

"What the hell are you doing up?" She leans against the cantankerous fridge and crosses her arms. "You should be resting."

Mike is well into middle age now, but April's still his older comrade. Part running buddy, part mother figure. The complexity of their old relationship unwinds, a little, in the old familiar kitchen. What are they to each other now, these two survivors?

"I'm sorry, April. I couldn't sleep so I made myself some tea. I hope that's okay."

April pats him on the shoulder. "Of course it is—this was your kitchen way before I moved in." She eyes his mug. "That the oolong?"

"I think so."

"Been here since Splinter brought it home. If some kinda horrific mold hijacks your brain, I take no responsibility."

Mike takes a sip. "It's all on me." He lets it linger in his mouth. Weak, but palatable. "Tastes like home," he says. "Honestly, it's the best cup of tea I've had in a million years. Can I fix you one?"

She reaches for a jar of instant coffee. "Tea doesn't do a thing for me these days." She dumps a heap into a mug and hits it with hot water. "I run on high-octane."

Mike watches her tilt the kettle. The sleeve of her robe rides up, exposing a gunmetal gray forearm instead of creamy skin. Then he clocks her hand: flesh-colored yet mottled with shiny patches where the outer layer's rubbed raw. Little clockwork joints. It's a prosthetic. And not a new one.

April catches him staring. She raises the arm, wiggles the fingers. "What, you never saw a state-of-the-art cybernetic enhancement before?"

Mike shifts his eyes to his teacup. "Sorry."

"Don't be. Got one just like it for my leg. Well, no. That one has toes instead of fingers."

She waits for him to laugh. But his mind serves up the startling image of a hand jutting from her ankle. With these back alley cybernetics, you never know.

"Souvenirs from the last time we saw each other." April sips her coffee, then raps her artificial knuckles on the table. "When the weather's right, I can pick up radio signals from the Bronx."

This time, Mike laughs. April's expression grows warmer, her facial scars bunching up. Mike thinks of a bulldog's neck. She reaches across the table and squeezes his hand. For a moment, he gets to be the turtle from back in the day, and not the beat-up old hulk covered in bandages.

"I'm so happy you're alive, Mikey."

"You too, April. All this time, I thought . . ." The litany of what he thought over the past two decades is dismal and not worth voicing. The bitter solitude, the helpless pining. He doesn't know what to say. The unspoken hangs in the air between them. "Listen. I think we should get one thing outta the way. I shouldn't be alive. A fall from that height would have killed me when I was younger. Would have killed *anybody*." He shakes his head. "I'm still processing it." He looks at her. "But I know one thing: I shouldn't be here right now, talking to you. I shouldn't be anywhere at all."

It's strange to air these thoughts out loud. He looks down at the hand holding the teacup, confirms it's solid. A bone-deep ache shudders through him. He winces. He suspects his body knows it's on borrowed time. That he has been granted some extension that can be revoked at will.

April goes to the fridge and opens the door. "Well, I'm no Donatello, but it doesn't take a genius to see your mutation has progressed over the years. You're bigger, stronger, faster. Tough enough to survive a sixty-story plunge to the cement."

Mike absorbs this theory. It ought to reassure him. Even excite him. Greater mutant abilities means a better chance of taking out Hiroto. But he feels disconnected from himself, as if one part of him— the part at his core—is sprinting ahead of the turtle he is at heart. And what's at the end of the race? Some horrible mutation, an evolution into a truly monstrous form?

He thinks of his river crossing. Maybe one day he'll crawl back into the slime, a twisted, malformed wretch.

April retrieves a carton of eggs and shows them to Mike. "Real eggs—not the synthetic crap we're usually stuck with—courtesy of our friendly neighborhood black market."

She produces an empty bowl from a cupboard and cracks an egg on the rim.

"You know it's better to crack eggs on the counter," Mike says.

She cracks another egg with a flourish. "Don't take my simple joys from me."

He nods at her prosthetic. "That thing ever hurt?"

She shrugs. "Every day."

They go quiet.

"Hey, this happens to be a *fresh* batch of eggs, too," April says after a moment. "We wouldn't want salmonella to finish what Hiroto started."

Mike growls softly at the mention of Hiroto's name.

April whisks the eggs. A dollop of yolk hits the side of the fridge. "Word on the street is, you really rattled his cage."

"Rattling cages wasn't the plan."

"Well." April lights the stove, slides a pat of butter around a pan. "You'll get another chance at him. You're healing insanely fast."

"My head's not. Everything's fuzzy. And I can see . . ." Mike trails off before he mentions his brothers. "I mean, I can't see how I got back here. Back to the lair."

April pours the egg mixture into the pan. "Hold that thought." She sets the empty bowl in the sink. "Casey!" she shouts. "Breakfast!"

Mike's heart surges. He feels like he could lift off the floor, float up through the sewers, rise above the city itself. The life of the solitary drifter, the ronin, recedes into a distant speck.

"Holy shit," he says, "Casey's still alive, too?" Impressions of Casey Jones slide through his mind: the hockey mask, the Louisville Slugger, the ramshackle wit and street-born toughness.

Elsewhere, a sofa creaks. A silhouetted figure appears in the doorway to the kitchen. Scraggly hair; wiry, muscular frame.

"Casey," Mike says, voice hushed with awe.

The figure steps fully into the kitchen. It's not his old friend but a young woman, her dark hair pulled back into a ponytail.

"Michelangelo," April says, "I'd like you meet my daughter—Casey Marie Jones."

Casey holds out her hand. But Mike only stares. He sees it all at once: the wry energy of her father, Casey Jones, and the tough city-bred kindness of her mother, April O'Neil. All of it wrapped up in an eager, sharp-eyed face. He looks down at the hand. The girl's muscular arm, wrist, and fingers are wrapped in white fighter's tape.

Mike takes her hand. Her grip's firm. "You been training?"

April snorts. "Can't keep this one out of the dojo."

"We kinda already met," Casey says to him, "back there in the tunnel. Though you were a lot less conscious and a lot more bloody at the time."

The girl talks fast, like her parents. Mike catches himself staring at her again and looks over at the busted cabinet instead. Something stirs his heart, an unfamiliar warmth. Casey's so young, so full of life—Michelangelo and his brothers used to be just like this. But he isn't sad. The stirring in his heart might actually be joy. He's not sure. It's been a while.

"This is so weird." Casey takes a seat at the table. "I've been hearin' stories about you turtles all my life, but I never thought I'd get to meet one of you for real."

Mike can't stop looking from April to her daughter. "*Casey*," he says after a while.

Casey raises an eyebrow. "Yep, that's me." She looks at her mother. "He supposed to be the funny one?"

April cracks another egg on the rim of the pan. "Like I said—lots of catching up to do."

22

THE TERRORIST SURVIVED THE fall.

Captain Ikusa's words echo inside Hiroto's head.

The terrorist survived the—

THWACK.

The heel of Hiroto's palm makes contact with a Foot soldier's nose. The ninja drafted into this sparring session stumbles into the wall of the penthouse dojo and slides to the floor. Hiroto grins, thinking of Ikusa's quick and astonishing report. He tries to conceive of a being that could survive a fall from his tower. He has seen images of the cratered pavement. This turtle simply got up from the cracked cement and walked away.

A second fighter attacks Hiroto alongside a third. Masked warriors, highly trained, both of them wielding heavy batons. They do not wait to attack one at a time. Their training lets them ease in and out of the flow of combat, two soldiers fighting as one. Hiroto reads their silent coordination, his footwork responding to their strikes. None of the batons touch his tattooed skin. Hiroto fights these armored soldiers bare chested and openhanded. He wears only simple black gi pants and fingerless gloves. His long hair is tied up in a bun.

The terrorist survived the fall.

Hiroto laughs. He ducks, spins, cracks a soldier's faceplate with an elbow, shatters the second one's knee with a kick to the side of her leg.

"What is wrong with you?" he screams at his soldiers.

The injured soldier slinks away. Her broken limb trails along the tatami mat, deadweight at a sickening angle. She does not dare cry out. Another takes her place from the ranks of a dozen handpicked warriors. The fighters advance on their master with fierceness and intent. To show hesitation, to pull punches for fear of hurting him—Hiroto has executed warriors for such offenses. Yet this afternoon he senses weakness. Its stench fouls the air of the dojo.

"I said show me a decent fight!"

He reaches out and snatches a baton before his opponent can react. The tattoos on his arms look beautiful in motion. As fluid as his fighting style. The fighter goes on the offensive, aiming a flurry of kicks at Hiroto's upper body and head. Hiroto dances backward through the barrage, then comes down on the fighter's shin with the baton. Bone snaps. The man limps away. Hiroto flings the baton at the back of his head.

"Don't *ever* turn your back on me!"

He looks at the half dozen ninjas waiting in the wings. "Try to kill me! Or I will toss you off the tower one by one so you can fly *like a turtle*."

Batons rise.

He glances up at the camera mounted to the corner of the wall. Like all his sessions, this one's beamed in real time to the TV arranged above his mother's stasis tube. She will bear witness to the fighter he has become.

The ninjas surround him. Hiroto feels the air-conditioning blasting across his sweat-soaked face. He catches a glimpse of his frame, poised and glistening, in the floor-to-ceiling mirror that lines the dojo. His training, his nutrition, his recovery—all of it is perfectly coordinated to produce the enviable body that he sends whirling toward the nearest opponent. For a moment, Ikusa's words go silent inside his head. Hiroto's instep makes contact with a fighter's neck, the pliable flesh just below the base of his helmet. A strangled cry, a baton hitting the floor, a second fighter coming at him, a third, a fourth. No sounds but heavy breathing and the flat smacks of skin on rubberized flak.

"That's it," Hiroto says. A warrior spins to sweep Hiroto's leg and Hiroto stamps down at the precise moment to shatter the man's ankle. A kick to the head sends his opponent sprawling across the tatami. Hiroto's limbs are spears in one moment then hammers the next. He swoops down with magnificent fury upon his warriors. There is no more indecision, no more impotent rage. There is only the purity of combat. It washes his mind clean. The fight progresses underneath him, around him, within him. Fallen batons litter the dojo floor. He is the apotheosis of his family's ambition. He parries a roundhouse kick and snaps a leg. The notion of this turtle, this invader, slips to the back of his consciousness. It is no more or less important than his other daily administrative tasks. It is a number on a ledger, a cell on a spreadsheet, a pile of birdseed in his palm. He has been so preoccupied, so pent-up, but now he is finally starting to relax.

Hiroto finds himself in tactical positions a split second ahead of his own initiative. His body is in thrall to some force beyond its ken. He parries, feints, lashes out, draws blood, cracks ribs even through bulletproof breastplates.

"Come on!" he roars at the trio of soldiers still standing. Bodies litter the floor at his feet. In the mirror he catches sight of his captain as he steps into the dojo. Fully armored, the captain stands tall and clasps his hands behind his back to watch the fight.

Hiroto's arm extends to deliver a strike to a vulnerable soldier. At the same time, a baton tags him on the shoulder. Hiroto whirls around. One of his soldiers has slipped behind him and landed a blow. Perhaps Hiroto let his attention falter upon seeing his captain enter.

The room falls silent. No one cries out from the floor. The remaining fighters hold their breath.

Hiroto stares at the warrior who tagged him. He is a big man for a ninja. Highly skilled to move with such grace and quickness.

Tension stiffens the warrior's body. He glances at his captain, then back to Hiroto.

"An excellent strike," Hiroto says, bowing his head. The ninja seems to relax. He returns the bow. "What is your name, soldier?"

"Juan, sir."

"Juan. What did I ask of you during this session?"

Juan's eye flicker to the other two ninjas.

"Don't look at them," Hiroto says. "Look at me."

"You asked us to try to kill you."

"I did?"

"Yes, Master. Just now. A second ago, I mean."

"I see." Hiroto wipes the sweat from his brow. "And was that what you were doing? Trying to kill me?"

Juan shuffles his feet. His eyes roam the dojo. "I wasn't," Juan stammers. "I wouldn't, I mean, I would never . . ."

"You caught me off guard, moving to my blind side. You could have caved my skull in. And yet you tapped me on the shoulder."

Juan swallows. Hiroto tries to focus on the soldier's discomfort and indecision. He glances at his captain. Then he sweeps his gaze across the broken figures on the floor. This audience of downed fighters knows what's going to happen. The captain knows what's going to happen. Juan knows what's going to happen. Yet Hiroto feels a creeping sense of emptiness. The spell of the fight has been broken. He has been cast back down to Earth after a brief moment of ascendance.

Hiroto tries to smile at this anxious soldier. He suspects it appears lopsided and wrong. Juan takes a small step back.

"Do you think me a coward?"

"No, of course not. You are master of the Foot Clan!"

Hiroto sighs. "Yes." He picks a baton up off the floor and idly twirls it. Juan flinches. The smell of blood is in the air. A fallen soldier twitches nearby. Hiroto tries to stay present in the moment, but there is a mutant turtle out there, prowling the city. This distraction gnaws at him. In one quick motion he rears back and swings the baton into Juan's shin. The man cries out and collapses in a heap. Looming over the man, Hiroto brings the baton down on Juan's neck. A horrid wet keening sound escapes his lips. The baton comes down again and again. In the mirror Hiroto glimpses his arm working like a piston. Up and down, up and down. Eventually, Juan's faceplate shatters to pieces that embed themselves in his swollen flesh. Hiroto wonders what would happen if he never stopped. Perhaps in some infinite recursive loop of pulping this man's face, he could clear his mind. Or perhaps not. He tosses the baton away and gets to his feet.

"Clean up this mess," he says to no one in particular. Then he beckons the captain to follow him and leaves the dojo.

Coward.

The severed head rests atop a pike that rises above the great marble table. A pair of ravens pick at graying flesh, removing gobbets. A third sucks at an exposed sinew like a wet scarlet noodle. The teeth are remarkably white and intact.

Hiroto indicates a seat for the captain beneath the pike. The ravens make a fuss, beating their wings. A half-chewed mass of skin falls to the table. Startled, the captain stares at it, then looks at his master, letting it be. Hiroto watches the man try not to let it bother him. He is doing an admirable job.

A servant arrives with a towel draped over his arm and a bottle of sake on a tray with a glass. Hiroto takes the towel, wipes his face, then lets it fall to the floor. The servant sets the bottle and glass on the table, retrieves the towel, and exits.

Hiroto sits next to the captain. "I like to pour my own drinks," he says. He tilts a splash of the cold plum wine into the glass. "I honestly don't know why."

He raises the glass and peers at the rotting head through its contours. The desecrated skull swims behind the clear, slightly viscous liquid. "In the stories told of great leaders, they often seem so decisive," Hiroto says. "A throughline of cause and effect dictates their great victories, their lasting achievements." He sips the sake. Cold and delicious, coating his throat, landing gently in his belly. "When I think of my grandfather and my mother, they seem to have always operated this way."

The captain raises an eye to a raven circling with a dangling piece of lip like dried fruit in its beak.

"But when we look back upon their paths to greatness, there is so much we don't see, like the endless time-consuming irritations." He pauses for another sip. "Of which this turtle is a prime example."

The sake loosens his thoughts. Perhaps not being more open to expressing himself is where he went wrong with Ikusa. So very wrong. He lets out a breath, releasing tension in his body. He will call for a massage later. And a sauna. "The turtle has changed things, Captain Fukuda."

"I will locate the rogue mutant," the newly appointed captain declares.

Hiroto twirls the glass slowly in a pool of its own condensation. A sudden bolt of frustration nearly makes him crush the glass in his fist. He closes his eyes and sips and takes himself back to pummeling that soldier's face. Then he opens his eyes and tries to untangle the knot within.

"Your predecessor and I were close once, as children, you know," Hiroto says.

"I do."

"But in recent years, we no longer knew each other, at all. Our connection was lost. I would like to avoid that with you. Start off on honest footing."

Hiroto glances up to follow a raven as it glides down from the apex of the dome to alight upon the wet-looking crown of the bare skull.

Coward.

He lowers his gaze to Fukuda. "When your predecessor came to me with news of the mutant turtle, I was conflicted. Part of me relished the chance to test myself against it."

At this admission, the captain looks taken aback. He composes himself, eyes narrowed between the severe angles of his horned helmet. "Surely you would destroy it in single combat, Master."

Hiroto swirls the liquid in his glass. Obsequiousness. What else had he expected? He barely knows this man, this Fukuda. His thoughts pull tight, and he can feel the muscles in his face growing taut. He glances at the head on its pike, purplish in the light cast down from the dome. We are all of us meat stretched over bone, he thinks. Every Oroku. His mother, his grandfather; Shredder's own father, his grandfather before him. Every Hamato, too. And here Hiroto sits, prevaricating over forging a personal connection with his new captain, like some sort of angsty teenager. He puts down the glass and swigs straight from the bottle. Then he lets it drop to the floor.

"Sir," Captain Fukuda says, "if it pleases you, my troops will turn this city inside out to hunt this creature down and bring him to you, so that you may face him in combat."

"Yes," Hiroto says. He clenches a fist and imagines bringing a steel baton down on the turtle's face. In this fantasy he is flooded with vivid, technicolor emotions. Each point of impact as he caves in the mutant's skull fires all his nerve endings at once. "That is exactly my wish."

Hiroto looks up at the ravens circling the skull. He listens. No whispered insult comes from the mouth of his old friend. He thinks of the way Ikusa died screaming. While he was flaying the skin from

Ikusa's back, his mind transposed the man's anguished cries onto the joyous shouts of their shared boyhood. Hiroto is surprised when his vision blurs. With an index finger, he swipes tears from his eyes before they can wet his cheeks.

His old friend had been a good man. It had been a waste to kill him. It had seemed necessary at the time, and the act itself had brought him a brief narcotic solace. But now he can scarcely remember his reasoning.

"Yes, Master," Fukuda says. Hiroto knows the captain is waiting to be dismissed. Itching to prove himself. But there is something else stuck like a splinter in the back of his mind. He has allowed himself a brief moment of vulnerability with this man, this relative stranger. Has it been cathartic? He does not know.

"Go now, Captain. Bring me that turtle. And never forget, you are newly raised to your rank in the wake of Captain Ikusa's failure." He nods toward the skull on the pike. A raven pecks at the remaining eye. "Ikusa was my friend. You are not. Imagine what I'll do to you if you fail me, too."

A second raven perches on Ikusa's jaw. The two birds fight over the eye.

"Dismissed, Captain Fukuda."

23

CASEY MARIE JONES BELCHES. Michelangelo laughs.

April glares. "Thought I raised you better than that, young lady. We have a guest."

Casey is standing at the kitchen counter with her mother and Mike, all of them eating scrambled eggs and hot sauce.

"Aww, come on, April," Mike says. "There's been about a million burps in this kitchen." He glances over at the table. Casey watches his eyes. She can practically see him tumble back into the past, call up some memory of his life here before she was born.

"I mean, one time me and Raph drank a six-pack of root beer each and had a whole burping *contest*. Cracked up Splinter like you wouldn't believe."

Casey rinses her plate in the kitchen sink. Eggshells litter the counter. A greasy pan sits on the stove's one working burner. "After two hours of kendo, that breakfast hit the spot."

"Yeah," Mike says, "I almost forgot what real food tasted like."

Casey sets her plate on a checkered towel. "That's about as good as it gets in Rock Bottom."

"I heard that name out in the streets," Mike says. "We used to be proud of where we lived, you know." He gestures around. "And we lived in a *sewer*."

"It's just a nickname, Mikey," April says. "The top is the city's elites. Foot City penthouses, Chrysler Building, Empire State. Then you got the rest of the high-rises and the brownstones and the nicer walk-ups. Rock Bottom is the streets and below. Our people."

"And then there's the rest of us," Casey says.

"The rest of us?" Mike arches his brow. Casey tries not to stare. It's strange to watch the face of a giant mutant turtle contort this way. He's gotta be two hundred pounds, easy. Big as Crunch and Scrape, only a lot stronger. Hell, he walked away from that epic swan dive. Got right up out of the cratered pavement like he'd been shaking off a rough night. And now he's in her kitchen—his old kitchen—covered in bandages, eating her mom's fresh egg stash. She feels like he stepped out of a dream.

"Rock Bottom's the battlefield," she says, "and the rest of us underground, we're the resistance."

"Which we'll tell Mikey all about after he gets more rest." April says. "Why don't you grab him some clean linens."

Casey turns to Michelangelo. "You see how she asks questions with a big fat period at the end?"

April sweeps eggshells off the counter into a wastebasket covered in faded band stickers.

Casey gives Michelangelo a nudge. He's gazing at the wastebasket like it's a priceless piece of art. "Come on, let's get you some sheets."

She leads him out of the kitchen, through a brick archway, down a wide corridor. The lair has always seemed to Casey like a place stuck in time. She imagines the workers who built it as burly men in suspenders and hats covered in grime, speaking in old New York brogues.

"Drier than it used to be down here," Mike says. He skims a finger along the grout between bricks. "Cleaner, too."

"My mom's a neat freak," Casey says. "You should see her lab."

"Ha," he says quietly. "Donnie's lab was like a hoarding situation."

They turn a corner and enter a sprawling dojo. Polished steel glistens from a weapons rack. There's a weight bench, dumbbells, a heavy bag, a battered fighting dummy clad in the black uniform of the Foot Clan. A nest of silver pipes twines above their heads. Track lights beam an orderly glow onto the tiles and tatami mats.

Casey crosses the floor. Michelangelo's no longer at her side. She turns to find him taking it all in. She thinks back to the moment she found him. Broken katana poised to slice open his gut. Hacking up blood. So damaged he couldn't end things on his own terms.

The muffled sounds of subway trains rumble in distant tunnels.

Casey goes to the weapons rack. "Blows my mind to be standin' here with you, y'know? I heard so many stories about you. Seen a million old pictures. You guys were like superheroes to me." She lifts a katana from its cradle. "I even tried to learn martial arts as best I could to be like you, even though I had to do it all on my own."

His feet shuffle quietly across the tiles at her back. "Kendo, huh?"

"Been doing it since I was little. Other stuff, too. Hard not to, when you grow up in the middle of all this." She demonstrates a fighting stance, brandishing the blade. "This ninja warrior shit always gets me pumped."

Michelangelo frowns. "Not sure *pumped* is the goal."

Casey feels like an idiot. She replaces the sword in the rack. Then she leads Michelangelo to a small wooden table covered in a white cloth.

"I know some of the history, too. Things like Bushido . . ." Casey removes the cloth to reveal a leather-bound diary, four colored masks, a pair of nunchaku, a sharpened sai, a long bō staff, and a broken katana. She glances at Michelangelo. ". . . and seppuku."

He doesn't flinch at the mention of ritual suicide. She knows he'd been trying to perform some feudal Japanese death ritual back there in the tunnels, and figured maybe he'd want to talk about it. Seems weird to avoid a thing like that when you're trying to get to know someone.

Instead, he turns his attention to the masks and weapons—the last physical remnants of his brothers—and his father's diary.

"These are all very personal to me." Mike pauses over the altar of artifacts. "Thank you for bringing them."

"Sure. Once I saw what . . . er, *who* you were, I didn't want to leave anything behind, especially considerin' what you were about to do." Casey picks up the broken katana. She doesn't want to push him so hard he shuts down. But there is an irresistible urge to drag such an awful act into the open. At least to get him to acknowledge it. She doesn't know where this desire comes from. She tells herself to drop it. But she can't. "I think I understand why you were going to, you know. The honor of it."

Michelangelo closes his eyes. "Did you say anything to your mom?"

The change in his tone, the brittle anxiety in his words, fills her with regret. She wishes she'd left it alone. She feels, suddenly, like a kid poking her head into a grown-up conversation. "No. Nothing. Things've been pretty rough around here for the last few years, so to see a little bit of hope in her again . . . I didn't want to ruin it."

He nods, lets out a breath, opens his eyes. "Thanks."

She tries to puncture the heaviness. "Hey, I gotta ask you something else. Did you jack a bike outside a rathole bar on the Lower East Side, by any chance?"

Michelangelo narrows his eyes. Casey looks back at him, waiting for the turtle to put it together.

"No way. That was *yours?*"

"My pride and joy. Any chance it's still in one piece?"

Michelangelo winces.

Casey is stuck with the loss like a punch to the gut. But she does her best to shake it off, picking up the weathered diary. "You can make it up to me by tellin' me about this. My Japanese ain't the great-est, but I understand enough to know that *this* is special." She flips pages. "Crazy martial arts styles I've never seen. And, like, important life lessons, or whatever."

"Something like that. It was my father's, once. Now it's mine." He looks at her. "What's up with these clean sheets, we ever getting to them?"

"Just one more question, then it's clean sheet heaven, I promise."

Michelangelo sighs. "Shoot, kid."

"Where have you been all this time?"

Michelangelo rubs the fabric of his old orange mask between his fingers. Casey listens to the distant trains come and go. After a while, he speaks.

"You have to understand, after everything went down, I thought I had no one left in New York. I didn't know what to do. So I just started walking. I walked over the bridge, wandered around Brook-lyn in a daze, kept walking till I hit the airport, and stowed away on a flight to Japan. When the plane landed, I kept walking. I thought maybe I could find some answers, or some meaning, anything to explain what had happened in my life. Why I'd lost so much."

"Did you find answers?"

"I found the mountains."

Casey watches that glazed look come over him as he inhabits a memory. Then she pretends to study the diary, waiting patiently for him to call upon the words.

"I'd seen photos of snow-covered mountains," he says after a while. Casey shuts the book and looks up. "But I'd never set foot on one before. Being cold-blooded, I didn't have a chance. I figured the mountains had called me to them so I could meet my end."

"So—" She stops herself. *So this isn't the first time you've tried to die.*

Mike meets her eyes for a moment, then glances down at the journal in her hands. "I came to a Shinto gateway in the middle of the wilderness. I dug a little hole in the snow, thought I'd wait around to either get enlightenment or freeze.

"It could've been days, a week, maybe longer. I don't know how long I lay there, but enlightenment never came, and my mutant body wouldn't die. Eventually I started to hear my . . ." he trails off.

"Your what?"

He peers at her like he's relieved to get something off his chest. His shoulders relax. Then, after a moment, his body tenses back up. "I started to hear voices telling me that my destiny was incomplete. That I needed to find shelter and stick things out.

"Eventually, it got warmer. The mountains gave me lots of time to look deep in my soul for answers. I read and reread my father's journal, hoping to find some kind of truth that would lead to balance. Maybe even a final peace. I spent years alone up there, thinking it was where I was supposed to be. Whether it was a reward or a punishment, I had no idea."

There is pain in his voice. Perhaps a hint of regret. Yet Casey finds herself awed by the tale. Mike's life has been so different than hers. She has known loss—everyone in Rock Bottom has—but Mike has explored deep within his own mind, while at the same time journeying to a harsh, far-flung wilderness. She knows she's viewing it through a different lens. But it sounds epic and transcendent in a way she'll never know, living down here.

"I wasn't alone on the mountain," he continues. "There were villages full of people who led quiet lives and didn't want to be bothered by the outside world. We knew about each other but had an unspoken agreement: I left them alone, and they left me alone. It was good, and it worked for a while. But then the others came.

"I didn't know if they wanted the land, or wanted the villagers for cheap labor, or if they were just evil. It didn't matter. The results were the same. Death and destruction.

"They came for me, too, in my tiny hut in the middle of the forest. The men who found me called me a monster, and they attacked me with clubs and fists and axes with dull blades."

Mike's voice is low and measured. His body is very still, almost frozen in place. She doesn't dare say a word. She recognizes that it is not a tale of some glorious battle.

"I didn't resist," he says in a flat, distant tone that she finds unsettling. "I let them beat me. I thought . . . enlightenment and death—maybe for me, they're the same. Maybe that's my final lesson, you know? And I would've been content to let things end there, until I saw the looks on their faces. These men were laughing. They weren't afraid of the big bad monster in the woods. They were going to take my life just to take a life. Not for honor, or out of fear . . . but for fun. That's when I got mad. Really mad."

Mike closes his eyes and breathes out slowly. "I, uh . . . I hurt those men, Casey."

She waits. He does not elaborate. Quick-hit images of unspeakable violence flash in her mind. Blood in the snow. Cries in the night. She finds that she is clutching the journal with white-knuckled intensity.

"My brothers and I were raised with respect and honor. We were trained from birth for redemption for our family. That fight on the mountain made me realize that the battlefield was my destiny to the end. Father's book laid out the path I was meant to walk. To learn and master all forms of martial arts. To adapt to every challenge." He is speaking faster now, words tumbling out. Casey's heart begins to pound. "I was the last of my clan. Masterless. A ronin. And it was up to me to restore our family's honor. To kill the last son of the Oroku family."

Casey taps a finger on the last page of the journal. Two heavily underlined words are written in English, obviously by Michelangelo.

NO PEACE.

She runs her fingers over the words. "What's this mean?"

"Means I still got work to do."

She closes the journal and sets it on the table next to the turtles' weapons. "Then my crew's gonna help you."

"Same crew that let your bike get stolen?"

Casey waits for the smirk, but Michelangelo's face is set, his eyes cold. Her anger flares. "You just got your ass kicked out of a tower. Maybe this lone wolf thing isn't working out for you. And—"

"Casey."

"—you just spent the last twenty years crying because you lost your friends and now—"

"Casey."

"—that you suddenly have some again you're like, 'Leave me alone,' which makes no sense at all because—"

"Casey!"

She stalks over to the fighting dummy and hits it with a one-two to the gut.

"Look," he says, "I appreciate the offer, but I won't be responsible for anyone else getting killed because of me."

She whirls around. "Well, too bad, 'cause I wasn't asking. You stirred things up, Michelangelo, and because of that, we got a shit-storm comin' down on Rock Bottom." Casey feels righteous fury take over. Michelangelo might be a legend around here, but her crew's had her back in a million different scrapes. She doesn't owe this tur-tle shit. "So fight with us, or else go on being lonely somewhere else."

Michelangelo's eyes narrow to slits. For a second, Casey's entire body tenses. His mind's all over the place. A few days ago he was two seconds away from pig-sticking himself with a broken katana. He sees her eye the weapons rack across the dojo.

Then he breaks into a wide smile. The creases of at the corners of his mouth displace a bandage on his chin. He starts to laugh.

"What's so funny?"

"Anybody ever tell you, you're a lot like your mom?"

"Once or twice."

"Well, you're a lot like your dad, too."

Casey looks at Michelangelo. His eyes are fully open now, windows into a world she never knew. Besides her mom, she'd never met anyone who even knew her dad. And now this turtle is standing before her, a link to a time in the city she can scarcely imagine.

She feels her face get hot and turns away.

"Come on," she says, "let's go find you those sheets."

24

OROKU KARAI HAD NEVER known peace in life. The storm at the center of her being had never stopped raging. Hiroto peers down through the glass of her chamber and wonders about his inheritance. His own storm rages dark and deep within, yet its core eludes him.

He places a hand against tepid glass warmed by the chamber's fluid. "That day at the retreat," he says softly. "When I fought Ikusa, and you were so disappointed in me that you pelted me with grapes and then stormed off." He pauses and glances over his shoulder. At the other end of the penthouse's main floor, past the dining table where his old friend's pecked-clean head is a bone-white orb, a four-person IT team is installing a holographic projector. Cameras on tripods encircle a mat. He turns back to his mother, keeping his voice low. "Why?" He doesn't know what compels him to ask about this now. He suspects it's at the root of the halting way he tried to open up to Fukuda. The shame of that aborted, childish moment of vulnerability has hounded him for days. He wants to root out what's inside him and kill it, and his mother holds the key. "What was the point? You knew how hard I trained. You could have just pointed out my mistakes so I could have worked on them in the dojo." He looks into her preserved, perfect face. He moves his hand up so that it encompasses her slender neck. "Instead you chose humiliation." He shakes his head. "Why?"

He waits for the admonishment in the form of the only word she ever flings at him. *Coward.* But it does not come.

Her eternally placid expression changes. Yes: the flutter of an eyelid. The twitch of a lip.

Hiroto sucks in a breath. "Mother." His voice is a whisper.

Her mouth opens to reveal a black yawning void where her lips had been pressed together for so many years. Hiroto finds his heart quickening. His insides churn. He has not felt such turmoil and excitement since the day he saw the mutant turtle on his security feed.

"You have no children."

Her voice is different than the mocking lilt that utters *coward*. Hiroto knows that was all in his head. But this—this is Oroku Karai's voice, coming back to him from some other place. The glass is no buffer. It does not even muffle her words. Their clarity is astonishing. He looks behind him. The IT team is busy setting up the projection system. No one glances his way. No one has heard Karai speak. He lets out a shaky breath and gains control of himself. Pride swells. He has mastery over his mind and body that he did not possess as a young man.

"Not yet," he says. "But there's plenty of time."

His mother's mouth gapes at him. The words are not formed by the movement of her lips. They are flung up at him from her dark throat through an immobile mouth.

"So you do not understand."

"You're right. I don't. Enlighten me, Mother."

Her leg moves through the fluid and her knee bashes against the glass. Hiroto flinches. Her body undulates, racked with some kind of seizure. He turns to a monitor and pulls up her dashboard. Vitals normal. Stable across the board. Technically she's fine.

"We just want them to be better than ourselves."

Hiroto turns back to the chamber. "A better *fighter*? I was twelve years old!"

Her body goes perfectly still. Her back is arched, her eyes closed, the O of her mouth unchanged. "There is weakness inside you, Hiroto." She sounds terribly sad. "I saw it then. I see it now."

Hiroto leans over the chamber. "Who is the weak one, Mother?" Flecks of spittle hit the glass. His rage is a quivering dullness in his mind. He can't untangle his thoughts. "I am out here. And you are in there."

Laughter comes from somewhere deep within Oroku Karai. The glass of her chamber vibrates like a tuning fork. The resonance hurts his head.

All at once, his mother's body goes limp. Her mouth closes. Hiroto glares at her inert form, telling himself he's glad she's gone quiet. He listens to the ministrations of his IT team across the penthouse. Someone drops a piece of equipment and it rattles against the floor.

He glances over his shoulder, then shifts closer to Karai's chamber with caution. "Mother?" He taps the glass, but she does not move.

Serene, in repose, she floats. Eyes closed, tendrils of dark hair drifting.

"You don't know me," he tells her. His palm slaps the chamber. "I have the *will*, and the *ability*, to do what you and grandfather could not! I have—"

A throat clears softly behind him. Hiroto whirls around. An IT technician with a scarred cheek, round face, and frightened eyes clasps then unclasps his hands.

"We're ready for you now, Master."

Beyond the technician, Hiroto's gaze travels past the shining skull and the conference table to where a circle of holographic cameras surrounds a red mat half the size of a boxing ring. Three technicians make final preparations. Their hands manipulate images on a massive screen. Ravens spiral in low to alight upon the cameras. A technician rushes to shoo them away. One bird shits on the red mat.

"Very well," Hiroto replies. "I'll be right over."

The technician bows, hesitates, then moves back toward the camera setup. Hiroto turns to the stasis chamber. "There is more strength inside me than you will ever know."

Hiroto descends from the chamber's platform. The hem of his crisp white robe swishes against the steps. He crosses the main floor. The farther he gets from his mother, the more whole he feels. The appearance of the mutant turtle might have disrupted his psyche in unnatural ways, but he will set things right.

At the perimeter of the cameras, Hiroto pulls up his hood. He looks at the lead technician. "Ready?"

"Yes, Master."

He steps into the center of the red mat. "Then let us begin."

The technicians' hands go to work on the screen. Hiroto straightens his spine. The lights brighten as the broadcast ring flickers to life.

25

A HIGH-PITCHED WHINE TAP dances over white noise. From the teeming stacks of Battery Village to the walled-off northern tip of the island, millions of heads turn skyward. Traffic snarls every avenue and the major crosstown arteries as elevated vehicles hover in place and the gas-powered procession at street level halts. A moment later, Oroku Hiroto appears, cloaked in a shimmering digitized sky. The holographic projection, bluish-white against the darkness, rises to dwarf the skyscrapers of Manhattan. If he were to reach down and extend his arms, this godlike manifestation could embrace the whole of the city from the East River to the Hudson.

Nestled halfway up the stacks, two old drinking buddies regard the apparition from behind half-lidded eyes. "Would you look at that," Jasper says. "Pollutin' our sky."

The impossibly massive Hiroto image flickers.

Ezzie raises a glass. "To technical difficulties."

The image clarifies, and Hiroto begins to speak. His voice hijacks every street corner speaker and booms across the city. "Citizens of New York. My people. For nearly two decades, I have kept you safe and protected. Under the aegis of the Foot Clan, you have prospered."

Jasper raises a glass. "To prosperity!" Ezzie clinks it with her own.

"Hear me now, friends," Hiroto says. "And heed what I have to say."

Outside Hilty's Pub on the Lower East Side, a linebacker-sized man leans against the brick wall. He watches the towering hologram and chews a cinnamon-flavored toothpick.

A second big man joins him, brushes dirt from the front of the first man's vest. "That ain't food, Crunch."

"Mmm." Crunch spits out bits of splintered wood. "This puts me on edge, is all."

The door swings open. Two normal-sized humans spill out into the night. One holds up a smartphone and shakes his head. The other speaks. "Hiroto's already jammed comms."

Scrape removes a battered flip phone from a vest pocket. "Switch to the burners."

Hiroto's hologram snaps its fingers. Every screen in the city—from the digital billboards of Times Square to computers in Soho apartments to televisions in the big-box stores of Fourteenth Street—flashes with an image of Michelangelo. Dressed in black, bloodied from battle, scowling with anger, the mutant turtle sneers out at the city.

"There is a monster in our midst, my fellow citizens," Hiroto says. "This creature—this assassin—attacked the very tower from which I deliver this message to you now. It came from beyond our walls with one terrorist mission in its animal mind: to kill me, and by doing so, tear down all we have built together."

Under the awning of a bodega on the corner of Third Avenue and Second Street, Casey Marie Jones snorts. "*Together,*" she mutters. As if Oroku Hiroto gives a shit about the New Yorkers he subjugates. She lowers her eyes to an old television screen in the window of the deli. Michelangelo looks like a rabid monster. She picks out subtle edits to the likeness. Froth at the corners of his mouth, bloodshot eyes, sharpened fangs for teeth.

"I care nothing for my own life," Hiroto says. "And I would gladly sacrifice it for the protection of this city. But I also believe that as we move toward a greater future, the responsibility to uphold our values and defend our city must be shared equally among us."

A young deserter from the Foot Clan moves quickly up Sixth Avenue toward Central Park. When the clanking of synjas in lockstep echoes down from Fifty-Ninth Street, the young man changes direction. He pulls up his hood and sticks to the shadows. But everywhere he looks, the mutant turtle who almost killed him stares into his soul. He begins to run. The synjas' glowing red eyes shine out of the darkness. A cry builds from deep inside him. Nowhere is safe.

"No stone will be left unturned until the beast is captured," Hiroto says. "And I will personally execute final justice. Until then, the city will be under martial law."

Outside Hilty's, Breaker approaches his bike. "This is getting bad."

"We gotta go underground," Crunch says.

Scrape flips open his ancient burner. "I'll text Jones."

"You will see my Foot soldiers out in force for your protection," Hiroto says. "Heed them, for their will is my own. If you see something, say something. And know this: Anyone foolish enough to harbor this terrorist insurgent, and by doing so, put millions of your fellow citizens at risk, will *suffer*. I want you to consider carefully what you have heard, and to do what you know in your heart is right." The apparition bows, then blinks out. His final words resound across the night sky.

"Only compliance, vigilance, and unity will bring peace."

26

FIRE RAGES. THEN THE world splits open with a roar that sounds like a living thing, like a monster. Michelangelo is struck by it, hurtling backward, away from the fire at great speed. He bashes through the buildings of Manhattan like an artillery shell through plywood.

Eventually he drops out of the sky and crashes hard, skidding to a stop in a snowy clearing. He stands, surprised to be alive. He understands this place to be Hokkaido, Japan. His father and brothers emerge from the darkness of the forest. Broken and bloody, they move with the unhurried pace of the dead.

Their vacant eyes stare at him.

"You failed us." Their voices overlap with strange dissonance. "The sun has set and Oroku Hiroto is still alive."

Michelangelo finds that he can't respond. There is no excuse he can make. The accusations are true. Hiroto lives, therefore he has failed.

"You are all that is left. You must honor us. You must balance the scales. You must."

The four phantoms continue to chant "You must" as a mob of angry humans digs its way up from the ground. Not zombies but not living men, their bodies reshaping as they move toward him, changing from men to women to men again, of every race. They are all of humanity at once, and they will never accept mutants in their world.

"Freak!" the mob cries. "Monster!"

Michelangelo has no argument for this either. He is so very tired of fighting. So he flees. Away from Hokkaido, down the coast, across the sea, away from Japan, to mainland Asia.

The miles fly by in seconds. Yet the ghosts pursue.

"You have failed your family!" they say as he crosses the ocean.

"You have failed the Hamato Clan!" they say as he makes his way through Korea.

"You have failed yourself!" they say as he flees on horseback across the Mongolian steppes.

"*You did not deserve to survive.*"

Michelangelo finds himself trapped in a cage with the mob of humanity. He has no choice but to fight them. His body won't let him give up and die, not even in this dream. No matter how much he wants to be done with it all, forever.

He delivers killing blow after killing blow, but the mob does not die. They crowd him, the pressure overwhelming, pinning his limbs, their rank breath fouling the air.

Michelangelo can only watch as a new figure emerges from the shadows. It approaches the cage and slinks effortlessly through the iron bars.

And then, Michelangelo is at the mercy of Oroku Saki, the Shredder, a flesh-kissed skeleton dressed in rags and tarnished armor.

Michelangelo's heart beats faster. He's cold. Afraid. Alone.

Shredder raises his bloody arm, points to Michelangelo, and says only one word:

"Death."

Mike bolts upright. A strangled cry escapes his throat. The sheets are twined around his legs. There, in the darkness of his bedroom, a massive figure rises, razor blades gleaming from his armored shoulders . . .

Mike gasps for air. His hand slams the nightstand. Once, twice, and then he finds the lamp's switch. The ancient fluorescent bulb fills his old room with wan, flickering light. No ghoulish Shredder is standing over him. He lets out a long breath and tries to slow his racing heart.

According to the old alarm clock next to the lamp, he'd managed to catch about forty minutes of shut-eye.

No going back to sleep now. He glances at the yellowed stack of old comic books piled on the floor. Then he looks at the nunchaku draped over a peg on the wall. He doesn't feel like reading or working out. His thoughts wind around themselves like the sheets around his bandaged legs. The dream lingers, bleeding into the reality of the lair, distracting him with notions of the past and the future. He tells himself to be in the now. To simply exist.

But his mind is caught in a feedback loop. Trapped like a turtle in a cage, with a half-dead mob pinning its arms and legs . . .

"You're not real," Mike says.

He tucks his legs underneath his body, releases the tension from his muscles, closes his eyes, and breathes in for two, out for two. In for three, out for three. In for—

"Hey," Raphael's voice chimes in from the shadows, "Mikey looks like he's got gas, don't he?"

"I'm trying to meditate," Michelangelo says without opening his eyes. He waits for his brothers to leave him alone. But he can feel the shift in the air. All three of his brothers, revenants somehow taking up space in the room. Their presence feels like a subtle change in temperature, a breeze that should not be. He sighs and opens his eyes.

Raphael leans against the wall, one foot on the stack of comics. Leonardo stands at the foot of the bed, arms crossed. Donatello sits on the corner of the mattress. Vibrant, almost alive, yet still cloaked in shadow. They all stare at Mike expectantly.

He doesn't want to talk about his dream. Or anything in particular. He sticks a blank expression on his face and waits.

Donnie cracks first. "So. April. I can't imagine how good it must feel to talk to her again."

"You could appear to her like you do to me," Mike suggests.

Leonardo sits down next to Donnie. "It doesn't work like that."

Mike scoots back against the cheap, creaky headboard. "Getting kinda crowded here, guys. And why the hell not, Leo? There some kinda ghost code I'm not aware of?"

Leo doesn't respond. Mike tamps down a smile. Once Leo decides what's proper behavior, he doesn't like to be challenged on it. Same as always.

"I gotta admit," Donatello jumps in, "Casey Marie's pretty damn impressive. Tough. Street smart. Perceptive."

"Sure," Leonardo says, "but Mikey's right—we're gonna take another run at Hiroto, we don't need to be worrying about her, too."

"I mean, it's not like she's deadweight," Mike says. He agrees with his brother, but he can't shake what she said to him. Leo might be right, but so is Casey: He brought Hiroto's wrath down on all of them. He can't ask them to just take it while he resumes his suicide mission.

"She's a kid," Leonardo points out.

"She's seventeen," Mike says. "And already taking on the Foot Clan." He looks at each brother in turn. "Sound familiar?"

"Apples to oranges," Donatello says. "We trained our entire lives."

"Plus, she ain't no mutant, bro," Raphael adds. "She's human. Fragile. And I don't care how old she is. She's still a kid. Casey and April's kid!"

"And we were Splinter's kids!" Michelangelo shoots back with an intensity that surprises him. "And Karai was Shredder's, and Hiroto was hers . . . and here we all are, back to square one, back to—"

"Hello?"

The voice comes out of the shadows. Mike's reflexes kick in and he grabs Raphael's sai from the nightstand and leaps from the mattress.

"Whoa!" Casey steps into the dim light of the bedside lamp, fingers in a peace sign. "Easy!"

Mike tosses the sai on the bed.

"I didn't mean to scare you," Casey says.

"You didn't."

"I just came home to check on Mom real quick, and then I heard you, and . . . is this some kinda ninja thing I should know about, talkin' to yourself in the dark?"

"No. It's not."

There's a long silence. "Okay," she says, "well, there's no door to this room, so I could hear you talking, and you seemed . . ." She trails off. "Anyway." Casey produces an ancient flip phone. "My crew hit me up on the burner. City's under martial law. We're gonna meet up, figure out what to do next."

"Mm. Maybe not a good idea."

"I wasn't asking for permission."

"I know. Just watch your back."

"Uh-huh. Listen, Mom wants to see you in the lab. Straight ahead out of this room and to the left. Don't get lost."

"I know the way."

Casey gestures at the mattress. "How are those sheets working out for you?"

"Scratchy as hell. It's good to be home."

Casey leaves the room. Mike listens to her footsteps fade. He waits for a moment, absorbing the silence. Uneasiness grows like a fungus, speckled mold dancing across the walls around him. He smells a hint of chrome and blood—Shredder's razored armor, its essence permeating the room. Mike sighs. At least he knows by now what it is to be haunted.

He wanders down the dark corridor toward April's lab. He turns over Casey's news in his mind. *Martial law.* The phrase conjures up armies of red-eyed synjas, jackboots marching in unison, barricades across Union Square and the Bowery. Guilt is like a metallic tang in the back of his throat. He brought this down on Rock Bottom, on every good citizen. The selfishness of revenge, its untold ripples in society—all of this is too big for Mike to untangle now. His fingertips brush the wall's cement. Framed photos of his family peer out of the darkness.

The reinforced door to the lab is ajar. He puts a hand against its cool steel, thinking of Donnie's explosive powder mishap that led to its installation.

"April?" Mike pushes open the door and steps loudly inside so he doesn't startle her. "Casey said you wanted to see—"

His voice catches in his throat. The lab is a marvel. Esoteric machinery crammed against the far wall hums with electric life. Thick power cords run up and down the walls to coil in spiraling clumps along the ceiling. Banks of monitors welded to steel supports jut from the cement walls. A massive electron telescope looms in the corner, its thick neck bent toward a tray in which some invisible force stirs up a puddle of water. He moves past racks of old keyboards with makeshift keys of various colors, test tubes, Erlenmeyer flasks, what looks like the medical bay of a space station.

April's voice hovers in some vague distance. "Hey, Mikey. Come on in."

He barely hears the words. His feet move of their own accord, drawn by the room's centerpiece: a spherical robot head staring out of round, dead eyes. The head is propped on a small table, wires spilling out in a sterile parody of gore. Small mechanical arms perform minute tasks with tiny needles upon the head's open panels.

Mike finds the word. "Fugitoid?"

"Yep." April pats the disembodied head. "Professor Honeycutt himself. All that's left of him, anyway."

"Holy shit, April. You gotta stop doing this to me. I don't know how many more surprises my heart can take after that twenty-story swan dive."

April frowns. "It was way more than twenty stories, Mike, are you serious?"

"Who do I look like, Donatello?"

"It's basic spatial reasoning, not math."

Mike lays a careful hand on the slope of the robot's forehead. "Man. Fugitoid. Unbelievable."

"Sorry," April says. "I was hoping to ease you back into everything. I have a feeling things are about to get crazy around here."

"*About to?*"

"Yeah. I know."

"Then I think it's time we get busy with all the catching up you keep talking about."

She looks away. "I don't know how much bad shit you've already got in your head."

Mike wonders if Casey ended up telling her mother everything about how she found him. "A little more's not gonna hurt."

"You sure you want to revisit that night?"

"I've blocked so much of it out over the years. But I'm tired of running," Mike says. "Lay it on me, April."

NEW YORK CITY: SEVENTEEN YEARS AGO

"ALL SYSTEMS CROSS-CHECKED."

Professor Zayton Honeycutt calls out updates without taking his prehensile arms from the control panel. Metal fingers dance across the keys. On the screen, equations and symbols of what Leonardo thinks of as theoretical physics blur past faster than any human or mutant could analyze them. But Honeycutt's large round eyes ringed in chrome feed data to his android brain with no figurative sweat. Leonardo marvels, for the millionth time, at the technology that has allowed Honeycutt's brilliant scientific mind to survive inside the android shell long after the death of his human body.

"You are ready for flight."

Leonardo shifts his attention to his brother Donatello, at the control panel next to Honeycutt, skimming the preflight checklist. He takes in the weathered bō staff strapped to his brother's back. The juxtaposition of the turtles' ancient ninja weaponry with the high-tech futurism of the Hamato Clan's Manhattan headquarters always feels a little out of joint to Leonardo, as if time has come partially unstuck in this place. The average New Yorker would never know the extent of the clan's operations in this former sugar factory. Stretching several stories underground and connecting to the city's official and unofficial tunnel systems, the complex houses dormitories and training facilities for the clan's elite strikers.

"You will have to remain radio silent for the entire trip to avoid detection." Honeycutt's voice is oddly soothing. "And be sure to run on cruising power as soon as you're over the ocean to preserve the electrical charge. It's a long flight, Donatello, and needlessly expending your fuel cells without a backup power source—"

"Will make it an even longer swim," Donatello says. "Got it, professor."

Leonardo turns his back on the control station. His brother's jokes grate on his nerves. He looks out across the hangar, a hollowed-out space in the middle of the old factory. A half dozen pillars of blue light carry energy from a fusion core deep within the bowels of the complex. On a pedestal in the room's exact center sits the experimental, long-range aircraft that Honeycutt and Donatello designed. Leonardo has never liked it. The contraption crouches bug-like and menacing while Hamato technicians swarm around its base.

He likes the ship even less now that Donatello has installed a cloaking device to allow incognito passage to Japan. His mind serves up increasingly extreme ways to keep this journey from happening. Sabotage the ship. Sabotage *Honeycutt*. Get everybody sick. Beg. Plead. Cajole. Bribe.

Leonardo shakes his head. The wrongness of this whole endeavor—and the fact that it's happening without his approval—makes him feel like a worthless leader.

Oroku Hiroto, the new master of the Foot Clan in the wake of his mother's death, just decides to extend an invitation to parley out of the blue? To hold peace talks to end the war between the Oroku and Hamato clans?

No.

From anyone else, Leonardo might have taken the offer at face value. Normal people grow tired of war, after all. *He* is tired of war. But this young Hiroto, and the rest of the Foot Clan's generals, are not normal people. They are oath breakers who already defied a truce. And that betrayal had cost Raphael his life.

Leo knows what's coming next. He tries to listen to Honeycutt and Donatello bantering about flight prep to block it out. But the impressions of Raph's last night on Earth come flooding back, as they always do. Foot soldiers swarming out of nowhere. Thanksgiving dinner on the floor of April's apartment. Rich smell of gravy in the air. Splinter, broken and bleeding, on the white tablecloth. And Raphael, suddenly gone. An absence never to be filled.

"Yo. Earth to Leo." Mikey's voice breaks his reverie. Leo turns to find his brother and Splinter standing next to him. "You hear what Father said just now?"

"I'm sorry, no."

Splinter clears his throat. Leo notes the downcast eyes of the old rat, the gray of his drooping whiskers. His father's aging has accelerated since Raph died. The bulky, ill-fitting flight suit makes his head look gaunt, fur stuck to an elongated skull. Leo finds himself immeasurably sad. He tells himself to snap out of it.

"Remember," Splinter says, "our strikers cannot appear to take an aggressive posture in New York while we are simultaneously engaged in peace talks with the Foot Clan in Japan."

"Understood," Leo says. "Father, please listen to me. I know we've been over this from every angle. And I know your mind is made up. But you have to know that Hiroto's parley can't possibly be legit."

"Amen," Mikey says. "He's an Oroku. They all lie."

The hard edge in his brother's voice hurts Leonardo's heart. *Grow up*, they'd told him over the years. Then Raph died. Now Leo wishes he could get the funny, optimistic Mikey back. But the party dude has left the building.

Splinter looks away, considering his words. "In the past, yes," he says. "But Hiroto has lost much in this war, just as we have. I know what you believe, my sons, but I must consider that perhaps the young master tires of all the senseless bloodshed as much as I do."

"You should at least let Mike and I come with," Leonardo says. "It would be better if we were all there to protect you."

"I said the same thing to Donnie," Mikey says. "He fed me some crap about the fuel calculations being precise, so there needs to be as little added weight as possible. What he means is, you don't believe in the parley, so you're gonna screw it up."

Leo looks at his brother. Mikey's face is pinched, his brow knitted in the expanse of green forehead above his orange mask. He looks weary and frustrated, so far from the Mikey of old he might as well be a new mutation. Leo glances at Mikey now, but what else is there to say? Splinter and Donnie are flying to Japan, Leo and Mikey are staying in New York, and Raphael is never again going anywhere at all.

They had been a proper family once. It had been Leo's job to keep them together.

Splinter raises his dark, fur-hooded eyes and gazes unblinking at the son he raised to be a leader. "Oroku Hiroto's predecessors honored many ancient traditions," Splinter says. He places one hand on Leo's shoulder and one on Mikey's. "And he is respectfully asking, so I am willing to try. But we will not let our guard down. Do not worry."

Honeycutt propels himself out of his seat. His bottom-heavy legs carry him to Splinter's side. Mikey raps his knuckles against the robot's round metal head. "Hey, Fugitoid"—short for Fugitive Android, so called because of his escape from Baxter Stockman's clutches—"you think this trip's a good idea?"

Honeycutt whirs with indecision. "I have not been asked for my counsel."

"I'm askin' you now," Mikey says.

"Let it be," Donnie says.

"You are ready to depart," Honeycutt says. "Systems check is complete."

"Come on, Father. Let's get this done," Donnie says, placing a gentle hand on Splinter's back. Leo feels a rush of indignance. Splinter might be old, but he isn't decrepit. Sometimes his brothers act like their father is made of tissue paper.

Leo crosses the hangar floor with the others. All around him, Hamato Clan loyalists and strike team guards bustle about. Leo nods at a familiar face: Monahan, a burly Hamato veteran with dragon tattoos winding up his bare arms, eyes shielded by ochre shades that match his hair. Leo gestures for the man to lead his strike team squadron outside the compound. Monahan gestures back: *Understood.*

Mikey nudges him. "Good call. If the Oroku scumbags are gonna try anything, it'll be when we're divided."

"We need more eyes on the street," Leo says. He hesitates. Lately he's been feeling more estranged from Michelangelo. Perhaps Donnie and Splinter's excursion will give them a chance to bond. "Hey, bro, listen—you wanna go out on patrol later, just me and you?"

They reach the center of the hangar and cluster at the base of the ramp leading to the aircraft.

Mikey's expression is unchanged. "Sure," he says.

Leo is stung by his brother's apathy. "Great."

Splinter strokes his whiskers. Leo notes a slight tremor in his hand. With a wave, Donatello heads up the ramp to the hatch. "Catch you guys later," he says.

"Be strong, my sons," Splinter says. "We will see you all again soon."

Leo watches the old rat follow Donnie inside. The door closes, and the engines come online with a low hum. The ship runs nearly silent, but Leo can feel the energy of the fusion lifts. An opening in the ceiling above the ship begins to dilate. The old factory shudders.

As Leo moves away from the ship, he turns to his brother. "They're gonna be fine. Hiroto's still a kid."

Mikey grunts. The unspoken hangs between them like lingering energy from the ship: A kid whose mother's in a coma thanks to Raphael. A kid who wants to consolidate his power in the clan.

The ship rises from its platform. The night sky's a round cutout washed in city light.

"Yeah, just a kid." Mikey's eyes trace the ship's ascension. "A kid with Shredder's blood in his veins."

Leonardo paces the compound's command center. Patrolling with his brother like old times turned out to be a pipe dream—he's far too busy. The weight of leadership presses down on him in Splinter's absence. Transmissions from the strike team squads he's dispatched come and go. Fragments of reports from the perimeter and the rooftops. Everyone on edge, reporting every sanitation truck or maintenance van.

"Let's get some drones in the air," Leo tells a young technician in front of a computer. "Kid looks like he's never needed a shave."

"Yes, Master Leonardo."

"You can just call me Leo."

"Yes, Master Leo."

Leo ping-pongs around the octagonal chamber. Honeycutt's positioned at a monitor, esoteric devices linked to his android brain via thick cords. The unblinking round black pools in his head absorb endless strings of code unfurling on a screen. Mikey's next to him, lounging, staring at a comic book without turning the page.

Leo goes to the far side of the chamber. April O'Neil and Casey Jones sit at a small table, sharing one of the Antonio's pizzas they brought from downtown.

"Yo, Leo," Casey says, gesturing toward the half-eaten pie in its box with the lid flipped up. "Go crazy."

He reaches for a slice out of habit, then decides he's not hungry. "Let Mikey have mine."

Casey whistles. "You feelin' okay, boss?"

"Donnie and Splinter are going to be fine," April says, reaching for a pepperoni slice. "And they'll be back before you know it."

"I know," Leo says. "But thanks for coming by, anyway. It's good to have you here."

"'Course," Casey says. "Nothin' good on TV tonight anyway."

Leo taps the table twice then strolls away. Cross-chatter ebbs and flows. Leo takes in the reports from the strike teams outside. He recognizes Monahan's voice among the terse, overlapping conversations.

"—need some eyes on the big rig—"

"—public works trucks but I'm not seeing any workers—"

"—stage one alert—"

Mikey puts down the comic.

"—top one, you copy—"

"—something's—"

Leo and Mikey meet each other's eyes as screams cut through the chatter. Leo rushes to a comm.

"Monahan, what's happening out there?"

Static.

A moment later, the team leader's voice comes through chop on the line. "We got incoming . . . everywhere . . . backup . . . Bleecker and—"

There's a wet *thunk*. Static rushes back. Mikey tosses the comic aside and leaps from his chair.

"Somebody give me something," Leo calls out.

"Perimeter alarms going off all over the place," the young technician replies. The strain in his voice sends it into a higher register.

"Foot Clan ninjas coming at us from all angles," a woman calls out from her workstation. "Here, and at other Hamato outposts throughout the city."

Mikey's frantically keying a comm. "Blackbird Six, this is home base. Hiroto played us! Foot Clan's coming in hot, over."

Silence.

"Blackbird Six, abort mission! It's a trap. Confirm receipt." He pauses. "Talk to me, Donnie."

Honeycutt pipes up. "Your brother's cloaking device requires strict radio silence, Michelangelo."

Mikey looks at the android blankly. "You saying we can't tell them to turn around?"

"They will not receive the message," Honeycutt says.

Michelangelo slams a fist on the console. "You gotta be kidding me!"

Leo takes a breath. He tells himself there's nothing he can do about Splinter and Donnie right now. "Listen up, everyone! Lock down the outer doors. Defensive positions at every access point."

"This is Baxter Stockman's doing," Honeycutt says. "He found a way to track me and chose his moment carefully."

"Why didn't you see this coming?" Mikey shouts at the android. "You spend all day *eating* code, can't you predict this shit?"

"Easy, Mikey," Leo says. Casey and April are at his side. Casey stuffs the last bit of a folded pizza slice in his mouth.

"April," Leo says. An explosion comes over the comms. The young tech rips off his earpiece with an anguished cry. Powerlessness claws at Leonardo. The strike team out on the street is getting cut to pieces. He needs to get an accurate assessment of the enemy's strength. Whether Stockman or Hiroto ordered the attack, he's past caring. He locks eyes with April. "Take Casey and Mikey, and get Honeycutt to the safe room. The professor's under the protection of the Hamato Clan, and Stockman will not get him back. Not today, not ever."

"Screw that!" Mikey shouts. Leo's brother is practically vibrating with rage. "I'm not leaving you here alone."

"Me and April got this, boss," Casey says. He lowers his hockey mask, its battered old visage streaked in blood and grime from his lone vigilante days.

"Sewer defenses breached!" a technician calls out.

"Coming at us from all angles," Mikey says. He clutches his nun-chaku. "I been telling you guys—the Foot Clan are nothing but liars, and we still got caught with our goddamn pants down!" He glares at Leo as if it's his fault.

Leo gets on a comm. "Strike team, pull back to the main com-pound. Sewer levels are not safe, repeat, sewer levels are not safe."

He takes a moment to watch Casey and April escort Honey-cutt toward the door to the command center. Then he turns to his brother. "Take a team with you and hold the sewers. If they swarm us from below, we're done."

Mikey doesn't move. Leo reads hesitation in his eyes. These past years, something grew between them, something gnarled and sour, pushing them apart. And now there's no time to rip it down, start again.

"Go!" Leo snarls. Only half of him is here in the command center. The other half is vapor, traveling out through the labyrinth of the compound, visualizing breaches and organizing fixes into concise commands. Splinter has trained him for this. He won't let his family down.

Mikey gives Leo a nod and opens a comm to summon his team. "Hernandez, you alive? Over."

A second explosion roars through the speakers. At the same time, the command center trembles. Leo widens his stance to keep his balance. Cups fall from the console, coffee splashing across the tile floor. Dust rains from the ceiling. He swipes it away from his eyes.

"Bay doors breached!" someone calls out.

There's a shriek of metal tearing itself apart. A series of loud crashes as the superstructure caves in. Leonardo gathers himself. They're here. Inside. Some Hamato Clan people are surely dead, killed by falling masonry or the first wave of Foot Clan ninjas.

He looks around at his people in the control center. The young tech coughs up dust. The others wipe their monitors. One man he doesn't know is lying on the floor, curled in a ball. The comms are spitting static. Cries are coming from inside the compound, echoing down the halls outside the room.

Casey reappears in the doorway. Leo curses. They didn't get far with Honeycutt. "We got bogies blastin' through everywhere."

Leo draws his katanas. The old familiar grips are molded to his hands. He finds a cold knot of rage inside him. Mikey grins.

"Then let's go out and meet them."

The open-plan kitchen and dining hall is adjacent to the hangar on the ground floor of the old sugar factory. Long modular tables are arranged in rows that give way to a buffet-style counter where steam trays and carving stations sit under hot lights.

The compound is being infiltrated from above and below. Leonardo pushes thoughts of this devastating violation out of his mind. There is only the battle in front of him now. Beside him, Mikey twirls his nunchaku with idle menace. Casey grips his Louisville Slugger. A hockey stick and a cricket bat bristle from the golf bag slung over his shoulder. April is right behind them, shielding Honeycutt. A dozen strike team personnel are fanned out in a V with Leo at its apex, their silver tonfa emanating the blue flame of destabilizing energy.

Footsteps thunder across the ceiling. Down come the muffled cries of a fight being joined on the floor above. Across the dining hall, three garage-size doors delineate the factory's old loading docks. A strike team woman in a yellow hood shows Leo a tablet device: the security feed from just outside. Ninjas are swarming the door. Then, abruptly, they back away.

"Steady," Leo says. "They just planted a charge."

"Come on, come on, come *on*," Mikey mutters, shifting his weight from one foot to the other.

Casey nods at the screen. "Never seen Foot like these before. Heavily armored and—"

A percussive blast rocks the dining hall. Leo feels it like a punch to the gut. The garage door blows open, hurling molten steel into the dining hall. The right flank of the strike team vanishes in a pink mist. Fire rages in the ruined doorway. The heat flows across the room and scorches Leo's face.

"Hold!" he calls out. He waits for the Foot ninjas to extinguish the fire and clear the way. But then dark figures begin to appear in the flames. Tall, broad-shouldered silhouettes, moving with an eerie grace.

"What the hell are those things?" Mikey says.

"They can't be human," Leo says.

The infiltrators form a pack. Dozens of red eyes glow as they emerge from the flames, metal frames shimmering in the heat.

"Terminators," Casey says.

New Stockman tech, Leo figures. So that's what the mad scientist's been churning out in his lab on Roosevelt Island.

"Motor oil or blood," Mikey says. "They gotta bleed something." Leo wants to beg his brother to run, hide, *survive*. After Raph, the notion of sending his remaining brothers into harm's way makes him freeze with terror. But he knows there will be no stopping Mikey from hurling his body at these metal ninjas. The knot in Leo's stomach is a new organ, a throbbing mass of rage and despair. He should have worked harder to convince his father and Donnie not to leave. He should have blown up the goddamn airship.

Bright red eyes move through black smoke. These ninjas' approach is inexorable and slow.

Casey reaches back and draws his hockey stick from its make-shift quiver. Leo knows it's reinforced with a steel core, just like his baseball bat.

"The class is Pain 101," he shouts, "and your instructor is—"

"Casey!" April cries out from behind them. "Wait!"

Casey launches himself into the phalanx of advancing ninjas. Leo watches through stinging eyes as Casey swings the hockey stick into the side of the lead Foot soldier's head. The wood splinters on impact and the stick breaks in two.

The soldier trains his red eyes on Casey.

Leo and Mikey charge the soldier. But they're not fast enough. The soldier's metal fist plows into Casey's chest. As if blown by a sudden hurricane wind, Casey sails backward, his limbs flung out in front of his body. He smashes into a cafeteria table and cracks its molded plastic bench. His body sprawls at an awkward angle. The hockey mask hangs askew on his face.

Leo knows the punch could have broken Casey's ribs, punctured a lung.

This is no place for nonmutant fighters. Anyone without enhanced strength is dead.

Leo holsters his katanas—edged weapons will be less effective against armored robots—and in one smooth motion plants a side-kick into the robot's gut. The impact reverberates up his leg. The robot is knocked off-balance. In a split second Mikey is behind the metal soldier, wrenching its head back with the nunchaku's chain. With a vicious twist, Mikey rips the head from the steel tendons that make up its neck. Sunbright sparks erupt from the jagged, glinting wound.

Mikey squares up to the next Foot soldier. Leo turns. April is at Casey's side. The other members of the strike team are engaged in their own battles. A robot lifts a fighter by his neck and the man's legs kick until the robot clenches his fist and the man goes still. The robot discards him.

"Get Honeycutt out of here!" Leo shouts. April manages to get Casey off the ground with the Fugitoid's help. Leo meets April's wide eyes. In this moment, he knows there is nowhere he can direct them to. The safe room will be a death trap. These terminators will rip apart the reinforced doors.

"Leo, watch your six!"

Mikey's voice brings him back to the fight. Leo whirls around, honed battle senses coursing through him. He contorts without knowing exactly why. A robot's long katana blade slices through the air in the place his head had just been. Leo draws a sword of his own in time for the robot's torso to jerk back the other way. The swords clash. Metal shrieks. Mikey staggers, almost tripping over his leg. A pair of robot ninjas press their attack. Nunchaku blur the air and smash into a metal shoulder. Armor splinters, flying bits dancing in the firelight.

Leo spins and catches the soldier's chin with his elbow. The tip of his katana skitters across a hardened breastplate until it catches in a divot. Leo exploits the weak spot and inserts the blade with a grunt of exertion. Red eyes flicker and go out. Leo withdraws the blade. It's covered in viscous fluid.

"Target acquired." The Foot soldiers' voices ring out in eerie metallic unison. They key in on Honeycutt. April stumbles under Casey's deadweight.

More robots are streaming through the blown-away door. Leo kicks one over to Mikey who takes its head off with a vicious overhead strike.

"Too many," Mikey says. His face is stained with oil. Leo drops to the floor and sweeps the legs out from under a Foot soldier. The robot hits the ground. Tiles crack under its weight. Leo brings the hilt of his katana down on its faceplate. Red eyes shatter. Mikey wrenches its arm from its socket and caves in its chest. The smell of scorched chrome and a battery acid tang fills the dining hall.

Leo catches a blur of movement. Suddenly, Honeycutt is among them.

"Get back, Professor!" Leo screams at the Fugitoid. But Honeycutt doesn't move. He faces down a Foot soldier. His noodle arm extends and his hand goes up.

"I know it's me you've come for, Stockman." Honeycutt modulates his voice so that it booms through the chaos of battle. "I'll self-destruct before I let you hurt my friends or imprison me again. This is your only warning."

As one, the Foot soldiers whirr to a halt.

"Holy shit," Mikey says. A soldier withdraws a sword from the belly of the strike team woman in the yellow hood. She crumples to the floor. The robots turn their backs in crisp unison, like some infernal dance team. They troop toward the shattered garage door and vanish into the black smoke.

Mikey looks at Leo. "You believe that?"

Leo surveys the carnage. Dead strike team littering the floor. Pools of blood. Stray metal bits. Lost weapons. April sitting on a bench, propping up Casey. Honeycutt's big round eyes staring at everything and nothing.

Leo turns back to the doorway. "I don't like this."

A new sound fills the room, the rattling, off-kilter whine of a busted air conditioner.

Leo's weary mind trips over itself. How many times can he tell Casey and April to get the hell out of here? How much more Stockman tech can he and Mikey fight off? He looks away from the strike team's mangled bodies. So much loss. And for what? He finds that he no longer cares what happens to Honeycutt. He just wants to be with his brothers, like the old days, leaping across the rooftops, laughing at dumb jokes, scarfing pizza, training in the lair with Splinter.

The sound gets louder, an incessant buzz tunneling deep into his brain. Shadows move inside the flames. Too high and too fast to be Foot ninjas.

The moving shadows flit into the light. Metal spheroids, each with the sharklike smiles of Baxter Stockman's mousers. Hundreds of small floating orbs cluster in shifting formations. Stockman's new antigrav engines send pulses of corrupted air through the dining hall. Queasiness turns Leo's stomach.

Leo clacks his katanas together, swipes metal on metal like he's a chef sharpening knives. "Hey, Mikey."

"Yeah?"

"I'm sorry I haven't been the best brother lately."

"Nah, Leo. I been all messed up." The mousers descend. Articulated, spiderlike limbs sprout from ports in their sides. As they hit the ground they begin to skitter along the tiles. The noise of their tapping spike-tipped legs drowns out the engine drone. Mikey lets his nunchaku twirl gently in his fists. "Been no good to anybody." He meets Leo's eyes. "You got nothing to be sorry for."

There is so much more he wants to say. But the mousers are almost upon them.

"You ever wonder how many of these things we've killed in our lives?"

The lead mouser begins to beep like an alarm clock. The red light inside its jagged maw blinks faster.

"I wonder about lots of stuff," Leo says. He understands, now, why the robot ninjas abruptly retreated. They're too valuable to Stockman to be used as suicide bombers.

Mousers, on the other hand—he's probably got a surplus of those. And if he can't have Honeycutt, he'll make sure no one else can.

"Yeah? Like what?" Mikey asks.

The alarm sound spreads through the ranks of the mousers. The interval between each beep gets shorter and shorter. Leo doesn't know how to answer his brother. Suddenly, the world is such a vast and unknowable place.

"Clock's ticking, dude," Mikey says.

"I wonder how Raph's doing," Leo says. "I mean, I think about him all the time. And I wonder—"

The sound and the heat and the light are so magnificent they take his breath away. The world goes brighter than anything he's ever seen. And then he is falling in every direction at once. He reaches out for his brothers and finds them everywhere.

27

"AFTER THE EXPLOSION . . ." MIKE trails off. So much is packed into that word. So much loss. He thinks of the last thing he heard before everything went white. Leo saying *I wonder.* He swallows, looks at April. "How did you end up here? In our old home?"

"Didn't happen overnight, that's for sure." April positions the syringe's long needle against the meat of Mike's left shoulder. "Took a rescue team a couple of days to find me and pull me out of the rubble. They got me to the hospital, which is where I woke up about a week later, only to find out I'd lost my husband, my friends, my home, my arm, my leg . . . and oh yeah, surprise, I was also pregnant."

April stops talking for a long moment. Mike can hear the pain in her voice. He doesn't prod her to continue.

The needle bites his flesh.

"Ow!"

"Seriously?" April snorts.

"Just hurry up. I hate needles."

"Then stop squirming, you big baby. I only need a few more vials."

Mike sighs. "I get that you scientist types can't help poking and prodding everything, but am I even gonna have any blood left after this?"

"What are you, five years old? This is barely any blood at all."

Mike glances at the vial his vein is feeding. Almost full.

April readies the next one. "Look, we're doing this because I need to see what your advanced mutation is doing to your body.

But I can get you a lollipop when we're done if that makes you feel any better."

"I can get my own lollipops."

The syringe clicks as April removes the full vial. Mike's blood sloshes. He feels a little queasy and turns away as she loads the next one.

"Anyway," April continues, "while I was putting myself back together, Hiroto was taking control of New York. He used the threat of rising water levels as an easy excuse to get the city to let him build a giant wall around Manhattan, which also cut us off from the world. After a little isolation, the street gangs and the cops declared war on each other and fought for what seemed like forever. All they managed to do was weaken each other, which made it easier for the Foot Clan to step in and take charge. Restoring law and order, right? The mayor welcomed it at first, but he regretted it before too long. When the governor and the president stopped taking his calls, he gave up and fled. To Jersey, I think, before they sealed off most of the tunnels."

The blood flows faster as Mike's heart pumps harder. He's furious, hearing how Hiroto took over his home.

"Things were getting really bad in the city," she continues, "and I wanted to control what Casey Marie was exposed to as much as I could, so I moved us down into the lair. Well, it was more like I hid us away down here, but that was okay. With the store destroyed and everyone gone, this place was all I had left to remind me of . . . you know. Better times."

April presses a cotton ball to Mike's arm and swiftly removes the needle. "All done. Keep pressure on this until I tell you to stop."

Mike clamps the cotton to his flesh with a fingertip. He nods at Fugitoid's head. "How badly damaged is he? Is Professor Honeycutt still in there?"

"I don't know. I think so. I hope so."

"Have you checked?"

"Do you mean, have I tried to activate him?" April pauses. "I haven't. I'm pretty sure Stockman found him last time by hacking the security firewalls Fugitoid had developed to keep himself hidden during the war. Reactivating him might be like blasting another 'Come kill us' signal to the bad guys."

Mike nods. "How'd you find his head?"

"A handful of Leo's strike team survived that night. They recovered the head while combing the wreckage for survivors."

"Strike team," Mike says. He tosses the cotton toward a wastebasket and misses. April glares at him. "Poor bastards." In his mind, he can hear the screams cutting through static, men and women being killed in the streets outside the compound. Their last moments amplified on speakers in the command center. Pain and fear and agony. He looks at April. "Any of 'em still kicking around?"

April comes at him with fresh cotton and a bandage. "Most of them died fighting the Foot Clan while Hiroto consolidated power. The ones that are left command resistance units around the city." Mike scratches the bandage on his upper arm. April raps his knuckles. "Don't do that. Let it heal. If you feel an itch, slap your forearm instead."

Mike does so. It works. He grunts. Learn something new every day.

April organizes vials of blood in a tray. "How about you?"

"How about me what?"

"Casey Marie said you went to Japan."

"Yeah."

"How did you—"

"I don't want to talk about it." Images from his last moments with Leo as a living, breathing turtle are surfacing in his mind. A film reel of things he doesn't want to relive, things he's been shoving down deep for many years.

"All right," April says. He watches her load one of the vials into the port on a machine the size of a small refrigerator. The silence between them grows heavy. Mike listens to the muffled dripping of some unseen leak, the rumbling of distant trains. He knows he could talk about the ghosts of his brothers. How sometimes it's nice having them hitch a ride on his consciousness. But other times, it's a cruel reminder of the family he let slip away.

"It's not your fault, you know," April says after a while. She busies herself by typing on an ancient keyboard while an overhead monitor displays scientific gibberish. Mike figures it's an excuse to keep herself occupied while she draws him out. "The counselors I worked with called it survivor's guilt." She moves to rearrange medical equipment on a battered metal table. A hazy memory surfaces: the long-ago afternoon when Donnie scavenged that table from a shuttered public school in Alphabet City.

"I know what survivor's guilt is," Mike says, resting his elbows on his knees, his body tense. "Listen, you got enough blood? Anything else you need from me?"

April comes up behind him. Mike feels her hands on his shoulders. She leans forward and gives him a hug. He doesn't move. "It took a lot of therapy and a lot of tears, but I finally realized there was nothing I could have done to change what happened. But that doesn't mean I have to accept what's happening now."

Shame wells up, brings heat to his face. April's attempt at comfort makes him feel his failure more acutely. He didn't ask for this. "Not to be a jerk, but I don't want to talk about anything unless it's a way to kill Hiroto."

"You're in luck." April walks over and pats Fugitoid's head. "Because I think I figured out how to beat him, once and for all."

"Then you need to tell us about it right now, Mom." Casey Marie walks into the lab. Mike's impressed. He hadn't heard her approach.

April turns to her daughter and gasps. "Casey Marie!"

Casey's lower lip is puffy. Dried blood stains the corner of her mouth. Her knuckles are smeared with glossy brown hydraulic fluid.

April rushes over. "What happened?"

"Nothing major, Mom."

"Synja," Mike says.

"Goddammit, Casey." April clutches her daughter's upper arms, peers into her eyes.

"I'm fine," she insists.

One at a time, four young men troop into the lab behind Casey. Instinct sends Mike out of his chair. From across the room he squares up to a massive bruiser. Bald, leather vest, abs of a gym rat and arms of a heavyweight. He's joined by his mohawked twin, an Asian kid with stained knuckles, and a guy bundled up like it's the dead of winter.

"You must be the crew I've heard so much about," Mike says.

The bald guy looks Mike up and down. "You must be the reason all hell's breaking loose in Rock Bottom."

28

THE SHREDDER COMES TO Oroku Hiroto in a dream. He is the size of a mountain, with each razor blade on his armor as big as a house. Hiroto is lost among the folds of his cloak, forever climbing—

He wakes with a start. The penthouse smells of jasmine, a scent pumped in through the vents. He sits up, sweaty and disoriented. Underneath the jasmine, he detects dying embers and rot. He makes a mental note to get rid of Ikusa's head. It's a good thing Stockman's arsenal works better than his appliances.

Track lights come on along the floor as the room senses his movements. Hiroto walks naked to his massive walk-in closet and pulls on a pair of loose-fitting trousers. Low light follows him as he makes his way to the back of the closet. He types a code on a keypad. A door swings open with a click. Inside, rows of shelves are illuminated. His eyes roam gold ingots, swords forged by long-dead craftsman, the battered armor of his Oroku ancestors. Hanging among these heirlooms is Oroku Saki's ragged purple cloak. Hiroto reaches out and caresses the coarse fabric. Like the Shredder himself, the cloak is scarred with the remnants of a thousand battles. Hiroto removes it from its hook and wraps it around his body.

Outside on the rain-soaked balcony that surrounds the penthouse, he puts up the cloak's hood. The lights of the city—his city—are like stars in the sky, too many to count. He imagines Shredder standing on some precipice, this very cloak flapping in the wind, gazing across Manhattan for the first time, alive with opportunity and potential. If only he could see this tower now, the culmination of Oroku ambition. Hiroto fastens the cloak's clasp then walks to the edge of the balcony. He closes his eyes and lets the breeze and the gentle rain embrace him. He knows it ought to bring him a sense of peace. This is what people do to calm themselves. They close their eyes and breathe. The rain taps out a rhythm on the windows at his back. It does not bring him peace but neither does it cause irritation. Even wearing his grandfather's cloak does not enhance the experience. He considers summoning a few warriors for a sparring session to help organize his thoughts but dismisses the idea. There are things he can do, out here, alone.

Hiroto listens to the sounds of his city. The din of life in New York. Millions of heartbeats, conversations, screams of fear or joy. All these sounds harmonizing in a symphony that honors him, a living reminder of his success.

He opens his eyes and tells himself to enjoy this moment. Yes, the turtle is still at large. But he will be caught, and Hiroto will slay him for all to see. And witnessing his triumph from beyond: the mountainous Shredder of his dreams, looming over everything. His dreams are no great labyrinth of psychodrama and symbol. He is perpetually haunted by the deeds of his forebears. So be it.

Without premeditation, Hiroto surrenders to an impulse. He steps toward the balcony's edge, then over, landing on the flattened top of one of the horizontal spikes that extend from the penthouse. The spikes are just wide enough for a man to walk on. With nothing between Hiroto and the city below, lights open up beneath him in a dizzying panorama. He tells himself to fully appreciate the beauty of Manhattan's music.

But it doesn't sound like anything at all. Not really. He pretends it's some kind of grand orchestra, but he knows it's simply the dissonant overlap of random chance.

The raindrops quicken. Hiroto lowers to a squat and lets the rain dance across his body as he peers down into the city. He lets his grandfather's ruthlessness and his mother's imperiousness course through him. He directs a sneer at the millions below, living out their meaningless lives in the shadow of his family's achievements. An indignant rush makes him lightheaded. He grips the wet edge of the spike. The citizens of New York owe their entire existence to him. He gives them everything they need.

Hiroto spits over the side of the spike, his spittle vanishing in the rain. He imagines the little gob of saliva splashing down atop some poor soul's head. The citizen looking up, wondering if he's just been shat upon by a pigeon, never knowing he has been struck by the expectoration of a god made flesh.

Hiroto says this out loud: "God made flesh." Quietly, at first. Then louder. "God made flesh!"

He rises like the Shredder of his dreams, towering above all. The rain intensifies. He paces up and down the spike with his arms outstretched. "I am your master!" he shouts. "I am your god incarnate!"

What does a deity feel inside? He pictures a white-hot flame at his core, some heavenly dispensation. Does a god wrestle with the man he is and the man he is supposed to be?

"I am god!" he screams into the night. "*I am god!*"

He likes the way this feels: the cloak, the scenic drama of the rain, the shouted invocations. He swaggers along the spike. For a moment, he feels free. Then a peal of thunder rolls across the sky and he remembers the goddamn turtle. He pushes back the cloak and lets the rain sting his chest. His thoughts sharpen and travel down fresh pathways.

On a whim, Hiroto leaps from one spike to another. He crosses eight feet of empty air, a thousand feet above the streets below. He hits the top of the spike and slides on rainwater before he finds traction. Poised like this, one errant step from plunging over the side, Hiroto stretches out his arms and feels the power of the storm on his taut muscles.

"Karai!" he calls out. "Mother! Do you see me now?" He steps to the edge of the spike and rises up on his toes. Millions of lights sway before him. No more sky and earth, only the city. "Do you see what I have done?"

Hiroto looks down at his people. "I have built this world!"

Thunder cracks in response. The elements pay him heed. He raises his arms to the sky. "Would a coward do *this*?"

Arms outstretched, he lets himself fall forward. The sky slides out of view. There is only a womb of light. He falls through the heartbeat of the city.

The shrill whine of a miniature jet engine cuts through the roar of the storm. The sound builds. A metal talon clamps his ankle and arrests his fall. Like a god, he cannot die. His angels—tall, winged androids—will react to his biometric implant and leap from their alcoves to save him. He laughs. Stockman tech to clean his floors, Stockman tech to pluck him out of the sky. He looks up at the impassive hunk of metal as it drags him through the rain.

"I am immortal."

The android says nothing. It has no speech protocols.

Hiroto laughs so hard he coughs. Rain streams into his mouth and he swallows. It tastes like nothing at all.

29

". . . AND THAT'S IT," APRIL says. "It could all be over in just a few more weeks."

"Oh," Crunch says. He's leaning against the wall with his arms folded. "Is that it?"

April glares. Casey Marie's crew is motley as hell. And the monster twins are oozing steroids out of their pores. She knows these idiots let Casey get wasted with them in that shithole biker bar. She also knows they'd die to protect her. Anyway, resistance folk aren't usually business casual types.

Hell, she'd been engaged to a guy who wore a hockey mask around the city while he dispensed vigilante justice with sports equipment.

She looks from the 'roid-head twins to the guy with the mustache to the strange silent one.

The mustache guy—Breaker, she suddenly recalls—nods. "Um. Okay. I see the possibilities here."

April scoffs. Not like she expected a round of applause for her brilliant plan to take down Hiroto, but this is a tough crowd.

"April," Michelangelo says, "the whole thing is crazy. I mean, I get the concept, but c'mon—it's like a billion-to-one shot."

April's hands go to her hips. She'd expected Mike to be so rabidly on board she'd have to hold him back. "Billion-to-one or not, I think it's our *only* shot. You know better than most what kind of firepower and technology Hiroto has access to. We need to level the playing field, and there's no other way."

"There are too many variables, too many moving parts." Mike looks at the wall. "And too many lives could be lost."

"That's true with *any* plan!" Casey barks, slapping Michelangelo on the arm. "We're fighting an evil empire here, dude. They're not gonna roll over and die just so we can feel good about ourselves!"

"Right on," Scrape says. He moves a toothpick from one side of his mouth to the other. "I like the plan. Stockman and Hiroto both gotta go down. Makes sense to do it this way."

April watches Mike pace the lab's dull floor. Getting Casey's crew on board is helpful. Getting the last remaining ninja turtle on board is vital.

"Okay," Mike says, like he's talking to himself, "so Baxter Stockman's got his own headquarters, fortress, *whatever* on Roosevelt Island, and we need to attack it and shut him down before we can take out Hiroto. To do that, we gotta activate Honeycutt during the attack, and *if* he wakes up, maybe he'll be able to knock out Stockman's tech?"

Mike looks around the room as if waiting for somebody to set him straight. When no one speaks, he shakes his head. "April, I'm sorry, but it's like I said—there are just too many damn *if*s, and that makes it way too risky. I'll find another way to take Hiroto down."

Mike leans against the wall. April tamps down her impatience. Guys leaning against walls are getting on her nerves. But she's not going to sway him by losing her cool. She keeps her tone measured. "Every plan, no matter how good the odds, has risks. You know that."

"And it's still got better odds than a hundred-year-old mutant attackin' Hiroto directly," Casey added. "I mean, we saw how that went."

"Hey!" Mike says. He points at Casey. "That's not fair!"

Casey shrugs. "Neither is life. And just so you know? We don't need your permission on this, *Mikey*."

Breaker whistles. Crunch and Scrape glance at each other. Lug inspects a fridge full of test tubes.

"This isn't about permission," Mike says. "This is about reality. Do you all have a death wish, or what?"

Casey snorts. "Look who's talking."

April watches Mike blink as if her daughter has just slapped him across the face.

"We were already dyin' before you got here, turtle," Scrape says. "You just made things worse."

Mike turns to the big man with the menacing slowness of a jungle predator on the hunt. "From where I'm standing, it was already pretty bad."

Scrape's huge body vibrates with barely controlled anger. "We used to be able to go underground till the heat died down. Now they're raiding our safe houses. Not just a few soldiers, either. *Synjas*."

"They're pulling people right off the streets," Breaker says. "My cousin's just gone. Disappeared."

"I saw a kid miss curfew by three minutes," Scrape says, "running to get home, and a synja blasted him to hell with no warning."

"Yeah?" Mike says. "Did you just stand there watching it go down?"

Scrape takes a step toward Mike.

"Enough!" April bellows. The factions are digging in, and Mike looks like he's about to punch a hole in Scrape. She won't let it degenerate further.

The lab goes quiet. "Casey," April says, "take your friends into the kitchen."

"What are we gonna—"

"Get them a goddamn snack!"

Casey shrugs. "Hope you guys like black market eggs."

"Not the eggs!" April says.

Casey leads them out of the room. Scrape's small eyes linger on Mike, who stares placidly back. Then he follows the others out the door.

April crosses over to Mike with a slight limp, favoring her prosthetic leg, to rev up his sympathy. She doesn't have time to play fair. She takes hold of his arm with her prosthetic hand. "Come with me, Mike. There's something else I want you to see."

"I know what you're doing, April."

"Do you?"

"You're trying to guilt me into agreeing with you."

"Am I?"

"April. Listen. They're gonna get killed out there. Brawling with the Foot Clan on the streets of Rock Bottom is one thing. I can get down with that. And they need to defend themselves, sure. But your own daughter. Casey. I won't . . ." He trails off. "You need to let me do my own thing here."

April leads him out of the room. "You heard them just now, Mikey. The city's under martial law. The Foot Clan's cracking down on the resistance, and people like those muscleheads back there? They're not gonna take it lying down. Neither is Casey. With or without you, or me, or my blessing, my daughter's gonna fight. And it's not just street brawls. It's bigger than that now. There's nothing we can do about it. What we *can* do is help keep her alive out there."

Muttering to himself, Mike follows her down a dim corridor, toward the abandoned station where Donnie once kept his half-finished projects. A rusted yellow van winks at them from the darkness. She can feel the change in Mike's body language in the darkness. He's taking in the spirit of his brother, she thinks. Still present in what Donatello left behind.

She guides him toward a massive truck-sized lump covered in a blue tarp. Rats scurry away as they approach. The distant trains rumble and a fine silt hangs in the air.

"This isn't one of Donnie's," Mike says, "is it?"

"Nope," April says. "This is mine. I've been prepping for a long time, getting ready for that one last fight I knew was coming."

She takes hold of the tarp with her prosthetic hand and drags it off the massive hidden object. "Couldn't have dreamed we'd have *you* on our side for it. That was definitely a surprise." Metal begins to reveal itself. Olive drab matte finish. Homebrew military hardware. One final flourish, and the tarp lies on the floor.

"I think Donnie would approve, don't you?"

April watches Mike regard the machine she's been working on for years. Seeing it through his widening eyes, her pride swells.

"Donnie would have absolutely loved this," he says after a while. There is tenderness and awe in his voice. "What is it?"

April smiles. "Just a little something to even the odds."

The revealed behemoth is a heavily armored personnel carrier. Its exoskeleton is all intersecting planes, modeled on stealth aircraft designed to fool radar. The wheels were scavenged from an old monster truck and are shielded by steel wells. A pair of hatches provide the only entry and exit points. Thick wires run from its underbelly to monitoring equipment in the corner of the darkened chamber. A low hum suffuses the air, punctuated by faint beeps. Mike runs a hand along a riveted seam in the vehicles armor.

"It's watertight," April says.

"No shit?"

"Drives through a brick wall and goes for a swim." She gives it a gentle pat. "All in a day's work for my sweet baby."

He turns to her. "Needs a name."

"I already used *Casey* for my daughter."

"How about *Splinter's Revenge*?"

"I'm not calling it that."

He shrugs. "I thought it was good."

April smiles. "So, you're in?"

"I'll think about it," Mike says. "No promises."

30

MIKE DOESN'T CARE IF he dies. This is what he tells himself as he rounds a bend, one dark tunnel giving way to another. His feet slosh through fetid muck. Far from the lair, wandering the sewers, he turns April's scheme over in his head.

It still sounds crazy. Even with that armored rig of hers, a ragtag bunch of street fighters who call themselves the "resistance" does not stand a chance against Stockman's tech on the scientist's home turf. Not to mention Hiroto's army.

As for Michelangelo? There's no expectation of a long happy life when you're driven by vengeance. He knows he will die. But he won't take anyone he loves down with him. He has to do this alone.

There. He can tell April he thought about it, but his mind is unchanged. Another turn, another stinking tunnel. Hundreds of tiny eyes shine in the dark. He thinks of Splinter.

Mike assesses his mobility as he walks. Limbs in working order. Strength and speed on point. Body aches faded. He's mostly healed from his dalliance with the pavement. If he sneaks out of the lair and makes another run at Hiroto tonight, then it will all be over by morning. Either Hiroto will be dead and April's assault plan will be moot, or Mike will be dead and he won't be responsible for what April and Casey do next. Either outcome offers absolution.

"That sound good to you guys?"

His voice echoes through the labyrinth of tunnels. Mike waits and listens. Distant trains come and go. Dripping water, rats moving through the sludge, errant clanks of unknown origin. The sounds of the undercity are the same as they ever were, but his brothers stay quiet.

"You guys pissed at me for something? Did I offend your delicate sensibilities somehow? Just let me know and I'll start my apology tour."

Nothing.

"Raph. You in particular, you're a jerk. I hope you know that." Mike strolls along, warming up to his end of the conversation. "What, don't tell me you guys think April's onto something with this crackpot scheme." Pause. "Seriously? *That's* why you're giving me the silent treatment? You want me to entertain this bullshit? A few days ago you were all like, *Casey's just a kid, Mikey, blah blah blah.* What happens when she gets herself killed by a mouser on Roosevelt Island, you gonna make her part of your ghost crew?" He shakes his head. "She's got a whole *actual* life ahead of her."

His shell brushes a pipe and he grimaces. The shrapnel wound still aches. He wonders if he's healed with some metal piece stuck inside, trapped forever. A fragment of the city becoming part of him. That would be all right.

Mike returns to the lair and hears the heavy bag getting worked over in the gym. He creeps in to see Casey Marie shining with sweat. The piece of electrical tape Leo once stuck over a hole in the bag's fabric is still there. From the doorway, he watches her unload a combo. Right kick, left jab, right cross. The bag swings. She takes a breather.

"Her technique's decent," Leonardo's voice says from a shadow at the far end of the room, near the entrance to the dojo proper. "But she's developed some bad habits. She telegraphs her jab. Oh, and she drops her guard. Splinter would never let her get away with being so sloppy."

Raphael snorts. "Give it a rest, Leo. That kid is a buck twenty soaking wet, and that bag's at least two bills. All things considered, I think she's doing all right."

"Maybe," Leo allows. "But I'd be interested to see what she could do with ten years of real training."

"Me too," Raph agrees. "'Cept we ain't got ten years."

Mike shakes his head. If anything's guaranteed to call forth his brothers' spirits, it'd be the sight of someone clobbering the heavy bag in their old gym.

"I wonder why she cut her hair so short?" Donatello chimes in.

"I dunno about her hair, Donnie," Mike answers. "You guys want me to show her some actual fighting techniques?"

"I mean," Leo says, "if she's gonna be out on the streets regardless, I think it's time to find out what she's willing to learn."

"Fine. But this is not 'training.' I'm no one's sensei. I'll just give her some quick pointers right now."

He waits for Casey to tire herself out, noting her movements. Then he approaches. "Well, besides getting your cardio in, that was just about useless."

Casey looks over. "Whoa!" She grabs a towel from a pile on a small table, wipes her face, tosses it aside. "I didn't hear you come in."

"I'm a ninja, remember?" Mike looms over her. She takes a step back. "You ever fight anyone skilled with that garbage?"

Casey Marie narrows her eyes. "I never had some ninja master to show me anything, and I still kick ass all over this city."

Mike holds his arms out wide. "Okay. Show me."

"Wait. What?"

"Hit me. As hard as you can. Right now." Michelangelo pats his chest. "Let's go."

Raphael laughs. "I love it."

Casey steps forward, fists raised. Then she stops. Her hands relax. "No, listen, I don't want to hurt you. You almost died a few weeks ago. You can't be all healed yet, and I'm not gonna make things worse."

Mike tamps down a smile. He keeps his face stern. Then he shows her his back and starts to walk away. "Nothing but a kid pretending to be a warrior. Figures."

He waits, feeling her energy shift. He turns around just as she snarls and launches a flying kick, yelling "HAI!" as she takes to the air.

Mike steps to his left and watches her sail past him. "Good thing you yelled first, or you might've actually caught me off guard."

Casey lets out a feral shout as she unleashes a volley of punches and kicks at his face. He blocks them all with a precision both methodical and gentle, like he's barely moving.

"You're fighting angry, kid. Anger makes you sloppy, and sloppy slows you down. Which means you're giving me all the time in the world to do"—Mike leans out of the way of Casey's punch, grabs her wrist, pulls her forward, and uses her own momentum to throw her to the ground—"*this*." He pauses. "I wouldn't get up if I were you."

"Whatever," Casey mutters. "Watch this." She kicks up to her feet, bends her knees, flips neatly over Michelangelo's head and lands in front of him in a fighting stance. Then her torso begins to rotate. He sighs as the telegraphed roundhouse kick comes and goes.

"Watch *what*, how to miss and leave yourself exposed to a counterattack?"

Casey feints then throws her body weight behind a hard punch. Mike grabs her wrist with two fingers and flips her into an armlock.

"And now you're done." He shoves Casey face-first into the wall. "Feel free to take some time to think about how you could've done this differently."

Casey shouts and punches the wall with her free hand. A chunk of masonry comes loose.

"Whoa, take it easy on the bricks, kid. They're old." Mike twists, increasing the pressure of the armlock.

"You would know," Casey says.

"What was that?" Mike twists a bit more.

"Okay, okay! I get it! I gotta be tougher!"

Mike releases her arm. "You don't get it at all. *Tougher*'s not the point here. You're plenty tough. But even the greatest warrior can't punch their way out of every confrontation. Sometimes, it pays to be subtle. Fluid. Elusive. Avoiding strikes instead of delivering 'em. Let your enemy wear themselves out while you remain in control."

Casey massages her wrist. "Fine. You made your point. Are we done here?"

"Look," Mike says. "I don't know you and you don't know me, but you're April's daughter, which makes you family. You got some skills, yeah, but you also got a lot to learn, or you're gonna get killed out there."

His mouth is outpacing his thoughts. Whatever happens with Hiroto, the city is a dangerous place. Casey's going to be fighting for her life, whether he likes it or not. He can't keep her out of every battle. So in the interests of saving her life . . .

"I might be willing to teach you what I know."

"Ha!" Raph calls out. "Manipulatin' you is so easy, it ain't even fun."

"But if I do this," Mike tells Casey, "I'm not gonna take any of your shit. No back talk, no attitude, and no . . . whatever that sound was that you made when you punched the wall. I tell you what to do and you do it. Got it?"

"Wait, what? Seriously? You'd show me stuff, like a real teacher?"

Mike hesitates. It had been easy to embrace the notion of his honorable death in the darkness of the tunnels. Now, under the bright lights of the lair, with this eager kid standing before him, it's like something's gone soft inside him. It worries him—might be another stalling tactic, some weakness in the recesses of his soul. He does not know. But there is a rightness to this path, too, he thinks. Even if it delays his vengeance.

"It's *sensei*," Mike says. "Not teacher." Hearing himself say this aloud cranks up his nerves. Splinter had been a true sensei. But him?

Then she wraps him in a tight hug and his angst subsides. "Right! A sensei!"

His ribs scream in pain—body's still knitting itself together. So this isn't a stalling tactic. He just needs a little more recovery time. Casey lets him go. The pain eases.

"We'll start first thing tomorrow," Mike says.

"I'll be ready. Thanks, Michelangelo. I mean: thank you, Sensei." Casey bows and leaves the gym.

"Bring some music! It's too damn quiet in here."

He picks up her towel from the floor and tosses it on the little table by the heavy bag. "You guys happy now?"

"Yes, *Sensei*," Raph says.

"The role you were born to play," Leo says.

Donnie laughs. "For real, though, Mikey—the kid needs you. This is good."

"Yeah, well, I feel like an imposter." He peers into the shadows, makes out the impressions of his brothers. "You guys really think April's onto something here, huh. Taking out Stockman first."

"Come on, Mikey," Donnie says. "When you got to the city, you didn't know about April and Casey. A solo run at Hiroto was all we'd been thinking about for years."

"Now it's different," Raph says. "But it's like you're the last one to notice."

"Of course I noticed!" Mike sinks a right hook into the side of the heavy bag. "April being alive, her and Casey having this kid—it's got me all messed up, Raph. What if I go along with this crazy plan and they die out there? What if I *watch them die* out there? Then what?"

"Then at least you were there," Leo says. "With them at the end. Like you were for me."

Mike stills the swaying bag. He leans his forehead against the worn fabric, feels the frayed edges of that old piece of electrical tape. "Ah, shit, Leo."

"They need you," Donnie says.

"They're family," Raph says.

Mike sighs into the bag.

31

"I WANT TO LEARN to sneak around like you," Casey says. "Become a silent killer." It's been three weeks since Mike became her sensei. They spend a lot of time meditating, and not nearly enough on actual training, in her opinion.

She hefts a rusty forty-five-pound plate and slides it onto one end of the barbell perched over the bench. Mike sets up a matching plate on the other end.

"You're not ready for that," he says. "You haven't mastered breathing yet."

"I know how to breathe." She lies down on the bench and slides under the bar.

"I know how to breathe *what*?"

Casey grumbles. "I know how to breathe, *Sensei*."

Michelangelo smiles. A genuine smile, like he's starting to remember how to enjoy life. Big difference from when she found him in the sewer, bloody and hopeless, broken blade aimed at his gut.

"Come on," he says. "Twelve reps. Three sets. Go."

Casey grips the bar. At first she'd been giddy that this legendary ninja had offered to teach her. She's never had a proper instructor before, forced to make do by cobbling together lessons from videos and whatever books her mother could find. But for a supposed party dude, Michelangelo is a stickler for procedure and respect. He moves to spot her. She glares up at the rippling muscles of his tough green flesh. His bandages are long gone, the last of his wounds healed.

She lifts the bar with ease. She's stronger now. Recovering faster too. Their daily gym and dojo sessions are irritating and boring, but they're working.

"I'm going stir-crazy," she tells him as she counts in her head. *Two reps. Three. Four.*

"If you can talk to me, you're not working hard enough."

She drops the bar onto the rack and sits up. "I'm serious, Sensei. Every day we waste down here, the Foot Clan destroys another family, the synjas come down hard on another resistance cell. People are disappearing by the hundreds and we're down here rotting."

"Your mother's still working on Fugitoid. Plus we gotta make sure everyone's on the same page, or this won't work. And it's not exactly easy to coordinate right now with all the infiltrations."

Casey raises an eyebrow. "You said *we*. Don't try to deny it."

Mike shakes his head and loads two more plates. She lies back down and curls her calloused palms around the cool metal bar. She imagines Mike in the old days, spotting one of his brothers on the bench. Or maybe even her father.

He snaps his fingers. "Be present."

Casey doesn't move. She wonders how much her father could bench. In the photos she's seen, he's wiry and compact, with coils of muscle running just underneath his skin. Not a bruiser like Crunch or Scrape.

Mike's voice softens. "Okay," he says. "Sit up."

She does.

"What are you thinking about?"

"I was just wondering about something."

"Some ridiculous technique you saw in a kung fu movie?"

She flicks at a piece of torn cushion on the bench. "What was my dad like?"

He blinks. "Oh." He looks around the gym as if hoping to tag someone else in. "Wouldn't your mom be the one to ask about that?"

She stands and retrieves two more forty-five-pound plates. With a curious expression, Mike watches her carry them over and feed them to the bar. "Are those heavy for you?"

She lies down on the bench. "Not really." She lifts the bar and barely notices the weight. "Mom can't tell me everything. I want to hear about him from you—when else would I have a chance to talk to one of his friends?"

She fires off five quick reps. The mechanical motion—up, down, up, down—brings a sense of order to her thoughts.

Mike doesn't bother spotting her. "I don't know what to say. He was a good man."

"Yeah. I've heard that from my mom a million times." She pauses. "I need more weight."

Mike peers at her for a moment. Then he adds a fifteen pounder to each side. Casey raises the bar without strain.

Mike whistles. "You been taking some of Crunch's go-go juice?"

She lets the bar drop with a clank. "Him and Scrape don't touch that shit."

"Yeah, they look totally natural."

She sits up again. "Quit changing the subject, Sensei. I hardly know anything about my dad. And I want to."

Mike sighs. "All right, Casey. We'll max out your bench press another time." He tosses her a towel even though she's not sweating. "I suddenly feel like taking a walk."

East of Bowery, Michelangelo prowls through sparse evening crowds in his black hooded ensemble with Casey at his side. She catches their reflection in the window of a shoe store, a pair of walking shadows. But Mike's figure is a strange, hulking presence. She's sure the Foot Clan patrols will spot him.

"How are you doing this?" she whispers, keeping a watchful eye on passersby. There are only so many Foot soldiers and synjas to go around, but they could materialize anywhere. "We're right out in the open and no one's given you a second glance."

"You wanted to learn how to be invisible, right?" They move through a holo-ad that dangles from a storefront awning, translucent protein shakes that flash in her vision then fade. "Well, most of the time, being invisible is as simple as not giving someone a reason to notice you."

They part as a woman in a loud floral-print Hawaiian shirt and a tattered cardigan darts between them. She grunts what might have been "Excuse me" as she shimmies past.

"That doesn't make sense to me," Casey says.

"Okay. What color was that lady's sweater?"

"I don't know."

"She walked right past you, and you didn't see it? It was green. You just had no reason to notice it until I asked."

"Yeah, but a lady's cardigan is one thing. You gotta be the most hunted dude in Rock Bottom."

Mike shrugs. They turn a corner. A man sitting cross-legged and shirtless in front of a graffiti-tagged ATM machine shakes a paper cup that jingles softly.

"People don't see what they're not looking for," Mike says. "And a lot of the time, they don't see what they don't expect to see. Donatello told me once about an experiment about this called 'The Invisible Gorilla,' or something. Anyway, point is, if you don't stand out, you're less likely to be seen. Pretty simple."

"But the rest of it is still some kinda secret ninja shit."

"You're catching on."

They walk quietly for another block. Casey lets the hum of elevated vehicles wash over her. It's nice to be out of the sewers. The pavement is damp from a recent downpour and the air is as fresh as it gets on the Lower East Side. Steam issues from an orange cylinder that splits the traffic flow on Third Street.

"Your dad reminded me a little bit of my brothers," Mike says, "all mixed together. That's one of the reasons I liked him, you know? He just felt like family. He had a big heart. Hated bullies. Was always there for anybody who needed him. I know telling you that he was a good man might sound dismissive, but that's what he was. And it was my honor to know him."

A Foot patrol approaches from the other end of the block. Four soldiers plus a red-eyed synja. Mike steers Casey down First Avenue. A malt liquor forty-ounce rushes past them in a blaze of amber light. Casey can't help but glance over her shoulder, though Mike keeps his eyes forward.

"Once," he continues, "your dad and my brother Raphael got into an argument about weapons. Casey liked sports equipment, and he used stuff with a little bit of a reach. A baseball bat or a hockey stick, right? Raph told him it was because he couldn't hack it in close quarters. So, your dad went out the next night and took down three muggers with a pair of Ping-Pong paddles because they were shorter than Raph's sai. We laughed about that for days."

Casey Marie stops walking, closes her eyes, and tries to picture her father. She knows what he looked like—her mom still has a handful of photos—but he's never come alive in her imagination. Before now.

"Thank you, Sensei," Casey says. She opens her eyes. Then she leans over and gives Michelangelo another hug.

"Hey, easy," he says. "I'm not going anywhere."

32

"CASEY, IS THAT YOU?"

April's voice comes from the lab when Mike get back to the sewers. He peeks in to find her inspecting Fugitoid's still-dormant head.

"Nope." He steps into the room. April's hunched over a panel in the back of the android's metal skull. She pokes at exposed circuitry with a tool that resembles a screwdriver grafted to a cell phone. Her face is covered in fine metallic silt. Three empty mugs and a half-finished pepperoni slice clutter the table next to Fugitoid. "Telecom lines were up and Casey got a text. She went to check in with those goons of hers."

"Uh-huh." April narrows her eyes and jabs with the tool. Sparks fly from the panel.

"Should you be wearing goggles?"

"I know what I'm doing. And don't call them *goons*, Mikey. They're decent people."

He tamps down his impatience. "You getting close with Honeycutt?"

"Almost there." She straightens and sets down the tool, swiping a hand across her forehead. It comes away speckled in silver. "And I've been coordinating with the resistance commanders as best I can. The attack plan's coming together." She hands him the pizza slice. "Here."

"April. You shouldn't have." He scarfs the pizza. Cold and delicious.

Raph's voice pipes up. "You ever wonder how many slices we've eaten in our lives?"

"I think we can figure it out," Donnie says.

Mike ignores his brothers as Donnie does math out loud. He polishes off the slice.

"You could be more involved with them, you know," April says.

He wipes his fingers on a rag hanging off the edge of the table. "With who?"

"The resistance. It would be good to have your input, seeing as how you've actually fought Hiroto. More or less."

Mike shakes his head. The word *resistance* conjures up Casey's drinking buddies. Profoundly inexperienced and unserious fighters. Plus that one weird silent guy. "I still don't like the idea of putting so many lives at risk. I think if I go myself, a quieter solo infiltration, I could—"

"Are you kidding me?" He winces at the sharpness in her tone. She steps out from behind the table. "You can't still be so far gone."

"What?"

"This death wish of yours! Casey Marie told me about finding you in the sewer. She told me what you were about to do."

Mike fights the impulse to turn his back and leave the room. He roots himself to the floor and averts his eyes. "That was about honor. I thought I'd failed my family."

His head drops. The darkness of the place he'd been in—even the memory of it brings shame. The despair of those moments gnaws at him again. He raises his eyes to April.

She places a hand on his forearm, giving it a light squeeze. "It's okay, Mikey. Just remember, you have people who love you."

He nods. "You gotta understand—for a long time, there was no one."

She offers a gentle smile. "Listen, I wanted to tell you, what you're doing for Casey Marie is wonderful. You know Splinter—he was there for you four, but he was there for me and Casey, too. For everyone he thought of as family, up until the end. And Casey Marie's never had that. She's only had me. I want her to be more balanced, but I can only do so much. She's got all her dad's courage, but she doesn't really have a way to direct her skills and soothe her anger. I've already seen such a difference in her thanks to you."

Mike lays a hand atop April's. He imagines hitting the heavy bag until this confounding swirl of grief, shame, and relief subsides. But he stays put.

"I think Splinter would be very proud of you," April says.

Mike's face grows hot. He turns away, wipes his eyes. "Why'd you have to go and say that."

"Speaking of Splinter," April continues. "I need to know what happened to him and Donnie. Casey told me what you said about your time in Japan. In the mountains. But there's so much you left out."

Mike takes a breath. "I know. I'm sorry. It still hurts so much. You'd think, after all this time, I'd . . ." He shakes his head. "But you're right. You're family, and you deserve to know." He steps away, paces to the corner of the lab, gathers himself. Then he faces her.

"After the ambush in New York, I stowed away on a plane to Japan. That much you know. But before I walked into the mountains, I went to the village of the Hamato Clan. I knew it was a longshot, because so much time had passed since the battle here, but I thought if I could warn the elders, they could get word to Donnie and Splinter, and . . ." He shakes his head. "Maybe keep them safe. Anyway, one of the elders—Master Shinichiro—he welcomed me in, and I told him everything that had just happened back home." He meets April's eyes. "I told him about you, and Casey, and Leo. And then, when I was finished, it was Master Shinichiro's turn to tell me a story."

SEVENTEEN YEARS AGO

THE AIRCRAFT HATCH OPENS with a hiss of depressurized air. Donatello ushers Splinter out into the night. Together, they walk down the ramp into what feels like an alien landscape. Fifteen hours ago they had departed from the hangar inside the old sugar factory. Strike team personnel bustling about, the smell of chrome and oil and sweat hanging in the air. A simmering miasma of stress and activity. In this place, snowcapped mountains rise into an endless sky full of stars unclouded by city lights. The air is crisp and clean. Beyond the clearing where the aircraft rests, the Hamato Clan's village cascades down a gentle slope. Fires burn in braziers that cast a flickering yellow haze across the snowy paths.

Donatello breathes deep. "Why do we live in a sewer, again?"

Splinter lays a furry paw on Donnie's back. "There is no place on Earth with air as sweet as this. I miss it very much."

"As we miss having you here, Splinter-san." A gray-haired man in purple robes emerges from the shadows of the forest. He greets Splinter and Donnie with a bow.

"Master Shinichiro," Splinter says. "It is good to see you, my old friend. It has been far too long. You remember my son, Donatello?"

Donnie bows to the man. Like Splinter, Master Shinichiro is elderly yet moves with the grace and measured intent of the lifelong warrior. Donnie can imagine both of them dropping the old-guy act in an instant and unleashing deadly violence. He smiles to himself.

One day, Donnie and his brothers will be like that, too. Grizzled veterans of a million battles, clapping each other on the back and toasting old times.

He shakes his head, corrects himself: Donnie and *two* of his brothers, anyway. Raphael won't be with them ever again. It's amazing how his mind allows him to blissfully ignore this fact. Then, when reality returns, the loss bites hard.

"Of course," Shinichiro says, bringing Donnie's attention to the present. "Greetings to you both, and welcome. I look forward to having a long conversation once we have concluded the business at hand."

"Ah yes, the business of peace," Splinter says. "I remain cautiously optimistic regarding young Master Hiroto's sincerity in this long-overdue endeavor. Some of my sons do not share my optimism."

"We left the biggest skeptics back in New York," Donnie says. "I'm somewhere in the middle."

Shinichiro laughs. "As am I, my young friend. It is good to be hopeful, yet vigilant. Thankfully, our scouts have found no signs of deceit by the Foot Clan. From all we have seen, they are preparing for peace talks in earnest."

Donnie lets Shinichiro and Splinter take the lead and follows them into the village. Fresh snow crunches beneath his feet. Three-story dwellings line the path. A full moon casts its pale light upon clay-tiled rooftops. Flags bedecked with the Hamato insignia—three black orbs inside a white circle—flutter in the mountain winds. His thoughts turn to Leo and Mikey. He wishes they were here, walking quietly down this path at his side, absorbing these rare moments of silence the city never provides. Yet, another part of him is glad for the time away from his brothers. Ever since Raphael died, he's felt the need for space. His hours in the lab get longer and longer, his patrols with his brothers ever shorter.

Shinichiro shows them to a neat house in the center of the village. "We will celebrate your arrival soon, my friends. But first you must rest. The business of peace requires a fresh mind."

Inside, Donnie and Splinter bed down on mattresses placed atop tatami mats. Within seconds, Splinter's breathing eases into a steady, quiet rhythm. Donnie's exhausted from their journey, yet sleep does not come easily. The silence of the remote village tickles his mind. Even in the underground lair, the sounds of the city creep in. There are always subway trains rattling, the muffled noises of the Lower East Side drifting into the tunnels. Here there is only the vast emptiness of the sky with its millions of stars, the full moon hanging in the darkness. It's all a bit like scenery in a play.

Donnie sinks into a memory. Once, long ago, the four of them snuck into *Phantom of the Opera* and watched a couple of the big numbers from the shadows alongside the stage. Donnie lets the atmosphere of the theater seep into the dark room, the hush of the audience, the spotlights' heat, the mask of the Phantom himself. Slowly, the music comes back to him, low tones slithering through the mountains that surround the village while he syncs his breathing with his father's. After a while, there is no more house in a mountain village and no more theater, only the depths of a dream.

Dawn finds him standing alongside Splinter and Shinichiro in a long-neglected, snow-covered cemetery nestled among dense evergreens. Red-brown torii gates rise above snaggled rows of ancient headstones.

As his breath puffs white into the frigid air, Donatello feels suddenly very far from home. He's had enough space and wishes his brothers were here. He reaches back for the comforting weight of the bō strapped to his shell, running a finger along its taped grips. Turning in a slow circle, he regards the weathered stones around him, the worn carvings, the names of the dead. Behind them, a handful of Hamato warriors stand ready, their wary eyes scanning the tree line.

"I hope young Hiroto chose this location out of ignorance, not malice," Splinter says.

"Yeah," Donnie says. "A resting place for the dead really sets the wrong tone."

He watches his father's eyes close as Splinter begins to meditate where he stands. Donnie keeps his mind occupied by seeking out fractals in the snowdrifts and pine needles and the never-ending patterns of branches against the gray sky. What would it be like to live in a place like this? Maybe they can all retire here someday.

After a while, a small delegation emerges from the forest and crosses the cemetery. One old man flanked by two young warriors. As he gets closer, Donnie marvels at how thin this man appears. It's like one of the dead has escaped its grave. His shiny black hair is tied back in a neat bun. The delegation stops a few paces from Donnie and Splinter.

The old man bows deeply, careful to keep the sweeping sleeves of his tunic out of the snow.

"I am Ambassador Hara of the Foot Clan, at your service. Master Hiroto sends his warmest wishes and kindest regards."

"We assumed the young master would be leading this delegation," Splinter says.

"Yes," Shinichiro says. "An incredible display of bad faith."

Hara looks horrified. "Oh, no, not at all! Master Hiroto is overseeing the final preparations for the grand feast we will share once an agreement has been reached!" He turns to Splinter. "I am sure Master Hiroto is on his way here now for a proper greeting. He is quite serious about peace, you know."

"And he finds planning the feast to be more important than the meeting itself?" Splinter asks. Donnie can hear the subtle shift in his father's tone. Next to him, Master Shinichiro's body is rigid. Beyond the tree line, a cluster of birds takes to the air and wheels away toward the distant peaks. Donnie flexes his fingers. He knows this is wrong. They all do.

"I could not speak to such matters," Hara says. "I am but a simple man, doing as my master commands." Hara glances from Donnie to the Hamato warriors at his back. "I notice you are all armed. One of the conditions of this gathering was to meet with no weapons, as a show of good faith toward the peace we wish to achieve."

Donnie calculates that he could incapacitate Hara in three seconds. His two bodyguards in eight. He figures Raph would have shoved a sai into the man's heart by now.

"I do not recall agreeing to that," Splinter says. "These weapons are merely ceremonial. However, we have no wish to make you uncomfortable. We will stand aside until your master arrives, and then we can conclude our business."

"We can conclude it now!" Hara insists. "I was given permission by Master Hiroto to finalize all terms before his arrival so that an agreement may be expedited."

"It is generous of Hiroto to have given you such authority so that he might see to the details of the celebration," Splinter says. "Nevertheless, we will wait to see if Master Hiroto arrives armed before we give up our weapons." His nose twitches. "In the meantime we will enjoy this fine morning air."

Hara pales. "Please, be reasonable. You may collect your weapons after the summit. We seek only peace."

"As do we, Hara. This war has lasted generations. A few more minutes will not matter."

Hara backs away, bowing as he goes. Donnie feels a strange sense of calm. He can already taste the battle in the back of his throat. Blood and steel and fear.

"Father," Donnie says softly, "we should kill these three now."

Splinter sighs. "I let my desire for peace blind me." He turns to Shinichiro. "We are a couple of old fools, my friend."

Shinichiro places a hand on the hilt of the katana at his side. "It will be an honor to fight alongside you again, Hamato Yoshi."

Hara's face twists into a thin smile. A half dozen men on horseback gallop into view and plunge down from a ridge atop the clearing's eastern edge. The Foot Clan standards flap from poles extending from the backs of their samurai armor. Donnie draws his bō. The weight of it in his hands, the perfectly balanced staff, connects him with home. A piece of his home and his brothers, here with him on the other side of the world. He closes his eyes and directs a silent message of love at Leo and Mikey. Then he opens his eyes to find one of the samurai outpacing the others. The horse rears up before them, its rider's armor bristling with ornamental blades on its helmet and gauntlets. Donnie is startled. It's clearly the ancient Oroku armor that inspired the armor of Oroku Saki—the Shredder.

"So!" The warrior's voice is that of a teenager. "The prodigal mutants return."

"Hiroto," Donnie says. "We came in peace."

Hiroto peers down from his horse. "Which turtle are you?" He shakes his head. "It doesn't matter. But I can tell you one thing: By now, you are certainly the last of your kind."

Donnie goes numb. Of course: If Hiroto set the trap here, the Foot Clan will be striking the Hamatos in New York.

Donnie surges with adrenaline cut by an undercurrent of anxiety. "You could never take down my brothers."

Hiroto shrugs. "Believe what you want. It doesn't matter anymore."

Splinter steps forward. "Do you have so little honor?"

Hiroto considers this. "I honestly don't know. That's a question for my mother, and my grandfather. Too bad you can't ask them. But really, what does honor matter if none of you are left to scold me about it?"

Donnie does not believe for a second that the Foot Clan has already triumphed over Leo and Mikey and the entire Hamato strike team. He can see a future where they defeat Hiroto and his men and fly back to New York in time to shore up the defenses around the lair and the compound. Of course, there are infinite futures, and in many of them, his brothers are already dead. He can practically hear Raphael rolling his eyes at the stretch of his imagination into multiverse theory. With a single breath, his mind clears. There is only the present moment, perched on a blade's edge. Time slows. A light snow begins to fall, nothing more than brilliant motes in the brightening morning.

"Anyway, rat," Hiroto says, "we all have a role to play. Yours is to join your children in death. It's nothing personal. It just *is*."

Splinter frees his katana. The old master moves with the swiftness of a fighter half his age. Steel flashes. Ambassador Hara and his two delegates fall to their knees. A moment later, three heads spill forward from three necks and tumble to the ground. The air is a red mist.

Splinter's katana is parallel to the earth. His other arm extends toward the tree line. "Oroku Hiroto, while you still breathe, you will call me *Master Splinter*."

Hiroto laughs. "Grand warriors of the Foot Clan—*attack!*"

The field of the dead comes alive. Hidden doors in snow-covered crypts, hatches in the earth, false gravestones. Foot soldiers swarm from all sides, their cylindrical helmets puffing steam through vertical slits. Dozens of blades flash. Donnie notes the traditional weapons, the spear-like naginata and the curved ninjatō sword, juxtaposed with the soldiers' modern cold-weather fabrics.

He turns to one of the Hamato warriors who escorted them. "Go back to the village for reinforcements. We'll hold them off till you return."

The warrior hesitates. "I cannot abandon Master Shinichiro."

The old man barks a command. "Go!"

The warrior bows quickly and rushes from the clearing, opening up a Foot soldier's belly with a swipe of his blade as he runs. Entrails steam in the snow. Donnie twirls his bō with easy flips of his wrist as he watches through narrowed eyes. The soldiers are nearly upon them.

"Show them no mercy!" Splinter calls out.

"Not a problem," Donnie says. "Mikey was right. Orokus are all liars. We never should've trusted Hiroto."

Splinter takes a running leap off a grave marker. As he comes down, his katana cleaves the helmet of a Foot soldier. Splinter withdraws the blade, lands in a crouch, and spins. A soldier drops his ninjatō and clutches his throat as if trying to contain the blood that pours over his fingers to stain the snow.

"I would not have brought a weapon if I trusted him," Splinter says. Donnie moves like a whirlwind. He cuts a ragged swath through the cemetery, his footwork churning the crimson snow. Subtle applications of his body weight imbue his staff with the deadly power of an edged weapon. He breaks ribs and crushes windpipes. Bodies crumple at his feet. A soldier wielding a kama—a short scythe—feints with his blade then delivers a swift kick that Donnie barely manages to parry with his bō. An ankle snaps like a crisp celery stalk breaking in two. The soldier stays upright on one leg and swings the kama. Donnie catches it with his bō, flips it out of the soldier's hands, and knocks him out cold with a kick to the jaw.

He pauses to get his bearings. His mind races with strategic calculations. Hiroto and his guardsmen have retreated out of the fray to the margins of the cemetery. They watch from their horses while their standards flap in the wind.

Splinter darts among enemies with balletic grace. Donnie marvels at his father's fluidity. With great economy of motion, the mutant rat sweeps the legs of one soldier, cuts his throat where he lies, and then flings himself at two others, stunning them with a flurry of jab-like kicks before stabbing one through the heart and decapitating the other.

Splinter's voice echoes clear across the cemetery. "If you choose not to stand aside and allow me access to your master, I will cut my own path!"

Donnie sprints ahead to join his father. Sensing his presence without looking, Splinter crouches as Donnie thrusts his bō through the empty air above his father's head. The staff meets the exposed neck of a Foot soldier and the man staggers away. Splinter removes the man's left foot with a swipe of his katana. The man shrieks at his exposed bone. Splinter rises to his full height and drives his blade through the man's heart.

"These guys are seriously lacking discipline," Donnie says. He flings a gangly soldier to one side with his bō. The man flees. He joins his father at a blood-soaked gravestone, so weathered the name of the dead has worn away.

"But not numbers," Splinter says.

"Splinter-san is right." Shinichiro, breathing hard, reaches their side. "We must not let our guard down. By now my men will be riding back from the village."

The remaining Foot soldiers rally around Hiroto and the other horsemen. One group hangs back to guard their leader while a second wave charges.

Splinter rushes out to meet them. "Keep pressing forward, my son!"

Donnie has never seen his father possessed with such feral, single-minded intensity. A cold knot of worry forms in his chest. How many times has Splinter warned his children against letting their emotions guide their tactics? He flanks around a scarred obelisk and confronts

a fighter wielding a pair of short swords. With one eye on his father, he blocks a downward slice with his bō. The short sword slides down the staff and opens a gash in his hand. Blood spurts from the wound. Enraged, Donnie shoves the fighter back with a flat-soled kick to the chest. Then he leaps upon him. All notions of technique and restraint desert him. Again and again, he raises the bō and brings it down. The fighter collapses. The swords fall from his grasp. The staff caves in his helmet. Bits of skull emerge from the slurry of hair and scalp. Brain matter speckles Donnie's tunic. He flashes to his brothers and finds that he's screaming himself hoarse.

A burst of searing heat explodes in his thigh. There is a wounded Foot soldier crumpled at his feet. He had not even seen the man. Now the hilt of a small knife protrudes from his leg. He rips it out, ignoring the pain, and drives the blade into the soldier's eye. The man twitches and goes limp.

Donnie turns to see Hiroto remove his mask. The master of the Foot Clan is a mere boy. He knew this, of course, but it's jarring to see the face of a smiling child overseeing the morning's carnage.

"You know nothing of honor!" Splinter cries out.

Hiroto's smile widens. He puts his arms out in an exaggerated shrug. "Welcome to the new world, rat. Everyone you've ever known and loved is dead."

"Then I have nothing left to lose!" Splinter raises his gore-spattered katana. Dead soldiers litter the ground at his feet. His fur is matted with sweat and blood. "Come and face me like a true warrior, boy! Meet your fate at my blade like your grandfather before you!"

"Sure," Hiroto says. He gestures to one of the samurai on horseback, who raises a small horn to his lips. The single note resounds across the clearing.

Donnie sees the men emerge from the trees and take positions beyond the last row of grave markers. His body floods with adrenaline and fear. "Father!" he calls out. "Get behind me!"

But Splinter does not heed him. Donnie wonders if he hears or sees anything at all besides Hiroto.

"Archers!" Hiroto calls out.

The newly arrived soldiers raise their longbows and nock their arrows.

Donnie races to shield his father. At the same time, Splinter launches his katana like a javelin. "For my family!"

Hiroto's arm comes down. "*Loose!*"

The volley of arrows arcs into the morning sky. Donnie reaches Splinter at the same time his father's katana strikes Hiroto's left shoulder. Hiroto screams. A second volley goes up while the first noses down toward the middle of the cemetery.

The first arrow bites into Donnie's forearm. The second just above his knee.

"My son!" Splinter calls out. Commanding himself to float above the pain, Donnie looks back at his father. Splinter takes one arrow to the chest, then another to the side of his neck. Donnie reaches for his father. An arrow strikes his belly and grinds against the bone of his hip. Agony flares and his vision blurs. He can't believe it has come to this. Part of him is still floating above it all while his body absorbs arrow after arrow. He can see their shafts protruding from his flesh. The pain fades to a dull hammering blow each time a new arrow finds its mark. It is all happening so fast. He watches Splinter fall to his knees, then collapse face-first into the snow. He tries to speak but blood rises in his throat and pours from his mouth. If only he had more time. All around him, arrows rain down on Foot soldiers. Hiroto is killing his own men, too. Donatello's hatred for this kind of dispassionate slaughter is a pure white light that expands like the rays of the sun across the cemetery to the mountains beyond. The arrows no longer announce themselves with pain. He is down in the snow, but it is not cold. He watches Hiroto pull the blade from his shoulder. His armor has protected him. Hiroto tosses Splinter's katana to the ground like trash. Donatello is simultaneously within his body and without, drifting like smoke above the forest. He can see the Hamato reinforcements arrive to chase Hiroto and the Foot Clan from the field of battle. He realizes that Hiroto had not been lying: His brothers are here, too, in this strange new place, and he opens his mouth to tell them he has come to join them.

33

"AND THAT WAS IT," Michelangelo says. "Shinichiro lived to tell the tale. Donnie and Splinter didn't. I went to Japan seeking the last of my family, only to find ashes and my father's journal. I was too late to save them, or even be there with them at the end."

Mike's shoulders slump. Telling the tale has sapped his energy. He's put himself in the minds of his brothers a million times. Lived the last moments of their lives as if they were his own. It always carves out a little piece of him, expands the hollow in his soul. He sits down in April's swivel chair, lets out a breath. All around him, visions of snow linger like TV static. He blinks to clear them away.

"Master Shinichiro offered to let me stay there with the clan. But all those warriors only reminded me of everything I'd lost. So I turned toward the mountains and just started walking."

April pulls up a chair of her own. He sits in a kind of stunned silence while she cries softly. No tears come to his own eyes. None left, he figures.

"If I knew you were alive, April, it might've been different. I could have stopped Hiroto before it got to this, maybe. I don't know. I'm sorry."

"Don't, Mikey." She picks up a rag and wipes her eyes. "There's no way you could have known. You're here now, that's what counts." She tosses the rag on the table next to Fugitoid's dormant head. "And the way Casey Marie has taken to you—it's amazing to watch. I've never seen her connect with anyone like that." She takes his hand.

Mike hesitates. He thinks back to Casey on the bench, adding plate after plate to the barbell like it was nothing. "Listen, April. About that . . ." He doesn't know how to bring this up. Easy enough to just keep his mouth shut. But it's already spilling out. He has to know. "Don't take this the wrong way." He can hear Raphael snicker quietly. "But that connection—is it, I don't know, by design, somehow?"

She narrows her eyes. "I don't understand what you mean."

Mike sighs. No going back now. "I mean, *your* design."

She frowns, shaking her head.

"Casey has extra abilities, April!"

She withdraws her hand and gets up from the chair.

"The first time I had her in an armlock, if she'd had a bit more training and knew anything about leverage, she could have broken my grip. I could sense her strength, all coiled up inside her." April turns her back to him. He rises from his seat. "I can lift a motorcycle with one hand. She shouldn't have been able to so much as *wiggle*." He pauses. "And there aren't enough weights in the gym for her to bench-press. She's too strong for a human." April's head bows. Her hands go to her face. Her silence stokes his anger and his weariness drops away. "Did you think I wouldn't figure it out? I'm the one training her. Every day I see her do things she shouldn't be able to do. Why would you keep that from me?"

He watches as she shakes her head. "I wasn't keeping it from you. Not exactly."

"You didn't *inject* her, did you?"

April wheels around. "*Hell no!*" Her prosthetic finger jabs his chest. "You know me better than that. I would never do that to my child."

"Then what the hell's going on?"

She musses her hair on one side then tucks it behind her ear. "You don't want to know."

"Would you just tell me?"

She takes a breath. "I've run thousands of tests on her since I first noticed she was different. As far as I can tell, trace amounts of mutagen were passed on to her from her birth parents—who happened to have nearly lifelong exposure to it from the company they kept."

Ghosts erupt into chatter in his head. He shoves away his brothers' voices, trying to grasp her meaning. "Wait, *us*? Seriously? We *contaminated* you?"

His brothers go silent. Their combined angst gathers between his eyes. His head aches.

"You didn't know, Mikey! None of us did."

"Shit, April." He looks at his palms, the leathery reptilian flesh scored in lines of age. Massive hands, thick fingers, not quite like anything else on Earth. He doesn't remember life as a baby turtle. His entire consciousness has been shaped by mutation. He raises his eyes to April's. "Does she know?"

"I can tell she's becoming aware that she's different, but I haven't told her everything."

At this, his brothers make their outrage known. Mike grimaces in pain. "She has to be told the truth."

"Soon, Mikey. I promise. The thing is, she's already reckless. I don't want her thinking she's invincible."

He weighs her words. Then he shrugs. "She's your kid."

"Thank you," April says. "Now, I need to get some food in me, and a few gallons of coffee. We can talk more in the kitchen. I have some friends coming over later that I want you to meet."

34

THE WAR ROOM IS an offshoot of the lair, a musty chamber Leonardo once crammed with monitors tuned to local news and weather. Now the big clunky screens sit dormant. A dozen members of the resistance's top brass gather near a table papered with city maps and blueprints. Behind them, a whiteboard on wheels is shoved up against the wall. Next to the whiteboard, a vending machine's smeared glass displays empty compartments.

"What happened to all the snacks?" Raph says.

"I remember hauling that stupid thing down here," Donnie says. "I forget why we even did that."

Leo sighs with pleasure. "Good to see the old whiteboard again."

Raph snorts. "Here we go. You love that goddamn whiteboard."

"It's a war room!" Leo says. "You gotta have a whiteboard."

Mike lets them talk. Their chatter soaks him in nostalgia, and it gives him a pleasant shiver. He'd forgotten about this place. It's like opening up a hidden door in his mind, stepping back into a better time. The four of them sharing a pie from Antonio's, Leo yelling at Raph for wiping grease on a rare blueprint of the Cloisters, Donnie laughing at some late-night public access show on one of those old-school TVs.

"Hey." Casey Marie rushes into the room and bops him on the shoulder.

Mike tries not betray that he knows a secret that concerns her. He feels like she can see through him—into his head, into his heart. "Hey."

"Smooth," Raph says.

Leo agrees. "Very natural."

Casey shoulders past him to the map table. A middle-aged man with a steel-gray beard and a bit of a paunch gives her a nod. Like the other resistance leaders, he wears fatigues. He clears his throat.

"For those who don't know me"—he glances at Mike—"I'm Commander Avallone."

He recognizes the name from April's lightning-round briefing on the resistance. Avallone is the ostensible leader, now that the disparate groups are making efforts to coordinate operations. The commander opens a manila folder and scatters photographs across the table.

"He should be using the whiteboard," Leo says. "Then everybody could see."

"Why don't you marry the whiteboard?" Donnie says.

"We've distilled years of surveillance down to inform a fairly linear operation," Avallone begins. One of the photos catches Mike's eye. He picks it up. It's an aerial image of a familiar strip of land in the East River—Roosevelt Island—except the landscape has been completely remade. Parks, schools, restaurants, the communities of Northtown and Southtown, all the people who lived there—all gone. What remains is a fortress surrounded by rubble. It brings him back to Master Splinter's history books, grainy photos of bleak European battlefields pocked with shell holes and trenches.

"Shit," Mike says.

"Usually people save their complaints until *after* I outline the plan," Avallone says.

"Sorry." Mike tosses the photo on the table. "I'd heard about Stockman's base, but I didn't realize he leveled the whole island to build it." He rubs his eyes. Every new and dismal piece of New York that reveals itself gives him a migraine.

"His lack of respect for historical preservation is surely his greatest crime," Avallone says, giving Mike a withering stare.

Mike puts up his hands. "Sorry, Commander. Please, continue."

Avallone nods and glances around the room. "We have enough rafts with cloaking devices to get our squads in position on the shoreline completely unseen."

"What happens when we get there?" Casey asks. "Cloaking devices are good, but once we hit the beach, Stockman'll be able to see us."

Avallone doesn't look annoyed by Casey's interruption. He gestures to an Afro-Latino man with the name Zaragoza stenciled on his fatigues.

"Some potential good news here," Zaragoza says. "From what we can tell, Stockman's external security seems fairly limited. I honestly believe he thinks no one would dare mount a serious attack on the island."

"They're going to get themselves killed," Donnie says.

Leo agrees. "They're underestimating Stockman because they want this to work so bad."

"So," Mike says to the room, "you're saying you really have no idea what kind of weaponry he has hidden away, or what kinds of traps he might have waiting on the perimeter of the island."

Another resistance lieutenant groans.

Avallone huffs. "Something you want to add, Carlson?"

"Yeah." Carlson's a short, squat, dark-haired woman with a thick Bronx accent. She pushes past Zaragoza and Avallone to glare up at Michelangelo. He notes the scar on the side of her face, a wet-looking mass marring her left cheek. "All due respect, but you haven't been here five minutes." She looks to Avallone. "Who's leading this mission, you or the turtle?"

"I'm not leading anything," Mike says. "But I've faced Stockman before. Many times. I know how dangerous he is."

"So do we."

"You got eyes inside that fortress?"

"We inventoried everything he imported to the island over the last decade. O'Neil's been figuring out what he might've been building."

"So, the answer is no. Every aspect of this plan is guesswork."

"Nothing wrong with that," Raph says.

"I heard Hiroto threw your ass out of his tower," Carlson says. Her face is flushed. The scar darkens to a deep crimson. She looks again at Avallone. "We taking orders from you or him now?"

Mike slams a fist down on the table. The wood shatters, spilling photos and maps onto the floor. The room goes silent. "I'm trying to keep you alive," he says. "All of you."

"Simmer down," April says, laying a hand on Mike's shoulder.

"Now they *have* to use the whiteboard," Leo says.

"Sorry about the table," Mike says. He turns to address Carlson. "You're right. You've been putting in work out in the streets while I've been MIA."

She shows her hands in a gesture of apology and backs away.

"We good?" Avallone asks.

"What happens if Hiroto sends reinforcements to the island?" Mike asks.

"There's no love lost between Stockman and Hiroto," April says. "They consider their partnership a necessary evil. Stockman isn't going to reach out for help except as a last resort. Maybe not even then. Hiroto would lord it over him forever."

Mike wants to point out that this is more specious reasoning based on armchair psychology. But he holds his tongue.

"Once our advance teams hit the beach," Avallone says, "they'll lay down suppression fire from various key positions so that Stockman won't know which direction the real threat is coming from.

And we finally have our own direct communications system up and running, so we'll be able to keep tight with all our movements."

Zaragoza kneels down and hands the mess of photos to Avallone. The commander shuffles them, finds what he's looking for, and holds up a top-down shot. Someone else passes him a dry-erase marker. Avallone draws on the photograph as he speaks. The photograph bends at awkward angles.

"Don't even say it," Raph says. Leo grumbles.

"While the first wave is keeping Stockman's defenses busy"— Avallone marks one corner of the map—"our second wave will blow the main doors on the south side of the building, as well as smaller entrances on the east, west, and north sides. Once we've completely overwhelmed any remaining exterior guards and taken out what we believe to be gun towers in the south, half of each squad will be ready to breach."

"What if the doors can't be blown?" Leo's voice asks. Mike repeats the question out loud.

"In the unlikely event that we have any difficulties with the doors," Avallone says, "we have secondary wall breach options here, here, and here." He draws three circles on the photograph. "Satisfactory?"

Leo's ghost has nothing to say. Mike shrugs.

Avallone continues. "Once the teams are inside Stockman's compound, the striker airborne squad will drop in to support the ground teams, as well as cut off enough of the power systems to repel any counterattack while we complete phase two."

"Airborne?" Mike asks. "You have a plane to drop skydivers from?"

Zaragoza says, "We don't have any planes, no. That's why our airborne unit will be climbing to the eastern side of the Manhattan wall and deploying to Roosevelt via enhanced wingsuits. O'Neil will pick up the briefing from here."

Mike lets out a dark laugh, echoed in his mind by Raph's cackles at the absurdity of this mission.

Zaragoza grimaces. Condescension creeps into his reply. "Absent a plane, which we don't have, BASE jumping via wingsuit is not only our best option, but our only one. Unless you have a better plan, that's how it's going to be. Now, O'Neil, the floor is yours."

"Thank you, Commander Zaragoza." April pauses, shooting Mike a look. "When everything is knocked out, I'll be rolling through the main gates in the AFV—that's our armored fighting vehicle—and heading straight for the largest generator I can find. We're going to need all the power we can get to reactivate the Fugitoid's head. Once he's fully powered on, we should be able to communicate directly with Professor Honeycutt's consciousness, get him to access Stockman's network, and take full control from there."

"Thank you," Zaragoza says. "Taking control of Stockman's network is our key objective, people. He designed all of Hiroto's systems, from the robot army to the toaster in his kitchen. If we can find a back door, and I'm confident we can, we'll hobble the Foot Clan. And then we can finally take this city back."

"And what if we can't wake Professor Honeycutt?" Michelangelo asks.

"Then we go to plan B," April says. "We blow up as much of the place as we can on our way out and start the fight all over again the next day."

"This is so not good, bro," Raph says.

"What are you talking about?" Donnie says. "This is exactly the kind of plan you lived for. Run at the bad guy, break stuff, see how it shakes out."

"Maybe," Raph says. "But that don't mean I think it's the right kinda plan here. Stockman's a crazy genius, and I don't think these guys know what they're walkin' into."

"I can't believe I'm saying this, Mikey, but Raph's right." Donnie says. "What do you think, Leo?"

"I think it's gonna be a bloodbath. But it's already in motion. They're going to attack with or without you, Mikey—and they have better odds *with* you."

"I know," Mike says to his brothers. "What am I gonna do, sit around the lair while they go out and die?"

"Thank you for that vote of confidence," Avallone says.

"Inside voice, bro," Donnie says.

"Goddammit." Mike looks at the commander. "Sorry. I just meant, I'm in."

April shakes her head. Casey gives him a curious look.

Raphael laughs. "Maybe if you ask that Zaragoza guy real nice, he'll give you one of them wingsuits."

35

ROOSEVELT ISLAND, A NARROW strip of land that splits the East River between Manhattan's Upper East Side and western Queens, has blossomed and withered over the centuries. Mike remembers exploring the ruins of the Smallpox Hospital on the island's southern tip, vaulting over fallen masonry, interpreting bygone graffiti tags like cave drawings. Donnie had played the tour guide that long-ago night, droning on about the many hospitals and the prisons that had once operated on "Welfare Island". But by the time he and his brothers set foot there, massive, looming apartment buildings had sprung up all over the island. New development projects grabbing scarce city land. The island's northern tip boasted a park with a lighthouse.

Now the lighthouse is gone. Mike imagines Stockman's robots toppling it into the fetid river. Maybe the low concrete slab he's hunkered behind had once been its foundation. He doesn't know. Doesn't care. There is only the assault, the relentless need that whispers: *Keep going.*

Next to him, Breaker raises his head to peek above the crumbling parapet. Mike grabs the shoulder of his body armor and yanks him back down. An instant later, a directed-energy blast splinters the concrete where his head had been. A striker on Breaker's left cries out and slaps a hand to his face. Mike curses. Shrapnel. The assault's barely five minutes old and they're already taking injuries.

"Man," Breaker says. His eyes are wide. Combat isn't what he expected. Mike figures it's something generations of soldiers have discovered the hard way. Dreamt-of glory doesn't mean shit when you're pinned down in the muck, surrounded by the screams of your buddies. "Why the hell did we come in at the northern end?"

"You think the south is a whole lot more chill, Break?" Scrape asks. Mike glances to his right. Casey, her crew, a handful of strikers in full armor—all of them taking cover. Casey's aped Mike's look: lightly armored black bodysuit, boots, belt filled with low-yield explosives and smoke bombs, and a thin black mask that he'd gifted her during a training session. Bitter thoughts creep in as bright red pulses sizzle across the top of the wall. He's her sensei and he's landed her in this shit.

Nobody moves. Mike swivels his head. The river creeps along in glacial swirls, sludge curling around sludge.

"It's our job to take out anything that can sneak-attack the other units as they come in," Casey says to Breaker. Mike takes in the tone of her voice. Steady, slightly quick patter. Tamping down her nerves, focusing on the nuts and bolts of the mission to quell fear. "Relax, Break. You're with the A-Team here. We got this."

"Don't jinx yourself, Jones." Breaker clutches his pulse rifle like it's more weapon than he's comfortable with.

"Jinxes are bullshit," Casey says.

"Stay frosty," Mike says. "Stockman's gonna be throwing whatever he's got at us."

"*Stay frosty,*" Raph mimics.

"I've always wanted to say that," Leo chimes in. "Never got the chance."

Mike ignores his brothers. He taps the comm unit on his belt. "April. This is Michelangelo. You in position?"

Garbled static hisses through the comm. April's voice is buried in there somewhere.

"April? April! Come in!" Nothing. He punches the concrete slab, makes a knuckle-shaped dent.

"Whoa," Crunch says. "Easy."

"Bad idea," he mutters. "This whole goddamn mission."

"She'll be here," Casey assures him. "In the meantime, we can take out those tower guns. Half the crew circles to the right and the other half—"

"No." Mike cuts her off.

Casey's eyes narrow. "Sensei, we have a job to do."

"Lay down suppression fire and wait for my signal."

"Mikey, hey," Leo says. "Take a step back."

"You're not flying solo here," Donnie says. "You can't just stash her behind this wall."

"Drop smoke," Mike tells the assembled team. "Lots of it."

He leaps over the concrete slab. Behind him, Casey calls out orders. The bursts from the tower guns track him in seconds. Now he can see the walls of Stockman's compound rising above the blasted landscape. Reading the trajectory of the pulses, he dives, rolls, finds cover behind a pile of bricks. The beams corrupt the island's bad air, flitting so close he can feel their heat. A crimson bolt catches him in the side of his left thigh. Body armor and fabric disintegrate in its wake. The glancing blow scorches his tough skin. He dismisses the pain.

Smoke bombs erupt. Black clouds drift across what used to be Northtown. The tower guns go quiet. Recalibrating their targeting, Mike figures. They won't stay down for long. Thin rifle pulses from Casey and her crew fizzle against the compound walls.

"Some kinda shield is displacing the beams," Donnie says. Mike peers through the dense smoke creeping across the battlefield. To his right, a system of haphazard trenches runs to the river. It's as if a giant claw has raked the ground. He hits the dirt and army-crawls, staying flat to the earth, keeping rubble between him and the compound wall. The smoke envelops him. In darkness, the ground drops away before him. His hand finds empty space. He propels himself forward and tumbles into a trench. His shell hits the ancient roots of dead trees. Leaping to his feet, he feels suddenly young and alive. Despite the horrors of this place, it beats sitting around the lair and hiding in the sewers, waiting. When three bone-white androids emerge from the smoke, he smiles. He draws his tonfa and his body feels like it's glowing as he attacks them before they can level their small-caliber weapons. Lightly armored scouts, he figures. Their guns fire. Bullets slam into the walls of the trench. Mike works in close, dispensing surgical tonfa strikes. The androids come apart. Too easy. In seconds the trench floor is littered with components. He wades through a pile of scrap.

"Don't get cocky," Leo warns.

Just ahead, smoke wreathes a pale white object that hovers above the trench. Mike readies himself for flying attackers. Mousers, or something worse. Then the object advances and the smoke wisps away like bits of torn fabric.

"That's a new one."

The robot sentry is twelve feet tall. Six crab-like legs clank as it wends its way through the trench. Two arms extend from a torso that rotates atop its lower half like some hellish bug's abdomen. Each arm culminates in a bladelike point.

Mike tucks away the tonfa and draws Leo's broken katana and Raph's sai.

"Damn straight," Raph says.

Mike notes vulnerabilities in the robot. Joints, articulations, mechanical weaknesses.

"Prepare to be eliminated," the robot says in a soulless voice.

Donnie laughs. "Why did Stockman program all these things to talk?"

A panel opens in the front of the robot's round featureless head and a long gun emerges. Mike rushes forward. The first blast singes his shoulder. He weaves across the smoky trench as the pulse rifle chatters. His brothers' weapons are hot in his hands, their blades quivering like hummingbirds. Then he leaps. Bright red bursts send clods of dirt flying in his wake. He plunges the splintered blade into a mass of lights in the center of the robot's chest. Sparks fly. He wraps an arm around the metal torso, ramming the sai into a vent at its back. The robot's upper body swings viciously back and forth. Mike's legs sail out behind him as he clings on. Held fast by the sai, he withdraws the broken katana. Severed wires fray and dance in the sparks. Again and again, he drives the blade into the robot's power supply. The gun stops firing. The panel slams shut. The crab legs stagger and the massive sentry begins to tilt. Mike tries to pull Raph's sai out of the vent but it won't budge. He refuses to leave his brother's weapon behind. The crab legs buckle. The metal body groans as it sinks into the trench. His shell scrapes against the packed earth of the wall. With a scream he pulls the sai free and scrambles away—

Except an immense pressure on his leg holds him in place. He stows the weapons and claws at the earth. But the crab leg comes down on him as the robot crumples into a gnarled fist of broken metal. He knows he's strong enough to free himself. But there's no leverage in the tight quarters of the trench.

"You got this, Mikey," Leo says. "Brace your back against the ground and find a better grip."

Mike grits his teeth. "Thanks." He strains against the cold metal.

Beyond the wrecked sentry, mechanical footfalls resound. He presses his body up against the implacable crab leg. It must weigh a thousand pounds. Through the maze of twisted metal, he spots two more android sentries. He throws an arm behind him, winces at the bad angle. He can't reach his tonfa.

Suddenly there's a flash of movement in the smoke.

"I got you, Sensei."

"Goddammit, Casey—get out of here."

He watches her scramble through gaps between the fallen robot's legs, quick as a rabbit darting into its warren. The two sentries fire. Shots ping off the dead robot. Casey strikes the first one with a kick that takes its head off.

"Good form," Leo says. The second sentry releases a volley of tiny missiles. Thin white contrails paint the air. Casey flanks around the first sentry and the missiles impact the headless robot. Casey dives out of the way. Mike averts his eyes at the flare of the explosion. He turns back in time to see Casey plant her hand on the ground and spin to her feet with a windmill kick like a breakdancer. The sentry lunges at her, swinging a bladed hand. She feints and dances behind it, aiming a kick into its lower back. As the robot bends, she takes it by the arm and flings it against the wall. It lands in a smoking heap.

"I think she's better than you, bro," Raph says.

"Student becomes the master," Donnie says.

Mike struggles to free himself. The muscles of his upper back go numb. "Shut up."

Casey works her way back through the twisted limbs. She lunges, bracing her back foot against metal. Together, they shift the massive limb, and the pressure against Mike's leg eases. He slides out from under the fallen robot. He takes stock of his ankle and knee. Joints intact. Nothing broken.

Casey extends an arm. He gazes up at her. "I thought I told you to stay put."

"You did. I didn't listen."

He waits a moment, then takes her hand and stands. "Don't do that again. Understood?"

"Yes, Sensei . . ."

36

"DÉJÀ VU," DONNIE SAYS. Mike and Casey Marie, along with her crew, are stranded behind a retaining wall on the west side of the island. They've been playing decoy, moving through trenches and craters, drawing out defenses, so Commander Avallone's forces can focus on breaching the gates of the fortress.

"See, if you'd used the whiteboard . . ." Leo says.

"I wish we were still alive so I could kill you," Raph says.

Explosions shake the island. Dirt and gravel rain down on their heads. The turret guns atop the compound shoot bursts that sweep across the rubble-strewn expanse. Mike's body stings where pulse blasts have grazed his flesh. He looks at Crunch. The big man's face is a mask of dirt and sweat. Crunch turns over on his belly, jabs his pulse rifle through a gap in the ruined wall, and fires. Then he turns back around, shaking his head.

"These pulse rifles don't do shit."

"Not against that shield," Breaker says.

"It's like we're shooting pop guns at a tank," Scrape says.

"Pop guns?" Casey says.

"Scrape was born in the fifties," Breaker says. "But yeah." He slaps the side of his rifle. "Pop gun."

"I'm working on it," Lug says quietly. Mike swivels his head to the unassuming man in goggles and a hood. The pulse rifle is disassembled in his lap. A case of pocket-size tools is open at his side. He works at the insides of the rifle with a pair of tweezers that emit a soft blue light and jabs at circuitry like he's a picky eater selecting the choice bits.

"This is why I like blades and batons," Mike says. "You don't have to perform surgery on your weapons."

A massive explosion sends their hands covering their heads. Clods of displaced earth arc up over the retaining wall. Lug continues his work unfazed.

"Guy's cool under pressure," Donnie says. Mike can feel his brother admiring the handiwork, one machine freak to another.

Scrape shifts his massive bulk. "Whatcha doin' there, Lug?"

"Making improvements."

"Great," Scrape says, handing over his rifle. "Do mine, too." An artillery round lands nearby. Shrapnel batters the wall. Everyone curls inward, waiting out the rain of debris.

Mike takes in Casey and her crew. The rest of the strikers have been dispatched to strategic positions up and down the island. The whole squad is stretched thin. He keys his comm. "Avallone, this is Michelangelo, do you read? Over."

Nothing but static. He imagines the wingsuit team getting torn to pieces by those tower guns, bodies hitting the dirt like sacks of meat. If he doesn't take out those turrets, the whole mission goes up in flames. And everybody dies.

"Yo, Lug," he says, "can you make this goddamn radio work?"

Lug doesn't look away from his pulse rifle. Circuitry unfurls across his lap. He selects a pair of needle-nose pliers from his kit and snips a yellow wire. Mike shakes his head. He's half convinced this guy's just improvising.

One of the turrets opens up. He feels the pulse impact the island in little staccato quakes. Screams drift across the rubble.

Casey turns to him. "What's the plan, Sensei?"

Mike thinks fast. "There's gotta be a manual override, some way to kill that shield."

"Yeah," Donnie points out, "buried somewhere deep inside the compound."

Mike jabs his finger into the comm button again and again. "April. April, come in." Nothing. He growls in frustration.

"I can't reach anyone," he yells to Casey. "Where the hell is your mom?"

"She'll be here! She knows what she's doing. We just gotta focus on what we can control."

Mike gives her a nod. The girl's cool head under fire is an asset, but he wonders what will happen when the trauma she's put a lid on boils over. He thinks of her parents and suddenly sees food spilled across a dining room floor. Memories of Casey and April's Thanksgiving come and go, the last time they were all together.

A strange hissing sound brings him back to the present.

Lug is crouched behind a small V-shaped gap in the wall, firing his pulse rifle. The recoil knocks his whole body backward. He situates himself and fires. Again, the kick sends him reeling.

Breaker peers through a crack. "Holy shit." He steps aside so Mike can take a look. Lug fires again. Mike watches the compound take the hit. At the point of impact, the shield burns white. There's a split second of pushback, then the pulse impacts the wall of the compound. Bits of Stockman's sleek, ugly polymer splinter off into the ashen sky.

Donnie shouts his approval. Mike grimaces at the pain in his head.

"Better give me that before it blows your ass into the river," Crunch says. Lug hands over the pulse rifle.

The roof turrets' heavy guns open up. Mike braces himself, but the impacts are distant.

"South end of the island," Scrape says.

Mike nods. "Locking on to Avallone's troops." He thinks for a moment. "Lug, can you mod the rest of the rifles?"

Lug grabs Crunch's rifle and begins opening a panel.

"Right," Mike says. "Do that. The rest of you, keep up suppression fire on the walls and anything else Stockman throws your way. We gotta draw some of the heat from the southern front."

Casey asks, "What about you, Sensei?"

Now he wishes she would quit calling him that. "I'm gonna go deal with those tower guns so the air team doesn't get shredded."

"I'm coming with you."

"No, you're gonna stay here, keep up suppression fire, and work on getting your mother on the comms."

"You'd still be stuck under that robot if it wasn't for me," she points out.

Mike frowns. "That won't happen again."

"Not specifically that! But something will. Something always does." The planes of her face go taut and he sees her father in her cheekbones.

"I need you here to protect your crew."

Scrape laughs. "We're good, Sensei."

Mike ignores him. "I need you to guide them, Casey."

"Bro," Crunch says. "We know what we're doing."

"Yeah," Breaker says. "She can go with you. We'll hold it down."

Mike glares at him until he averts his eyes. "Fine," Mike says. "But tell Zaragoza to hold off on the airborne drop until we give the okay."

"Roger that," Breaker says.

Casey shoulders her rifle. "Covering fire, guys. Don't mess this up."

37

THE UPPER WALLS OF Stockman's fortress are ridged with polymer, uneven battlements carved by a madman's hand. Mike kneels at the edge of a tiered crenellation, reaches down, and clasps Casey's wrist. With a single effortless lift, he deposits her on the rooftop at his side. The moment her feet land her eyes go wide.

"Synja!" She fumbles with her rifle.

Mike wheels around and unleashes a shuriken before he can even register the android's approach. The silver star whirls through the moonlit gloom. The black-clad android's red eyes level an unblinking gaze as it sprints toward their position.

The throwing star passes through the synja as if it's an apparition. The robot does not stop.

"What the hell?"

Casey fires her weapon. Perfect shot, center mass. The red pulse follows the star through the synja's chest.

Mike recalls the streets of Manhattan, the garish advertisements that peel off the sides of buildings to leer at passersby. Cartoon milk cartons, happy little antidepressants, mustached beer dudes. He relaxes.

"Holo-ninja."

Casey doesn't lower her weapon. "You gotta be kidding me."

The synja expands to fill his vision—then vanishes. At a distant point on the rooftop, the holo-ninja respawns and begins its loop anew.

"Means Stockman's bringing his entire force to bear on the troops down below," Mike says.

Mike gets his bearings. From his vantage point on the summit of the outer wall, the compound's layout resembles a cramped military base. Spotlights draw lazy circles against wisps of dissipating smoke. Rows of Quonset huts give way to hangars and barracks armored in drab gray polymer and steel. One cylindrical building bristles with antennas and satellite dishes. Another emits a shifting, iridescent darkness that makes his eyes hurt.

"Some kind of dazzle camouflage," Donnie says. He can sense his brothers' ghosts all around him, roaming the rooftop, keeping watch.

"Um." Casey points into the sky to the west, toward the Manhattan wall. "We got a problem."

Mike follows her gesture to a mass of floating specks barely touched by moonlight. Their progress is achingly slow, two dozen fighters plastered against the night sky. Beyond the airborne team, the lights of Foot City seem to hover in the smog, indistinct as traffic in a rainstorm.

"I told those guys to hold off the assault!" Mike growls. Tension gnaws at his mind. The dominoes are falling, everything racing toward the inevitable bloodbath. "Stupid attack plan!"

"Easy, Sensei," Casey says, "it's not their fault. Comms are probably jammed across the board."

"Better hurry," Donnie urges him. "Wind currents are strong. The airborne team's gonna be in range of those guns in no time."

Across the rooftops, the turret gun swivels to draw a bead on the specks in the sky. Mike grabs his tonfa and activates the EMP. The gun emplacement keeps moving. Either the range is too limited or the cannons are operating on a frequency immune to his weapon's pulse.

"Michelangelo," Leo's voice rings out. "*Move.*"

His brother's tone cuts through the noise in his head. Some things never change. He turns to Casey. In his peripheral vision, the holo-synja comes at them, red eyes glitching. He ignores it.

"Can you take that one?" he points to a turret about a hundred yards down the battlements.

"Yes, Sensei." No hesitation. He meets her eager eyes. The last vestiges of his anxious protectiveness fall away like moorings from a dock. Casey's not as fragile as a human. And it's up to the two of them to prevent a massacre. He reaches into his belt and produces a half dozen grenades the size of golf balls. He gives her five. "Give them a little twist to arm them." He mimes the motion. "Then you got three seconds till they go off. Time your throw and get the hell outta the way."

She takes them. He notes the slight tremble in her hand. "You're only keeping one."

"I've had more practice. Go!"

She takes off running, scrambling over the uneven polymer, rifle slung across her back. His own target is across the compound, on the opposite wall. In the sky, he can just make out the shape of wing-suits splayed like flying squirrels. He leaps off the battlements onto a building shaped like a flat-topped silo. A hidden panel opens with a click and a whirr. A minigun emerges and its barrel spins. Mike jumps to a lower rooftop. In the air, bullets hit his shell. His trajectory is altered and he crashes down to the metal surface. He tells himself it's no big deal. This is nothing compared to his fall from the tower. He rolls and rights himself. The bullets lodged in his shell send weird vibrations up his nerve endings. Not pain. More like a sensation that should not be. He reaches for an antenna, uses it to slow his momentum. He swings a quarter-turn and launches himself across a helipad.

Just ahead, the turret gun opens up. The airborne unit scatters. Now he can make out their limbs and heads. A laser burst flares in the darkness. An airborne fighter whirls out of formation, tumbles toward the river. Mike roars as he propels himself across empty space. His legs clear the pitched roofs of Quonset huts below. Behind him, the minigun chatters away. His body shudders as he hits the wall on the compound's western edge. The turret is just ahead, a dome-capped cylinder that rises to twice his height.

A sudden explosion sends a plume of liquid flame into the night sky. He hopes Casey got out of range before the gun blew. April's face flashes in his mind. Her mouth twisted in rage and sorrow. He shoves it away. No time for that now.

His own grenade is hot in his palm. He gives it a twist, rolls it toward the base of the turret, and races to shelter behind a battlement. The explosion sends metal bending outward. The smoke clears. The turret leans, its base a mess of frayed, sparking wires and scorched chrome.

But then the twin guns recalibrate, compensating for the bad angle. One barrel is out of commission. The other fires. An airborne fighter spins away into the night. Mike rushes the turret. He draws the broken katana from its scabbard.

"What the hell is he doing?" Raph asks.

"Uniting his body and soul in purpose," Leo says.

Mike flips in the air, gathering torque. He slashes downward as his body uncurls. The broken blade eats through the gun barrel's steel flesh. Sparks fly. Mike hits the ground, pivots, rushes back toward the battlements. The remaining cannon tries to fire—and explodes. Its barrel peels back like a metal banana.

"Wow," Leo says. "I honestly wasn't sure that was going to work."

Mike stows the blade. "Then why'd you say that shit about body and soul?"

"Leadership."

Mike trains his anxious gaze along the opposite wall. What remains of the charred turret belches dark smoke. Spotlights rake the undersides of clouds. A figure moves among the polymer ridges. It pauses. Then two quick bursts of light flash in Mike's direction.

"Flashlight on her rifle scope," Donnie says.

Casey Marie.

Mike feels himself relax. He turns to the west as the first wing-suited fighters come in for a landing atop the wall. He winces as they hit metal, bodies tumbling. Moving quickly, he helps them up, meets their unfocused eyes until they gather themselves. He finds Zaragoza by the ruined turret, deftly unclipping his wings. The suit falls to a puddle of nylon at his feet.

"Commander," Mike says. "How was your flight?"

"Shitty," Zaragoza says, nodding at the smoking turret. "Thanks for the assist."

Mike quells the urge to tell Zaragoza to get his ass down into the compound. The quicker the airborne team disables Stockman's defenses from within, the more lives will be saved in the main assault. He defers to the commander as the man organizes his team.

"All right," Zaragoza says as the fighters coalesce around him. Wingsuits slough off their bodies like husks of dead skin. "Let's get down there and kill anything that moves."

38

THE SKY IS ALIVE with mousers. Mindless spheres with jaws of interlocking blades emit a piercing mechanical whine like some hellish cicada swarm. Impossible to count in the pale light from the smoke-obscured moon—Mike guesses they number in the thousands. Stockman must have warehouses full of them. And he's just unleashed them all on the main thrust of the invasion force. He watches as tubes extend from the compound's walls, spitting never-ending streams of bots.

The south end of the island is littered with the smoking wrecks of android sentries and broken, crumpled synjas, their red eyes gone dark. There are dead humans, too, resistance fighters perforated by miniguns or eviscerated by androids' blades. An acrid layer of smoke like a thousand chemical burns hangs heavy over the island. Mike feels their loss in a distant way, a dark pall rather than acute pain. Casey Marie is at his side, unscathed. He is ashamed that to him, her life is worth a million resistance fighters. All brave souls, he is certain, but none of them are family.

"What are those things?" one of the resistance fighters shouts.

"Mousers!" Mike yells back. "Find cover and fire at will!"

Behind a pile of cinder blocks draped with the body of a purple-haired fighter, Mike draws his tonfa and fires off the EMP. Inert mousers clank to the earth around him. More take their place. At this rate, the tide will never turn. Stalemate is the best the resistance can hope for. And stalemate means Stockman wins.

Avallone comes skidding in beside him, breathing hard, clutching his pulse rifle. Screams come across the blighted land where the invaders are pinned down. "We need a new strategy for these things. We'll never get through them like this." Avallone looks at Mike. "I'm going to order a retreat."

The tonfa grows hot in his hand. He triggers the EMP. A handful of mousers die. Fewer each time, he notices.

"The signal's getting weak," Donnie warns. "It's not meant to be spammed like that."

Mike gives it a rest. "It won't do any good," he tells Avallone. "These little bastards will never quit. They'll just follow us." He thinks back to the last time he fought with any of his brothers. Leo, standing at his side, facing down a swarm. "Plus Stockman can blow them up any time he wants. We have to keep the team scattered. We cluster together, it's all over."

A silver orb crests the corpse atop the cinder blocks and zeroes in on Mike's head. He shoves the tip of Raph's sai into its maw, skewering it, then casts the dead robot aside. "I hate these things so much."

"Then I'll divide our force in half," Avallone says. "Take a few squads to the north. If the mousers self-destruct with us all together like this . . ."

The comms crackle. Avallone's eyes go wide.

"Sorry I'm late!" April's voice comes through, clear and steady. "AFV got stuck at the bottom of the river. If you can still call it a river."

"Mom!" Casey Marie shouts into the comms. "It's about damn time! Where are you?"

"Check your six."

Mike peers over the dead fighter's torso, ignoring her face. The monstrous AFV rumbles into view, its armored chassis shedding reeking muck and tendrils of seaweed. Metal shrieks and crumples as the vehicle's massive treads crush fallen androids and synja limbs.

"*Splinter's Revenge!*" he yells.

"It's not called that," April says.

Mousers swarm the heavy assault vehicle. Then a new sound hits Mike, worms into his brain, makes his body go numb. An alarm-clock beeping sweeps through the ranks of mousers as they fire on the AFV. His heart pounds. The rest of the world fades to a grainy, slow-motion distance.

"Mikey!" one of his brothers tries to snap him back to reality. The voice does nothing. He feels soaked in trauma. The cold blood in his veins freezes his body in place. The intervals between the beeping get shorter and shorter.

"You gotta warn her!" his brothers are shouting at him now.

"We have to get out of here," he hears his own voice, meek and quiet.

"What?" Avallone's hand is rough on his shoulder.

The mousers cluster around the AFV, coating it in a mass of writhing silver.

"April!" he screams at last. Then he remembers to key the comm. "April!"

"I see 'em, Mikey," she says. "Don't worry—this baby's got an EMP that'll make you shit your pants." Through comms, he can hear April slam down an unseen switch. "Eat shit, you little monsters."

The EMP goes off in a silent explosion. Mousers drop dead, pelting the ground like steel rain, bouncing with hollow thuds. Immersed in the out-of-tune melody of the falling robots, Mike comes back to himself. His heart rate slows. Shame rises: The awful sound triggered a full-body flashback that rendered him useless. A true warrior would have shrugged it off and stayed in the fight. What if Casey Marie had died because he froze?

The last mouser drops. A cheer sweeps the ranks of the resistance fighters. Avallone delivers a tough slap to Mike's bullet-pocked shell. Mike shakes off the last vestiges of the flashback. He keys his comm. "April, you good?"

Her head pokes up from the hatch atop the AFV. "I ever tell you how much I hate these things?"

Mike wades through piles of fallen mousers, kicking the dead orbs out of his way. Casey joins him alongside the vehicle. The smell of fuel oil and river sludge thickens the air.

"I gotta get Honeycutt to the power source." She nods at Avallone. "Want me to get the door for you guys?"

"A little more time and we could have breached it," the commander says. He sticks a fat cigar in his mouth and flicks open a silver lighter.

"We'll be right behind you," Mike calls to April. She disappears back into the belly of the AFV.

He turns to Casey. "Bring in your team right behind your mom. I'll take the rear to make sure there's no other surprises out here. Stockman's gotta have some other nasty tricks on deck."

Avallone struts off in a puff of white smoke to organize his troops. Crunch, Scrape, Breaker, and Lug appear from behind ruined barriers and piles of rubble and drift over to join Casey. Mike watches the AFV rumble to the polymer-coated doors of the compound. A pair of large caliber guns rise like pop-up headlights from ports in the front of the vehicle. The guns open fire. The sound is deafening. The polymer holds for a moment, then begins to fray under the onslaught. Bits of the doors peel away in strips. Some kind of optical mess on the underside of the shredded polymer plays havoc with Mike's vision. He narrows his eyes.

"Fascinating," Donnie says.

The guns go quiet. Barrels spin in place, then retract back into their ports. The AFV advances. Even half obliterated, the polymer pushes back against the vehicle. The treads kick up river muck and gravel in a wild spitting arc. Then the doors begin to give. The nose of the AFV presses through as the polymer collapses inward. Avallone leads what remains of the resistance fighters in a tight formation behind April's vehicle. Casey and her crew weave themselves in with the larger squad. The doors go concave. The treads bite. The AFV breaches the walls, and fighters pour into the compound in its wake. Mike falls in behind them, casting a last look across the field of the dead.

"I told you this was a good plan," Raph says.

39

BAXTER STOCKMAN'S INNER SANCTUM is a cavernous industrial space. A maze of pipes winds overhead, connecting platforms housing the esoteric machinery that powers Stockman's robot empire. The walls are crammed with alcoves and cubbyholes, a teetering, precarious interior that reminds Mike of the shanties of Battery Village. Ticker tape spews from dozens of slots, printing columns of symbols. Old filing cabinets, drawers half open, spill yellowed papers and creased blueprints. A supercomputer sprawls out from its nerve center in one corner of the vast room, towers of monitors lashed together by tendrils of wire. It's a glimpse into unbalanced brilliance, the homespun genius in severe isolation. The space reminds Mike of those old 16-bit side-scroller games Donnie used to play till dawn while guzzling energy drinks. A boss level writ large.

"I'm seeing *cyberpunk nightclub*," Donnie says.

Mike gazes around while the rest of the invasion team secures the room. The emptiness feels staged. This is Stockman's brain come to life. No way's he's abandoned it to his enemies so easily. Machines click softly. LED lights flash red, orange, blue.

April's voice comes over the comms. "I think I see the access point. How's it looking out there?"

Mike defers to the commander. "Avallone?"

"My people have been over every corner of the room. Nobody's here. You're clear to proceed, April."

Casey sidles up next to Mike, her crew shuffling warily at her back. "I don't like this, Sensei."

"Be weird if you did." Mike walks slowly across a concrete floor polished to a high sheen. He moves through rows of lab tables. Prototypes sit in silent, vaguely gruesome array, polymer limbs and silver exoskeletal faces behind glass. "No way Stockman just abandons his life's work."

Casey shudders. "Place gives me the heebie-jeebies."

Crunch picks up a metal hand. "Smells funny, too."

"Like . . ." Scrape sniffs the air. "Cereal."

Crunch drops the metal hand on the floor. Lug bends down to peer into the lens of an electron microscope, its cylindrical body the size of a hot water heater.

On the other side of the room, just inside a breached section of wall, the AFV's hatch opens. April climbs out with a hard plastic case the size of a microwave. Honeycutt's dead round eyes stare out from an opening in the side of the case. Anxiety surges. If April can't wake the Fugitoid up, all this will have been for nothing. He watches April move toward an alcove.

"Honeycutt . . ." The voice is a soft purr that somehow resounds through the chamber. "Honeycutt is here . . ." A figure appears before a tower of monitors. He's a young Black man in a crisp white lab coat. His eyes are magnified behind thick lenses—nerd chic. *Stockman.* Mike is surprised—Stockman ought to be a much older man. He had imagined someone twisted by isolation, not this neatly dressed, eager-looking young scientist. Maybe he created some kind of youth serum. Mike's hand goes to the hilt of his brother's sai. He judges distance and angle. Stockman puts his hands in the pockets of his lab coat.

There's a mechanical click as a dozen fighters' pulse rifles are raised to draw a bead on the scientist. At the same time, Avallone and a small squad rush to shield April and Honeycutt.

"Don't move." Zaragoza comes out from behind a row of humming machinery, leveling a pistol at Stockman's head. His airborne troops stream into the chamber behind him.

With aching slowness, the scientist moves his hands above his head. A vacant smile is plastered to his face.

Mike narrows his eyes. Something's wrong. Stockman's face freezes, then jumps to a thin-lipped smirk.

"Glitch," Donnie says.

Mike flings a shuriken. The silver star passes through the scientist's lab coat and buries itself in a monitor behind him.

"Hologram," Casey says.

The scientist's avatar turns to Mike. "Android 11-E threw you out of Hiroto's tower." His tone is measured, matter-of-fact. "You walked away. I have seen all available footage." The avatar pixelates and goes blurry. It blinks. "Divert power," it commands. The avatar sharpens.

"Stockman," Mike says. "It's over. Show yourself."

The avatar's vague smile returns. Its teeth are blindingly white. "Your mutation is evolving. I have seen it in my dreams. Give yourself to me and your friends' deaths will be painless."

Mike draws the sai. "Screw you."

The avatar turns its head toward April and Avallone's protection detail as they make their way toward the wall—"I'm sorry, Miss O'Neil, but I cannot let you do that."

The avatar snaps its fingers. Mike transfers his nervous energy into a dead sprint across the chamber in April's direction. "Protect her!" he calls out to Avallone's team.

At the same time, the avatar blinks out of existence. The chamber trembles. A baritone rumbling comes from deep within the compound. The sound of heavy objects sliding, like a giant pushing furniture across the floor. Just ahead, Avallone and six fighters close ranks. April and Honeycutt disappear behind them. Mike is almost there when the walls open up. All across the chamber, the dimensions of the cluttered interior begin to shift. Hidden panels and trapdoors appear. Filing cabinets and bookshelves betray their falseness as they give way to dark openings from which iterations of robot sentries flow. Modern synjas spring forth and engage the resistance fighters. Pulse rifles chatter. The room resounds with the clanks of metal limbs. Four-legged, doglike androids leap at exposed throats. A chorus of screams rises and bounces around the high-ceilinged chamber. Red flashes hammer erratic lines into the walls.

Avallone fires at a synja and takes off its left arm in a shower of sparks. The robot keeps coming. Mike jumps and hits it with the side of his shell, knocking it off course. The fighters surrounding April battle a polymer-coated sentry with whirling blades for hands. Mike drives Donnie's bō down into the synja's face, skewering its head. The red eyes blink out.

A pulse blast grazes his arm. Mike grunts at the searing pain. He drops into a half-spin and takes out the legs of a crab-walking automaton. A segmented metal tail like a scorpion's aims a silver spike at his head. He rolls away. A synja's katana takes a chunk of green flesh out of his shoulder as it narrowly misses his throat. He springs to his feet, twirling the bō as a diversion, jabbing with the sai, turning from the crab to the synja, delivering short sharp thrusts. Metal pieces fly. He tries to find April in the chaos but another synja is coming at him, swinging a pair of short swords, and his unconscious mind ticks off the rhythm of his strikes and feints. The three robots attack as one in vicious synergy. With the shattered katana in one hand and the sai in the other, Mike's limbs work among explosions of sparks. More sentries close in. The world is a writhing, glinting mess of red eyes and metal weapons. Steel bites his forearm. Mousers buzz in from overhead, released like party balloons from on high. One of the robot dogs leaps, its steel jaws and needle teeth clamping onto Mike's elbow. He kicks a synja's wrist and its sword goes spinning away. The mousers descend. Mike finds himself at the center of a cyclone of mechanized attacks. April is gone. Casey is out of reach. There is only pain and flickering steel.

40

APRIL CLUTCHES THE FUGITOID'S head, safe in its case. Her other hand rests on Avallone's back as he advances. She can feel his body swivel as he targets fresh enemies. The pulse rifle has no recoil as he fires with precision. The port is just ahead, a large socket built into the wall, a charging station for one of Stockman's creations. It should jumpstart Honeycutt and give him access to the compound's mainframe.

In theory.

The dark-haired woman guarding her left flank cries out. She is pushed into April by a charging automaton. A limb spins, a blade lashes out. The fighter parries with her rifle. The gun is cut in half, its barrel superheated red at the severance point. The other fighters close ranks. April's breath catches as the woman steps outside the relative safety of her squad and draws a sword. The automaton recalibrates itself, limbs sprawling low, as its blade hand swirls about the woman's ankles. She screams as she collapses. There's the shriek of metal on metal as her sword finds its mark. And then she is out of sight.

"Fifteen feet to the power source," Avallone shouts back to her. He takes the head off a synja with a single shot to the neck. Its body keeps coming. The fighter to her right takes it apart with a rapid-fire burst.

"Mom!" Casey Marie's voice crackles over the comms.

April's heart leaps. "Casey. Find some cover!"

"Sensei's in trouble. Thirty feet away from you on your three o'clock." Her daughter's voice degenerates into static. April turns her head, searches the chamber. Halfway to the lab setup, she can see a scrum of robot dogs, sentries, automatons, all of them swarming obsessively like ants around a fallen food scrap.

She slaps her palm against Avallone's back as he fires at a smoking wreck from which a metal hand twitches. "Mikey's down. We gotta help him."

"Negative, O'Neil. We're taking you to the access point. We gotta end this."

"They're killing him!"

"He knew the risks."

A wretched indecision grips her mind. She keys her comm. "Casey, can your crew get to him?" Silence. "Casey?" Nothing.

April tries to push Avallone, to get him to move faster, but her protective detail fights methodically, picking off sentries, clearing the lane. Progress is achingly slow. The access point is ten feet away.

April holds her breath as if she's diving off the deep end. She pulls Honeycutt's head from its case and cradles it like a football. Then she flanks around Avallone's broad shoulders and sprints for the power source.

"April, what the hell?" He reaches out for her. She feels his fingertips on her shoulder and then he is right behind her. Rifle bursts flash past her. Her feet barely touch the cement, the flexion of her arches springlike and quick.

Then a massive armored cyborg slides into view, blocking her path to the access point. Seven feet tall, gleaming silver, with a face—

—a face of corrupted flesh, wormlike coils of skin winding around small red eyes, the neck's ropelike tendons intertwined with cables. Man and machine grafted into a swirling conglomerate of polymer and living tissue.

"Stockman." The name escapes her like a gasp as she tries to slow her momentum.

A hiss escapes the scientist's ruined mouth. "*Honeycutt . . .*"

His fist connects with the side of April's face and the world goes white.

41

CASEY MARIE FIRES AS she runs. Mousers come screaming in. Breaker sprays them with covering fire. The rifle, modded by Lug, turns them to molten scrap. Casey dodges twisted knots of fiery metal that plummet to the floor, pocking the cement. Crunch and Scrape flank her to either side. Crunch shoots at the mass of robots swarming the place where Sensei went down. An automaton blows apart. Its leg goes spinning into the back of a resistance fighter who collapses on the cement.

Scrape fires indiscriminately. A pair of sentries turn, kneel, return fire. Casey throws herself to the floor as shots zip over her head. She thinks distantly that she could break a bone, being so reckless with her body, but nothing hurts. In fact, she feels amazing. Coursing with adrenaline, strong as Crunch. She scrambles to her feet and yells over her shoulder at Scrape.

"Don't hit Sensei!"

Scrape holds his fire. Casey stares into a synja's red eyes. She's moving faster than she's ever moved before. In seconds, she's across the chamber floor and launching herself at a robot on the scrum's edge. Her training flits through her mind. All the forms and patterns Sensei drilled into her, the wisdom from Splinter's journal. To strike these robots at close range with her fists and feet ought to leave her bones splintered, her body broken. Yet in the back of her mind, she knows she will not be hurt. At least not in that way. This is not a source of pride or excitement. It is just a thing that is.

She takes a sentry by its neck and smashes it to the ground. A mouser swoops at her head. Crunch swats it away. Her mind serves up ancient techniques, feeds tactics to her nervous system. Her clenched fists cave in a synja's faceplate and its eyes go dark. She reaches down and wrenches a robot dog off her sensei's upper body and flings it away. Then Crunch and Scrape are beside her once again, helping to lift Michelangelo off the ground. Blood stains his face. His left eye is swollen, the tough green skin nicked and scored with a hundred cuts.

He looks in Casey's eyes, nods once, then draws his nunchaku. She pulls Crunch and Scrape out of the fray as a silent fury overtakes her sensei. Robots come apart at the end of his chain-linked batons. He wades in their components and stains them with the blood from his wounds. The greater battle raging in the chamber dulls to a muted, slow-motion scene, window dressing for Michelangelo's systematic dismantling of Stockman's robotic cadre.

Then she raises her gaze to the far end of the chamber, where a massive cyborg is taking fire from Avallone and a half dozen resistance fighters. The cyborg's armor reacts like the shields on the perimeter wall, sublimating the pulses.

Casey hears herself scream when she spots her mother lying in a heap at the cyborg's feet. Without thinking, she motions to Breaker, and he tosses her his modded rifle. She lines up the cyborg in her scope and squeezes the trigger.

42

APRIL'S HEAD IS THICK and confused. She moves like she's underwater. Her unfocused eyes are trained on the monster who struck her down. Baxter Stockman. Rendered inhuman by his own experiments. Polymer and metal and skin and bright red pebbles for eyes. She manages to hoist herself up on an elbow. Honeycutt is still cradled against her belly. Stockman is distracted, taking a withering barrage of rapid-fire pulses. Distracted yet unfazed, his armor absorbing the bright crimson bursts.

Stockman knows what she is here for. He has positioned himself in front of the power source, blocking the port. He looks down and trains those red eyes on her. Even above the chaos of the battle, she can hear him speak.

"April O'Neil. Give me Honeycutt or die screaming. Like Casey Jones before you."

April knows he is baiting her. The minute she lets her rage propel her to her feet, he will cave in her skull with that metal fist and the last thing she will ever see will be his awful face. She tells herself to stay down—but feels herself rising. Behind her, Avallone is screaming for her to get the hell away from here. She ignores him. She has a prosthetic hand of her own. With Honeycutt's head under her human arm, she flexes her metal fingers, curls them into a fist.

"This is for my husband," she says.

Then a pulse hits Stockman from the side. Instead of being absorbed, the burst lingers, frozen in a weird trembling state against

his chest. Stockman frowns. April looks over and sees Casey advancing with a pulse rifle raised. Before she can tell her daughter to back off, Casey fires again. Stockman cries out in surprise. The pulses slip behind his shield. He staggers away from the wall.

The power source is right in front of her, a dangling cable calling her name. She rushes forward and jams the cable into the side of Honeycutt's dormant head. She sends a prayer to a god she quit believing in years ago.

The robot skull grows warm to the touch. In seconds, it's too hot to hold. She rests it on a shelf inside the power source and backs away. A moment later, Casey is at her side. April watches as Honeycutt's eyes flare with sudden radiance. Lights on the side of his head blink faster and faster. She knows he's taking in information from Stockman's mainframe, processing faster than thought.

The speed of Stockman's sudden leap takes them all by surprise. Hydraulics in his legs launch him toward the power source. Before Casey can get a shot off, Honeycutt is in Stockman's hands.

"Yes . . ." Stockman says. "You came back to me."

Long-dormant speakers in Honeycutt's head emit a scratchy voice. "I know . . . what you have done . . . to this city."

"What?"

"I . . . have seen everything."

Fugitoid's eyes are as bright as the sun, full of power. Full of life. Full of anger.

Baxter Stockman goes rigid, as if some kind of poison is flowing from Honeycutt's head into his hands, wending through his cyborg body.

"For my family."

Stockman screams in agony.

Mike appears at April's side. "Get back!" She catches a glimpse of his huge green body covered in wounds as he plants himself in front of her and Casey and begins pushing them away from Stockman and

Honeycutt. Mike looks at Avallone and the handful of fighters left alive. "All of you, back!"

"For my friends!" Honeycutt's voice is louder now.

Stockman's head is thrown back. A frisson hits the air, a current of energy that passes between Honeycutt and Stockman like a million tiny droplets of shimmering mercury. His scream grows in pitch to a piercing cry.

"For *everything!*"

April cranes her neck to see around Mike's enormous shoulders. Stockman's armor is infected by a curious haze, as if the polymer has gone out of focus.

"What the hell?" Casey looks at her, shocked and confused.

April puts it together. "Stockman's body is held together with nanotech. It's a smart material, essentially. And now Honeycutt's got control of it."

Stockman's armor is indistinct, a quivering mess of vibrating particles. His shriek is an inhuman whine, full of glitches and hiccups. His skin blurs into the disintegrating armor.

"Looks like the nanotech was *all* that was holding him together," April says. "You might not want to watch this part."

"Wouldn't miss it for the world," Casey says, peering intently at the dispersing cloud that had been Stockman. The mist is shot through with airy puffs of gray and pink, what had once been blood and organs, torn apart cell by cell.

His voice dies away. Honeycutt dangles from the power cord, no longer gripped by Stockman's hands. A formless cloud lingers in the air, moving like a fog bank rolling in from the sea, flowing across the chamber. April, Mike, and Casey watch as it invades the supercomputer, undaunted by its solid exterior. Honeycutt mutters to himself.

All across the chamber, androids power down. Synjas' eyes go dark. Stockman's robot forces grind to a halt.

"Honeycutt's in control now," April says softly. Her cheek aches from Stockman's punch. All she can do is marvel at the series of events that has led them all to this moment. She takes her daughter's hand and pulls her close.

"Mom," Casey protests but doesn't move.

Breaker comes jogging over. "Comms are clear. Stockman's tech is shutting down all over the city."

Crunch wraps a piece of gauze around a bloody slash in his forearm. "Gonna be a lot of people pissed about their vacuum cleaners."

Nobody says anything. April looks around the chamber. Resistance fighters tend to the injured. Robot detritus litters the floor, piles of scrap metal and smoking husks. The walls are lacerated with scorch marks from pulse rifles. She closes her eyes. So much death.

"Should we celebrate?" Casey's voice is flat.

"No," Mike says. She listens to him walk away.

43

ON MANHATTAN'S SOUTHERN TIP, the dive bar nestled in the stacks above Battery Village is empty except for its two regulars. The old man coughs into his napkin. The woman pours him two fingers of whiskey. He balls up the napkin and leaves it crumpled in front of him on the table.

The woman shakes her head. "Swear you was raised in a barn."

The man shrugs. His voice is strained. "Could be, Ezzie. Too long ago for me to remember."

She grunts and sips from her smudged glass. A bike roars past, nosing its way down Main Street. She catches a glimpse of neon yellow, and then it's gone. "Goddamn kids."

Jasper drains his glass. "Back in my day we had respect or we got the belt."

"Thought you couldn't remember all that."

"The welts do the rememberin' for me."

She pours him a refill. Whiskey splashes the table. Then she lifts her glass. "To everything we forgot."

Clink.

Jasper runs the back of his hand over his mouth and settles in his chair. Ezzie notes the dirt crusted on his suspenders. "You're about due for a wash, Jasper. You and your clothes both."

He snaps a suspender and grins. "That why nobody else ever comes in here?"

"That's more due to your personality."

He laughs. "I figured."

Through the missing wooden slat in the wall, Ezzie gazes out at the lights of Lower Manhattan. She tries to recall the last time she crossed the village to walk in the shadows of the skyscrapers. Suddenly, the view changes. She frowns, rubs her eyes, and leans forward. "You see that?"

"I can't see anything, Ezzie."

She stands and peers through the gap in the wall. "Half the lights in the city just went out."

"Hell," Jasper says, "you wanna talk about a blackout, I remember—what year was it now . . ."

She straightens up. "Hasn't happened since the Foot Clan took over. Say what you will about the man himself, but Stockman tech does the job."

"I saw him once, you know." Jasper scoops up his napkin and coughs into its soggy mess.

Ezzie scoffs. "Nobody's ever seen him."

"That ain't true! It was—"

Ezzie watches his head turn toward the door. Jasper's a decrepit old geezer, but he has the ears of a bloodhound. She watches the darkened archway. A moment later, a skinny little tweaker kid she knows from down the stacks steps into view.

"Hey, you heard the news?" He moves into the wan light of the bar and holds out an object in his hand.

Jasper starts. "The hell you do, Benny?"

Ezzie gasps. The kid's brandishing a severed head.

Benny tosses the head on an empty table. It lands with a heavy *clank*. Ezzie takes a closer look. The dark metallic sheen gives it away.

"It's one of those *things*." She looks at the kid. "You manage to get the jump on a goddamn *synja*?"

"Nope," he says. "They're powering down everywhere." He mimes a robot slowing down and freezing. "All at once, just going dead like somebody pulled the plug. Craziest thing I ever saw."

With that, he's gone. The head stares blankly from the table. Jasper reaches out with his fist and raps on the top of its skull.

"I'll be goddamned," he says. Then he looks at Ezzie. "City's about to go *pop*."

44

HIROTO HAS WORN THE cloak of his grandfather. He has kept his mother alive and shouldered the mantle of familial responsibility. His rule over the entire city is a testament to the expansive man he has become. He has loved his citizens and murdered them, set them free and oppressed them. And now, the universe has presented him with the capstone to his achievements.

"The turtle survived for a *reason*," he says to Captain Fukuda. "I am being tested."

The captain strolls with him through the penthouse, past scurrying technicians. "Yes, sir," Fukuda says.

"You say that," Hiroto says, "but do you really understand? I'm just coming to terms with it myself." A raven buzzes past their heads. Hiroto opens his hand. The bird feasts on a pile of seed and departs.

"You were saying the turtle has opened your mind," Fukuda says.

"Sir." A young, clean-shaven technician comes running up. Hiroto does not stop walking. The technician falls in beside them, fidgeting. "Sixty-seven percent of the city has gone dark. All cybernetic organisms, android sentries, and synjas are offline."

"Yes, yes," Hiroto motions as if flicking away a fly. "Stockman tech has run its course, failure was inevitable someday."

"Oh." The technician stops short. His puzzled face twitches. "Okay . . ."

Fukuda chimes in as they leave the technician behind. "Our satellites show mass destruction on Roosevelt Island. There's a high probability that Baxter Stockman is dead."

"Did you see that?" Hiroto smiles at his captain and lowers his voice. "That kid thought I was going to be upset at this news. He was probably terrified." He calls over his shoulder at the stunned technician. "It's about time Stockman was put out of his misery!"

Fukuda narrows his eyes slightly. "You're not upset. About any of this."

Hiroto turns to his captain. "The turtle coming back from the dead has given me an *opportunity*, Fukuda."

He continues his circumnavigation of the bustling penthouse.

"Sir," Fukuda says, "I want you to know that I remain fully dedicated to tracking down the turtle and delivering him to you. If you'll just give me—"

"Quit self-flagellating, Fukuda, it doesn't suit you." Irritation gnaws at Hiroto's thoughts. "You're not listening to a word I'm saying. I'm *glad* you have completely failed at the single task I have assigned you."

Fukuda remains silent.

"The turtle will come for me, Fukuda. And my tower defenses have been reduced to human ninjas. He'll cut right through them." He leads Fukuda over to a contraption that appears to be half dentist chair, half MRI scanner. Five technicians in lab coats oversee final preparations. "All I have to do is wait for him."

Fukuda nods. "And when he arrives?"

"Ah." He scans the faces of the technicians, picks out a young Asian man, and steers him toward Fukuda. "Ryu Mori here is the head of the research and development team down on the thirteenth floor."

Mori bows to Fukuda.

Hiroto claps Mori on the back. "Tell him, Mr. Mori."

Mori clears his throat and looks from Hiroto to Fukuda. "Captain, I feel duty bound to tell you that what Master Hiroto has ordered me to do may cost him his life. From a development perspective, we are at least a year away from a prototype that I would consider safe for contact with a human subject."

Hiroto groans. "Enough of this, Mori, Captain Fukuda doesn't need your endless disclaimers. You've already informed me of the risks, you are absolved of responsibility."

Mori leads them to a table on which sits an empty glass-and-steel box.

"I don't follow," Fukuda says.

"Just wait," Hiroto says. An indescribable feeling takes over. He locates warmth at the back of his neck, perhaps even excitement. He watches Fukuda's expression change as Mori slides his finger along a tablet screen.

The inside of the box comes to life. Billions of previously unseen, nearly microscopic particles glow, then coalesce into a small dagger. The dagger splits, and one blade becomes two. The blades lengthen until they stretch from one corner of the box to the other.

"Nanotech," Fukuda says.

"Yes," Mori says. "Stockman is—"

"*Was*," Hiroto corrects him.

"*Was* a master of the nanoscale." Mori taps the screen. The dagger fizzles into nothing, then reshapes itself to form a gauntlet. The fingers curl, flex, then close into a fist that rockets forward and punches the glass wall of its enclosure. The glass cracks.

"I thought all Stockman tech has been compromised," Fukuda says.

"My team has been reverse engineering his nanotechnology," Mori explains. "This operating system is proprietary, totally severed from Stockman's power sources."

Fukuda turns to Hiroto. "And you plan to use this as a weapon to kill the turtle."

"Not just a weapon," Hiroto says. "Mori assures me it can be fashioned into armor."

Mori swallows. "In theory, yes, but to control the armor, we must inject you with nanobots programmed to interact directly with your brain. There's no telling what kind of side effects the bonding process may have."

Hiroto beams at Fukuda. Overhead, ravens circle. "You see, Captain. It's beyond a weapon, beyond armor. I am occupying a new way of being. Do you understand now? A whole new plane of existence, something my mother and grandfather could never even glimpse, not in a million years."

Mori and Fukuda exchange a look. Hiroto takes a seat in the white leather reclining chair. A technician straps down his arms and legs.

Mori wheels over a small rolling cart that holds a second, identical box. A hose connects the box to a wicked, pistol-like syringe. "Sir, you do understand that I will be introducing an unpredictable foreign element into your brain?"

"*Yes*, Mori, get on with it."

Mori lifts the syringe and holds it to Hiroto's neck. He looks at Captain Fukuda, who regards him with vague curiosity. Hiroto knows the captain masks his feelings. Whatever is written on the captain's face, Hiroto figures it only hints at the depths of emotion churning inside him.

The sting of the needle bites into the flesh of his neck.

Hiroto is no stranger to pain. But this is an internal scouring, billions of microscopic machines prodding every cell on the way to his brain. His vision goes white. The technological virus courses through him. He screams. And yet, through the agony, he finds a wellspring of joy. This pain is like nothing he has ever experienced before, and the purity of the feeling is like coming home after an eternity away. He has been searching for something like this all his life. The nanobots converge in his brain and bond to his neural network. He can feel every single one. He clenches his jaw and breaks a tooth. His screams turn to cries of ecstasy.

The porch of the Oroku family's mountain retreat is an expanse of smooth, lightly varnished wood that juts majestically from the back of the main house. Hiroto sights his best friend, Ikusa, down the blade of his blunted ninjatō. Hiroto's hand is slick with sweat and the sword's hilt is clammy in his grip. His heart pounds.

Something hits the side of his face. It doesn't hurt. He knows better than to let his attention become divided. He keeps his eyes trained on his opponent. Tall and lanky, Ikusa stares back. When his friend is in deep focus, he never seems to blink. Ikusa has been training hard, and it shows. Hiroto is overmatched in front of his mother and the Hamato generals. But Ikusa has been letting him gain the upper hand to save face.

Thwack.

Out of the corner of his eye, he sees the projectile fall to the deck. A fat purple grape. His mother's favorite fruit.

It takes a moment to dawn on him. His mother is pelting him with grapes, as if he is some lowly circus performer who has displeased her. He finds that he can't move or turn his head. His feet are roots attached to the wooden slats of the deck.

Ikusa bends to retrieve one of the grapes. When he straightens, his face is hidden behind a silver helm lined with razor-like protrusions. Only his eyes are visible, and they are the eyes of a much older man. The figure grows taller, his blade sharper. A purple cloak sprouts from his back. He holds out his hand, clenches his fist, then opens it to offer the grape to Hiroto.

"Eat," his grandfather tells him.

Beyond the vast porch of the retreat, the sun dips behind the mountains. Cool night air drifts across Hiroto's face. His grandfather's eyes are kind. Hiroto takes what's in the Shredder's fist without looking at it. The crushed grape is warm and sticky.

"Go ahead," his grandfather says.

Hiroto closes his eyes and licks the purple smear off his palm. It tastes better than anything he's ever eaten in his life. When he opens his eyes, the turtle stands before him. A hulking green monstrosity with a black mask across his eyes. The turtle brandishes his grandfather's sword.

"Coward." The turtle speaks with his mother's voice.

"Come and see," Hiroto replies.

The turtle swings the sword.

Hiroto blinks and he's back in his penthouse, strapped to the white leather chair. Mori stands by his side with concern etched into his face.

"I was worried about you, Master Hiroto. Your vital signs skyrocketed."

Hiroto takes stock of his body. He doesn't feel any different. The long spiral of pain and the hallucination are like a half-remembered dream.

He glances at Fukuda. "How long was I out?"

Fukuda's brow furrows. "A few seconds at most. You blinked a few times, and here we are."

Hiroto recalls the progress of the nanobots, their interminable journey to bind with receptors in his brain. Crying out in agony, then pleasure. "Did my screaming not alarm you?"

Mori taps his screen. "You didn't make a sound, Master." He pauses. "I would like to debrief you, to record your experiences."

"Some other time, Mori." Hiroto raises his head off the leather and looks down at his arms and legs. Nothing seems out of the ordinary. "Is the interface with the nanobots secure?"

"My readings indicate that it is. The command nanites are actively connected to your brain, so you should be able to control your armor with but a thought."

Hiroto considers this. "You're telling me I can just . . ."

"Manifest," Mori says. The young scientist stands next to Captain Fukuda, both of them waiting expectantly. Behind them, his ravens glide in lazy circles through the jasmine-scented air.

Hiroto takes a deep breath in and lets it out. A voice from his hallucination echoes in his mind. *Coward.* He accepts the voice, sits with it, lets it flow through him. He can feel the particles come alive, tickling the inside of his skull. A strange ache swells behind his eyes, nausea localized in the back of his face. His body twitches and strains against the straps.

"Master . . ." Mori peers at the screen. "Your brainwaves are highly abnormal."

Come and see.

Hiroto glances down at his arms. The flesh ripples as if an invisible hand is kneading his skin.

"Your face," Fukuda says, eyes wide. He backs away from the chair.

Hiroto feels a great dispersal of energy from his pores. He gasps at the sudden release. Particles dance in his eyes. The taste of hot coins rises in the back of his throat. Then his body goes rigid. A klaxon blares. Technicians rush around their bank of screens and tend to their equipment.

Waves of pleasure sweep through him. He feels every part of his body expand. Fireworks pop behind his eyes. A silver sheen coats his bare arms. The straps explode off the chair, snapped by his growing bulk. His tunic is shredded. He leaps to his feet. Pure strength courses through him. The silver sheen clings to his musculature, an exoskeletal coating that he wears like a second skin.

"Come and see," he says. His ravens squawk madly, flying in erratic bursts. Technicians rush to abandon their posts at the machine. Mori only stares at him in astonishment. Fukuda backs away farther as Hiroto tests his legs. He takes one step then another. The coiled potential is incredible. And he knows this new evolution isn't merely armor—it's a weapon, too.

Manifest.

As he approaches Fukuda, he imagines sparring with his new captain. He imagines them both on the porch of the mountain retreat, displaying their skills for the high-ranking members of the clan. His mother is there, watching impassively, the glass bowl of grapes in front of her on the table. He feels a subtle shifting in the composition of his hand, as if it has suddenly multiplied its flesh. Twin blades grow from his knuckles, eight inches long.

He drives them into Fukuda's belly with a thrust so effortless he does not feel a hint of resistance. The man's eyes are beautiful in their shock. He lifts the captain off the ground, impaled on the blades, and tosses the weightless man aside. Laughing, he bounds like a puppy from one end of the penthouse to the other.

45

MIKE SITS ON THE bed in his father's old room. His bloodstained battle garb is tossed in a pile on top of his pads, mask, and tabi boots. He turns to his brothers' weapons. They are not the exact ones his brothers wielded when they died. Those had been lost to time. These are the ones they carried as teenagers, when they fought the Shredder. They had been in the lair when Michelangelo returned, distraught, after the destruction of the Hamato Clan compound. He had gathered them up in a daze and carried them across the world.

Mike cleans each of the weapons, places them side by side on the floor, and tries to meditate. But his mind remains clouded by death.

Death has been following him for many years.

His brothers. His father. Casey Jones. Friends he'd made abroad. And now, the bodies of resistance fighters sprawled across Roosevelt Island.

He'd killed so many, too. He can feel their presence in the room with him, souls lost and souls taken. The weight of their spirits is suffocating. His chest hurts. He feels hot and dizzy. He can't catch his breath.

After Stockman's defeat, Avallone and Zaragoza had refused to leave the island until their dead comrades could be collected and given a proper burial. This honorable act had sent Mike into a spiral of shame. Raphael's body had been carried away by the river before anyone knew to look for it. Splinter and Donatello are interred half a world away, in the tombs of the Hamato Clan. Worst of all, Leonardo had died by fire, and Mike hadn't even had the presence of mind to mark his passing. No funeral and no grave.

The fact that he hasn't thought of this in years makes it even worse. Another failure. Another thing he can never truly repent.

Mike begins to sob. His body is racked with pain. His thoughts turn to April and Casey Marie: family that survived. Family that gave him something to live for beyond single-minded vengeance. Thanks to them, his spirit has healed almost as quickly as his mutant body. He clings to this thought, lets it blossom inside him, edging out the violence and rage that masses like a storm cloud inside his mind.

He settles his breathing into a soft, easy rhythm. Sounds of the undercity come and go. After a while, he begins to find his center and regain some measure of peace. Gently, he works to encourage it.

Hours pass like minutes. For two days, he meditates in silence. The pain from his wounds eases. His mind goes mercifully blank. He feels no hunger or thirst.

And then his brothers' voices rise from the dark to steal his focus.

"You know, I think I was only in this room once or twice when father was still alive," Donnie says. "It looks exactly the same."

Raph sighs. "How much longer you gonna sit on your ass, Mikey?"

"Until I've found inner peace, that's how long. Now stop talking while I'm meditating."

Mike could hear Raph's growl coming from the shadows, near Splinter's dust-covered collection of vintage paperback novels: dog-eared Westerns that echo the stories of the samurai, mysteries that insist justice can always be found, romances that suggest love conquers all. Stoicism, justice, and hope for love—principles that once defined Splinter's existence.

For the first time in two days, Mike gets up from the lotus position. He goes to the shelf and begins to dust off the books. He can sense Leonardo in the corner, radiating disappointment.

"Raph is right, Mikey. Inner peace comes after Hiroto's dead. Not before."

Just like that, the Zen he's worked to cultivate over the past two days exits his system like a squid jetting its ink. "Don't lecture me about my own mind, Leo."

Leo's eyes are cold. "It's a plain old tactical reality. Why haven't you pressed the attack against Hiroto yet? You guys caught him completely off guard by taking out Stockman's tech. You're wasting your advantage!"

Mike quits dusting off the books. "I don't have to explain myself to you."

"Everyone just calm down," Donatello says. "We all know why Mike's been sitting here alone in this room."

"Is it 'cause he's a coward?" Raph asked. "That's where I'm thinkin' about placin' my bet. He always had trouble doin' the hard stuff."

The last vestiges of inner peace are gone. Mike clenches his fist.

"No," Donnie says. "It's because it's finally sunk in that he's the sole survivor. He's the last of us. That's a heavy burden to bear. Painful, too."

"Seriously, Mikey boy?" Raph's ghost snickers. "Is that why you've been stalling for two whole days? I kept my mouth shut long enough, bro. I knew you weren't strong enough to handle this kind of mission. You never were."

Mike slams the side of his fist into the brick wall. "You can go to hell, Raph!" He takes a swing at the spot where Raphael should be, but his brother is already gone, standing with arms crossed in a shadow across the room.

Mike rubs his sore hand.

"Do you feel better now?" Donnie asks.

"No," Mike says. "You know, I thought teaching Casey was helping, but right now I just feel used up. You all know what I've seen and done, and you all know I wasn't built for it. Killing hurts my spirit."

He takes a deep breath. "But I know damn well it's not over for me yet."

Mike sits back down on the bed and lets his head drop. The full weight of every year he's been alive without his brothers presses down on him, along with all the damage he's taken over a lifetime of war.

"After all this time," he says softly, "getting back to New York and discovering that April was alive, meeting Casey Marie and the resistance, seeing that they're fighting just as hard against the Foot Clan as we ever did, sacrificing just as much as we ever did . . . this isn't only about us or our family, not anymore. So, I gotta do this right. I gotta be sure that when I go up against Hiroto again, it'll be the last time. Because if I fail, more of these people are gonna die. Maybe all of 'em.'"

A long moment passes before Raphael starts a slow clap. "Cute speech, but I ain't buyin' it. Somethin' ain't right with you."

"The only thing that isn't right here is that empty space between your ears, Raph."

"That some kinda ghost joke? You always had the worst sense of humor, Mikey."

"Can it, Raph," Donnie says. "You're being a creep. Even for you."

Raphael shouts back at Donnie. Mike tunes them out, walks over to the pile where he stowed his gear, and gets dressed.

Bracers. Kneepads. Pants. Boots. Long-sleeve shirt. Thin body armor for an extra layer of protection. Hooded jacket. Belt half filled with smoke pellets, bombs, shuriken . . . and a mask. A thin strip of cloth that has no real-world function, but Mike can't imagine going into battle without one. It ties him to his family. To his cause. And to his grief.

"Hey, I got an idea," Raph says, addressing Mike again. "Another full-frontal assault like on Stockman's compound. That worked out pretty good. If it ain't broke, don't fix it, right?"

"Classic Raph plan," Leo says.

"And?"

"Those are the worst ones," Leo says.

"Yeah, right!" Raph shouts. "Just 'cause I got great ideas, you're—"

"What? Jealous? Of your stupid, impulsive—"

"Take your whiteboard and shove it up your ass!"

"How about we start with any plan at all?" Donnie says. "I haven't heard Mikey say a word about strategy, and he's the one who's—"

"Would you all *shut up!*" Mike screams. He doesn't care if April or Casey can hear him. "I want you to *stop talking*. To me, and to each other. I want you *gone*."

"You'd be lost without us," Leo says.

"No, I'd be a whole lot less stressed." Mike pulls the mask tight and knots it behind his head. "It's worse now than when you were alive, constantly telling me what to do. And what do I have to show for it?"

Leonardo doesn't answer, so Mike picks up the weapons that had belonged to his brothers. He holds the broken katana—Leo's blade—out for his brother to examine. "This. This is all that's left."

Leo looks away. "That's low, Mikey. We all did our part."

"Yeah, and to us, it was everything." Donnie adds.

Raph shakes his head. "Ungrateful jerk."

"I know what you did! I live with it every damn day, so I don't need you here to remind me! Leave now and never come—"

His brothers vanish.

"—*back*."

They had disappeared before. Once, during his self-imposed exile, they had stopped visiting him for years. But they never felt truly gone. Now, Mike feels an absence inside his head. A cavernous emptiness, both terrible and freeing. He can *think* again. And act without the weight of their expectations.

He picks up Splinter's journal from the nightstand, flipping to the back, where his own entries begin. He stares at the page that reads *NO PEACE* and considers the words.

After a moment, clarity arrives in the form of a truth Mike hasn't been ready to accept until now. He rifles through the nightstand drawer for a pen and scribbles something into the journal.

When he's finished, he goes into the kitchen and leaves the journal on the table for Casey Marie. Then he puts the lair behind him, all the while fighting the urge to look back.

46

CASEY MARIE SLOSHES THROUGH ankle-deep water in the labyrinthine sewers. Her shins displace the bodies of dead rats. Other,
larger things splash in the shadows. Humidity fills the tunnels. A rank
stench hangs heavily in the thickening air.

She doesn't know anything about the city's drainage system.
What is very likely a miracle of engineering is only apparent to her
now because it's failing. She figures it has something to do with the
death blow they'd just delivered to Stockman's technology. That
crazy bastard invented the hydroelectric system inside the wall that
surrounds Manhattan. The city's pumps must be connected to it
somehow.

Turning a corner, she crosses a threshold into the lair. There's no
reprieve from the rising water. An anxious, oppressive feeling settles in
her chest. She thinks of her mother's lab, all that irreplaceable work,
carried away, gone forever. And beyond her own losses, there's Rock
Bottom at large—the black market, the homes built in the catacombs,
the subway. All of it vulnerable to the water's inexorable creep.

"Mom?" she calls out. Her heart races. What if her mother is
trapped somewhere? She'd once read that it's possible to drown in
two inches of water. "You here?"

She steps into the kitchen and stops short. There, on the table,
is Splinter's journal. That doesn't make sense. Michelangelo would
never leave his prized possession lying there, out in the open, for
anyone to see.

"Sensei?"

No answer. She tucks the journal into the pocket of her overcoat and sloshes through the lair. Bedrooms, dojo, gym, lab, war room—all of them empty. She heads beyond the living and working areas into the old, seldom-used storage tunnels. Soggy old board game boxes and swollen paperbacks float lazily in the water.

"Mom?"

She's about to turn around when the response comes at last. "Casey?"

"Mom!" She splashes in the direction of the voice. "Where are you?"

"Where do you think?"

Casey's hand goes to her face. "You moron," she mutters to herself. Beyond the storage tunnels is a side chamber that houses the lair's water pumps. As a little girl, her mother had warned her to stay away from them. That warning had crystallized into a childish fear of the dank, forbidding room that had never really left her mind.

Casey eases her way to the back of the dim chamber.

"Down here."

She finds her mother half submerged in a recessed pit, her upper body caked in grease and grime. Dark water laps at her waist. A pump's curved and rusted hatch is open and her mother's hands are deep in the guts of its motor.

"You okay, Mom?"

"I'm having a great time, Casey. Where the hell have you been?"

"Avallone's got me on riot control. The blackouts have the city on edge. We've had some looting."

"You get us anything good?"

"They're all out of water pumps."

April pulls her hands from the motor and wipes them on her pants. "I underestimated how much of the water management system was tied in with Stockman tech. These pumps aren't directly connected to the main system, which put extra strain on them the last couple of days. I've been trying to get them back up and running all day"—she wades over to the edge of the pit—"but I think they're history. I've neglected them for too long. Everything I need to access is rusted shut."

She plants her boot on the bottom rung of the access ladder and reaches for Casey. "Here, make yourself useful. Help me up."

Casey clasps her mother's prosthetic hand and hoists her to the chamber's main level.

"Where's Sensei?" Casey asks when April's standing at her side. April's jaw clenches subtly. "Mom? Where is he?"

"Mikey's not here, Casey. He left. I'm sorry."

"What do you mean he left? You just let him go?!"

"It wasn't like that. He didn't even say goodbye to me. I went looking for him to ask for help with the pumps and he was already gone."

Anger and disbelief rise in Casey's chest. There's so much that she still needs to learn from him. The resistance, her mother, they all need him. They're all finally making real progress, and her mother seems at ease in a way she hasn't in years. April is almost like a different person with her old pal Mikey around. They have so much shared history, so many memories. Casey has never seen this side of her mother before. And she's never felt so close to the father she never got the chance to meet.

Michelangelo did all that. And then he just left? Without saying goodbye?

Rage travels through Casey's body and out to her fists where it explodes in a vicious punch. The force of it takes out a chunk of the wall. Broken masonry splashes into the rising water at her feet.

"Casey Marie Jones!" Her mother takes her by the arms. "Stop it! You'll hurt yourself!"

"Oh, will I?" Casey looks at her hand then holds it out so April can see. Not even a scraped knuckle. "Will I *really*, Mom?"

Her mother doesn't say anything. She seems almost frightened.

"I know I'm different," Casey says. Her rage melts away. She can scarcely believe she's giving voice to the secret hunch that's been festering inside her for months. She hadn't planned to discuss this with her mother today. Maybe not ever. But now, here they are. She keeps her voice steady. "I think I've known it for a long time. Sensei looks at me when we're in the gym like he can't believe half the shit I'm able to do." She pauses, giving her mother a chance to interject. When April still doesn't say anything, Casey continues. "I'm just like Michelangelo, aren't I?" She can feel herself breaking down into sobs and tries to fight it but her body begins to heave. "A *mutant.*"

"Come with me." Her mother steers her out of the chamber. Together, without speaking, they slosh through the storage tunnels and into the kitchen. April gestures for Casey to sit in a chair before grabbing one for herself. Their legs are submerged halfway to their knees. Casey wipes her eyes and almost laughs. It's completely absurd.

Her mother takes a breath. "Yes," she says. "It's true."

Casey's mouth goes dry. The only sound is the water lapping at the cupboards under the sink and rushing through the tunnels with a low, ceaseless hiss. Even with her mother's confirmation of what she already knows, Casey finds it hard to believe. To grow up certain of one identity, then to find herself inhabiting another, is impossible for her to wrap her head around. "How?" is all she can say.

"Your dad and I were regularly exposed to a low dose of mutagen over a long period of time, being around Splinter and the turtles. That kind of long-term exposure . . . I think it infected us. Changed us, but just a little. And then, when I was pregnant, those changes essentially changed you. Mutated your DNA."

Casey can tell her mother is trying to make it sound clinical. Or natural. But it isn't quite that way, and they both know it. She does her best to process the explanation, and imagines the seep of mutagen into her parents' pores like the water's slow progress up the walls of the lair.

"When were you going to tell me?" Casey asks.

"Years ago," her mother assures her quickly. But Casey can see in her mother's eyes that this isn't true. April shakes her head, corrects herself. "Never. I don't know. I just didn't want to face it. And I kept finding other things to do. Then Mikey showed up."

"Did you tell him? Does he know he did this to me?"

"Casey, no. Michelangelo didn't do this to you. Or to us. Mutagen's properties are still pretty much an undiscovered country. No one knew this was something that could happen."

Casey peers at the palms of her hands. She thinks they look different now, the lines slightly altered, the skin hinting at reptilian scales. She blinks and they go back to normal. Just her mind playing tricks. "Will I do this to anyone else?"

"Nothing in my research suggests so. The turtles were changed from direct contact with mutagen. You were born this way." She takes Casey's hands in hers. "And you're perfect."

Casey's brow furrows.

"Mom?" Her voice breaks.

"What is it?" Her mother reaches up to lift her chin, wiping away fresh tears.

"Will it kill me?"

"Oh, sweetie, no." April leans over and pulls her daughter into a tight hug. "This won't kill you. I promise. But it's not going to let you live forever either."

Casey nods. "I know."

Her mother lets her go and sits back in her chair. Now there are tears in her mother's eyes. A rare sight. "You still need to be careful."

"I will." She pauses. "Hey, Mom?"

"Hey, Casey."

"Can we stop sitting in a room full of water now?"

Her mother stands. "Probably a good idea."

Casey follows her mother out of the kitchen. She pats her pocket, feeling the shape of Splinter's journal. "Once I get you to the surface, I need to find Sensei. He's gonna need my help."

April turns abruptly, water splashing above her knees. "Casey. I need you to hear me on this. Long before I met the turtles, long before you were even born, there was a war raging between the Hamato Clan and the Foot Clan. Mikey and his brothers trained their entire lives to end it. That's their family's destiny, and if Mikey feels that he needs to finish it alone, we have to respect his wishes."

"To hell with that," Casey says. "It's like you said, Mom—he's a part of us both. Literally. In our blood, like family. I'm with him to the end."

"I understand. But right now, the city needs you more." She leans over, cups her hand, splashes water against the wall of the tunnel. "The main pumping station on the East Side is in Kip's Bay. That's where I'm going. The secondary station is down under East River Park, just past Grand Street. Maybe that weird guy you're friends with for whatever reason, the one who modified the pulse rifles on the fly . . ."

"Lug."

"Of course that's his name. Maybe he can help you get the motors back online."

Casey thinks for a moment. "All right. Let's go un-flood this dump."

47

MIKE PRESSES THE NINJA'S finger against the glass of the bio-metric scanner. He's kept the man alive in case the system locks out dead tissue. When the door clicks and the red light atop the scanner turns green, he aims a swift kick downward. The man's neck breaks against the ball of his foot. He drops the limp hand and opens the door.

Hiroto's penthouse is a dizzying array of multitiered platforms and long, open expanses. Floor-to-ceiling windows look out upon a sky filtered through Foot City's canopy, making the space feel like the bridge of some massive generation ship. Mike's eyes dart around the hangar-sized chamber. He catalogs neat living quarters and exotic luxuries. What appears to be an orange grove fed by transparent irri-gation tubes arranged in artful spirals. Sparkling trapeze-like perches for dozens of ravens that circle the underside of the domed ceiling. A marble table the size of a tennis court, a supercomputer with a bank of monitors as long as a subway car. He moves slowly past tables cluttered with half-empty bowls of birdseed and bottles of sake. A huge television at the edge of a sunken living room plays an episode of a sitcom on mute. The three-sided sectional sofa is littered with blankets and throw pillows. It looks like someone has been lounging around here for days. He glances down. The floor tiles emit soft light that follows him as he moves through the penthouse. He cracks his bloody knuckles and sniffs the perfumed air.

"What is that, Hiroto?" he calls out to the empty room. "Jasmine?"

Mike's startled by a fluttering in midair, just off to his left. Then black wings are beating against his face. He swats at the raven. Squawking, the bird departs, soaring back up to its perch. A single feather drifts to the floor in its wake. Mike touches his cheek and his fingertip comes away wet with blood. "Lousy bird clawed me . . ."

He starts to walk up a set of stairs, gliding a hand along the ornate wrought iron railing. His knee protests. He tries to calculate the number of kicks he threw on the way here. Where's Donnie when you need him? For a moment, he feels his brothers' absence like a deep ache in his bones. Guilt threatens to swamp him. They ought to be here for this. For the end of things. He thinks of Raph's sneering provocations, Leo's cold eyes, his own anger unleashed on his brothers' spirits. When did they all become so sour?

A sudden, searing pain slices the back of his neck. One of the ravens ascends from behind him, then dives-bombs his face. Mike gets a forearm up in time. A sharp beak pecks at his tough skin. Mike flicks his arm, trying to dislodge the raven without hurting it. Then the bird opens its beak and clamps down.

"All right," Mike says, "that's it."

With some deep reserve of quickness, he snatches the raven by its feathery body. It wriggles in his grip, yet its warmth and smallness give him a moment of strange calm. He is careful not to hurt it. The bird's head peeks out the circle of his thumb and forefinger.

"What's this?" Buried in the feathers of the bird's neck is a nodule. A metal implant of some sort.

"Ow!" A second raven is on him now, jabbing its beak into the top of his head. He releases the captive bird and swats them both away.

As the ravens take to the air, he pauses to swing his left arm, working his sore rotator cuff. At least this time, the tower guard he fought through on his way here had been human Foot soldiers and not synjas. He'd have a lot less left in the tank for Hiroto if he'd had to dismantle androids on the way up.

He steps lightly across a plush rug, the pilings swallowing his feet like a pleasant massage from a fuzzy anemone. Blood leaks from a wound in his thigh. Goddamn shuriken. A coward sniped him from the shadows of a stairwell. He'd pulped that asshole's face with the broken katana's hilt.

He stops to examine a gilt-framed portrait of the Shredder in his full armor. It's an oil painting in which Oroku Saki is standing on a wooden deck of some sort with blue-green mountains for a backdrop. Upstate somewhere, maybe. Mike shakes his head. This place is infecting him with some weird nostalgia.

"Remember when we used to go to April's farm in Massachusetts?" he says. His brothers don't reply. He moves past a small, neat alcove hung with swords in ivory scabbards. Except for the ravens—six of them now, following his movements, gathering in the air above him—the penthouse is quiet. For the first time, he wonders what he will do if Hiroto is simply gone. His mind churns with visions of Hiroto lifting off the roof in a helicopter, cruising out over the forsaken river, landing on some estate's manicured lawn in Connecticut.

Above him, the ravens break ranks. A dozen more of their brothers and sisters swoop down from their distant perches, their wings folded back in sleek aerodynamic formation.

Mike's tonfa are in his hands. Twin batons, his most nonlethal weapons. He swings wildly, hoping to discourage the birds, scatter them for good. The piercing squawks of an irate flock drill into his head. A storm of black feathers obscures his vision. One claw gouges a wound in his forehead, perilously close to his left eye. Another takes a swipe at his shoulder. He turns in a circle, fighting them off, but it's no use. The birds simply regroup, dive, and swarm. Mike begins to breathe hard. His heart rate spikes. He's tired from battling his way up to the penthouse. It won't take much for these birds to sap his energy for the fight with their master.

A beak latches on to the skin above his elbow. The bite is sharp and fiery. Mike growls in pain. He thinks of the birds' metal implants. On a hunch, he activates the EMP in the tonfa. The invisible pulse blazes through the maelstrom of feathers and claws. The ravens seem to tremble midair. He half expects them to plummet to the ground. He braces himself for the sight of an avian massacre at his hand. Tiny puffs of white smoke issue from the nodules, ribboning to the ceiling and dissipating quickly. As the pulse runs its course, the ravens begin to soar, imbued with a sudden freedom. He watches as they forsake their perches, scattering to the far corners of the penthouse.

"Hiroto!" he bellows. Exhaustion begins to cloud his mind. All at once, this place makes him feel claustrophobic despite its vastness. It's like being trapped in Oroku Hiroto's head. "Where are you hiding, coward?"

"Coward?!" the voice that calls back is strong and confident. "That's what *she* calls me, you know."

Mike follows the sound. He turns a corner past the entrance to a dojo where a tatami mat is covered in faded bloodstains. Just ahead, atop a raised platform, a tall figure in silver armor stands next to what looks like a glass-topped coffin connected by thick cables to a bank of machinery.

Mike stops walking. For years, he has been rehearsing this moment. Visualizing it during meditation. Bolting upright, waking from nightmares in which Hiroto appears before him as he does now. In feverish isolation, he has created worlds that branch out like parallel universes, all stemming from this tableau: Michelangelo, the Last Ronin, standing ten paces away from Oroku Hiroto, the man who murdered his family.

He has listened to his mind replay iterations of the cold scripture he will deliver unto Hiroto. The last words his mortal enemy will ever hear. He has spoken them aloud, written them down, crossed them out, scrawled them over again, sent shreds of burnt paper into the cold mountain air as invocations to the spirit of vengeance who has guided him to this moment.

Yet now he finds that he cannot say anything at all. He is at a loss. So he reaches into his belt and launches a shuriken. Hiroto dodges it easily. The star vanishes into the depths of the penthouse. But it opens the floodgates.

"Seventeen years," Mike says. His voice is hoarse. "It's been seventeen years since you killed my family."

"Which one are you, by the way?" Hiroto asks. He doesn't move from beside the coffin. "I can't tell you mutants apart."

"All you need to know is, I'm the one who's gonna finish this. The last of the Oroku bloodline ends tonight."

Hiroto raises his hands. Mike reads exasperation in the gesture. "I just want to know what to call you."

Mike figures Hiroto's playing games. Some stalling tactic. He opts for another Raph plan and hefts his brother's sai as he approaches the platform head on.

"I want to thank you, mutant, " Hiroto says. He lets this statement hang in the air between them. "Your return to the city changed my life."

Mike continues to advance. He draws Leo's broken blade. His eyes move from side to side, anticipating an ambush from some hidden weapon.

"It's become hollow, sparring my finest warriors." Hiroto shakes his armored head. "I don't say this to boast, but I've far outpaced my grandfather." He steps behind the coffin. "I know he respects what I've been able to do." He places his hands on the glass and leans forward. "But my mother?"

Mike reaches the bottom step and begins to ascend.

"My mother remains a proud, stubborn woman. Her own rise was cut short, and in her bitterness she refuses to acknowledge what

I have built." He makes a fist and slams it against his chest. "The man I have become."

Mike is close enough now to study Hiroto's armor. It's a skintight suit of a dull silver that has no shine to it, metallic with a matte finish. And it sends optical distortions out into the air. Every time he blinks, the armor seems to flow like liquid metal in different swirling patterns that dive and swoop along the contours of Hiroto's body like the ravens circling above. An abstract mirror. A secret weapon. Mike breathes deep, grips his weapons, and readies himself for the unknown.

Hiroto puts up a hand. "Wait. Please. I need you to hear this. You have given me the opportunity to show her who I am. Your death will have *meaning* beyond your wildest dreams."

Mike does not stop. He does not care what Hiroto has to say. He is barely listening. From the top of the stairs, he can see there is a human shape in the coffin. A prone form submerged in some viscous, transparent fluid.

"*WAIT!*"

Hiroto brings an armored fist down on the coffin. Shards of glass explode outward, flung by a sudden gust of compressed air.

Mike acts on an impulse. He scrambles to one side and with two deft strokes of the sai cuts the wires connecting the coffin to the machines. At the same time, he stabs a softly beeping monitor with the katana. Sparks fly. A sheet of flame rises like a theater's curtain at Hiroto's back as the gas from the coffin ignites. A secondary explosion sends shattered glass across the platform. Jagged shards pepper Mike's armor. One piece nicks his face as it spins past his head.

"No more talking," Mike says as he leaps. One foot on the top of a machine, one on the end of the coffin, and he's coming down on Hiroto, blades trained on his neck. In a split second, Hiroto's armor ripples down his forearm and his knuckles sprout twin knives. Metal shrieks as Hiroto's blades catch Mike's. Hiroto throws his body into a sideways lunge and with his momentum tosses Mike against a railing. He lands on his feet, drops into a ready stance, and gains control of his weapons.

He coughs as smoke fills his lungs. Flames lick at his ragged cloak. His body feels heavy and slow. Too much toxic gas and heat up here on this platform.

Before him, Hiroto sprouts razor-tipped gauntlets. Liquid metal, Mike figures. Some kind of nano-carbide shit that Donnie would know all about.

Suddenly, a corpse rolls out of the ruined coffin. It hits the floor with a wet *shlump* and turns over before splaying out. The body is charred and blackened, but the face is mostly unburnt. Mike blinks.

"Karai," he growls.

Raphael's killer. He hopes his brother can see her now. He looks from the woman's body to her son as the silver armor grows three linked trident-like spikes on his forehead. A bastardized version of Shredder's helmet.

Mike shakes his head. "You got a messed-up family, Hiroto."

Then he vaults over the railing and lands on the cool surface of the marble table, one level below. Etchings of esoteric symbols dance across the marble.

Hiroto leaps down from the platform and lands with a slight bend in his knees. Mike coughs and spits a dark glob of phlegm. His lungs feel tight, his breathing shallow.

"At least the Orokus are *human*," Hiroto says. He glances at the platform where the smoking body of his mother lies. His armor convulses.

Mike considers Hiroto's mental state. He's agitated, frustrated. Mike figures he can use that to his advantage.

"Your mother was right about you." He chokes out the words from a raw throat. Flames leap like a stag from the platform that held Karai's tomb, catching a tapestry adorned with the red Foot logo. In seconds, the pillar that holds the tapestry is ablaze. A nearby bottle of sake explodes. "You *are* a coward." He jabs a sai at the platform. "At least your mother had honor."

Flames dance across that plush rug. Mike's vision blurs. Hiroto goes out of focus. Mike's mutation gives him some mammalian traits that mingle with the reptilian. Intense heat is the worst of both worlds. He feels like he's moving through boiling water.

"My mother fought and killed your family because it gave her purpose," Hiroto says. The armor clinging to his cheeks and forehead goes slack. Then it tightens into a severe, high-cheekboned visage. For a moment, Karai's face emerges. Then Mike blinks and it snaps back to Hiroto. "If you consider that *honor*, then you are as lost as she was."

Mike propels himself across the marble and lands a series of devastating strikes with his edged weapons. Hiroto barely bothers to deflect them. The blows should have eviscerated him, yet it's like stabbing at wet cement, constantly evading and reforming.

Hiroto catches Mike with a hard kick to the gut. Mike staggers back, his wind gone. In the haze of his pain, Hiroto's eyes steal their intensity from the eyes in the oil painting. Oroku Saki's features shimmer across his face.

"When you first arrived, I could scarcely believe it." He advances toward Mike. The knives protruding from his fists grow several inches. The flames branch off into white-hot tributaries of flame, rivers that flow toward the sunken living room and the supercomputer.

Mike gasps for air. He coughs up a bit of vomit and spits at Hiroto. His mind reaches for a Donatello plan, scans for weaknesses in the confounding armor. But there aren't any that he can see. It's a seamless, ever-shifting offensive and defensive weapon.

Summoning a reserve of strength, he backflips off the edge of the table and lands in the shadows of the orange grove. Off to his right is an open expanse that leads to the windows, lined with rows of minimalist shelves where hundreds of sculptures sit with little placards.

Hiroto follows him off the table with a movement that looks weightless. "But now, do you know what I think?"

Without any physical advantages, Mike settles for a Leo plan. As much as it pains him to engage with Hiroto's bullshit, Mike decides to give him what he wants, then reel him in.

"What?"

Hiroto lashes out with astonishing speed. One of his knives slashes Mike across the face. He tastes blood. Mike hits the floor, rolls, and when he comes up, Hiroto is already delivering a kick that drives Mike into one of the shelves. Ceramic vases crash to the floor and shatter.

At the same time, an explosion sends scorching plumes of chemical smoke billowing from the computer. Shrapnel clatters across the tiles. A pungent, burnt-plastic odor scorches the air.

"I think I always knew you were out there." He takes another swipe at Mike but it turns out to be a feint. Mike doesn't see the flying knee coming. Hiroto is so fast, his movements flowing like his armor. Mike feels his orbital bone snap. One side of his face goes numb. He backs into a shelf and knocks it over as he stumbles and falls, landing hard on his shell. Pain wracks his body. For a split second, all he can see are ravens circling like vultures in the desert. The dome is so far away.

"I could feel your presence like some vile chore I neglected to complete." Hiroto's voice brings Mike back to himself. "Nagging at me across the years." Mike crosses his arms to block an axe kick and scrambles to his feet. A quick glance over his shoulder reveals the windows a few feet behind him. "And I knew that one day you would come back when I needed you most."

"Sure," Mike says, slowly backing up as Hiroto stalks him down the row of museum artifacts. He catches sight of Buddhas and pharaohs, ancient copper weapons and clay pipes. "That makes sense."

"You know, if I were you . . ." Mike almost stops dead as Hiroto's face takes on a bulbous new shape, the armor puffing out into a distinctly reptilian mien. He is looking at a simulacrum of his own face. "I never would have let my father and my brother go all the way to Japan to die in a trap a child could have foreseen."

Bile rises in Mike's scorched throat. He swallows hard to keep from puking. He tells himself to stay focused, but it's as if Hiroto has drawn him deeper into the labyrinthine recesses of his mind. "But I'm not you." The silver face smiles. The armor erupts with razor-tipped ridges. "Because I'm alive . . ."

Mike's shell bumps against the tempered glass. Hiroto is silhouetted against the raging inferno consuming his penthouse.

". . . and you're dead."

Then the blaze reaches some deep and powerful element of the supercomputer. The explosion is all kinetic energy, a violent cyclone that whips outward from the center of the penthouse and blows every pane of glass out into the night sky. The floor and the ceiling trade places as Mike flails through empty air. A silver form rushes past him. Mercifully cool air fills his lungs. The darkened, crippled city reaches up, once again, to claim him.

48

BREAKER MOVES THROUGH WAIST-DEEP water, holding a flashlight above his head to keep it dry. The Grand Street pump station is an old, decrepit pit. Black mold speckles the walls. Sediment and muck squishes under Casey's feet at the bottom of the brackish water. Something swims past her, its tail breaking the surface before flicking away. She tries not to think about it.

Breaker shakes his head. "Lug says it's no good, Jones." His voice is doubled by an eerie echo.

"Are the pumps rusted here, too?" Casey asks.

"No. But they're a lost cause anyway. Crunch and Scrape pulled every lever in the substation, and Lug and I checked the electronics as best we could. And yes, before you ask, we double-checked everything."

Casey fights the urge to tell Breaker that nothing's a lost cause; there's always hope. That would be some laughable bullshit. This is the fifth set of pumps they'd tried to reactivate. They've managed to bring two online. Not enough to make a dent in the rising water.

"All right, fine," Casey says. "Let's move on to the next set."

She sloshes over to a massive steel cylinder fed by tubes the size of waterslides. Crunch hoists Lug out of the water. He climbs on top of the pump. Scrape hands him a toolkit. Then Lug cocks his head and cups his hand next to his ear.

"What's up, Lug?" Crunch asks. "You get some water in your ear?"

"No," Breaker interprets. "Comms." He pauses as a static-laden squawk fills the chamber. "Rock Bottom's reporting an explosion over at Hiroto's tower."

"What?" Casey says. "Seriously?"

Scrape snorts. "Hiroto bein' dead doesn't mean shit if we let the city sink to the bottom of the river."

"City can't sink," Crunch says.

"You don't know that."

Lug unscrews a panel and flips it open. He pokes around inside the pump for a moment, then gestures at Breaker.

"Uh-huh." Breaker nods as Lug points at the wall. He turns to Casey. "Looks like most of these pumps are connected to the main station in Kip's Bay. We gotta bring those online first, and it'll cascade from there."

"Right," Casey says, wading toward the stairwell that leads to the Grand Street access tunnel. "You guys go help my mom get those pumps up and running."

"Where the hell you going?" Scrape calls after her.

"Sensei might be in trouble," she shouts back.

Violent splashing comes up behind her. A rough hand on her shoulder spins her around. Crunch is a monstrous shape backlit by Breaker's little flashlight.

"Look, Casey, we all love you, but you gotta stop with this *Sensei* shit. The dude's a warrior, no doubt, but he's on his own death trip here, and he don't need you making some noble sacrifice for his sake. I guarantee you no part of him wants that, either."

She wriggles out of his grasp. "You don't understand."

Scrape cuts through the water, lifting his knees in a stilted run, to block her way. "Listen, Casey, you stubborn little shit. We're in the middle of a catastrophe here, and we need you. The city needs you."

She tries to flank around him. He sidesteps to remain in her path. "You guys can manage just fine without me, as long as you got Lug."

"Fine," Scrape says. "I only said all that just now as a pretense, because what I really want, and I think I speak for everyone here, is for you to *not die.*"

Casey just looks at him. She could come clean right now, tell them all she's a mutant who can punch through walls without bruising her knuckles.

"Thanks, Scrape," she says instead. "I don't want you to die either."

"Or anybody else in Rock Bottom. Right?"

She looks down at the flashlight beam refracting in shimmering coins along the water. "Right."

"So help us."

Something eases within. She sends a silent wish to her friend and teacher, her sensei with whom she shares an impossible bond. It might be goodbye. She hopes it's not.

"Nothing's a lost cause when there's hope," she says.

Crunch bursts out laughing as he splashes toward the stairs. "Beautiful, Jones."

49

MIKE PLUMMETS ALONGSIDE THE man he has come to kill. The night air is bracing as it whips past. His thoughts race, his mind on overdrive. He survived this once before. He can do it again. Still, scenes from his life play behind his eyes. A dress rehearsal for death. He sees his brothers as they were: teenage mutants, vagabonds and scamps, roaming the city, ensconced in brotherhood and endless jokes. He blinks away the past—*not yet*—and moves his body like a skydiver. Adjusting his fall by using the wind and the angle of his descent, he drifts closer to the edge of the building, a blur of glass and steel.

A deeply slanted rooftop comes into view below, quickly approaching. Mike splays his arms and legs and goes into a spin as he tries to edge toward it. A silver missile slips past him, falling faster: Hiroto with the same idea. Mike hits a second after his enemy, surfing the glass without smashing through, letting the slope carry him out from the tower proper. Faces in a generator-lit atrium glance at him. Mouths open in astonishment. Hostile architecture batters his speeding body: anti-pigeon emplacements, jutting bits of stone, rows of spikes. He feels every gash like a searing knife pressed against his flesh.

The silver missile comes and goes from view, and then Mike is upon the end of the slope. He reaches for his grapple but there's no time. He strains to grab hold of a jutting ledge, part of a Cubist windowpane, and grips it as his body tumbles over the side. Then he's dangling over empty space, the canopy curling above him like a great glass jellyfish.

Mike tries to come up with a solid Donnie plan. Rational and chess-like in its accounting for all possible outcomes. He hangs from one of the decorative window's severe angles. Then Hiroto slides into view, working his way around the other side of the window. A curtain flutters, and an alarmed face appears then withdraws. Hiroto swings like a pendulum, lashing out with a kick that dislodges Mike's arm.

"I can do this forever!" Hiroto screams into the howling wind.

Mike's grip falters. He launches himself forward, driving his shoulder into Hiroto's exposed midsection, wrapping him in a hold and using his bodyweight to pull Hiroto from the ledge.

Together, they somersault down floors lit in washes of emergency reds. It's all happening so fast. Mike tries to position himself to use Hiroto's armor to break his fall and absorb the shock. The world spins. They hit the very edge of a cantilevered rooftop garden, a concrete abutment that shreds half of Mike's body armor. He can't see where they're headed as they keep falling. He only knows it will hurt.

Hiroto laughs and laughs. They smash through a rooftop water tower. The wooden top disintegrates like paper. Hitting the water inside knocks the breath from Mike's lungs. He loses his grip on Hiroto and punches through the bottom of the tank. The rooftop is waiting for him. No time to brace for impact. His vision explodes with starbursts of white light. His shoulder pops out of joint. For a moment, he can't move. He smells blood and the tar of a city roof. His body twitches. Water pools around him.

A kick to his side flips him over, sends him sprawling. Ribs definitely broken. Breath catches in his throat.

Hiroto looms over him, seemingly unscathed. Then Mike's eyes go to a long, jagged gash in Hiroto's forearm. Through the haze of his pain, he zeroes in on this flaw as a point of attack. He tries to retrieve a weapon but his arm won't obey his command. Hiroto frowns and examines his armor. Liquid metal flows over the wound. In seconds, a gauntlet of unbroken silver encases his arm.

Hiroto goes down on one knee and leans over Mike's prone form. Mike lashes out feebly. His arm flops across his chest.

Hiroto's audible breaths come in quick succession. His body heaves as if he's hyperventilating. Mike feels his mind begin to drift away from the rooftop, soar above the city in search of old familiar downtown streets. In search of home.

Hiroto forces out words between breaths. "This . . . is going . . . *to hurt.*"

Hiroto makes a fist. Mike stares up at the knives as Hiroto passes his hand above Mike's body as if he is performing sorcery.

Then he works the twin blades slowly into Mike's flesh, underneath his ragged armor, just below his collarbone. The pain is immense and all-consuming, nanotech steel inside his body like some squirming thing both hard and soft. Mike screams, and the world slips away.

50

THE MAIN PUMP STATION in Kip's Bay is a netherworld of old brick lined with filthy black grout. Rusted pipes leak runoff into the floodwater.

"Mom?" Casey calls out as she leads her crew through a stone archway. The water is above her waist. She figures she might as well swim. Leaning forward, she keeps her face out of the sludge and dog-paddles.

"That's FDR Drive above us," Breaker says, flipping over into a lazy backstroke. "The old highway."

"Thanks, Break, that's super interesting to me right now," Scrape says. He remains standing. The water's only up to his thighs.

Crunch ducks to avoid a sign that says AUTHORIZED PERSONNEL ONLY.

"Mom!" Casey calls out again. She propels herself through another archway. Etched inside its capstone is the year 1874. Beyond the archway, the station opens into a chamber the size of an Olympic swimming pool. A bare bulb casts a cone of light down on the floodwater's choppy surface.

"Hold it right there!" The gruff command comes out of the darkness at the margins of the room.

Casey straightens as best she can, sets her feet down in the muck of the floor. Crunch and Scrape move to shield her.

A man in a black wetsuit sloshes slowly into the light. He's flanked by several others holding pistols above the waterline.

"You can't be here," the man says. "Turn around now and go back the way you came."

"Oh shit!" Crunch says. He lifts his massive knees and splashes into the light. "Yo, Otter!"

Casey looks at Breaker. "Otter?"

He shrugs.

The man in the wetsuit squints. Then his face relaxes. "No way. Crispy Crunch!"

The two men clasp hands.

"What the hell you doin' here?" the man called Otter asks.

Crunch gestures back at Casey and the others. "We're here to get the pumps running, since you're obviously messing it all up." He points at Casey. "And we're looking for her mom, you see a lady with a prosthetic hand kicking around anywhere?"

Otter motions to his team to lower their weapons. Then he splashes toward Casey. "You're April's kid," he says. She notes the augmentation around his left eye, a ring of metal embedded into the socket.

"Yeah," Casey says. "Is she around here somewhere?"

Otter glances at Crunch, then back to Casey. "So, here's what's up. Me and my engineers are working on the main pumps. I think we got a good shot at reversing the flow before the water gets to street level. Problem is, there's a couple of switches that need to be manually operated, and they're down in a flooded chamber." He pauses. "It's a maze down there."

Otter averts his eyes. Casey's anger flares. This guy's scared to tell her what she already knows.

"How long's she been down there?" Casey asks.

"A while," Otter admits.

Casey turns to her crew. "You guys help them with the pumps." She starts to swim toward an access hatch on the opposite wall.

"Jones!" Scrape calls after her. She doesn't stop.

Breaker catches up with her, his limbs carrying him through a smooth forward crawl. "Just let April do her thing!" he swallows water and begins to cough.

Two of the engineers rush to block the access hatch.

"You're going to have to shoot me!" Casey calls at them.

"Jesus Christ," Otter says. "Let her go."

One engineer pulls open the hatch to reveal a tunnel bored into the stone. Water spills out into the chamber.

The second engineer hands her a penlight. "It's waterproof," he says. "We gotta close the hatch behind you."

She takes the penlight with a nod and crawls inside the tunnel. The hatch slams shut at her back. Instantly, the air changes. A humid closeness makes her breathing feel shallow. She's not claustrophobic, but her heart starts to pound. She clicks on the light and begins to crawl along the wet stone. A thin stream of water soaks the base of the tunnel. She crawls for half a minute. Then the tunnel spits her out into another half-flooded chamber, much smaller than the first. She turns in a slow circle and plays the light along the glistening walls. No visible hatches or exits. She takes a breath and plunges into the floodwater. The flashlight's beam is dampened by the murk. Particulate sludge floats through the light as Casey moves it around the slime-crusted floor. In a moment, she finds a staircase that leads to a deeper level of the station. She surfaces, gulps air, and swims down with the penlight clenched in her teeth.

The stairwell is infested with floating cockroaches. She focuses on keeping fear at bay. Panic will only waste oxygen. But calmness eludes her. It's not like she can perform a breathing exercise down here.

The stairwell takes her to a large underground room packed with massive, turbine-like fixtures fed by rusted pipes. Her lungs are burning. She's certain she can hold her breath longer than a human, but she still requires oxygen. If she doesn't find her mother soon, she'll have to turn back. She pushes deeper into the room. Her front teeth ache from clamping down on the penlight.

Suddenly, she registers light up ahead: sparking, pulsing, much brighter than a flashlight. She recognizes it as some underwater version of an acetylene torch. Frantically, she paddles toward it. In a moment, she picks out a lone figure in a diving mask working to cut away a rusty obstruction jamming a bank of levers. Casey moves her light across the figure's prosthetic hand.

She fights the urge to yell out "Mom!" as she closes the distance between them. Her mother releases the trigger on the torch and the radiance dies away. Then she removes the breathing tube from her mouth and places it in Casey's hand.

Casey removes the penlight and pops in the breathing apparatus. She takes a long drag of oxygen. Her body relaxes as the urgency of her flight response subsides. One last time she fills her lungs before passing the hose back to her mother.

April motions to the rusted levers. Then she points at her daughter's arms.

Casey nods. Her mother needs her strength to free the switches. She reaches for one of the levers and braces her feet against the side of the switch box.

All at once, the chamber shudders. The water churns. Her penlights floats away from her grasp. Disturbed sediment weaves in and out of tiny bubbles.

Something happened up on the street, or in the station above them. She thinks of her crew. Then she forces the thought from her mind. Reaching out, she grabs hold of the penlight. Her mother goes after the welding torch.

Crumbling masonry drifts down around them, jagged chunks of stone dislodged by the disturbance above. Casey watches them come to rest on the floor. She shines her light along the ceiling. Cracks and fissures run the length of the chamber. It won't take much force to bring the whole thing down on top of them.

She shoots her mother a look. April points at the switches. Clock's ticking.

51

THE PAIN FROM HIROTO'S nanotech blades judders through Mike's shoulder. The knives are moving inside him, dissolving and reconstituting, ripping his musculature to shreds. For a moment, the world does the same. The sky is burning with fractals, mirrors of his confused pain. Then Hiroto withdraws the blades and their absence is a rush of arctic cold. Mike cries out. Hiroto kicks him and he rolls toward the rooftop's edge.

Mike lies still and gathers his strength. The twin puncture wounds send jolts of agony through his torso. He bears it and lets Hiroto unload on him, cracking his ribs, while he puts his thoughts together. No use matching Hiroto blow for blow. Not with that armor. It's time for a Leo plan. If he can't find a weak spot, he'll have to make one.

He pats empty pouches on his belt. Anxiety grips him. Did the fall from the tower knock all his secondary weapons loose? Hiroto is babbling on, looming over him, menacing him with the knives. He tries to tune him out but the voice slips through.

". . . and perhaps I'll keep you alive after all, like her, to bear witness . . ."

With the tip of a knife he draws a thin searing line across Mike's forehead.

Mike grits his teeth, makes his eyes go out of focus, and lolls his head, playing at being incapacitated. Finally, he finds his last explosive charge, a plum-sized grenade. With speed that takes Hiroto by surprise, he grabs Hiroto's wrist and jams the explosive between the blades on the back of his hand.

Then Mike rolls over and puts his shell between his exposed body and the grenade.

The blast sends him caroming off an HVAC unit. The world goes silent except for a piercing whine that bounces around his skull. His body protests, but he manages to stand. The agony is beyond anything he's ever felt. Halfway across the rooftop, Hiroto is down on one knee, staring at the bare skin of his hand as if seeing it for the first time. Liquid metal snakes up his wrist but seems to glitch. The armor sends stringy tendrils of silver along his palm. They fail to link together.

Mike sprints across the wet tar, drawing Raph's sai. Hiroto turns to face him. Mike jukes to one side, then skids forward in a low crouch. With a hyper-quick jab, he rams the sai into Hiroto's exposed hand.

"Here's a gift from my brother."

Hiroto cries out. Mike spins around to deliver a kick, but Hiroto has already recovered. He dodges the blow and elbows Mike in the face, sending him sprawling across the tar.

Hiroto holds up his hand and regards the weapon impaling his palm. Then he pulls it out without making a sound. At last, the armor begins to flow and stitch itself back together. Mike makes a mental note: The armor is self-repairing, but Hiroto's flesh is not. Underneath that nanotech lattice, the wound remains.

Hiroto snaps Raphael's sai in half and tosses away the pieces. "Never mind all that," he says. "I'm just going to kill you."

Mike pushes himself to his feet. He finds that his left arm dangles, the knife wound rendering it useless. Hiroto sprints at him and lowers his shoulder. Mike sees himself evading the charge with ease, but his body moves half as fast as he'd expected. Hiroto's razor-tipped armor catches him across the face, ripping open a gash in his cheek.

Blood flows. Mike knows he can't keep this up forever. "You talk too much," he rasps.

Whatever Hiroto says in return is lost amid the deafening sound of another massive explosion. Mike knows without looking that the fire has spread from the penthouse, igniting some other section of the tower. To actually divert his attention to the tower now would be suicide.

And yet Hiroto turns to look. Perhaps he thinks Mike has grown too weak to attack. Perhaps he thinks his armor will shield him. Perhaps he is simply transfixed by the destruction of his empire.

Without thinking, Mike takes advantage of this mistake. He launches himself into the air and grabs hold of Hiroto with both arms. Razors press into his flesh as he carries Hiroto over the edge of the building.

There's a moment of pure weightlessness as they hang in the air. Debris from the tower falls around them. A burning office chair plummets past them. Then they pick up speed and outpace it. Mike narrows his focus to one thought: No matter how much pain he is in, he will peel himself off the pavement and drive Leo's broken katana straight through Hiroto's armor.

The impact deletes all thought. There is only blackness. Then a stuttering dose of reality, light and sound hammered into his skull.

The colors of the world are all wrong. A switch has been flicked in his brain. He sees three of everything. On his hands and knees, he vomits blood. A silver shape comes out of the haze, staggering and swaying before him. He manages to narrow his vision, to sharpen the edges of the figure before him. The armor is worn visibly thin. Hiroto's body shows through in patches. Where the nanotech has peeled away like torn paper, sparks are sizzling and popping.

Mike gets to his feet. Hiroto lifts a hand, swipes with an oddly curved blade. Mike grips the hilt of Leonardo's katana. His heavy

eyelids close, and for a moment, the thought of simply falling down and going to sleep takes over. He blinks and fights the urge.

He coaxes his voice out through his swollen throat. "For Leo."

He rams the broken blade into a gap in Hiroto's armor on the left side of his abdomen.

Hiroto grunts and wraps his hands around the hilt jutting from his body. He regards it as if he can't believe what is happening to him.

Mike collapses to the pavement. His eyes close. It would feel so good to let go. But he can still hear the sounds of the real world—and what he hears is Hiroto's goddamn voice. He opens his eyes.

Hiroto is laughing as he pulls Leo's blade from his body. It's a strangled sound, phlegmy and awful. The sword clatters to the ground. Hiroto falls to his knees. Then he begins to crawl toward Mike, trailing blood and bits of silver that writhe on the blacktop. His razor-like protrusions scrape along the street as he pulls himself along.

A few feet away, Mike spots a manhole cover. Some animal notion of home drives him toward it. Somehow, he manages to slide it off and pitch himself down into the sewer. He splashes into a foot of water. Lying on his shell, he watches as if from behind a smeared pane of glass as Hiroto shimmies into view, a silhouette inside a circle, outlined in sparks. Then the silhouette pitches forward and plunges into the water.

Mike finds that he is gripping what is left of his brother's bō staff. The fall has broken it in two and splintered the severed edges. Half swimming, half crawling, he makes his way to Hiroto's prone form.

The nanotech has reconstituted itself in places, strands of silver crosshatched in thin weaves. Some are grotesque corruptions, bulbous growths and confounding patterns, creating, erasing, starting again.

The faceplate has diminished. Hiroto's eyes stare into space.

With his good arm, Mike lifts the bō. He positions the splintered end of the staff at the puckered entrance to Hiroto's stomach wound.

The pale, swollen flesh seems to swallow the weapon as Mike leans to drive it into Hiroto's body.

Hiroto wheezes. Blood leaks from his mouth. Mike collapses on top of him. Hiroto presses a curled, twitching blade into Mike's upper back. The pain is a distant thing.

"For Donnie," Mike says at last. Then he closes his eyes.

52

DEBRIS FALLS FROM THE ceiling while Casey and her mother work to free the switches. Chunks of concrete ease dreamily down through the flooded chamber. Casey shoulders them out of the way, shielding her mother from the heaviest pieces. But the chamber has been shaken to its core. Cracks like dendrites spread across the ceiling. A slow hailstorm of loose stones clouds the room.

A cave-in is coming, and soon. Casey knows she's strong, but even Sensei couldn't dig himself out from a million tons of water and concrete. She turns her attention to the bank of switches. Her mother dissolves rust with the knifelike flame of the white-hot torch. Casey wrenches the lever into place.

The chamber shudders again. She doesn't bother with a hit of oxygen, just moves down the row of levers. A long flat piece of concrete tilts into her mother's face. Casey shoves it aside. A jagged edge catches the breathing apparatus and rips it from her mother's mouth. Frantically, April reaches out for it. She clamps down on the mouthpiece, breathes—and turns to Casey, wide-eyed through her mask.

Bubbles jet from a gash in the tube. Casey's thoughts race. No way her mother can swim all the way back to the main chamber before she drowns. There's only one way out of this.

Casey's no good at meditation. She can't clear her mind on command. Panic swells in her chest. For a split second, she wishes herself someplace else, where this isn't happening. Her mother rips off the face mask, eyes wild and pleading. Casey gathers her strength and grips the next lever in the bank of switches. She braces her legs and pulls. It does not move. Debris scrapes her back and she winces at the pain. She thinks of Sensei rising from the crater in the pavement after a fall that should have killed him. The same mutagen courses through her veins. She can do this.

Her muscles strain. She tightens her core and drives with her legs. The lever gives way. She slams it home and moves on to the final switch. How long has her mother been without oxygen? She has no sense of time. Her own lungs are screaming.

She swims around behind the lever, presses her shoulder against it, and kicks off the wall like a swimmer in a race.

The lever creeps forward. A metallic *clank* reverberates through the flooded chamber. The system activates with a long, low rumble, like the engine of a massive ship. Pumps spring to life all over the station. With a great sucking sound, water begins to rush out of the chamber. A sudden current drags Casey toward a drainage pipe embedded in the far wall. She hits the grate that covers its opening. A moment later, the current slams her mother into the grate at her side. She moves to shield her mother's body from the stones riding the slipstream. They pelt her in the back, one stinging blow after another. Then the water sinks below her face. Her own gasps are all she can hear. As she pulls air into her lungs, she finds herself standing with her feet on the floor. Water laps at her knees. Next to her, her mother is doubled over, coughing. She holds her mother close as her heart rate slows.

"It's okay, Mom. I got you."

Casey can breathe again. Her mother is alive. For a moment, she basks in the knowledge that these two things are all that matters.

"I am so—" Her mother is interrupted by another coughing fit. Water sputters from her mouth. She holds up a finger. Then she continues, "—pissed at you. What the hell were you thinking?"

"I was thinking I'd find you trying to fix some old broken thing. And I was right."

"Casey Marie, you could have been killed."

"*You* could have been killed, Mom!"

"Yeah, but I'm *old*, Casey." She holds up her prosthetic hand. "I've *lived*. Loved your father. Had you."

"So I'm supposed to let you die because you've had a good run?"

"No, you're supposed to . . ." Her mother grabs hold of her sodden hair, bunches it together, wrings it out. "I don't know. I don't know what anybody's supposed to do anymore." She sighs then meets Casey's gaze. "Speaking of old broken things, Mikey has no idea about this, but I injected him with a tracker when I drew his blood."

"What?" Casey pushes her slick bangs away from her face. "How do we get the signal?"

"It's a standard resistance frequency, we just need a radio."

Casey takes off toward the stairwell. "Breaker has one upstairs!"

"Wait!" April sloshes over and wraps Casey up in a hug. Then she breaks the embrace so she can look into Casey's eyes. "Be careful. Please."

"Only because you said *please*!" She turns to go. The steps are slippery with wet sediment. She bounds up them anyway. A lightness she hasn't felt in a long time carries her to the main chamber. They've handled the flood. Rock Bottom is safe. Now she's going to track down Michelangelo, and everything will be all right in the end.

53

NOISE INVADES THE SWEET, peaceful darkness. With great reluctance, Mike claws his way back from oblivion. His eyes flicker open and he makes out a round cutout in the tunnel's ceiling: the manhole he crawled into. The pain that courses through him is all-encompassing. He wears it like a shroud. One of those hairshirts ancient penitents wore to punish themselves. He tries to catalog his many wounds and quickly gives up.

He manages to turn his head. To the right there is nothing but a pool of water and a few scurrying rats. To the left, Hiroto lies sprawled and moaning. His armor is peeled away like torn flesh. He doesn't move.

The noise grows from a distant gurgle to a thunderous roar. The air quality shifts. A single pigeon flies out of the darkness and soars up through the manhole cover. Mike watches it vanish into the night sky. He feels removed from everything that is happening. When the great wall of water comes racing into the tunnel and carries him away, he accepts it with no fear or regret.

Water pushes its way down his throat. There is nothing he can do about it. His battered body slams against the tunnel walls, opening more raw wounds and scrapes. Then he is shot into the air, expelled as if from a cannon.

His body splashes down in a pit of sludge outside the wall, in the shallows that buffer Manhattan from the East River. The knee-deep muck cushions his fall. The river's stench brings him back to the moment he returned home and first set eyes on Hiroto's abomination. A moment later, Hiroto splashes down next to him.

So it began and so it will end.

Mike pushes himself to his knees. All around him, runoff from pipes jutting from the wall swirls in the muck. With his good arm, Mike reaches for his one remaining weapon: his nunchaku. Blood dribbles from his mouth. River slime sluices through his fingers.

He tries to stand. The weight of his body forces him back to his knees. It's too heavy. Half crawling, half wading, he moves toward Hiroto. The deep puncture wounds in his shoulder and back feel sizzling and infected. He wonders if some of the nanotech is still inside his body. Tiny flecks of digital intelligence scrambling his cells. The dark river and black sky overlap. Eventually, he reaches Hiroto. The man begins to stir. Hiroto rises, groaning with effort. Mike's brain screams at him to cut Hiroto down, but his limbs will not obey. He forces himself to his feet before the one who murdered his family. He tells himself to lift his arm and strike. Nothing happens. Hiroto goes in and out of focus. The silver armor, abraded and scorched, has ceased to spark.

Hiroto's eyes come to rest on Mike. "I cannot die," he announces in a whisper.

Mike chokes out a retort. "You're doing a pretty good job of it."

Hiroto's swollen lips curl into a sickly grin. "My angels will not let me."

Mike can't stomach any more bullshit. "You don't know any angels."

Crying out at the effort, he backhands Hiroto across the face. Hiroto's body follows in a half-spin. Churning the river sludge, Mike maneuvers so that he is behind Hiroto, gritting his teeth as he wraps the chain of his nunchaku around Hiroto's neck and pulls. Hiroto struggles feebly.

Hiroto tries to choke out some gibberish. Mike catches the word *immortal* and pulls tighter. His body begins to go numb. The pain leaches away, and in its place throbs a dull understanding. He is at the end of his life. Peace like a mountain stream settles over him. Not because he has fulfilled his destiny or kept his promise to his brothers, but for some other reason, some everlasting truth he can't yet grasp. For now, he lets the honor of his family fall across him like a shroud.

Hiroto claws at the chain around his neck. Then his hand moves down to a little pocket of silver nanotech embedded in his forearm. Mike thinks he should stop him, but he does not move fast enough. Hiroto slips a finger inside the pocket and presses down against his skin.

The suit erupts into sparking bolts of electricity. Mike is at the eye of a lightning storm that kicks the slurry around them into hypnotic patterns in the air. Electricity surges through his body and grabs hold of his heart. Mike and Hiroto are frozen in time, their bodies lit from within by an eerie glow.

And then the armor explodes.

54

RAIN FALLS ON HIS face. He is lying on his back, looking up at the sky.

"Sensei!" The voice comes from far away.

After a while, someone is hovering at the edges of his fading vision.

"I'm here, Sensei. It's me, Casey. Casey Marie."

Her face is obscured. She is a visitor from a place he no longer inhabits, but he remembers her. He tries to smile. She takes his hand.

"You're not leaving yet. Okay? We have things to do. Look." She produces a leather-bound book. "I brought Splinter's journal."

She tries to put it in his grasp. Then she sets it on his chest.

He pushes his voice out from a great distance. "I left it for you. To teach you all he knew."

"No." She rests a palm on his arm. "*You're* my teacher. I need you, and my mom needs you. We're your family."

"Yes," he agrees. "Always." His body is neither warm nor cold. Rain falls on his face, but he can't feel it. Somehow he slides a finger underneath the journal's binding and flips it open to the last page. "Last lesson is mine."

His finger leaves a bloody print on the final entry. What had once read *NO PEACE* now says *KNOW PEACE*, with the *K* and *W* scribbled in.

Casey's tears fall on his face.

"Most important of all," he tells her. In the night sky, a star appears. How strange. City lights stole the stars from view a long time ago. After a while, the star is all he can see. He drifts into its brightness.

55

APRIL FINDS HER DAUGHTER kneeling by Mikey's side, crying. She hangs back to let Casey grieve privately for a moment, then slowly steps into view. Her own tears come when she sees Mikey's ravaged body.

At least now, he's beyond pain. His eyes are open, gazing up at the night sky like he's trying to find a star where there are none.

She kneels down next to Casey Marie and puts her arms around her little girl.

Casey cries harder. "It's not fair, Mom."

She's right, April thinks: It's not fair that such a gentle soul had lived such a hard and violent life. She pulls her daughter closer.

"Oh, Mikey," she whispers through her tears. "Goodbye, my sweet friend."

56

ALL THE PAIN—EVERY OLD wound and aching joint—is suddenly gone, wiped away as though it had been part of a long and terrible dream from which Michelangelo is finally waking. He opens his eyes and finds himself in a warm bed, blankets pulled over his face. In the crook of his arm is the stuffed bear that Splinter had given to him when he was a child.

A shadow moves at Mike's side and blocks some of the light that filters through the blankets. The shadow edges closer until it's a few inches from Mike's ear.

"Mikey!" Leo's voice hollers, sending a jolt of surprise up Mike's spine. "Wake up already!"

"Yeah," Raph chuckles. "You gonna sleep all day or what?"

"You just had the longest nap ever, bro!" Donnie says.

Mike pulls the blankets down. The room he shares with his brothers is bright—too bright. Donnie must've scavenged some halogen bulbs for the lair. When his eyes adjust, he sees his brothers: Raphael, Donatello, and Leonardo.

They all look young. *Teenage* mutant ninja turtles. They wear no battle scars or armor plating. Just smiles and their everyday gear: belts, wrappings for their joints, and colored masks.

"Hurry up." Donnie stamps his bō staff twice on the ground for emphasis. "It finally stopped raining!"

"Yeah," Raph says, "and we're headin' topside for some fresh air."

Leo clears his throat. "And training. Come on, we're already behind schedule!"

Raph balls Mike's mask—bright orange and clean—and whips it at his brother, bouncing it off his head. "You heard him, sleepyhead. Get your lazy butt movin'—last one out has to do the dishes for a week!"

Mike feels his midsection and finds that he is whole. No wounds, no blood, no tattered remnants of body armor. Had the battle with Oroku Hiroto been the dream, or was this—

"Looks like we have our winner," Leo says as the others file out of the room.

"I think you mean loser," Raph calls back.

Mike laughs—a genuine, joyful laugh—grabs his nunchaku, pulls on his mask, and leaps out of bed to chase after his brothers. The last bit of his painful dream fades before he gets to the ladder that leads out of the sewer.

"No fair!" Mike yells as he climbs. "I wasn't ready!"

Raph's face appears in the open manhole. "Loser says what?"

"I'll show you I'm not a loser," Mike says as he emerges onto the street.

Raphael cackles as he begins to scale the nearest building. "Only a loser would say that."

"He's right," Leo calls out, already on the roof. "Look it up!"

Mike follows his brothers across the rooftops of the Lower East Side, chasing them for several blocks. The sun begins to peek out from behind plump, gray clouds. Mist hangs in the air, the pleasant aftermath of the rain. The best kind of day.

"Who's the loser now, dude?" Mike says as he races to close the gap. He passes Raphael in just three buildings, a new record.

"Hey!" Donatello hollers from above. Leo, Raph, and Mike stop and look up at a ten-story building half a block ahead. Donnie's sitting on the edge of the roof, waving at them. "I think you're all losers. And slow! Maybe you two could help Mikey with the dishes?"

Leo, Raph, and Mike glance at each other. "How the heck did he get up there so fast?" Leo asks.

Soon the four brothers are united on the rooftop, taking in the view. The Manhattan skyline cuts a beautiful image against the blue sky and positively glistens in the sun. After a few minutes of silence, Raph makes a gagging sound and punches Mike in the shoulder. "Phew! So much for the fresh air we were after, fellas—smells like Mike cut the cheese."

"Hey!" Mike rubs his shoulder. "I did not!"

"Yo!" A new voice exclaims from behind the turtles. "I think I gotta side with Mikey on this one, Raph. You know that old saying 'Whoever smelt it, dealt it'?"

Mike turns to see Casey Jones squatting on the top of an AC unit. "Casey! You're here!" Mike is elated. It feels like the first time he's seen Casey in years.

"Course I am, bud. Where else would I be? I mean, besides upwind. God, do I wish I was upwind right now . . ."

Another voice chimes in. "I cannot speak to Raphael's flatulence, but I will observe that New York City also has its own unique and pungent odor, does it not?"

"Yeah, it does," Mike says as he surprises Splinter with the tightest of hugs. "It smells like home, Father. I think I'm finally home."

EPILOGUE
ONE YEAR LATER

CASEY MARIE PUNCHES THE heavy bag, recently reweighted to five hundred pounds.

Left. Right. One. Two.

She aims for the strip of electrical tape.

One. Two. Left. Right.

She slips into a solid rhythm, ticking off instructions to herself in her head. *Mix the jab and the cross. Now uppercut. Now kick. Now do it all over again.*

Every day for the past year, Casey's been working hard to fill the hole Michelangelo had left in her life, honoring him through sheer effort.

She spins and kicks, punishing the bag with a satisfying *THWAP*. Her sweat spatters the fabric.

She places her hands on her hips. "How'd that one look?"

She waits a moment, then smiles to herself. Sometimes it feels like Michelangelo is hanging around the dojo, watching her, silently critiquing her technique. Sometimes, she even talks to him. But he never replies.

"Watch this one."

She torques her body into a vicious roundhouse kick. The chain connecting the bag to the ceiling snaps, and the bag slams into the wall and sags to the floor.

A slow clap echoes through the dojo. "Not too shabby, Jones."

She mops her brow with a sweat-drenched terry cloth. "This is actually a members-only gym, did you show your ID to the doorman?"

Crunch steps into the room and flips her the bird. "ID this."

Scrape, Breaker, and Lug file in behind him.

Casey tosses the towel into a wicker basket. "You guys here to fix my heavy bag?"

"Drinks," Scrape says, miming pouring a giant glass down his throat. "Hilty's. Now."

Breaker turns to the doorway and calls out into the tunnels, "By *drinks* he means *sodas,* April!"

"I gotta shower," Casey says. She thinks for a moment. "Also, it's like, *noon.*"

Lug walks across the room and peers at the broken chain dangling from the ceiling.

"We got business to discuss," Crunch says.

"Lemme guess," Casey says. "New gang popped up."

"Call themselves the Midtown Mafia," Breaker says. "Staking a claim to Tribeca."

Casey bursts out laughing. "The *Midtown Mafia?* Sounds like a drink with an umbrella in it."

Scrape examines the rack of weapons against the wall. "They been cutting out people's eyes."

Casey goes to the table, where Splinter's journal is open to a page illustrating a complex series of moves. "So, not that funny, then."

"Depends on your sense of humor," Crunch says.

Casey makes her way to the door. "You guys go ahead. I'll meet you there in a few."

After a long shower, Casey heads for the lab.

"Hey, Mom!" she calls out. "Anything interesting explode today?" She waits for a response. April's face is buried in a pile of disassembled electronics on her workbench. She musters a wave.

Casey walks over and gives her mother a quick side-hug. "How're the tests looking?"

April looks up. "Slight improvement, actually. Lots more to get done, though. Busy day." She wipes her hands on a rag. "You heading out for some sodas? Couple of root beers with the boys?"

Casey strolls to the other side of the lab. "In a bit. Any preferences for lunch?"

April goes back to puttering. "Get what you want, kiddo. I'm not hungry."

Casey smiles as she approaches a large terrarium. "Wasn't talkin' to you, Mom."

Inside the terrarium are four small turtles. A monitor on the table next to the glass enclosure displays strong vitals. They're having a positive reaction to the mutagen that April synthesized from samples of both Michelangelo's and Casey's blood. These little turtles aren't mutating yet. But they will. And Casey knows they're going to be amazing.

She leans in close to the terrarium. "Hurry up and grow already," she says. "I've got so much cool stuff to teach you."